THE PROBLEM IS
I FELL IN LOVE

A **MacaVelli** BOOK
SAN FRANCISCO

THE PROBLEM IS
I FELL IN LOVE

A NOVEL BY PAMELA M. JOHNSON

MACAVELLI

ALSO BY PAMELA M. JOHNSON:

FROM A HARD ROCK TO A GEM:
A MEMOIR OF A LOST SOUL

I'LL CRY TOMORROW

FORTHCOMING BOOKS BY PAMELA M. JOHNSON:

PROTÉGÉ

THE AUTOBIOGRAPHY OF ANTAAWN SING, DRUG LORD,
AS TOLD BY PAMELA M. JOHNSON
(The first of a trilogy)

DEATH ROW

LIFE AFTER DEATH ROW

WITHOUT FATHER

BIRTHWHISTLE

GHETTO PROPHET: THE IDEAS, PHILOSPHIES & OPINIONS
OF TUPAC SHAKUR (AN ANTHOLOGY) NON FICTION

MACAVELLI
Bringing the urban culture to the world & the world to the urban culture

An Original Publication of Macavelli Press
Macavelli Press Fiction, published by Macavelli Press
1550 California Street, Suite 6-262
San Francisco, California 94109

www.mavcavellipress.com

ISBN 0974657239

Cover Photo © Corbis

Cover/Book Design by Alian Design www.aliandesign.com

Library of Congress Cataloging-in-Publication Data

Library of Congresss Preassigned Control Number: 2005925740

Johnson, Pamela M.
The Problem Is I Fell in Love: a novel/Pamela M. Johnson.—Macavelli Press Trade pbk.ed
p.cm.

1. African-American—Fiction. 2. Young Women, United States—Fiction. 3. Businesswomen—Fiction. 4. Entrepreneur—Fiction. Publishing—Fiction. 5. Entertainment—Fiction. 6. San Francisco (Ca.)—Fiction. 7. African-American Business People—Fiction. 8. Realestate—Fiction. 9. Love & Romance—Fiction. 10. Black Love & Romance—Fiction. 11. Afircan-American Romance. 12. Urban—Fiction.

First Edition 2005

First Macavelli Press trade paperback edition April 2005

10 9 8 7 6 5 4 3 2 1

Macavelli Books are published by Macavelli Press, a division of Macavelli, Inc. Its trademark consisting of the words "Macavelli" and its drop down V is Registered in the U.S. Patent and Trademark Office and in other countries. Marca Registrada.

For information regarding special discounts for bulk purchases, please contact Macavelli Press at sales@macavelli.com.

For
Calvin

This book is dedicated to the man who noticed
my gift of writing before I did,
awakened me to it and encouraged me to write.
And for the role he played in assisting me
in making Macavelli Press happen.
I'm thankful that God placed us at that particular intersection
in our lives where we crossed paths and met.

Calvin, you are legendary, the epitome of success and
an inspiration not only to me but to all African-Americans.
As an entrepreneur I wish to follow in your footsteps.
Thank you for being there and for all that you've said,
much love & respect,

Pamela M. Johnson

ACKNOWLEDGEMENTS

This is my third novel in approximately a year and a half. Again, I am so grateful to God for giving me the talent to write and a whole lot of imagination to do it with. I am also grateful to have discovered my passion for writing and for God bestowing the gift upon me. I thank my attorney and financier, investment banker Calvin Grigsby (you wear soooooo many hats) for the role he played in motivating me and contributing in the way that he did, assisting me in making my goals manifest with *Macavelli* Press. I also want to thank Jack Romanos, CEO of Simon & Schuster, for listening to me and communicating with me in all those emails we sent back and forth. Thanks for your belief in me and for the opportunity, but I had to see first what I could do on my own. Now, I am distributed by the major book distributor Ingram, and wholesaler Baker & Taylor, and the black-owned book distributors Culture Plus, A &B, Afrikan World Press; with *Macavelli* novels distributed by all the major chain bookstores and our titles available in more than 500 independent bookstores throughout the country, and now with a fan base not even 9 months later—all this means a girl ain't done bad for herself (smile). Another special thank you to Sessalee Hensley, buyer for Barnes and Noble for the opportunity to be distributed by the bookstore chain for taking that initial one-thousand book order last year and I thank the chain for regularly ordering more novels. Walden Books thank you also for ordering hundreds of books at a time as well as Books-A-Million and to Borders thank you for believing in me enough as a new author to order an initial two-thousand copies of my debut novel, *From a Hard Rock to a Gem: a Memoir of a Lost Soul.* I did an initial print run of twenty thousand copies of my debut novel, *From a Hard Rock to a Gem: a Memoir of a Lost* Soul and thanks to you guys I moved those novels. Y'all moved a great deal of books for me, right on—let's do it again with this novel and the future ones (smile).

My sincere appreciation to all of the book clubs who've read my novels and have invited me to their book club meetings, (Mahogany Pages Book Club of Oakland) thank you so much for supporting me and my small press, *Macavelli*, and for purchasing a *Macavelli* book. To the book clubs, send me an e-mail so that I can personally thank your book club by name in my next novel. In addition, if you choose one of my novels as your reading selection for the month and want me to be present at your book club meeting when you discuss it, let's make it happen, contact me at publisher@macavelli.com. To my editors, Scott Tuckman and Benjamin Stockton, thank you so much for your edits to my manuscript and your editing advice, you are appreciated. To my distributors Ingram, Baker & Taylor, Culture Plus (Larry, Onika), A & B (Karen, Wendy, Kwame', Eric), and Afrikan World Press (Nati), the chain bookstores Barnes and Noble, Borders, Walden Books, Books-A-Million, e.t.c. around the country who are selling my novels, thank you so much for promoting and distributing my novels; I couldn't have achieved the success that I have without you. To the more than 500 independent bookstores that also make my *Macavelli* Press novels available to their customers, I thank you from my heart and I thank McClymonds High School in Oakland for their order of 100 copies of *From a Hard Rock to a Gem: a Memoir of a Lost Soul* and *Jefferson High School of Daly City* and all of the other schools who ordered a *Macavelli* Book. I also want all of the schools around the country to know that *I'll Cry Tomorrow—my novel* that addresses *HIV and AIDS* in the black community, an excellent discussion piece for students to begin a much needed dialogue about the dreadful disease is available to them at a discount. I wrote the novel in an effort to address the issue of HIV and AIDS in the Black Community and to begin a much needed discussion about the diseases. My goal is that the novel provides for a more comfortable so to speak discussion forum about AIDS and HIV, a subject that in 2005 is still taboo in our community, yet we have the highest numbers and those numbers are rising as Magic Johnson has been expressing all along. We need to educate ourselves about the diseases. I send out a special thank you to Bernard Henderson of Alexander Books, the first bookstore to put me on as an author and take books from me on consignment in March 2004, and the whole Alexander Book Co. on Second Street in San Francisco. Bernard when you took those first twenty novels from me my world lit up (smile) and then each week consistently you were calling me for twenty more novels, and then you started taking more and having those checks ready on time. I'd walk into the bookstore with a box of books—hand you the box and you'd say, "Wait a minute I got something for you," and there was an envelope with a check inside for the novels staring me in the face. It was crazy good; you really know how to treat authors. Bernard, thank you for upping me on this publishing game. I also thank Marcus books, the second bookstore to take novels directly from me as an independent author and kept calling back for more (thank you Marcus—Karen, Tamiko & Blanche) and Jerry Thompson of Barnes and Noble Jack London Square, Ralph and Focus 2000 Hair Salon in San Francisco for the love & support they've shown me and for all of the copies of my debut novels that they sold, amazing, and I thank them in advance for selling this novel as well; Hair Flexx of Daly City (Felita & Opal) and Mrs. Sarah's Creations, thank you also for selling my novels in your hair salons. Also, my sincerest appreciation goes out to all of the hair and nail salons around the country who sold my novels; A Time for Nails—Nail salon, hello Lee and Long, (if you are a hair and/or nail salon, bookstore or any other business and want to sell *Macavelli* Books email me at publisher@macavelli.com and I will make it happen). Furthermore, I want to thank Magic Johnson, Kevin Johnson & Underground Books in Sacramento,

San Francisco City College; Southeast Campus (Lori, Tamyra, Leo Sykes), John Adams, Downtown Campus, and Ocean Avenue Campuses for adding me to their Black History Month Concert Lecture Series Program and welcoming me to do a book reading/discussion and signing. I thank Malaika Adero for recognizing my talent and for the opportunity, Denise Stinson, Tracy Sherrod and I thank my incredible and brilliant assistant, my 8 year old niece Asha Amani Sanford (can't wait to read your children's book, *The Purple Pizza*); my other incredible and brilliant 6 year old niece Dominique Johnson—can't wait to read your book also (Asha and Dominique you two have so much leadership—you remind me so much of me when I was your age; remember there are no limits except for those that you impose upon yourself). My nephew, Angelo Marcel Johnson, *Rest In Peace* Black man; I love you. Last but not least, I want to thank twelve important people in my life, my beautiful nieces Candace Walker, and Angel Johnson, My sister Cynthia Johnson and my beautiful and true friends Melody Fuller, Brenda Gray, Inez Marshburn, Deanna Davis, Kecia Carrol, MD, Deborah Greer, MD, Jilchristina Vest, Machelle Berry and Lisa Rutledge. What can I say…words alone cannot express the love I have for you all and our genuine friendship. If a man or woman can have one person on this earth who they consider a friend they are blessed, I have the twelve of you, wow!

To my fans: Thank you so much for your support—you are appreciated. My novel, *From A Hard Rock to a Gem A Memoir of a Lost Soul* was urban fiction; my follow up, which is a spin-off novel to this novel, is *I'll Cry Tomorrow*—this novel deals with the theme of HIV and AIDS in the black community (this novel is a must read). My third novel is *The Problem Is I Fell In Love*, a black love story, followed by my fourth novel, another romance novel, *Protégé*—to hit stores soon. See you soon with my fifth novel, *Antaawn Sing, Drug Lord,* another urban novel followed by *Without Father* and *Birthwhistle* and many more…

Pamela M. Johnson
Publisher/Author
Macavelli Press

You may visit *Macavelli* Press on the web at www.macavellipress.com and email Pamela M. Johnson at: publisher@macavelli.com. I so look forward to hearing from you.

Public Relations for *Macavelli* and its authors is handled by www.thejohnsonagency.net

THE PROBLEM IS
I FELL IN LOVE

PROLOGUE

The problem is, I fell in love with a married man. I would never have believed that in a million years I would ever do such a crazy thing. It is so unreal to me. I'm a strong, intelligent, educated, independent woman with morals and values. I have it all together. I should have known better, but I somehow let it happen.

The funny thing is, not even two years earlier I had ridiculed and condemned my friend Camille for doing the exact same thing. Our friend Krystal had invited us over for one of her regular Friday night girls' dinner-sleepovers. These socials often take place at her house, and she invites the clique (herself, Camille, Utopia, and me) to get together and kick it.

We are all best friends. What we have in common, what binds us together, is that we are all college-educated, successful career women who grew up in the hood. None of us lives there now, but our families, friends, and our men are responsible for our regular visits back to our roots.

Unlike many of the friends we all grew up with, we managed not to succumb to the street life. Nevertheless, we had refused to date any man other than a Black man. We're all attracted to guys who are in the game.

A lot of our female counterparts who went to college assimilated, but we never switched up. We are down-to-earth Black women. We kept our shit real. We had dated thugs before, during, and even after college.

In college, we experimented with dating educated Black men, but we discovered there is nothing better than dating a brother who has a rough edge about him—some thug in him. That kind of man is always going to be more exciting than those tight-assed, briefcase-packing, proper-speaking brothers. Our thoughts on them are the same as our thoughts on O.J.: White women can have 'em. No harm done.

The ghetto females, a.k.a. " hoochies," from the block resented us. They said we thought we were better than they are. Wrong. They simply didn't like the attention that we received from the brothers on the block, or how the brothers got at us with a different sort of pick-up line: "Hey, College Girl, I want me a college girl, let me take you to dinner, College Girl." The hoochies didn't like that the brothers would take them to McDonalds, Popeye's, Del Taco, or some soul food or Mexican restaurant in the hood, *while we were taken* to exclusive restaurants on Sunset Boulevard, in Beverly Hills, Malibu, Pacific Palisades, or somewhere in the San Fernando Valley. The hoochies were also jealous of the way the brothers distinguished us from them, referring to us as "the Hollywood Crew." After I got my hair cut they said that I looked like Halle Berry; Utopia, Nia Long; Camille, Vanessa Bell Calloway;

and Krystal, Star Jones.

The hoochies didn't have anything on us. They could be divided into two classes, so to speak. First there were the hoochies, and then there were the "Ghetto Fabulous."

The hardcore hoochies are the "round-the–way" females from the block. Generally, they were not meticulous about where their clothes were purchased, and so they would mix-and-match styles. They'd wear a Ross fit, to a Macys, Nordstrom or Saks Fifth Avenue fit in a minute, depending on where they'd copped it, if from a booster or by boosting it themselves. When they didn't get the designer fashions, they sported imitation designer clothing, shoes and accessories: fake Prada, Fendi, and Gucci; and fake Movado and Gucci watches, purchased in LA's garment district. The second class of hoochies, The Ghetto Fabulous, actually tried to look like us. They regularly sported popular designer clothes, shoes and accessories like ours—the real deal. Like us, their closets also contained only the most expensive fashions from designers like Prada, Moschino, Fendi, Gucci, Jones New York, or Tomatsu (one of Hillary Clinton's favorite designers), as well as other popular and expensive clothing, watches, and accessory designers. They, too, did not mix their fits, but stuck with one designer from head to toe on any given day: hats, tops, dresses, slacks, shoes, shades, whatever. Not many of the hoochies had it like them. Like us, they were in competition with their men, wearing the likes of the same designers. Like us, they were distinguished-looking sisters—at least, on the surface they were.

The Ghetto Fabulous were few in the hood and stood out. But they still couldn't match us. For starters, they weren't educated, and they didn't have the style or class we did. When they sported their clothes, they didn't wear them with style and grace like we did. We wore our clothes with *attitude*. We knew how to present ourselves. Bottom line—a premium-grade hoochie was still a hoochie, and…well, they just looked "ghetto fabulous." We looked classy. Also, we smelled good, like Issey Miyake, Gucci Envy, Michael, Alfred Sung, Tiffany, and Mizrahi.

But looks weren't really what set us, the Hollywood Crew, above the Ghetto Fabulous. When they dressed up on the outside they looked something like us, but when they opened their mouths and spoke, brothers could see they didn't have the same class or education that we possessed. They always spoke in Ebonics. Our speech was different. We had a broader vocabulary. Don't get me wrong: Because we also grew up in the hood, we had ghetto in us as well. However, we knew when to let the inner ghetto show, and when to reserve it. At work, we remained the ladies that we are. When the clique chilled, we spoke—more or less—in Ebonics. College had educated and refined us. It took a lot of the hood out, but the hood was still at the root of our being.

College had also taught us independence, and that was a lesson the hoochies had never learned. Hoochies, whether they boosted styles or bought them for cheaper, were financially dependent upon their men. Sometimes our men bought our clothes, but more often than not, we would elect to pay cash or use one of our own credit cards.

When the brothers saw us, heard us, or smelled us, they knew we were different from the hoochies and the ghetto fabulous females. They were mesmerized by us not only because of our education and the way we carried ourselves, but also now because we played hard-to-get. They didn't love us any more than they loved the hoochies they dated. The thugs just liked the excitement of the chase that they went through to get us. If we had allowed the thugs to get inside our heads, as they often did with the women they went out with, we would be treated no differently. The thugs were gamers, and that's what gamers do. They just used a different approach to get at us because we were different.

Although some of the thugs were cute, we weren't interested in these scrubs. When they flirted with us, we just played with them and flirted back. We loved the attention. We are some beautiful sisters, and the attention we got from the brothers reminded us of how good we still look in our late twenties and early thirties.

No, we didn't just date any brother from the block. Most of them were some broke-ass nigguhs. We didn't want the broke ones; the guys posted on the corner, or the ones running up to cars making a little something-something. The brothers we dated had to meet a certain criteria. We dated the "cream of the crop," so to speak: the no-limit brothers, the brothers with money, the *ballers*.

These brothers wore the latest fashions, and were fitted from head to toe. On their tapered heads, they wore fitted hats. When they dressed casually, they wore Sean Jeans, Platinum, Fubu, and RocaWear clothes. On their feet were Tim's, J's, or Air Force Ones. On days when they really felt like being suited, they wore Armani, Gucci, Prada, DKNY, Dolce & Gabbana, Roberto Cavalli, and Versace suits. Underneath, shirts from the likes of the same distinguished designers were worn. Suits were topped off with classic ties from designers like Fendi, Kenzo, Valentino, Mondo di Marco, and Versace. When suited on their feet, the ballers sported the designs of popular shoe designers: Cole Haans, Allen Edmonds, Ferragamo, Barrett, Mezlan, Nando Muzi, Madeo, or Gucci and Prada were among the designer shoes in their collections. On their wrists, only the best was donned: Rolexes, Huguenots, Bvlgari, Movados, and Tag Heueurs. With all the fly gear, these brothers couldn't be sitting in just any ride. They always rode up on dubs and in expensive automobiles. Range Rovers, Hummers, Navigators, and Escalades were their preferred SUVs; BMWs, Mercedes and Jaguars were their cars of choice.

Like us, the guys we dated had ambition. They were men who wanted something out of life. They often spoke of getting out of the game: taking the money and investing it in legitimate businesses, stocks, and bonds. Some did, in fact, own real estate, and were also entrepreneurs. They didn't hang out on the corner; *others* hung out on the corner under *them*.

Our men were high-class, but deep down, they were still thugs. So, we all experienced problems with our men in the areas of commitment and fidelity. They didn't want to say "*I do,*" and became liars and cheaters. Somehow, though, still we loved them. No matter what them motherfuckas put us through, how much they stressed us out, or fucked with our heads, we always found it in our heart to forgive them, take them back, and continue loving them. We were all single again; most of us had our dirty work for those nights we wanted to get our groove on. Well, at least those of us who hadn't taken a vow of celibacy like I had, did.

Most of the times when the clique got together, discussions about men dominated. Tonight's discussion at Krystal's house was no different. We focused largely on Camille and the married guy, Jonathan, she was dating at the time. We jumped all over her for dating a married man. As long as I live, I will never forget that night.

Jonathan was a baller in the d game. But we didn't trip on the fact that he was a drug dealer. We were letting Camille have it: drilling her about the fact that Jonathan had a wife and four kids, she was one of many, she had no future with him, and that dating him was morally wrong. I was the most vocal and critical one out of the bunch, giving a speech about how wrong it was for her to be dating a married guy.

I held Camille in contempt for being an adulteress, some married man's Jezebel. I lost respect for her. Where were her values, pride, dignity, or her sense of family? After all, her daddy was a preacher, and his daddy before him, and his daddy before him. She attended First Union Baptist Church on Normandy and Figueroa. She never missed a Sunday, and she even sat in the pulpit, sometimes as a member of the church choir. Sometimes she had to give a speech, or read the church newsletter before the start of the service. She was there nodding her head in agreement when the reverend, her daddy, gave his many sermons about extramarital affairs and how they displeased God. Clearly, Camille knew that violating the marriage bed was wrong.

That Friday night, Krystal stood at the island in the middle of the gourmet kitchen, with the black knife in her hand, dicing yellow and green onions, red bell peppers, garlic, and tomatoes for her crab-and-prawn Creole gumbo. We talked about Camille's dilemma. Utopia, Camille, and I sat a few feet from Krystal at the round metal-based glass kitchen table, in the chairs with the white linen tiebacks. The table was covered with a white sheer table-cloth that hung down and touched the ash-blond hardwood floor. Krystal had purchased the table and chairs from The Pottery Barn, our favorite store. Camille's eyes were low. Her depression was obvious. She admitted the affair was driving her crazy.

Without looking up from her food preparation, Krystal spoke to Camille. "So Camille, how's life treating you?" *As if Krystal couldn't see for herself,* I thought.

"I'm cool."

"How are things going between you and Jonathan?"

"Cool, I guess."

"What do you mean 'you guess'?"

"Krystal, you know the situation, y'all know the situation," Camille said, glancing over at Utopia and me.

Krystal gazed towards Camille. She stopped chopping the vegetables, placed the knife with the silver blade and black handle down on the counter, and leaned forward. Her open palms rested on the island's dark grey ceramic. "So, do you think anything is going to come out of this relationship between you and Jonathan?"

"I don't know. I hope so. I mean, I love him… but I don't know," Camille said. A worried look was on her face. She was almost in tears.

Krystal resumed dicing the vegetables. "Camille, be careful. You are mess-ing with a married man. There is no telling what a person will do if they feel they are losing their family. His wife might hurt you. I see it all the time at work. Someone killing over love, crimes of passion."

Utopia had been listening intently to the discussion. "What is it about this man that you like so much, Camille?"

"I'm in love with him."

"What is it about him? What is it that he does, that has you so in love with him?"

Camille hung her head down. She stared down at her clasped hands—rolling her thumbs one over the other. She spoke, "I love everything about him. His strength, his attitude, his street savvy, everything— and I want to be with him. He loves me. She raised her head and looked around the room—making eye contact with me, Krystal and Utopia. "I know you guys don't believe it but really, he does love me. He knows you guys don't like him and that bothers him."

"How does he know that?"

Krystal and I looked at each other. Our mouths dropped open. "She *told* him." Krystal and I had spoken in unison.

"What?!" Utopia was indignant at this apparent breach of one of the informal but abiding principles of the clique: what was spoken by the clique, remained with the clique. "Why would you do something like that? You are our friend and what we say to you in confidence is just that. You do not need to be going off telling your boyfriend about what we think of him!"

Krystal and I shook our heads.

Camille sat speechless in the chair. She was holding her head down. I knew that in the end, Camille's relationship with Jonathan was not going to work and would likely have a bad ending. The sooner she got out of it, the better it would be for her in the long run. I didn't want to see my girl get hurt. She was my friend. I knew Camille loved the Lord. I figured that appealing to her sensibilities would be the way to get her to see the truth about dating a married man, and would make her understand that she did not have a future with him, so why waste her time? I joined the conversation with Camille, Krystal and Utopia.

"You're breaking the commandment God gave us at Exodus 20:14, that you must not commit adultery," I said flatly. Rolling her saddened eyes up and blinking them, Camille sat upright in the chair. She took in a deep breath and then released—as if to say, 'here we go again,' and we were getting on her last nerves. However, she didn't say anything. I left the table and walked into the hallway and to the bookshelf to retrieve Krystal's big black King James Version of the Holy Bible, with the gold cross on the front.

Like myself, Krystal was an avid reader. There must have been more than three hundred books on the tall red oak bookshelf. My eyes searched the shelf, and, locating the Bible, I removed it. I remained standing there, opened the Bible, and turned to First Corinthians 6:9. To assure that it was the scripture I was seeking, I read it silently to myself. Then, having felt satisfied, I hurriedly returned to the kitchen, anxious to show Camille God's word on adultery. Standing over her and sounding like a preacher behind the pulpit on a Sunday morning giving his sermon, I read the verse aloud:

"'What! Do you not know that unrighteous persons will not inherit God's kingdom? Do not be misled. Neither fornicators, nor idolaters, nor adulterers…'" I grabbed a handful of pages and flipped to the back of the Bible. They fell open to the book of scripture that I wanted to see: Revelations. Rushing, I thumbed through the stuck-together pages searching for Revelation 2:22. Frustrated because I kept turning to the stuck-together pages before or after the chapter and verse, I stuck my index finger in my mouth, licked it, and finally separated those stubborn pages. Now I was in control. I turned through the book until I found Revelation 2:22 and also read that scripture.

"'Look! I am about to throw her into a sickbed, and those committing adultery with her into great tribulation, unless they repent of her deeds.' See, it says it right here," I said to Camille, my accusing finger pointing at the scripture I had just read in the Bible that lay in my open palm. "Going with a married man is wrong, dead wrong."

I sat the open Bible in front of her on the table. She glimpsed at it uneasily, and pushed it all the way to the middle of the table. She began speaking; finally, Camille got in a few words. She contended that Jonathan didn't love his wife and that she, not her, was really his soulmate. Jonathan claimed that he and his wife were not compatible, and that he only married her because she became pregnant. Therefore, he wanted to do the right thing, and married her so they wouldn't have a baby out of wedlock. She said he was going to leave his wife soon, and by this time next year, they'd be living together. She even tried to convince us that he was not sexually interested in his wife, and he was only sleeping in the same bed that they shared every night.

"Is that what you believe, Camille? That they're sleeping in the same bed and aren't fucking?" I asked. She hunched her shoulders. "Well let me tell you, they *fucking*, and don't believe for one minute that they are not."

"Well, he said he hasn't slept with her in six months," she retorted.

"Wait a minute," Krystal said, throwing her hand up in the air in exasperation. She stepped out, barefoot, from behind the island and walked towards Camille. She pulled a chair from under the table and sat down. Placing her hand on her chin, she then turned and looked at Camille with a fixed gaze, right up into Camille's eyes. Her voice was soft, but clear and quite composed. "Camille, you know the way the game goes, you are a gamer yourself. The Camille I know is a strong woman and don't give a fuck about a man. She uses them to her benefit and moves on. Now, talk to me girl. What's up?"

"I know what it looks like and I know that you guys want the best for me, but in time you'll see that Jonathan and I are perfect for each other."

"But what happened, girl, this is not the Camille we know, expressing her love for a married man." I could hear hints of frustration seeping in around the corners of Krystal's calm demeanor… but only hints; her voice remained calm. "Camille, we got our game from you on how to deal with brothers like Jonathan."

Camille cut Krystal off. "I guess I just got caught up."

"Well you can get uncaught," Utopia snapped.

Scratching her head with one finger, Krystal stared off into the distance in deep thought. "Camille…" Krystal paused. She began to speak on a particular matter, but refrained. A frown was on her face. She fixed her eyes back on Camille's saddened face. "Nothing, I've made my point. I rest my case," she said breaking her silence.

"Ooh, Camille, all I got to say is watch him. Don't believe anything he says. Men are fucking dogs, liars, and cheaters," Utopia proclaimed.

Krystal stared back into the distance. "That's why I'm tired of dating black men, they too scandalous. I refuse to date another one. I'm gone find me a White guy, Mexican guy, or do like Kim Fields did and get me an Asian." Krystal stood up from the chair, walked back around the island, picked up the knife she'd laid down on the counter, and continued dicing the vegetables. "Seriously speaking, Camille, Jonathan is not leaving his wife for you. I'm not saying that they are never going to break up, but he is not leaving that woman for you. If he were going to he'd have done it by now. You been dating him for how long?" Krystal paused for a moment. "Get my point? Let him go. He's bad news."

"Um hum," Utopia chimed in.

Krystal went on. "You guys don't know this, but I dated this married guy once. I didn't find out he was married until five months after I started dating him and I stopped seeing him after I found out. Three months had gone by after our breakup and his wife who had been looking for me all this time finally caught up with me. She approached me one day about her husband." Her eyes were fixed intently on Camille again. "I was lucky. Ever heard of crimes of passion?" Camille nodded. "Anyway, to make a long story short, when his wife finds out about you, it's gone get real ugly. It won't be worth it. Girl, trust me, walk now, girl. You deserve better than being some married man's mistress," Krystal said.

"And all I got to say is if some shit go down between you and his wife, he gone side with her and not you," Utopia expressed.

"Of course he is," Krystal assented.

"But I love him," Camille declared again in a tone that was barely audible in her depressed state. The whole affair thing, his false promises were driving her crazy.

Krystal nodded. "We really don't have any control over who we like or fall for, but we do have control over who we date."

I thought about what Krystal had said about us getting our game from Camille. She was right. She gave us our game on how to deal with men, the gamers. She's the one who taught us how to get inside a brother's head and break him down mentally. She spoke on how to control our emotions in relationships with men. She even gave us our bedroom tips. Camille had more game than any female I knew. In college, she was an exotic dancer who performed at a gentlemen's club in West Hollywood, and later in Beverly Hills. She was the one who had the men head-over-heels in love with her and she played them, using them for their money or whatever.

Now, it was the other way around. Camille was being played. We'd never seen her weak for a man. The Camille we had known for so long would never have allowed her emotions to get involved with a guy like Jonathan. Had she dated a married man, she would have kept the relationship in perspective and never lost sight of the purpose she was with him for, be it the money or the sex. Jonathan was what we so regularly described as our "dirty work," or sex partner. He wasn't the kind of guy you'd get serious with, let alone give your heart to. He wasn't even kicking Camille down with money. She had always commented that the sex was good and how Jonathan was hung; however, these were not reasons to fall in love with a man or give him one's heart. Before their love affair, they were simply platonic friends.

Like it or not, I figured Camille wasn't ready to throw in the towel with Jonathan. She didn't see the truth. She didn't *want* to see the truth. What we said to her didn't matter: She wasn't coming to her senses, for love had blinded her. She'd known him even longer than I'd known DeMarco, who was to become the subject of my affair. Camille had known Jonathan for something like five years. I'd known DeMarco for two.

I had an inkling about how the mess had started. Jonathan dated Camille's play cousin before Camille slept with him. She had a history of sleeping with men that her friends had dated, or were currently going out with. However, she never crossed that line with the clique.

She hadn't crossed it yet, anyway. The way I saw it at the time, Camille simply couldn't be trusted. A line had been crossed. Knowing her history, and especially now that she would date a married man, I couldn't trust this bitch around a man I liked. Period. The truth is, this is how the clique collectively felt; this was a subtle consensus which each of us had independently reached. For instance, when we went out and knew in advance that a guy that one of us liked and wanted to get with was going to be at our destination, Camille, the potential "man-snatcher," was uninvited. As we saw it, we didn't need her serving as our competition. Among us, we had a "stay back" rule that we respected, an "I want him" understanding. As friends, this boundary was never crossed.

I would not have said anything to Camille's face, or probably out loud to anyone on the topic of the clique's consensus. However, subconsciously and on occasion, I didn't think of Camille as a true friend. When we were all kids, she moved to Jordan Downs, where she and Utopia became acquainted. Utopia then introduced her to Krystal and me. So, I regarded her as Utopia's friend and sorority sister, seeing as how it was through Utopia that we had all first met Camille.

Unfortunately, not two years later, I turn around and do the same god-damned thing. Her guy had two kids; my guy has three. Hadn't he ever heard of the word "protection?" Damn. You can get it over the counter, purchase it at damn near any store. Hell, birth control has reached its advanced stage by now. His bitch could have even gotten the patch. The truth is, all this really didn't matter to me. I was in love. Shit. Oh, well, I fucked up big. I know it.

Apparently, when I got with DeMarco, a case of amnesia had developed regarding the whole Camille situation and my convictions. Interestingly, Camille never criticized me for going out with DeMarco. She would put in her two cents from time to time, but she never came at me like, "remember when you told me nada, nada, nada," or "blah, blah, blah, blah, blah about dating a married man." She never even brought up the way I responded to her and how I treated her for having done the same thing. She remained a friend, which was surprising, given my initial friend-of-a-friend statement. I really appreciated this, especially after everyone—particularly my family—criticized my relationship with DeMarco. It is a funny thing how Camille has now broken up with Jonathan. She said she realized his promises to leave his wife would never happen, and she just grew tired of the situation.

I know that dating a married man is wrong. I try to psych myself out and make it a mind-over-matter thing. I tell myself that we are in control of our emotions and our emotions are not in control of us. I aim to convince myself that I don't like DeMarco. I pretend I don't like him. "*I don't like DeMarco*" has become my daily mantra; these are words I utter on the bus, on the train rides to work, and while driving somewhere. This rant continues even when I am brushing my teeth every morning: I will stare into the bathroom mirror with a twisted mouth full of mixed toothpaste and saliva, hissing and mumbling, "uh ahh don't like DeMarco!" Who am I kidding? I *am* in love with him. He is my constant thought, the one that brings a smile to my face, and the man who keeps me smiling when I'm in his presence.

To deal with my lust for a married man, I consulted with Reverend Miller at church. I had confessed and confided in him about going with a married man. In that black pin striped suit, starched white dress shirt, black tie and black suspenders for which he is so popular for wearing, he spoke in his southern Mississippi drawl. The good old reverend told me, "Gurl, what you doing lusting for a married man, it's a sin. Why you wanna do it? What you need is prayer, so God can get that sin off yo mind. Next Sunday, I want you to go up to the altar at altar call, and confess to God about this man. I'm gone pray for you, Sister Jones, things gone be aiight. Now, I want you to go up to that altar and talk to God. But you know you got to get down on yo knees tonight, you have to pray to God and leave it in his hands. Get on your knees and pray tonight to the Lord, ask Him for repentance. Ask him to remove the thoughts of that married man from your mind and for forgiveness of your sins."

Not pleased with the way the reverend handled the situation, I considered visiting a Catholic church. I had never been to a Catholic church, but I was willing to give my first confession there. Maybe the priest would go soft on me, in light of what was going on right now in the news, what with the Catholic Church and all the discussions about the priests molesting little boys. Hell, the sin the Reverend Miller told me I was guilty of was not nearly as bad as those violations! Who knows? I thought the priest might even grant me absolution.

I know that must seem silly. But it showed how my conscience was getting the best of me. "My friendship and working relationship with DeMarco is over, I swear," I said to myself. When I said it, I meant it; really I did. I tried to be strong. I forced myself not to call him. The struggle was softly and slowly killing me inside. Every time the telephone rang, I became enlivened. I answered it with anticipation of his voice on the other end….only to become dispirited again.

"Oh, hey girl, it's you," I would say. The disappointment that I tried to hide was all too clear.

After a few more days went by, he called.

"Hello?"

"Haley, how da hell ya doin'? Where in da hell ya been," he said jokingly, in that thick, fake Jamaican accent that he is known for emulating. I became nervous, anxious, butterflies flew around in my stomach. I found myself unable to give the speech, which I had practiced for days while waiting for the day where he would call. I had rehearsed this monologue in front of the mirror. I was prepared to tell him about himself, and end our little affair.

Instead, I found myself putting on my sweet sexy voice, "I've just been real busy, that's all. How you been?"

I closed my eyes and I see him right through the telephone line. In my mind's eye, I envisioned his handsome face, his dark smooth Hershey chocolate skin, his long loose black dreads cascading down his back, his full and nicely-shaped lips, and his half-smile. I see him behind the wheel of the Black Range Rover wearing a Versace, Dolce Gabbana or Gucci suit, his shiny Huguenot, Rolex or Bvlgari watch, the gold chain on his wrist lying next to it, and the silent strength of his character. I blush over the phone. The sound of his voice gets rid of the anxiety in my heart, and erases my ideas about cutting him out of my life. My mood soars. And there I am, back to square one. The prepared speech is now forgotten.

I ask myself when and how my feelings for DeMarco developed. Like the last three pounds I had gained, I looked up one day, and they were simply there. I have tried to make them go away, Lord knows I have, but they won't depart. I'm in a "Catch 22" situation! Again, I know that loving a married man is wrong. But, the truth is I don't want to end my relationship with DeMarco. I am in love. My heart literally aches when I am not with him, or when I do not hear from him for even a few days. You know what the problem is? The problem is, I fell in love.

One

When we met, I had no interest in DeMarco and he had no interest in me. We met at a recording studio in Los Angeles. He was the CEO and owner of the record label, Life Incorporated Records. I was the president of Eastside West Entertainment, the company that owned the studio where we met. Also, I was working on starting *Rage* Magazine, a hip-hop magazine. A mutual passion for the music and entertainment business ended up bringing us together.

Before I even met DeMarco, I had already heard the rumors about him from my cousin, Skerz. I had been away on a business trip in New York and hadn't been at Eastside West all week. My airplane had just landed at LAX when Skerz called me on my cell. He was excited, telling me all about his friend named DeMarco, who was a millionaire from the drug trade who had just moved into Eastside West headquarters while I was away in New York. He said DeMarco was now running his record label out of some office space he had subleased from the owner and president of Eastside West, my boss, Big Larry. Bubbling with excitement, Skerz talked about how DeMarco was what you'd call a baller's baller. He said that the ballers got their drugs from him. He said DeMarco was going to be the next Suge Knight or Irv Gotti in the music business, and would put the West Coast hip-hop and rap music scene back on the map.

Dumbfounded, I sat on the telephone listening to Skerz carrying on about this DeMarco. He hardly even let me get a word in. "He gone take over Big Larry's studio and show him how to run the shit, cause that nigguh don't know how to run it right. He doesn't even listen to you, Haley," Skerz had commented.

"He ain't takin' over shit," I expressed.

Before I was even finished with that one little sentence, Skerz's monologue continued. "Man, that nigguh, Big Larry, he playing. With a studio like the one he got, he suppose to be way farther than he is. He supposed to be a millionaire by now. Haley, you suppose to be rich. Man, Big Larry he just messing around. He playing. Man, watch my nigguh DeMarco though. He gone go up in there and have it cracking up in that motherfucka like it is suppose to be." Skerz's admiration and praise of DeMarco seemed to have no end. "That nigguh got money. He a balla, he sell pounds, I mean pounds of weed and drugs. He like the Michael Jordan of the drug game out here, or damn near close to it. He about his money and he know how to make money. Plus, he a real nigguh. Now, are you stopping by the studio tonight, Haley?"

"After I go home, put my luggage away, shower and change," I answered.

"When you see DeMarco, let him know you my cousin."

"Alright." And should I bow when I see him, I wanted to ask.

Two

The smell of chronic and the guys' shouting voices greeted me as I walked into the Eastside West building. The guys were in the lounge, watching the playoff game between the Lakers and the Sacramento Kings on the sixty-inch silver-and-black TV.

"Did you see that? Shaq is hell," a voice shouted.

"No, Shaq is a motherfucker," another yelled. Shaq had just dunked the ball, taking the Lakers into the lead.

I peeked inside the lounge. Animal, Dubb, Dollar Bill, Riff Raff, Big Larry, and a stranger with long dreadlocks were seated around the room. A crumpled brown paper bag, pint of Hennessey, a 16-ounce bottle of Coca-Cola with a lemon twist sat at Big Larry's feet. They were all drinking liquor from shot glasses. Riff Raff and Dollar Bill were permanent fixtures at Eastside West, carrying out odd jobs assigned by Big Larry in exchange for free studio time. I figured the stranger with the long black dreadlocks sitting next to Big Larry on the couch to be DeMarco. The stranger spoke. "Hey, where the weed at? Y'all smoked it all."

"It's gone man," Riff Raff said, in a voice that might as well have said, "What's to be done about it?"

The stranger who was holding two shiny silver meditation balls in one hand—rolling them around, playing with them—had a perplexed look on his

14

face. He reached inside the pocket on his suit jacket, and pulled out a large Ziploc bag full of chronic. Tossing the bag across the room to Dubb, "Here, roll some up for us," he said.

Dubb caught the bag in the air with one hand. "I know somebody around here got a blunt," Dubb asked aloud—not directing his question at anyone in particular. No one responded to his question. They were watching the TV. Dubb shouted his question again.

The stranger acknowledged him. He tapped Big Larry on the shoulder, and pointed towards Dubb. "Hey, Big Larry, you got a blunt for this nigguh?" Sitting next to Big Larry on the gray sofa and staring at the TV, using his fingers, he continued rotating the silver meditation balls constantly clockwise and counter clockwise in his hand. His fingers moved smoothly over the soft balls. His thumb pushed the ball toward his pinky.

"Look over there on that table; it's some blunts over there," Big Larry said, waving his hands in the air without removing his eyes from the TV. Dubb got up and retrieved the box of blunts from the table. Everyone's backs faced me, and their eyes were fixed on the TV. They hadn't even realized I'd walked in. Big Larry kept watching the game.

Big Larry, whose real name was Larry Scott, was the owner of Eastside West Entertainment. The company was housed in a huge building smack in the middle of the downtown district of Los Angeles on Wilshire. Eastside West was like the Taj Mahal of recording studios, I'm here to tell you. The entrance room alone was all decked-out. Upon entering the building, visitors were greeted by an armed security officer, who required a signature from them in his ornate black book with gold lettering, like a guest book you'd see at a fancy wedding. Surveillance cameras were present throughout the building, wired to Big Larry's home computer. He could see the goings-on at his studio, every square inch of it, from home by simply turning on his Dell desktop computer and remotely logging into the computerized security camera system.

The recording studio was located at the back of the huge building. To get there, you walked through the lounge area, passed by the newly remodeled kitchen—yes, a kitchen!—a Jacuzzi, fireplace, a twenty by ten-foot stage and the five swank suites that housed the visiting artists who were recording at the studio. On the nights when there were parties, artists and groups rehearsed and performed on the stage.

Just when you thought that you had come to the end of an impressive tour, you looked up and saw an invigorating mural of dead artists sitting behind the stage. It was a custom job painted by Bryan Keith, a talented and gifted L.A. street artist. He was a recovering heroin addict who used art as part of his recovery. Bryan had never taken a formal art class, yet began drawing at the age of seven. The mural was a custom job. Big Larry had provided him with pictures of all of the artists, and Bryan painted them on the mural. The mural was as big as a billboard.

As an artist, Bryan was right up there with Michelangelo. You could walk right up to it and see fine details in the musicians' faces and clothes. The mural itself was a Who's Who of Black artists: Tupac, Biggie Smalls, Eazy E, Marvin Gaye, Jimmy Hendrix, and Bob Marley were all on the mural. It was truly breathtaking and inspiring. When asked why he had the mural designed and why he started East Side, Big Larry would say, "The mural represents my admiration and appreciation of all those artists. It is my dedication to them. Each one brought something unique to music. Eazy E is the legend that started gangster rap. I can't imagine having a serious discussion about rap music without talking about him. Tupac and Biggie, they speak for themselves, as does Marley and Marvin Gaye. When people come in here and they see these dead artists on the mural, they'll be reminded of them, and give that moment of silence they rightfully deserve. All the rest, they were true to their art and contributed greatly to the history of music. Their music did a lot for people's souls." After giving this speech that he regularly gave to first time visitors, Big Larry would close by saying, "there is so much talent on the West Coast. I am here and open to the artists who are serious-minded and believe in their dreams, and are determined to have a successful career in music."

Originally from Chicago's south side, Big Larry came to southern California to escape the notorious Midwest gang life. He was a Gangster Disciple. He was recruited into the notorious Chicago gang life at a young age. His group was feuding with a rival gang, and many of his fellow members were killed. Larry wanted to get away from the nonsense and change his life, so he moved to the West Coast. Upon arrival, he didn't know anyone except his older brother, Raymond, with whom he moved in. His brother was in the Army at the time, stationed in California. Raymond was also a former gang member who had turned his life around.

After having several near-death experiences, Big Larry often commented that he was amazed with how he was still alive. On three separate occasions, his mother's home was sprayed with bullets. He had been shot at many times, and twice struck by a bullet. Big Larry's older brother would often tell him, "If you don't change your lifestyle, you won't be here by your next birthday." Big Larry said he'd respond, that it didn't matter because we were all going to die someday. At the time, he was banging, he didn't care about anything, and his attitude was he didn't give a damn.

Big Larry loved to tell stories about his life growing up in the Shy. His stories—no matter how many times you heard them- were always interesting and captivating. Each time he told them, he would speak with even more enthusiasm and excitement than before. Sometimes when listening to Big Larry speak, he sounded as if he still idolized the street life or even missed it now and again. I don't know; maybe he wanted the rappers to know he lived the life they rapped about, and that he came from a similar environment to their own.

One thing was for sure: Larry's stories, his enormous size, and the scar that ran from his ear to his neckline earned him respect. It was rumored that an opposing gang back in Chicago had kidnapped and tortured him. It was said that they left Big Larry for dead in a local park on Chicago's south side after slitting his throat. He had almost died.

As a teenager, lying in a bed for a second time at Chicago's County Hospital, Big Larry said his life and death flashed before his eye and he gained a new outlook on life. In that hospital bed, wounded, he re-evaluated his life's direction. Up until that point, like many of the brothers that lived the street life, the thug life, Big Larry had accepted that his path would have eventually led to his death.

"I could go on with that thuggish life or turn my life around," he told me one day when we were sitting up in his office, watching the traffic on the street below. "For the first time, I understood my brother's words: that if I kept living the way I was, I wouldn't live to see my next birthday. I realized life is more important than death. I wanted to live. I realized I had so much to live for, so much I wanted to do before I died. I was young. Clearly, for the first time, I realized I had two choices, continue banging and die young like most of my homies I grew up with, or change my ways and live this life to the fullest."

He chose the latter, and headed west to Woodland Hills, California, a suburb of Los Angeles. There, he met a former member of the hip-hop group Digital Underground, who had his own recording studio and record label. Big Larry learned studio engineering from him by recording sessions for some local rappers. After about six months of working at the studio, Big Larry had learned the art and the science of recording; he became the studio's sole engineer and a rapper on the record label. He said that after he arrived in California, he noticed the local rappers were speaking about the street life. He realized that he could rap like them 'cause he had a whole lot of stories to tell about growing up on Chicago's South Side. It wasn't easy.

After a couple of independent releases, Big Larry started producing for many of the local groups. Eventually, his name got out there as a producer who made tight beats and numerous underground rappers started buying his beats. He said that he then stopped rapping to pursue a career as a producer after signing a bad recording contract that restricted him—telling him what he could and couldn't do. Big Larry realized that being a producer in the music business was where the real money was. Using his royalties plus a well-timed inheritance, he became the owner of his own record label and recording studio, thereby founding Eastside West.

Because he was having financial problems about two years ago, Larry brought in two investors. Unfortunately, he was now feuding with them and they refused to offer financial assistance. In an attempt to save the enterprise and to cut costs, he reluctantly decided to sublease some of the office space within the five thousand square foot building to other musicians and artists. DeMarco, a prosperous drug dealer in the music business and one of the first people Big Larry met when he moved to southern California, happened to be one of those people.

Big Larry was 42 years old, stood at six-feet-four inches tall, and weighed 275 pounds. He was a handsome, light brown-skinned, big man with a baby face. He bore a striking resemblance to Quincy Jones. In fact, he looked so much like Quincy that people would joke, betting he could get back stage at one of his concerts without a problem if he said he was Quincy's son. Somehow, the long-faded scar that ran from behind his right ear down to his neck did not take away from his good looks. He was a well-groomed man. He took his dress and grooming seriously; both were always impeccable. His clothes were purchased off-the-rack at department stores like Macy's Men and Nordstrom's. However, he could have easily convinced people that his clothes were tailor-made, for they fit him so well. Even as a big man, he had that kind of physique. His clothes looked good on him. Working out at the gym regularly, he carried his weight well.

Big Larry often sported a Cuban cigar; however, he only lit it on those special and rare occasions. With the exception of his gold two karat diamond wedding ring (which he'd sometimes alternate with a gold wedding band), Big Larry didn't wear jewelry. He wore a trimmed full black beard and black mustache, and every two weeks had his nails manicured and he also got a pedicure. "Gotta stay looking good so my wife don't leave me," he'd often joke. Big Larry always smelled good—leaving behind a scent of Calvin Klein Eternity Cologne.

At the studio that evening, Big Larry's aunt, Esther, was in the kitchen doing some really aromatic cooking. She was an excellent cook. Every Friday, Aunt Esther prepared a delicious meal in the studio's kitchen. The end-of-week feast had been a tradition since the studio had opened more than eight years ago. When she got going, your mouth would be watering before you'd take three steps into the studio, and this night was no exception.

I went into the kitchen to say hello to Aunt Esther, who was in the newly remodeled brick red colored kitchen with the brown cabinets and windows trimmed in gold, working with the new shiny appliances. She was now bending over at the stove, wearing a white apron trimmed with ruffles, lowering the fire under the skillet of simmering smothered pork chops. Another pot of greens with salt pork and smoked neck bones was cooking next to a pot of Jasmine rice, and next to that, candied yams. As if all of that wasn't quite enough, cornbread was in the oven.

"Hello, Aunt Esther."

She looked up. "Hey Haley, how you doing, baby?"

"Good, and you?"

"I'm blessed."

"Aunt Esther, you got it smelling like Christmas up in here," I said, walking further into the kitchen, inhaling the heady vapors of the upcoming Southern banquet. She smiled.

"The food will be ready shortly," she said.

"Alright, I'll be back. I just wanted to say hello. I'm going to go in the lounge and watch the game with the guys."

"Alright," she said, turning back to her work, like a scientist in a laboratory.

I walked back into the lounge. This time when I walked in, Big Larry noticed me.

"Hey Haley," he said. The stranger looked back at me. Big Larry got up and gave me his usual greeting hug. Animal, Dubb, Dollar Bill and Riff Raff spoke; I acknowledged them by saying hello. Big Larry pointed at his six-feet-two-inch friend DeMarco—who was now standing up next to him, looking ten inches down at me- and introduced us.

"DeMarco, this is my girl Haley right here who I was telling you about, she the President of Eastside West. She runs everything around here—everything," Big Larry so proudly proclaimed. DeMarco smiled and extended his arm for a handshake. He was a handsome dark-skinned brother. Immediately I noticed his teeth. They were extra white. They were beautiful. I took hold of his hand and shook it, examining his perfect teeth. *People spent a lot of money at the dentist on expensive treatments and having them capped to get their teeth in perfect smiling condition like his*, I thought while staring at them.

Big Larry continued. "Haley, me and DeMarco go way back. He's one of the first people I met out here in LA when I moved here a long time ago, and he was one of the first executive producers to buy my beats."

"Is that right," I replied.

"Nice to meet you, Haley," DeMarco said.

"Nice to meet you."

Big Larry kept talking, "Haley, DeMarco knows everybody in the music industry, and he got hook up at the radio stations here in LA. Haley, his boy be wrapping vans. We need to get our van wrapped with our Eastside West logo and we need to put some of the rappers' pictures we be working with on the van. It would be excellent advertising for us." Pointing at DeMarco, he said, "DeMarco, give my girl Haley the number to the guy who be wrapping vans." DeMarco's eyes were fixed back on the TV and the game, where Shaq held the ball again, besieged by the other team's forward and center. Never taking his eyes off the television, DeMarco nodded. A moment later, a buzzer rang in the background on the TV, and the clock on the scoreboard was all zeros.

"It's halftime—food ready," Aunt Esther announced. Riff Raff and Dollar Bill were the first ones up and getting their plates; Big Larry quickly followed suit. One of them bumped into Big Larry on the way to the kitchen.

"Hey, hold on wait a minute, this is my shit I'm getting my food first, back the fuck up," Big Larry shouted, pushing his way into the kitchen ahead of them. When Big Larry got through fixing his plate, it looked like a feast for two. The greens were piled high on top of the rice. He had loaded onions atop the onion-smothered pork chops, piled up the candied yams, cut a large piece of cornbread, and sat it atop the yams. Everyone crowded around him so they could make way to the stove next. He resembled a quarterback in a huddle. "Back the fuck up nigguh, let Haley get in there first," Larry said, making his way from the stove to the kitchen table and chair sitting in the corner.

"I just want to taste some of your greens and a piece of cornbread, Aunt Esther," I said, stepping through the kitchen.

Despite his cussing and attitude, Big Larry was a good person with a heart of gold. He'd give you the shirt off his back. He talked rough, but there was really no vicious bite behind his bark—at least not with us. Larry and Aunt Esther were more like brothers and sisters. He was actually four years older than Esther. His grandmother, her mother, had raised them together.

"DeMarco, you gone fix you a plate," Aunt Esther asked, noticing that DeMarco alone hadn't made for the kitchen like lightning.

"He don't eat pork," Larry said while stirring his greens, rice, and cornbread together. "Somebody hand me the hot sauce," he yelled. Dubb handed him the bottle of Tabasco.

"Good, that's more food for us," Dollar Bill joked. DeMarco stared at him. He didn't even crack a smile.

"You don't eat pork, DeMarco?" Aunt Esther questioned him.

Big Larry grinned. "Didn't you see him just eating that vegetarian sandwich with the bean sprouts, tomatoes, lettuce and eggplant when he first got here?"

"I wish y'all motherfuckers would shut the fuck up and let DeMarco speak for himself, God damn," Aunt Esther said. "He don't look like no one that needs someone to talk for him." She turned to DeMarco. "I didn't know that you didn't eat pork. Had I known, I would have made some chicken for you. Are you the kind of vegetarian who eats chicken?" DeMarco nodded.

"How come you don't eat pork?"

"I just don't. I eat healthy. I mean our body is a temple and we have to be careful about what we put in it. But yeah, sometimes I eat chicken, turkey and fish, but not really that often, like a few times a month."

"Well DeMarco, do you want some of the other stuff I cooked like Haley fixed herself? Greens, cornbread, or rice or something," Aunt Esther appealed.

"I'm cool."

"Say man, DeMarco are you a Rasta," Animal inquired.

"What you mean?"

"I mean, you know, your dreads, are you a Rasta? You like the Rastafarian culture."

"I appreciate and like all cultures, not just the Rasta culture. But yeah, there's a lot of things that I do like and appreciate about the Rasta culture."

Dubb piped in. "How long you been growing your dreads?"

"Twelve years."

"Yeah, I notice a lot of those Compton nigguhs from Jordan Downs be wearing dreads, especially back in the days," Dubb said. With his head tilted to the side, DeMarco locked Dubb in his stare. I later learned when DeMarco first moved to Compton from the Bay, he moved to Jordan Downs; so, to everybody in the game, that's where he was from. He had come by way of East Oakland's notorious San Antonio Villa, a.k.a. "6-9 Ville."

Three

One Friday evening, I sat alone in Eastside West's lounge, talking to Utopia on my cell. I was ending my conversation with her when DeMarco entered. Dropping his coins into the coin slot on the vending machine for a bottled water, he asked if Big Larry was around.

"No, he's at home. He left about an hour ago. He wasn't feeling good."

"You know when he's coming back? I need to see him about something." He removed the bottled Evian water from the machine.

"Naw, I don't," I said, shaking my head.

"So how you doing," DeMarco asked.

"Fine, and you?"

DeMarco shrugged his shoulders. "Well, it really don't do no good to complain, but as my grandma says, I'll do."

"What's up with you?"

"Just a lot of bullshit. Some shit I got to take care of, that's all."

"Hmmm." DeMarco carried a worried and stressed look across his face. I could feel his thoughts. He was burdened about something.

"What's up with you on a Friday night," he asked.

"Nothing really."

"You ain't going out with your girlfriends—the ones that came here with you last time I saw you?"

"You talking about Krystal, Utopia and Camille? We tight. We've known each other for years. Actually, I'm going over to Krystal's house for dinner."

"Krystal, is that the one that looks like Star Jones?"

I giggled a bit. "Everybody says that about her. She does look dead on Star. We tell her that all the time."

"Isn't she a lawyer?"

"Yeah, she is. How did you know?"

"I thought that was what Big Larry said. Also, I know some people that know her. I know some people that know Utopia and Camille also. From what I hear, they dated a few of my boys. What kind of lawyer is Krystal?"

"She's a criminal law attorney. She's got her own practice."

"Is that right? Hey, tell her I might need her to look into something for me."

I filed that last bit of information away, figuring that it might mean something if DeMarco needed a lawyer. "Alright. So what about you, DeMarco, you kicking it with your friends tonight?"

He shook his head, "Naw, most of them gone to the Tyson fight in Vegas at the MGM."

"Is that right? I take it you didn't wanna go?"

"No, I did, but some other ass shit came up that I gotta take care of, so I didn't go." DeMarco appeared quite irritated. "I had a ticket to the fight and every thang. Man, I paid a lot of money for that ticket, four G's to be exact. I gave my boy my ticket at the last minute. He drove down. I would have given him my airplane ticket, but it wasn't in his name and you know since 911, things at the airport is really tight."

"Hmmm." *Must have been rather important, whatever it was he missed the Tyson fight for, for him to miss it*, I thought.

"I'm about to go home though and fuck with my kids. I need to spend some time with them," DeMarco said.

"How many kids you got?"

DeMarco held up three fingers. "You got three kids," I asked.

"Yeah," he said proudly, "How about you? How many kids you got?"

"None, but I got a lot of nieces and nephews."

"You married, Haley?"

"No. You?"

"Yeah, but she ain't here now, she's away. I'm a single parent. Been one for almost a year now."

"You got boys or girls or both?"

"Two girls and a son. I had one kid before I met my wife. I had full physical custody of her. I was raising her as a single father before I got married."

"Is it hard being a single parent?"

"It can be, but you just do what you gotta do—you know? Hey Haley, not to change the subject or anything, but check it out. I was in Borders bookstore in the Beverly Center the other day and I brought these three books on the music business. They got all kind of stuff in there on music publishing and independent record distribution. Wait a minute; hold on… I got the books here. Let me go and get them out of my studio. I'll be right back." DeMarco left the lounge. I got up, retreated into the kitchen, and took a seat at the glass bar with silver trimming. Big Larry paid a lot of money for that bar. One day he was ranting and raving about how bad he wanted it after seeing it displayed in a store window. The next thing I knew, Vogue Furniture store was delivering that bar. The lounge was located next to the kitchen, which was in route to DeMarco's studio. Shortly, he returned with three books, *Get It in Writing, Independent Record Distribution,* and *Understanding Music Business Contracts.*

He plopped the books down on top of the bar next to me. "Artists really need to educate themselves and read some of these books. Most of them sign contracts and don't even know what's in them. See, I'm like you Haley, I read a lot and if I don't know something, you can believe I'm going to learn about it." He pointed at the three books. "Haley, if you ever wanna borrow them, you can."

"I just might take you up on borrowing the one about independent music distribution."

"Here." DeMarco handed me the book. I tucked it into my Moschino tote. "Alright, after you finish reading it, I'm gone read it and then we have to discuss it over lunch or dinner, deal?"

"Deal," I confirmed. We shook hands.

DeMarco went on. "Big Larry says you starting a magazine?"

"I am, it's going to be called *Rage*. It's similar to *Vibe* and *The Source*. It's a hip-hop magazine."

"Wow! Starting a magazine is a real good idea. You can't go wrong with that. What made you decide to start a magazine?"

"Writing is my passion. It's something I do very well. I have a degree in public relations. I do a lot of PR for Eastside West, among a lot of other duties. Actually, I do a little bit of everything around here. I also write business plans. I wrote one for a jazz record label that got funded, and I wrote the business plan for *Rage*."

"You're a busy woman."

"Yes, that I am."

"Are you going to leave Eastside West once your magazine gets off the ground?"

"No, I'll still be here. Eventually, when the time is right I want to launch my own record label though. What's the name of your label, DeMarco?"

"Life Incorporated Records."

"Life Incorporated," I repeated. "Why Life?"

"I knew you were going to ask me that," DeMarco said. He smiled, looked me in the eye and went on, "I named my record label 'Life' because Life is about existence and mortality. Life is about growing, you know, and learning the lessons along the way. What you do today you won't do tomorrow. What a lot or rappers do today or how they feel and react today, they won't tomorrow. Life represents a continual process of growth. And this is what Life records represent. That's why I got all kind of artists signed to Life: rap, reggae… hell, I am even going to sign some gospel rap and jazz acts as the record label grows. I'm a philosophic person. I read a lot of books on Buddhism. It gets me through a lot of life's drama—you know, my own personal demons. Do you know the Philosophy of the Yen and the Yang?"

"Yeah, the never ending circle, infinity."

"Yeah, well, Life Records is about that. It's about living, it's about being positive, it's about being able to change what you are today and be what it is that you want to be tomorrow."

DeMarco appeared to be quite the philosopher. "I have read my share of books on Buddhism. There are some very interesting philosophies in Buddhism. Some really good things you can apply to your life, especially if you've been through it."

"Man, who you telling, I found refuge in the religion. Man, like I said it has helped me to get over a lot of my own personal demons. I used to gangbang and all that shit when I was a little nigguh and I even had my share of that life into my adult years. My life use to be crazy and my temper—ooh wee man, I use to have a temper. Thanks to Buddhism and the Bible, can't count out the good book, I have changed a lot from the way I use to be. I use to didn't give a fuck about nobody or nothing. Man, Haley, you wouldn't have liked me even just a few years back. I have definitely changed for the better."

"Well that's good!"

DeMarco nodded, and stared at me for a long time. I tried to stare him down, thinking that he'd turn his head first, but he didn't. Feeling uncomfortable, I turned my head and stared at the stove that was in front of me. I felt awkward. The room was silent. In my mind, I was thinking, *Okay, why is he staring at me long and hard like he is. I wish he'd stop*. It was as if he was looking through me. Then, standing right there before me he started doing these double takes and double stares, which were really making me feel uncomfortable. I decided it was time to come out of silence.

"DeMarco why are you staring at me like that," I asked.

He shook his head. "I don't know."

"Don't you know it's rude to stare at someone?"

He took another double take at me and raised his eyebrow. He ignored my comment. "Your hair looks nice like that…cut short. Makes you look like a darker version of Halle Berry." He finally changed the subject back to music. "Like I was saying, my artists now are rap and reggae, but I'm diversifying. I have my eye on this one female gospel artist I'm thinking about signing to my record label. Speaking of artists, who are some of the people you'd like to interview for Rage, Haley?"

Now we were both talking about our passions. "Well, my ultimate interview would be one with Nelson Mandela, or Muhammad Ali even. I'd like to interview Don King, Puffy, Suge Knight, Snoop Dogg, Al Pacino, and Dr. Dre. Too Short… ooh, man the list goes on. Oh yeah, I got an interview with Shock G. tomorrow. That should be a good one. He was the man who put 'Pac in the game."

"You got an interview with Humpty?" DeMarco looked impressed.

"That's right; I'm interviewing him for a Tupac tribute article that will appear in the next September issue of Rage Magazine. You know, the eighth anniversary of his death is coming up. I figured who else would be better to talk to about Pac but Shock G—the man who put 'Pac in the game. I just learned that he produced my favorite Tupac song, *So Many Tears.*"

"What? Shock produced that song?"

"Yeah, he wrote it and produced it."

"Well, well, well. You learn something new every day."

"I know, huh? I just found out he produced the song about a month ago. I did this interview with Money B. and he mentioned it during the interview."

"How did the interview go with Mon?"

"It went good, he was talking about how Digital Underground are real visionaries, that they started in 1941." DeMarco cocked an eyebrow oddly, so I went on to further explain. "Hip-hop wasn't made yet and there was no turntables, nothing. They all committed suicide and decided to be reincarnated later. They came back together in the '80s—Mon, Shock G, Humpty Hump, Tupac, DJ Fuse, Chop Master J, BlowFish, Sleuth, Kenny K. and Baby Dope. Mon said, 'it's a beautiful thing to know that through our transformation of 1941, we are still committed. Who knows? Perhaps once we achieve our goal of 1941, we will commit suicide for a second time and reincarnate in another forty, fifty, or sixty years… say, come back in the year 2050 or something.' That's what he said."

DeMarco looked at me incredulously. "Is that what he said?"

I nodded my head.

"Mon is a fool. I guess that's their philosophy. Shock must have came up with that story." DeMarco and I both laughed, and he continued. "Yeah,

Shock told them nigguhs that shit, he's eccentric."

"I know crazy huh," I replied.

"Yeah, but Haley, that Shock interview is going to be a good one. He is the man who put 'Pac in the game, you know, 'Pac's manager and his manager were friends. 'Pac's Manager told Shock's manager about him and both of their managers made it happen for them to meet. Hey, I got a question for Shock. Ask him to speak on Tupac's feelings about Biggie. Personally, I don't think 'Pac hated Biggie so much. When 'Pac was in New York filming the movie *Juice*, Biggie use to hang out on the movie set with him. He and Biggie was having like steak, and lobsters, and shit at Pac's expense—cause Biggie wasn't making money yet back then. They was friends." I nodded in agreement cause I had heard the same stories also.

"Yeah, Haley you should really ask Shock to speak on Tupac's feelings about Biggie 'cause like I said, I don't think 'Pac really hated Biggie. Shock could clarify some things for a lot of people. 'Pac is dead and gone now, so he really can't say nothing, but Shock, yeah, he the one who can clear it up. That Suge interview would be a good one too, though. When do you expect the magazine to be out?"

"It's still in its development stage right now. I'm at the point where I'm just kind of planning things. Rage probably won't be out for another year, the Shock interview will be in the September issue of the first year's run. It's on my editorial calendar, but everyday I am doing something towards Rage like interviewing celebrities and having photo shoots with my photographers."

"So you got a staff?"

"Right now, I have an art director, two photographers, two writers, and two editors. I need to bring on board a few more graphic designers, photographers, and writers. I've actually been doing a lot of the writing myself. Most of it in fact. I am going to put an ad up on Craigslist tomorrow for some more help to see if I can find some more people to work with me."

"What's Craigslist?"

"Craigslist is a web site, where you can find practically anything you are looking for. It is communities of talented people with different kind of skills coming together to help one another. On Craigslist, you can find an apartment, roommate, and pretty much whatever it is that you are looking for. I can go on there, for instance, and post that I am launching a magazine and I need art directors, graphic artists, writers, or whatever, and people with those skills will respond to my ad. It's a real cool site. You should check it out sometime. I found the photographer, the two art directors and the editors that I am working with now on Craigslist."

"That's cool. Later tonight, when I get home, I'll check it out. Like I said, you got a good idea with that magazine." DeMarco sat down on the barstool, folded his arms, and leaned forward against the bar. Biting the tip of his thumb, thinking, he said, "Starting a magazine is one of the best ideas I've heard in a long time. Everybody starting record labels, but no one's starting a magazine—that's a damn good idea, and you can write. Man, you are going to be able to barter a lot of services with these rappers—getting them to drop vocals in exchange for ads. You ain't gone ever have to pay for verses from rappers to get on your shit or any of your projects. You can even barter an ad for an ad with other magazines. Let me know if you need any help or anything. I could help you with promotions and getting interviews. By the way, I got a contact to Dr. Dre if you don't have one, if you want it. You mentioned he is one of the people you'd like to interview."

Now that would be cool, I thought. "Is that right, you got a contact for Dre?"

"Yeah, my boy is one of his staff producers. He could make it happen for you to interview Dre."

"I would appreciate that. For me to make *Rage* Magazine to the West Coast what *The Source* is to the East Coast—which is my goal—I need support from people like Dre."

"Wait a minute; let me call my boy right now and he can hook it up. He might not answer his cell though 'cause he probably in the studio. Dre be working them nigguhs;" DeMarco said, reaching inside the pocket of his soft Kenneth Cole black leather jacket. He pulled out his cell and dialed the number.

"Hey Eric, what's up nigguh?"

I could hear Eric's voice coming through the earpiece on the cell. He was talking loud. "DeMarco, what's happening, dog," he asked.

"Shit, just trying to make a dollar. What's up with you?"

"I'm like you nigguh—trying to make a dollar too."

"Hey DeMarco, nigguh, I need a pound."

"Alright, when?"

"Tomorrow."

"Alright, just come see me."

"Hey you got any chronic?"

"Yeah," DeMarco responded hesitantly. "Wasn't that the pound you was talking about you needed?"

"Naw, nigguh, I need a pound of coke and four pounds of chronic."

"You got the money?"

"Nigguh, I wouldn't be asking for it If I didn't. I know you don't fuck around when it comes to your dollars."

"No problem. I'll take care of you. Hey, Eric, the reason why I was calling is because I got this lady here, right? Her name Haley, she folks and she got this magazine called Rage and she wanna interview Dre. Wait a minute, hold on, I'm going to put her on so she can talk to you." DeMarco handed me his cell. "Here; my boy wanna speak to you."

"What's his name?'

"Eric?"

"Yeah." I took the phone. "Hi, Eric, I was talking to DeMarco and I told him that I wanted to interview Dr. Dre for the magazine called *Rage* that I'm starting. DeMarco told me had a contact for me to Dre, and he called you."

"Well, any friend of DeMarco's is a friend of mines," said the warm, welcoming voice on the other end of the phone. *What a break,* I thought…

"When you wanna do your interview? You wanna do it now? Well, wait a minute before I say that. Let me go and see what this nigguh is doing," he said.

My heart leaped. "You mean Dre would do the interview with me now? Over the phone?"

"Yeah, if he's feeling up to it. Hold on, let me see though if he's up to it. We just fucking around chilling at the studio you know—smoking chronic. Wait a minute, I think he in the kitchen, everybody in the kitchen." I heard a lot of voices in the background—so many people talking it was hard to make out what any one person was saying. The music and the tenor of the voices sounded like a party in progress. Then I heard Eric's voice on top of theirs.

"Hey Dre, nigguh, my folks got this magazine that she want to interview you for. She on the phone right now. You up to an interview right now?"

"I ain't feeling it right now. Who you say want an interview?

"My folks Haley—with Rage Magazine." I listened intently. Yes, the voice was definitely Dr. Dre's!

"I'll do an interview with her, but not now nigguh. I'm kind of fucked up right now. Give her Lisa's number and she can call her and set it up," Dre yelled back.

"Aiight, Haley?"

"I heard him." To tell the truth, I was a little relieved. I mean, I'd have *done* the interview if Dre had wanted to—you didn't pass up an opportunity like that!—but I was glad I'd have the chance to gather my notes and thoughts first.

"Wait a minute, hold on for a second," Eric said. "Hey, Dre, what's Lisa's number," he shouts.

"Nigguh, it's the same number that you call me at everyday," Dre shouts back. Everybody starts laughing.

"Fuck y'all," Eric said, good-naturedly.

Eric got back on the phone and gave me the number. I thanked him.

"Your quite welcome," he replies. He asked to speak with DeMarco; I handed the phone back to him, thanking him.

DeMarco talked for another couple minutes. After he clicked off, he turned to me. "What he say?"

"It's all good. I gotta call somebody named Lisa to set it up. Thank you DeMarco, I owe you one."

"I got some more contacts for you too—some more people you could interview for your magazine. You know you might want to do an interview with Seff Tha Gaffla and the underground rapper *Macavelli* from Oakland. Them two nigguhs are the kings of the underground. Them nigguhs be selling two and three hundred thousand records independently, underground. I got Seff Tha Gaffla's cell number if you want it. In fact, that nigguh owe me a song. I need to call him. I ain't got a number on *Macavelli*, but I can get one."

"I'd love to do an interview with Seff Tha Gaffla and *Macavelli*. I've been hearing a lot about *Macavelli* lately."

"Alright, I'll hook it up then with Seff Tha Gaffla and like I said I gotta get a number on *Macavelli*. I think my boy Creature Man got a number on him back home. What Eric say, call Lisa?"

"Yeah."

"Oh Lisa—that bitch, I think she like Dre's assistant or his publicist or something." DeMarco smiled.

Things were looking better for me now, than they had for a long time…

Four

It was Friday night. The clique —Utopia, Camille, Krystal, and I— were at Krystal's for our regular Friday night girls' dinner sleepover. Krystal lived in Ladera Heights, an older, but presentable and exclusive L.A. neighborhood. It was a popular residence for black professionals. Debbie Allen and Vanessa Williams once lived in Ladera. In fact, Ladera was where a majority of the well-to-do Black people lived in Los Angeles. The popular Black attorney and stockbroker, Tellis Mahon, also lived in Ladera Heights, as did a few well-known rap artists.

Krystal's modern 2500-square-foot home was beautiful. It was so spectacular, that Barbara Walters could have conducted one of those celebrity interviews in it, or someone could have had their wedding reception in there. The spacious living room had a white marbled floor and creamed colored walls with paintings resembling artwork done by Picasso. That room was equipped with a sixty-inch wide-screen television, state-of-the-art Boise entertainment system, a fireplace, and white glass patio double French doors with gold doorknobs that led out onto the wood deck. Beyond that, a sixteen-person Jacuzzi sat in a corner against the fence. A real socialite, Krystal was always giving something at her house. Baby showers for friends and family members or a birthday party for someone; when there wasn't a special occasion, she'd have a potluck in her home by organizing the event. Sometimes

Krystal would call us on the spur of the moment. I'd answer my phone and she'd be at the other end, "Haley, girl, this is Krystal, be here at six and bring a dish, I'm having a potluck." She'd also put the calls in to Utopia, Camille, and other friends and family.

For tonight's dinner, Krystal had it going on in the kitchen. The kitchen was just as state-of-the-art as the rest of her pad; they could have shot one of those chef's shows in there. She was cooking turkey wings simmered in cream of mushroom soup, yams, black-eyed peas, mustard greens mixed with collard greens and spinach, rice, and hot water cornbread for dinner. Dessert would be Mrs. Smith's Apple pie and Dryers' vanilla ice cream.

We were lounging around Krystal's family room, which was across from the kitchen. The Channel 7 news was on. She was watching television with us while she prepared tonight's meal. The TV was showing the video of Wynona Ryder shoplifting at Saks Fifth Avenue in Beverly Hills.

"Look at this white bitch," Camille exclaimed sarcastically, gesturing at the TV. "She give boosters a bad name. She don't even know how to boost. She just putting shit in a bag and leaves out the door. Man, that's a dumb bitch."

Camille turned toward us as the footage rolled. "Have you seen the whole tape? See how that bitch is acting like she lost or something? I mean she walks out the door, Security follows her out, walks her back in and she looks like a deer caught in some car's headlights. She has this 'what's the matter' look on her face. Read my lips: 'Bitch, you was stealing and got caught, now you looking dumb as hell,' that's what's the matter," Camille said.

"Something wasn't right about that whole thing," Krystal said. "The way she stole. Personally, I think she's a kleptomaniac. I mean it's not like she couldn't afford the clothes."

Camille was still indignant. "Can you believe that her lawyers are saying she wasn't shoplifting? They claim that's the way she shop. If I shopped that way they would put my black ass in jail and they would put your black ass in jail, your black ass in jail, and your black ass in jail," she said pointing at each of us, "but for this white bitch, they are saying 'oh that's just the way she shops?' Give me a fucking break. The bitch was stealing. The woman stuffs something like nearly seven thousand dollars' worth of clothes into bags and exits the store without paying for them, now come on," Camille said.

"That's real talk though," Utopia blurted out.

"Hell, yeah, that bitch was stealing," I said.

"Man, it's different laws for different people. It's about if you got money or if you don't," Krystal said.

"If she were black, she'd be locked up," Utopia said.

"Not necessarily. Today, it's more about having money that gets you different treatment and gets you acquitted," Krystal said.

"So are you saying that she wasn't stealing, Krystal," Camille asked?

"No, the bitch was stealing and there is enough evidence in my opinion to prove that." Krystal pointed at the TV screen, which was now showing Ryder in front of the magistrate.

"Oh, okay, you had me wondering for a minute."

Utopia asked, "You think she going to jail, Krystal?"

"No," Krystal responded.

The TV commentator moved on to a report on the stock market.

"Haley, girl, speaking of Wall Street and shit, when was the last time you spoke with Tellis?"

It's been a couple of months. I think he's probably out of the country or something on business."

"Why you ask?"

"Just wondering. I was driving through Beverly Hills the other day and thought I saw him, but when I made the block and got a closer look at the guy, it wasn't him. Is he married?"

"No. What you got eyes for Tellis, Krystal?" She smiled, 'Damn, the man do look good and he rich. If I got him, that would just be too damn lucky for a girl now wouldn't it!"

"You never know, you want me to hook y'all up?"

"No thank you, Haley, I can do my own hooking up. I know Tellis, too. From time to time I see him at some of the attorney conventions I attend.

Camille looked up. "Hey, not to be changing the subject or anything, but I want you all to know I owe thanks to Haley for always giving me reassuring words about how smart I am and encouraging me to be an entrepreneur like she is with her magazine, and helping Big Larry run his record label and all. I am pursuing my life long dream of being an entrepreneur. I am starting my own business." She had a wry grin on her face, way too big of a grin; we girls knew something juicy was coming. In a sultry voice, she went on. "It's called Uninhibited Films, an adult entertainment film company and an Internet web site, www.uninhibited.com. I'm meeting with this guy tomorrow who is going to design my web site."

"What?!" Utopia was all excited.

"You starting what?" Krystal asked, as if she hadn't properly heard.

"An adult entertainment film company, and a porn web site. There's a lot of money to be made in the adult entertainment industry. As you guys are already aware, I used to be an exotic dancer and escort in college. The money was good. There's even more money in owning an adult entertainment company and having porn web sites. Plus, I understand the business, and I've made up my mind I'm going to cash in on it."

Krystal was clearly intrigued. "Are you going to be in the porno's, or on the web site?"

"Hell naw, I'm going to be strictly behind the scenes. I'm going to be holding the camera filming the shit. And once it really gets going, there's gonna be someone else holding the camera for me."

"Fuck it, we all grown. We then all watched porno. There is a lot of money to be made in that business. I say go for it, Camille," I said.

"Yeah, fuck it, go for it, Camille. I hear Snoop making money from his porno," Utopia said.

"Whateva," Krystal stated, clearly lukewarm about the whole idea. "I realize your degree is in Film from UCLA, Camille, but are you sure that this is how you want to use it? Why not do documentaries or music videos or something?"

"Because making documentaries is not my interest. However, I am thinking about transitioning and making music videos. Haley, I could produce videos for your artist," Camille said.

Raising her eyebrows, Krystal spoke. "Well it looks like you got it all planned out Camille, go for it. I ain't one to kill somebody's dream and I ain't a hater. I'm sure you're going to be successful. I feel it."

Camille smiled. "Haley, you always be stressing that we should put our degrees to work for ourselves rather than someone else and I see you practicing what you preach by the leadership you bring to Eastside West and launching *Rage*. The truth is, Haley, you've helped me find myself and you gave me the confidence to go into business and I thank you for it."

"Oh, thank you Camille. I am glad to see you doing the entrepreneurial thing."

"Actually, Haley, I was wondering if you wanted to go into business with me and be my business partner in the adult entertainment company." I was taken aback. *Me,* do a venture like *that*? It just didn't fit. "Girl, you can make a lot of money and I just want to help you out and help you get the money you need to put into your magazine. I need your help on the business end, Haley. You are so good at business. Are you with me?"

"I ain't starting no porno company."

"Haley, come on. You are so business-minded and together, girl, we can be successful. I know the business. I used to be an escort in college. You wouldn't have to get involved at all other than helping me with the paperwork.

"No way."

"Why?"

"No way."

"Come on, girl."

"No."

"Why not?"

"Read my lips: I am *not* starting an adult entertainment company. That would make me like a Madame, wouldn't it?"

"Girl, you so crazy. Yeah pretty much. I'm only kidding. No, girl," Camille laughed.

"Haley, you can make the money, drop it into your business, flip the business, and get out."

"Camille, thanks, but no thanks, I'm not starting any escort service and I don't want to continue this conversation with you. Yes, I wish you the best of luck. Yes, I will help you put your business on paper, register it with City Hall, and incorporate it with the State. Yeah, I guess I can file your fictitious business name statement and all that for you, take care of the paperwork. What's the name of your company?"

"Uninhibited Inc. When the film first comes on, it will say *An Uninhibited Film*. I'm going to come up with a fake name to use as the producer, you know something like Chastity Innocence or Chastity Love or something. I'm going to be low-key about this business venture; it's not something that I'm going to broadcast. You know I don't want my parents to find out about it, and generally speaking, I don't want people in my business. People think when you doing something like that they got you figured out or something. They think you a freak in the bedroom. It's important to me that I keep my anonymity. I mean if the shit really takes off and I am really making lots of money at that point I really wouldn't give a fuck."

"Come on everybody, let's go to the living room and chat around the fireplace." Krystal announced as she headed in the direction of the beautifully decorated white and green living room. We all rose from where we had been sitting and, following Krystal, retreated there.

"We can listen to some music. What y'all wanna hear? I got Avant, Musiq, Bryan McNight, Tyrese and Luther. What y'all wanna hear? Oh yeah, and I just brought The Best of Al Green."

"Girl put on some Al," I said.

"Yeah! Put Al on," Camille said.

Now we were all lounging around Krystal's living room. She kept our wineglasses full with White Zinfandel. Between the glasses of wine, Utopia and Camille was also drinking Hennessey. By the time the food was prepared, nobody felt hungry.

"Whenever you guys are ready to eat, the food is ready," Krystal asserted after turning off the burners, then walking back into the living room. We talked late into the night. We fell asleep without even eating any of the turkey wings, yams, black-eyed peas, rice, and hot water cornbread which Krystal had prepared for us.

I was the first one up in the morning. The sun was streaming in the window. I looked at the black-and-silver Movado watch on my wrist. It was 9:30 a.m. I looked around Krystal's living room. Krystal was asleep on the leather chaise, and Utopia and Camille were asleep, sprawled out on the matching leather sofa. We were all best friends. Looking at them, a proud feeling came over me. I realized how much I loved them individually. They were the best friends that a girl could have. We had a bond. There was nothing that we could not talk about among us, and sometimes we probably did get in the others' business a wee bit too much… but even then, whatever it was that we expressed was well-taken. Sometimes, through our conversations helped each other to better understand our dilemmas. On occasion, one of us would fall out with another, but it didn't last long for all that huffing and puffing we did wasn't shit.

I look back at the clique sleeping. Last I remember before dozing off to sleep was that it was three in the morning, and we were talking about men: why we can't live with them, why we can't live without them. Krystal had lit the log in the open fireplace and we were chilling, talking, and listening to Al Green's song, "Simply Beautiful" on the CD player. Singing along with Al Green (it didn't matter if we were a little off-key; the wine was well into our systems by now), "if I gave you my love, tell you what I do, I expect a whole lot of love out of you. You got to be good to me. I'm gonna be good to you, there's a whole lot of thang's you and I could do, ooh, hay, hay, baby, yeah, yeah, yeah, ha, yeah… sing Al, Sing," Krystal was shouting. "Al is the man!"

The song served as background music to our conversation. Somebody must have pushed the repeat mode on the CD player, 'cause this is the only song that I remembered hearing throughout the entire night. It played over and over again, and was still playing now. I turned off the CD player, gathered my belongings, and on my way out, I whispered in Camille's ear that I was going home and asked her to call me after everybody else got up. I told her I'd come back and kick it with them.

Five

At Eastside West, the bills were piling up. Circumstances between Big Larry and his investors were worsening, and the situation was now beyond his control. Financially, Big Larry was in way over his head. He made a lot of money, but he spent a lot of money—too much money. He had a big overhead, and a lot of expenses. East Side's monthly bills were an extravagant $14,000, including the mortgage. The entertainment company was bringing in about $30,000 per month. For most businesses, this would have meant a great cash flow situation. However, Big Larry had owed so many people and had so many outstanding debts in addition to the staff salaries, utility bills and other bills, that the rest of the thirty grand was eaten up. After all bills —on the table and under it— were paid, Big Larry wasn't even taking home $1500 a month. His wife, an RN, had to put in extra hours at the hospital to make ends meet at home.

Big Larry and his wife, Stephanie, had purchased their second home and their mortgage was near $2000 a month. Then came their daughter's private school tuition, piano lessons, karate lessons, his new blue Cadillac Escalade truck, and the white Volvo sedan that his wife had recently purchased. It added up, and quickly at that.

Big Larry had vowed not to have another recording studio in the building, but because he was hurting for cash, he subleased space to DeMarco. At first, Big Larry, not wanting a competitor under his roof, put a stipulation in the contract to the lessee that he was not to operate a recording studio. But as the balance sheets bled red, Big Larry no longer had that luxury. He subleased DeMarco the space for his record label in the five thousand square foot building, thereby removing the non-competition clause from his lease.

But as I was to soon find out, even that only postponed the inevitable. Big Larry just had a blind spot when it came to expenses, and that laid him low.

When Big Larry finally decided to close his doors, I was the first one he had told. He called me at home one evening. I had just put the key in the door when the phone rung. I had been shopping at the Beverly center for most of the day. After unlocking the door, I ran into my house, dropping my brown leather Gucci purse and the four brown shopping bags with Nordstrom written across the front to the floor. The small Nordstrom bag that was inside the large one containing newly purchased Mac lipsticks rolled out of one of the shopping bags and onto the white carpet in my living room.

"Hello?"

"Haley, can you come to the studio? I need to talk to you."

"Larry, I'm in for the night. Can it wait till the morning?"

"I really need to talk to you tonight. Come on, I'll be here. I will be waiting for you inside the studio." I heard the urgency in Big Larry's voice. I knew Big Larry well enough to know that by the sound of his voice that something was also seriously wrong.

"I'm on my way." I hung up the phone. I went into the bedroom, took off my cocoa brown DKNY boots, and changed out of my brown DKNY pantsuit with the matching black turtleneck sweater. I then put on my gray GAP sweat pants and tank top, and slid the dark gray pullover nylon Fubu windbreaker jacket over my head. I fished out my gray and white Cheryl Swoopes Running Shoes with the dark gray design, located the car keys, and ran a pink claw comb through my hair.

Still looking in the mirror, I lifted up the back of the nylon Fubu jacket and my tank top and slid the back of my sweats down a little. I checked out the tattoo on the small of my back: a piano outlined in purple, with black and white keys. *Rage*, the name of my magazine, was written across the piano. I had the tattoo done about a month ago. "Damn, I'm tight," I said to the empty room as I checked out my body, particularly my flat stomach. "Janet Jackson, eat your heart out." I had been working out consistently for the past eleven months, four times per week, at the gym to get my stomach looking like that. Finally, in my 34 years of life, I had a body with which I felt pleased. And I damn well earned every tight inch of it. I left for the studio.

It was 7 p.m., and I remember thinking I could go to the gym after my meeting with Big Larry. I walked right back out the front door that I entered through only fifteen minutes earlier, and headed to the studio.

When I arrived at Eastside West, the front main door entrance was open. I walked inside. Beyond the main entrance was another set of white double doors that led inside the studio. This door always remained locked, but it, too, was cracked open. I turned the gold doorknob, opened the second set of doors, and entered the studio.

"Larry, hey," I yelled out. "Big Larry!" He didn't say anything. All kind of thoughts was going through my mind. Did Eastside West get burglarized? Was Big Larry held hostage? Recording studios in the area had been getting robbed. Perhaps I had arrived there while the burglars were still inside? I know he said that he would be in the studio, but in all the years I worked at Eastside West, it had never been this quiet. I could always hear music, guys talking… something. Tonight, there was nothing except the faint whir of the air conditioner. Eerie.

"Big Larry! Big Larry!" I yelled out loud again, and felt a chill that was not temperature-related.

At last: "Haley, I am in the studio." I walked down the long, burgundy-carpeted hallway.

"Hey Big Larry, what's up with you," I asked upon entering the studio. By now, a part of me really didn't want to know. He hadn't called to tell me he'd won the lottery, that much I knew.

"Man, Haley it's all bad," Big Larry said;. He sat facing the door in the black swivel engineer's chair, holding a pint of Tanguray Gin in one hand and a glass in the other. His back was facing the huge Tascam mixing console. I pulled up a chair, placing it next to him. I noticed a handgun sitting on the Tascam. I had seen guns before in the building, though not often. But the way that 9mm was sitting there spooked me. The huge window that separated the sound booth from the recording studio was in the background. All of the equipment was turned off and idle; this, too, was unprecedented. And why did I think that, just maybe, that gun had one round in the chamber…

"What, what's all bad, Big Larry?"

"I'm gone have to close shop."

"Huh? What are you talking about?"

"Yep, my investors, man, they ain't right. I am behind in the bills, the rent, everything, girl. I am losing the place. Haley, you know what's going on. You see the books." I liked Big Larry a lot. I had known him for fourteen years, and didn't like seeing him in such a bothered state.

"Larry, we ain't losing anything. How much money you need? I got something saved up."

"Haley, I can't take anything from you."

"Larry, how much money do you owe? It can't be all that bad."

"I don't want your money. I am letting the place go. I am tired. You know how rough it's been around here especially lately. I'm tired. I am so tired. I am tired of dealing with this nigguh, gangsta, killing shit with these rappers. Haley, we ain't just working with any studio gangsters." Big Larry looked me in the eye. "We working with *real* gangstas. These rappers, they real gangstas. I am tired of everything, the killings, and people dying. Every month it seems like there is another death another funeral to attend. In this business, you lose someone every month that you know, to someone behind a gun. Haley it's not just one or two things why I am throwing in the towel. It's not just the money. It's a lot of things."

"Larry, I feel you on what you're saying, but that's life —people dying. I mean, yeah, we see more of it cause we dealing with people who are in the game and we from the hood, but you can't let that stop you."

"Listen to me. Right now, I am at a point in my life and at the age where I just want peace. This company ain't bringing me any peace any more. The bills are enough of a headache, but I mean we got fights breaking out in the studio with the rappers, arguments, rappers getting killed, dropping like flies; Haley, this shit is supposed to be fun. It used to be fun, but it ain't anymore. I'm shaking the spot; I'm done."

"Larry, how much money you behind? What do you owe?" Larry didn't say anything. "Larry! Would you please talk to me? You keep keeping things from me. Five months ago, you take the books you say you going to handle the accounting—now you come back and you telling me all this. Let me see the books, Larry, so I can see what our financial snapshot looks like."

"Haley."

"Larry, please let me see the books."

"For what? I am behind something like sixty thousand dollars as of the 30th of this month." I felt cold; that was a far deeper hole than I had thought Big Larry was in, and I was already thinking deep. "I am going to take what little I have, and get the fuck out of here with my wife and child. I am going back to Chicago. The cost of living is cheap there and I can liquidate my assets and live comfortably with my family."

I thought, No! "Larry, I saw you build this studio. I remember when you put the sheet rock up. I remember when you put the nails in these walls. I remember when you painted the walls orange and when you put these high gloss hard wood floors in here. Larry, I remember when you built the stage, remodeled the kitchen, put the three bathrooms in this place, brought in the Jacuzzi on the freight elevator. I remember when the freight elevator broke and I called the Otis company in Sherman Oaks to come fix it and they sent us that ridiculous bill for $1500. I remember when you build the secret room that only like, what, five people know about. You *cannot* give all this up without a fight, Larry. This place was not only your dream Larry, it was mines—it's a lot of peoples—even the rappers who come up in here to record, it's there dream too. I got twenty G's saved. I am willing to put it into this business, into Eastside West Entertainment Incorporated, now all we got to do is go out and find some more investors."

"Haley, investors ain't easy to find."

I shook my head. "For a business like this, Big Larry, it ain't gone be that hard. This business is already making money. We've just got to cut expenses. Now what about your boy DeMarco, what you think he good for? What about your other boys Ron Ron, Animal and Benny? Come on, they all balling. I am certain we can get the money from them."

"Oh, you mean well, but look—I already been served with eviction papers. We, everybody got to be out of here by the end of the month."

"Larry, why didn't you tell me this before, earlier?!"

He made a fist and slammed it down hard on his thigh in frustration. "'Cause I thought I was gone find a way. I always find a way, but not this time."

"Let me talk to Ed the landlord, see if I can work something out with him for us to keep the place."

"You can try, but he ain't gone change his mind. I already talked to him. He won't listen. He has other plans for the building, said he was going to do something similar to what we were doing. Haley, I'm out of here. If you can work it out with Ed, it's all good and I wish you the best, but I'm gone."

Big Larry looked around the studio. He looked calmer now, but I knew better. It was controlled fury. "Yeah, it would be good for this place to stay here. Man, Haley, there is so much talent on the West Coast. Put this motherfucker back on the map, like when 'Pac was still alive, like when Death Row was in its heyday and had this motherfucker popping, Snoop, Dre, Tha Dog Pound, Suge, NWA. Even Too Short, Ice T, and DJ Quick did they thang. Haley, promise me you will make this place rock again, which is all I ever wanted to do. It is in your hands now. Get Los Angeles and the whole West Coast the recognition it deserves. Don't let the East Coast nigguhs keep shutting down the West Coast nigguhs."

Big Larry was rambling now. "It's a conspiracy. You see, they don't want the West to come up. That's why they won't let anybody from the West Coast come up after 'Pac. Truth is, 'Pac made it bad for the West Coast. His attitude, his character, the things he said and did. He was powerful in more ways than one. The world fears another 'Pac so they shut down the West Coast, even the music industry shut down the West Coast. What, you think all the talent is on the east and the south? Naw man." Big Larry just sat, shaking his head. "Haley, you have the intelligence, the education and the skills to do it. Please help the West Coast and its artists get the recognition it deserves. Would you promise me that?"

I had been stunned into silence. But I accepted the commission that I never thought would be handed to me. "Yes, Big Larry—I promise you to do all that I can to put the West Coast back on." Big Larry had spoken a lot of truth; he was right. It had been some time since West Coast talent had gained worldwide recognition, and it was our time. We were long overdue for our day in the sun.

"Haley, here's what I need you to do. I need you to schedule a meeting with all of the tenants in the building so I can make an announcement to them and tell them what I have told you. Let's do it the day after tomorrow. Naw, fuck it. Let's call an emergency meeting for tomorrow and have everyone here by 6 p.m. Make sure all of the tenants are here."

"It's done. Hey, let me ask you something." My voice trembled here —just a bit, but I knew; I could hear it. "Why is your nine on the Tascam?"

"Haley, I ain't gone even lie to you. I thought about killing myself. I was going to write a note and let everybody know why I had done it. I wanted my investors to especially know they were the cause of it, but I had a change of mind. I couldn't get my wife and daughter out of my head. I imagined someone ringing my doorbell at home telling my wife that I had committed suicide. I couldn't fathom that thought. Haley, it's because of my family that I couldn't do it."

I knew just how hard it must have been for Big Larry to admit the real reason that gun was where it was. He looked utterly spent. I walked over to the chair Big Larry was sitting in and gave him a hug. "Here's a big hug for a big man. Big Larry, did I ever tell you how much I love you?"

"You have."

"Well let me say it again, I love the hell out of you. I am so glad that you did not take your life."

"Haley, I love you too."

"Now Larry I am taking the gun with me. I'll give it to you later, alright? Don't argue with me."

"Alright."

I picked the gun up off the Tascam and headed into my office to get a bag in which to place it. A feeling of sadness overcame me. I realized that that the office would soon no longer be my own. I couldn't stop the tears. I thought about the promise I made to Big Larry about putting the West Coast music scene back on the level it use to be on. *Wow that's a big job, but with the right team and the right marketing and promotions budget, it could be done.* I was ready to take on a leadership role to make that happen. I knew I just had to stack the team right and get the correct financial backing. The wheels in my mind were already turning…

I knew that somehow, in some way, I had to connect with Dre and Snoop to make this happen; they were the new leaders of the West Coast. I thought about it: if it were not for Dr. Dre, there would be no West Coast producers being played in regular rotation on mainstream radio in the U.S. and abroad. He needed some help. One of the first things I needed to do was put together a team of damn good producers. Rappers come a dime a dozen, but good producers do not. I got up and left Eastside West, leaving Big Larry in his fallen empire. But I'd be back tomorrow. Tomorrow was a new day.

Six

The meeting was held the next day at 6 p.m. just as Big Larry wanted. All of the tenants came. Even Ed the landlord was there. I assembled everyone inside the recording studio for the meeting, as Big Larry had asked me to.

Big Larry sat on a silver aluminum stool, leaning against the wall. The stool had been left behind by a couple of the rappers who had painted the inside of the studio earlier that week.

With all eyes on him —everyone had pretty much figured this wasn't a social call— Big Larry began speaking. He professed his retirement. He was selling his house in Woodland Hills, moving back home to the Midwest to a place called Danville, a Chicago suburb. He said he could get at least four hundred thousand for his house and wouldn't have to spend half that much for a new home in Danville; he would even have more space. People in the room listened impassively. They had already figured out that Big Larry hadn't called this meeting to discuss real estate deals. Then he also announced to everybody in a jumbled, awkward rush of words, that they had to move for he was two months behind in paying the fifty-five hundred per month rent. On the thirtieth of the month, which was a mere eight days away, he would be three months behind. When he finished speaking, Larry asked if anyone had any questions. I could see that he was hoping no one did, but knew there would be many questions indeed. I swear, the guy was starting to stand up to move toward the door.

"Yeah, I got a question," DeMarco said angrily. He was the first one to speak. Everybody who was in the room fixed their eyes upon him. He was sitting on the black leather sofa inside the studio. Next to him, the other tenants—who were all musicians- sat and looked at DeMarco. Those who didn't fit on the small couch were huddled around it; DeMarco resembled a king sitting on his throne, his dreads regally flowing downward.

He was rolling two silver meditation balls around in his right hand. One over the other, over and over again. You could feel him thinking. As before a thunderstorm, I could feel the tension building. "I have been here for three months," DeMarco said carefully. "Why didn't you tell me this when you took my money, Big Larry? I paid you two months in advance and you took a deposit from me. Whatever hole you're in, you didn't fall in yesterday. Or the day before." His voice was smooth as ice, and just as cold. "When I gave you my money you knew what the deal was. You played me and I don't like to be played, and you know that," DeMarco said.

I noticed Big Larry trembling. He was nervous. And why not? I could tell by the look on DeMarco's dread-framed face he had good reason to be worried. Big Larry started fidgeting around on the stool. DeMarco fixed him with a steely gaze.

Larry finally spoke. "DeMarco, when you moved in here, I thought every thing was going to be alright."

"So you saying that you didn't know you was in the hole?"

"DeMarco, when you moved in here I thought every thing was going to be alright."

DeMarco may as well have been a statue. "So you saying that you didn't know you was in the hole?

"DeMarco, like I said, when you moved in here I thought every thing was going to be alright."

"Just answer my question, Big Larry. So, you saying that you didn't know you was in the hole? 'Cause if that's what you're saying again, that's bullshit."

"No, I am not saying that. However, I thought that I would be able to hold on to the place."

"Oh, you thought you was gone be able to hold on to the place. Man, you knew what was up. How you gone just be playing with people's lives like that, man? You should have at least been up front with me about it when you took my money."

"I can understand why you are upset, DeMarco—"

"Do you?!" DeMarco said, cutting Larry off. Yeah, he was pissed. "Man, you should have just been up front with me like I have always been with you. When you took my $5500, you knew what you was doing. Big Larry, fuck all this talking, man, just give me back my money."

"I hear you DeMarco, and I am already knowing that you want your money back. My business partner, Mike, is going to give you the fifty five hundred you gave me to move in here back," Big Larry said.

"When?" DeMarco was clearly unconvinced.

"He'll be here later, I'll find out when he's giving it back to you. I already talked to him about it. No need to worry, DeMarco."

DeMarco's eyes grew wide, eyeing Big Larry like a predator eyes his prey. "Oh I'm not worried. Trust me, I'm not worried." Laughter filled the room. Big Larry shifted uneasily on the stool that suddenly seemed too small for him. DeMarco continued, "I can't even believe that you fixed your mouth to say some shit like that to me. If that nigguh… what did you say your business partner name was?"

"Mike."

"If Mike don't give me my money back in a timely matter, he'll be worried. All I know Big Larry is I…want…my…money…back. I gave it to you in good faith, you didn't follow through, and I want you to give it back to me. You get it from your business partner Mike and then you give it to me."

"Alright, man, it's done."

"Anybody else got a question," Big Larry asked.

A few hands went up in the air. Not acknowledging them, DeMarco spoke out again. "Hey, wait a minute, man, some of the people who renting from you live here like my Brazilian boy Paulo. You telling everybody they got to be out by the thirtieth?"

"Yeah."

DeMarco shook his head. Dreads shifted around. "Well, that isn't enough time for him and the other tenants who live here to find another place to go. Man, you need to give them at least another month."

"DeMarco, is that how much time you need?" Big Larry asked.

"Hell, naw, I don't live here. I got a house, but not everybody has a house like me. Shit, all I need for you to do is to give me my fifty-five hun back and it's all good." Everybody started laughing again, but it did little to dispel the tension that hung in the air. I was a little surprised, because I thought that Big Larry and DeMarco were the best of friends. In the times when I observed them around each other, it seemed like they had love for one another. But business was business, I figured.

All the tenants chimed in. "Yeah, we need at least a month to find another place.

"I need two," someone yelled.

"Hey, Big Larry, I got another question for you. Let me ask you this," DeMarco said. "How many months behind did you say you are?"

"Two."

"So you have been collecting rent from your tenants and you haven't been paying it?"

"Man, I had to pay bills. The PG&E, the telephone, the water, the garbage. Man, it's been crazy."

"So you used the money they gave you for rent to pay your bills and you didn't pay the landlord with it?"

"Man, I… whateva. DeMarco, I don't know what's up with you, but I ain't gone let you keep on talking to me like I'm a bitch, and I am not gone keep answering your questions."

DeMarco became silent. He stared long and hard at Big Larry. He broke the silence saying, "Nigguh, you playing everybody. You used everybody's money to pay your bills?"

"Man, everybody benefited from me paying those bills. If I don't pay the PG&E, no body would have lights, nobody would be able to record up in this motherfucker. If I didn't pay the water, we would have no water for people to use the bathroom and flush the toilet and cook. I had to pay the garbage or else these little motherfucking mice would be running around the studio."

"Man, —"

Big Larry cut him off this time. "Look DeMarco, I am not gone answer no more of your questions. You not gone treat me like a bitch. I am not gone let you do it."

From the couch, DeMarco stared across the room at Big Larry. Sitting on the ladder, Big Larry stared back. The stare-down between them silently lasted for about twenty seconds. "All I know is I want my money back," DeMarco quietly said. I noticed DeMarco pull out a black rubber band from his front pant pocket, and use it to corral his dreads in a nice, tight circle as Big Larry paused. "If I don't get my money back I am going to get mad. And I am like the Incredible Hulk, you don't wanna make me mad!" Everybody laughed again. DeMarco got up and walked off, saying, "Man, fuck this shit." The tenants followed his lead. They left the room behind him. Big Larry just sat on his stool. I'll never forget that night. As I walked out, he was still there… sitting.

Seven

Friday evening came, not one moment too soon. One week had passed since the confrontation in the studio, but I still remembered it well. Like any other California corporation going out of business, Eastside West had to inform the State of California of its plans, not to mention reconciling its accounts to the penny. With Big Larry about to file the bankruptcy, there was so much to do in so little time. All throughout the week, I had labored over Eastside West's books alongside the accountant who did the internal audit, closing out those books, and wading through the million government papers necessary to officially and legally dissolve the entertainment company. And now, at long last, I hit that "Power" button on the front of the computer with a wearied finger to end my day's labors.

Tonight, Krystal was having the usual girls' dinner sleepover at her house, but that week of endless balance sheets, forms, scribbled calculations, and printouts had absolutely drained me. The party beckoned, but all I wanted to do—all I felt able to do—was head home and go to bed. As I walked down the stairs to my car, I decided to call Utopia from my cell and inform her I wasn't going to make it to Krystal's.

"Hello?"

"What's up, Utopia, it's Haley."

"Hey girl, where you at?"

"I'm leaving work, walking to my car."

"You on your way to Krystal's?"

"Girl, I'm not going to Krystal's tonight. I'm exhausted. I'm going home, light my candles around my tub and take a Victoria Secret Pear bubble bath, put on my PJ's and retire for the night."

"What?!"

"Yeah, girl, let everybody know I won't be able to make it. Tell them I will see them next time."

"Dang, Haley, you the life of a party. It isn't never the same when you aren't there. You know tonight Krystal got some guys stopping over?"

"Yeah, I know, I remember… but, Utopia, I'm way too tired."

"Man, alright, Haley. I'll let everybody know you ain't coming cause you too tired."

"Thanks."

"Now, go get some rest."

"Bye."

"Bye."

I got in my silver Range Rover with the black leather seats and hurled my Fendi briefcase in the backseat. It looked as worn as I felt. *Damn, it's time for a new one,* I thought, as I released it from my grip. I had owned that briefcase for eight years. I bought it when Eastside West first opened its doors, and I was on this thing about looking professional. So, the expensive briefcase was purchased. It was so old that it was falling apart. But, I paid a small fortune for that thing and was definitely getting my money's worth. Now, it was time for a new one. I put my key in the ignition, started the car, and pulled off. I hear Outkasts song, So *Clean and So Fresh* playing, as it is the ringing tone to my cell. Because I liked the song so much, my nephew had logged onto an .mp3 website over the past weekend, and downloaded the tone to my cell phone. I looked at the caller ID; it was Krystal.

"What's up Krystal," I answered.

"Girl, why you ain't coming over tonight? I got some eligible men stopping by! Remember Steven?"

"The attorney you told me about that works with you and who graduated from Southwestern Law School and is Mark's frat brother? He's single and he complains that he can't find a decent black woman to date?"

"Yeah, him. Girl, come on by and I can hook y'all up."

"What he look like?"

"Girl."

"I'm just asking. I mean I can't believe that a man with his qualifications is having a hard time finding someone, that's all."

"So what you think his looks got something to do with it?"

"Yes? I mean, to some degree they do."

"Haley, girl, it ain't easy for us or them."

"What he look like Krystal?"

"Haley?"

"Krystal?"

"Yes."

"What does he look like?" Krystal was quiet.

"Is he fine, I persisted?"

"Well, he got a big head," Krystal said.

"Uh uh."

"But, he real nice."

"Uh uh. I'm cool. I'll pass. Girl, I'm tired. I'm going home and going to bed. Talk to you later.

"Bye."

I tossed the cell on the passenger seat.

I hadn't driven two blocks when I again hear *So Clean and So Fresh playing again.* on my cell phone. *Damn Krystal, now she must be trying another approach to get me to her house,* I thought. I rolled my eyes. Shaking my head, I reached over and felt for the cell I'd tossed on the passenger seat seconds earlier. Unable to look at the caller ID because my eyes were fixed on the heavy traffic as I entered the 405 freeway, I answered, "What, Krystal?"

A voice that was decidedly not Krystal's spoke. "May I speak to Haley?"

Well, I knew it *wasn't* Krystal, but I had no idea who it was. "Speaking," I said.

"Hey, Haley, how you doing? This is DeMarco."

My mouth dropped open. This was unexpected. I stiffened up and shifted around in my seat before sitting straight up. DeMarco had never called me before. He barely even fixed his lips to say hello to me when he saw me at the studio. He didn't speak unless I spoke to him first, and if I said "hello" to him he'd respond with "hello" and leave it at that. The times I tried to initiate a conversation with him he replied with short answers. He showed no interest in engaging in a discussion with me whatsoever. If he were talking before I entered the room, he'd stop speaking upon my entrance. I figured he didn't want to be bothered with me, so I left him alone, ignoring him altogether. If I spoke, he spoke. If I didn't, he didn't.

Even after DeMarco called his boy Eric who worked for Dr. Dre to get me the interview, and we'd hung out once in the studio together, he still remained withdrawn from me. I remember how often he would stare. I would look back at him and do the same, figuring that he would turn his head once he was aware that I knew he was staring at me. Sometimes he did, but usually he kept his stare. It was almost as if he were looking through me. When he would look at me like that, I'd feel a little awkward, especially when I stared back and he still would keep his penetrating eyes fixed on me. Eventually, I would end up being the first one to avert attention, and so I learned to ignore what he did.

And now he was on my phone, unannounced and uninvited. Why? I put on my professional voice, "Oh, hey, DeMarco. I'm good. How are you doing?"

"I'm cool. I was thinking maybe you and me could work together and go look for some office space for a studio. I got most of the equipment and I could buy more. You could house your magazine in the same building as the recording studio and my record label. There are some places for rent in L.A. I got two of them out of the newspaper and my real estate agent gave me a two-page list of some warehouse spaces for rent. We can go and look at them."

At first I couldn't believe what I was hearing. DeMarco Speed wants to become a business partner with me, Haley Jones. Well, we do have many of the same dreams and ideas. Bottom line, DeMarco's passion for music was as keen as mine, for music and *Rage* alike, and we both were looking for opportunity. We were both enterprising people. *It might not be a bad idea for us to network and do something,* I was thinking. From my understanding, DeMarco did have money—something I was going to need to make my goals happen. When I'd mentioned to Skerz about Big Larry losing the studio, he suggested we ask DeMarco for the money. He said DeMarco had enough money to buy the place and keep it open—said he was balling like that. Skerz had named about six project sets in the city for which DeMarco was a major drug supplier.

"Yeah, we could do that. How much are these places renting for?"

"$1900 and $2500."

"DeMarco, I was looking in the real estate section of the Los Angeles Times on Sunday and I saw some places for rent also. However, I'm gone keep it real with you, I am not in a financial position to afford to pay anything on any space other than the one I got at home."

"It's cool, I can pay the rent. I just need you to help me find a place, and for you to be my business partner, help me run things. We can sublease, too, if we find a big enough place. Also, Haley, you know I got like fifteen hundred square feet of office space in Beverly Hills."

"You do?"

"Yeah, the only thing is it's located in an office building. We can't put a studio in there. But you can use the office in Beverly Hills if you want to. We can share it. But because it's office suites, we still need to find a studio. Actually, I'd like to relocate the office to the new spot we get. Have everything under one roof."

"How much do you want to spend for rent, DeMarco?"

"It doesn't really matter."

I repeated the question. I needed to know in my pursuit of looking for real estate what kind of rent he could afford and was willing to pay. "DeMarco. How much do you want to spend for rent?"

"Whatever, just find us a big enough place, something comparable to the space Eastside West had."

DeMarco was being evasive. Commercial rent was expensive in Los Angeles. There were some studios paying as much as six thousand dollars a month for rent. I continued my persistence. "Do you want to spend fifteen hundred, two thousand, twenty five hundred, three thousand, four, what?"

"Haley, it doesn't matter. We'll probably spend closer to four though cause I want a lot of space. We need enough space for me and you to have offices, and my boys D and Kameron, they need offices too. My other boy, Creature Man, he got his own record label also, but he doing his own thing. However, he might want to sublease from us. I'm going to see him later today. I'll check with him. Also, Haley, we need to make sure we have a lounge and a security room. I'm going to hire an armed security officer to monitor the cameras and provide security throughout the building."

"Got it. You know, if we had sixty thousand we wouldn't have to move anywhere. You and I need to meet with Ed and see if we could work something out with him to keep the place. I think we could work it out," I said.

"Yeah, we could do that. Call him and set it up. But if his ass ain't talking right, fuck 'em. We just get our own spot. Let's meet with his punk ass on Monday and see what he's talking about, after we go and check out some of the places I'm telling you about."

"Sounds good. I'll call him and set up a meeting."

"Oh, and I want you to know one thing, Haley."

"What?"

"I'm not like Big Larry. I listen. I used to hear you give him good business advice and suggestions about how he should do things and shit, and he'd never take it. If he would've listened to you he would have been better off, and his business would have been better off and wouldn't have suffered. If he'd listened to you he would have not lost the place. I've observed you at work, Haley. You're a smart woman, a strong sister. We need more strong sisters like you. I don't think Big Larry realized what he had on his team when he had you, that he had the Cleopatra or some other African queen with outstanding leadership skills on his team." I felt strange; DeMarco had hardly ever talked to me before, and now he was giving so much praise.

He continued. "What Big Larry should have done was what he did best, producing music and making beats. He should've let you do what you did best, which was run the business, instead of always overruling you 'cause he owned the place. He lost sight of why he hired you to be the president, and he lost sight of the success you helped Eastside West rise to. Had he not interfered with the way you ran things, that place would have boomed. We all saw it. You know another thing Big Larry did with y'all relationship that was so stupid?"

"What?"

"He showed division. Division is something that two partners can never show. When people see disagreement they capitalize on it, especially your enemies and this is how people and the tenants played y'all and put y'all up against the other. Haley, check this out, perfect example. When Big Larry was collecting the rent from the tenants in the building, he always got it late. However, the months you collected the rent and you let motherfuckers know up front that if they were late they paid a penalty, it got paid on time.

Everybody, well, not everybody, but a lot of the tenants started going to Big Larry saying that you was rude and disrespectful to them the way you asked them for the rent and the way you was talking to them and penalizing them. He relieved you from collecting the rent and took it upon himself to collect it. He sided with them. He started collecting the rent and they started paying late again, and he doesn't even slap a penalty on them or serve them with an eviction notice like you would have.

What Big Larry should have done when they came to him to talk about you was kicked 'em back to you. He should have reminded them that you were the president of the company and what you said was law. He should have had your back. That what business partners do. If business partners have a difference of opinion with one another then they need to take their differences behind closed doors and discuss them. Haley, if you tell me something, or how to do something that I am doing better, hey, I have no problem with it. I'll listen. If you can teach me something, I'll learn."

All I could think was, *Wow!* DeMarco said much, and made sense of it all. Those words won me over. The apprehension I had felt when I heard DeMarco identify himself on my phone was gone. DeMarco was right: how many times had I given Big Larry advice that could have saved him money, and even kept him from losing both the record label and recording studio? And how few times had he actually taken it? I didn't even know that DeMarco had taken notice of my discussions with Big Larry.

"So what time do you wanna hook up on Monday?"

I had to file the documents to dissolve Eastside West, and I had to pick up the documents to be filled out to incorporate *Rage* at the State Building. I figured I'd have DeMarco meet me there.

"I have to go down to the State building and drop off some paperwork around 9:30. Why don't we meet right after that, like at 10?"

"Where?"

"Just meet me in front of the Building and I'll ride with you."

"Alright, I'll see you at 10."

"Bye, DeMarco."

"See you in a minute."

As planned, on Monday morning at 10 a.m., I met DeMarco on La Cienega in front of the County building. I wore a tight black Gucci suit with a royal blue button-down collared shirt and a pair of black Gucci boots. The royal blue against the black looked dramatic. My pant cuffs hung perfectly over the boots. I had my Mac Currant-lined Diva covering my lips, Mac Caramel pressed powder on my face, and my Mac black mascara.

Upon leaving the building, I spotted DeMarco's Black Range Rover outside at the curb, parked beyond the black double automatic glass sliding doors at the building's exit. I walked outside. The front door to the passenger side of the truck opened. A tall, medium-built, handsome, dark-skinned brother dressed in all black stepped out and stood next to the open passenger door. DeMarco bent his head down, looking at me and waved me on as I walked towards the truck. "Hey, Haley," DeMarco called out. "You can sit in the front with me." Still standing next to the passenger door, his friend nodded hello and gestured for me to get in. I got in and he closed the door behind me. His friend got in the back seat, closed the door, and DeMarco drove off.

"How long you been waiting, DeMarco?" I asked.

"About five minutes." The light in front of us caught us. At the light, DeMarco played with the meditation balls. For the first time, I took a close look at the metallic spheres as he stopped at the red light, as there wasn't much else to do. I observed DeMarco as he crooked his fingers and rolled the two silver spheres in one hand. They were of equal size and, near as I could tell, of equal weight. As he rotated them in his hands, something inside produced a soothing set of soft tones—electronic or otherwise, I couldn't tell. Each ball made a different sound which, when combined, produced a calming and soothing effect over one's mind.

Holding the steering wheel with his left hand and the meditation balls in his right, DeMarco gripped the balls in his closed palm, lifted his arm and pointed his thumb behind him, "Haley this is D," DeMarco said while pointing to the back seat. "D, this is Haley. Me and D go way back. We have known one another since third grade. We grew up together. D is also from Oakland," DeMarco said. D's hand reached around the black leather seat from an awkward angle. I turned around, grabbed hold of it and shook it.

"How you doing," he said.

"Fine, and you?"

"I'm cool. I heard a lot about you, Ms. Haley. DeMarco talks about you all the time," he said. Just as he said, that DeMarco eyed him in the rear-view mirror. D chuckled. The light changed.

"Oh, really," I replied.

"Yeah, my boy speaks highly of you. Says you be writing business plans and doing public relations and shit. Said you had it going on and are a good person to know."

DeMarco interrupted, "I gotta make two stops. First, I gotta drop D off in Long Beach. After that, I need to stop by my boy's house real quick in Compton on the way back to L.A. Then we gone go and look at these places," he said, handing me the list of commercial properties for rent his real estate agent gave him. "Oh yeah, and my boy Creature Man, he ain't gone be subleasing from us. He renting a warehouse in Long Beach for his record label. I don't want us to be located in Long beach. I want us to have an L.A. address." There must have been more than fifty listings on the paper. Some were circled in red.

"I went through all of those places and I marked the ones that I think we should look at," DeMarco said. After we dropped off D, we went to see his boy in Compton as noon approached. I waited in the Range for DeMarco, as he was inside for about ten minutes.

Upon arriving back to the truck, DeMarco asked, "Hey Haley, you hungry?"

"Yeah, I'm hungry!"

"Alright, I tell you what… I know this real good Jamaican restaurant, Johon's, up here on Martin Luther King where we could eat. Do you like Jamaican food?"

"Uh huh."

"What you like?"

"To be honest with you, the only time that I have had Jamaican food is when I was in Negril. I had the Jerk Chicken. It was good. Oh, yeah, and I've been to Cha Cha Cha's on Sunset Boulevard."

"Yeah, but Cha Cha Cha's ain't Jamaican. It's more Southwestern, Brazilian cooking. They got some Jamaican dishes on the menu, though. The Jamaican spot I'm telling you about has real good authentic Jamaican food. The dude who owns it name is Johon. Johon is from Kingston, and he can cook his ass off."

DeMarco was still playing with the meditation balls, rolling it around in his hand. "How long you been using the mediation balls?"

"Now, I have practiced meditation balls for almost a decade. Eight years."

"I hear people say they are relaxing," I said.

With his eyes on the road, DeMarco nodded. Momentarily, he took his eyes off the road and looked over at me sitting next to him. "They're real relaxing and soothing. Sometimes, Haley, I be so fucking stressed out. The meditation balls soothe my body and mind. They relax me. They relax my thoughts, drown my worries, and release my stress.

"Is that right?"

He nodded. "They help release tension. Whenever I'm tired or have a lot on my mind, or sometimes when I am just relaxing, I play with them. If I'm stressed and I play with them, my body becomes relaxed and then energized pretty quick."

"Man, maybe I need some meditation balls if they do all what you saying they do," I said.

"Yep, they do. I'll pick you up a pair if you want me to, or I'll take you to Chinatown and we can grab you a pair. It would probably be better if I took you there. They come in five sizes so you need to try them out and see which one feels comfortable in your hand.

"I'd like a pair. DeMarco, seems like you know a lot about Chinese medicine? How did you learn about that and the meditation balls?"

"I'm a black belt in Taikwando. Also, about eight and a half years ago, I took three shots in my body. It fucked me up pretty bad. My boy, Niko, he was half Black and half Japanese. He introduced me to acupuncture and to my acupuncturist, Tamiko Yoko who's Japanese. She was his acupuncturist. He's dead now. Anyway, Tamiko became my acupuncturist. Since I met her, faithfully I see her once each month and sometimes more depending on how I'm feeling. She is the one who really introduced me to healing, Chinese medicine, these meditation balls and massage. She gave me books to read about Buddhism and Chinese medicine. I combined all of what she taught me what and I learned from reading, into my life. Acupuncture and Chinese medicine helped me to heal quickly, and it brings me balance. Sometimes I listen to meditation and relaxation tapes. They take me away from the bullshit of life in the inner city, you know?"

I just sat there thinking about all that DeMarco had said. I had gained more insight into this man in the past day than I had in all the months I knew him.

"There's the restaurant right there," DeMarco said pointing at the storefront building. Parking was tight. After driving around the block a few times, we found a spot across on a side alley and around the corner from the Jamaican restaurant.

When we walked in, the waitress and the owner, Johon, walked over to the door and met us. They greeted DeMarco by name, and he greeted them in turn, "What's happening Johon and Portia?" Johon first shook DeMarco's hand, followed by Portia. "DeMarco, where you been? Haven't seen you around these parts in a while," he said.

"Yeah, I know. I haven't been on this side of town in a while. I was talking to my business partner, Haley," DeMarco said pointing behind him at me. I was standing a couple of feet behind him. "Haley, this is Johon and Portia," DeMarco said as he pointed at them. Portia was a heavy-set, dark-skinned Jamaican woman, looking every part the cook. Her head wrap matched the brown-and-cream-colored dress she was wearing. A dark brown apron was tied around her waist. With his finger still pointed in my direction, DeMarco said, "I was telling Haley about your restaurant. She has never been here before and I want her to taste your food. It's the best in all of southern California and some of the best Jamaican food around."

"Yeah, mon," Johon said, winking his eye at me. I smiled back at him. DeMarco took a seat at the bar on the torn black vinyl barstool, which had some white cotton coming out of it. I noticed his hesitation before sitting down. He wore a blue Versace suit with a black long sleeve pullover sweater. On his wrist was a gold Huguenot watch and a gold chain. I glanced at his feet. He wore a pair of nice black shoes, although I am not sure of the brand name. If I were a guessing woman, I'd bet they, too, were Versace. I sat next to him on a barstool that resembled the one he was sitting on.

I was also apprehensive about sitting down, because I didn't want to mess up my clothes. However, I just figured, *fuck it*: if I made a fuss about it, then I would come across as bourgeoisie, which I am not. Besides, I'd been to Jamaica and had eaten in restaurants that looked worse. The small, dingy, hole-in-the-wall storefront restaurant with the mix-and-matched tan, white, and black chairs in the dining room would be considered a luxury restaurant if it were on the Island. The waitress handed us both menus. We opened them. Not taking his eye off of his menu, DeMarco asked the waitress what the day's special was.

"Today's special is the goat simmered in coconut milk, with mint leaves and potatoes over rice," she said.

"That sounds good." He was still looking at the menu. "Alright, let me have the grilled fish, rice and red beans and a side of jerk chicken. Haley, what you having?"

"I'll have the jerk chicken, rice and red beans."

"Did you like the coffee when you were in Jamaica?"

"Yeah, it was good."

"They got Blue Mountain here. You want a cup?"

"Yeah, I'll have a cup."

"We'll have two cups of Blue Mountain Coffee," he looked up and said to the waitress.

The news played on the small grimy, gray, seven-inch RCA black and white television that hung over the bar. Mob boss John Gotti had died, and they were broadcasting it. The newscaster reported Gotti's battle with throat cancer, and death within a prison hospital.

"He was stupid, too flamboyant, and he brought reproach upon himself," DeMarco remarked.

"Yeah, he was, mon," Johon was now standing behind the bar, twisting the hairs on his beard and watching the television, laughing. "He listed his occupation as a plumber, as flamboyant as he was," Johon said, shaking his head. "How you gonna wear three and four thousand dollar suits and say you are a plumber."

DeMarco spoke, "He loved the camera, that was a big downfall of his. He should have just stayed behind the scenes. A real gangsta don't want to be in front of the camera. Man, he had the power and he had his anonymity. You can't ask for more."

The waitress brought our coffee. Now the news covered an assassination in the Middle East. Sipping on his cup of coffee, DeMarco still talked about Gotti. "His son, he was just plain dumb. His daddy made all that money, and his dumbass son was still out there doing some thug shit, fighting on the streets and shit. Hell, when you get that big, you don't personally have to kick ass no more. You can have that shit done for you!"

The next story on television discussed a fight, which broke out at the Forum after a rock concert. We all watched. The newscaster commented that people were running wild because shots were fired, and people didn't know from where these shots were coming from; the scene was chaotic. The camera showed people running amuck, falling down, and getting trampled.

"Now, look at these motherfuckers," DeMarco contemptuously spoke. "They don't know if they running towards the gunman or away from him. Haley, if that was you out there among that crowd of people, what would you do?"

"I would make it back to my car."

"Yeah, but which direction would you go in?"

"What do you mean, which direction would I go in? I would go in the direction that my car was in."

"So you'd be out there running wild and crazy like them. You wouldn't know if you were running in the direction of the gunmen or not," DeMarco said.

"Well what would you do, DeMarco? Which direction would you run in?"

"Look, Haley, let me give you some game," he said turning his body into me. He touched my knee, "I would step in the cuts until I knew where the gunmen was and once I spotted him, I would go in the opposite direction. I would make sure that I was not running towards him."

"And what if you never spotted the gunmen?"

"I would still step to the side, let them dumb motherfuckers run over each other and trample each other, and when it was all clear I'd get on."

"Huh," Johon expressed approvingly.

"Here's your food," Portia said, placing it on a table in the dining room across from the bar. DeMarco and I retreated to the dining room. The food was excellent, just as DeMarco promised. It was real authentic Jamaican food. After we left the restaurant, our stomachs pleasantly full, we began our search for office space. Along the way, we made small talk.

"You married, DeMarco?"

"Yeah, but my wife, she's away." *Away, what does that mean? Away in jail, on vacation?* I thought. I didn't want to seem nosy, so I didn't bother to ask.

"I'd ask you if you're married, but I already know you're not," DeMarco said.

"How do you know that," I responded?

"I don't see a ring on your finger?"

"And I don't see a ring on your finger either."

"Did I ever tell you why I got married?"

"No."

"It's a long story. One day I'll tell it to you."

Again, I figured I wouldn't push the issue. *When the day comes, if it comes and he wants to talk about it, perhaps I'll listen.* Anyway, whatever it was he was going to say, I figured it was going to be a bullshit line anyway.

"See, Haley, this is what I was thinking. You know what I do. I'm getting older and it's time for my life to take another direction. I don't want to look up one day and be an old man in the game. I was thinking that you could become business partners in Life Inc. with me and I could help you with your magazine. You then already been to college and you got all those degrees. Man, you already done the hard part and the rest is easy.

"Is that what you think? I've already done the hard part?"

"Yeah, you finished college and got your degrees, that was the hard part. Now the rest is easy. With a woman like you on my team, Haley, I could go far. With a man like me on your team, you can go far. Hell, we can go far together! Let's merge and do our shit together. I will help you start your magazine. I'll give you the money you need to start it. I'm here for you. How much do you need to start your magazine?"

"I need about two hundred thousand dollars. Maybe a little bit more."

"How much would you make back?"

"Well, *The Source* and *Vibe* are charging twenty five thousand dollars for a full page ad. If we go to print with two hundred thousand copies, we can charge twenty five thousand per ad. Each issue of *Rage* will be approximately one hundred and sixty two pages. Seventy percent of those pages will be ad pages… that's like damn near one hundred pages of ad and the rest content, DeMarco. No, it's going to take some time to get a hundred advertisers, but when we do, we will generate more than two million dollars per issue in advertising revenue."

"Damn, is that right?"

I nodded.

DeMarco continued. "We will be printing an issue a month, twelve issues a year. It costs $135,000 to print two hundred thousand copies. Then we need about another $100,000 to promote *Rage*, billboard ads, magazine ads. We need to have a web site designed, commercials on BET, MTV, and the radio."

"If I give you the money would you make me a fifty-fifty partner?"

"Hell, yeah, I would."

"Then it's done. I'll give you the money. Let me organize some shit first, set a few of the other projects I'm investing in motion, and then I'll break you off. Plus, I need to think about the way in which we need to do this. We got to organize it in a way where I don't have to be exposed as your investor, but don't trip I got the money and if you helping me I have no problem helping you. Let's shake on it." DeMarco extended his handshake. I extended mine. Looking each other directly in the eyes, we shook hands firmly.

After we ate, we looked at five commercial spaces. Neither DeMarco nor I liked any of them. Either the locations were shitty—one was right under the flight path leading to LAX- or the buildings weren't suitable for what we had in mind.

Next, we headed over to meet with Ed Lee at his office. Our meeting was short, and lasted for about twenty minutes. When we arrived, his secretary, an Asian woman with long black hair, called him and informed him that we were there. Ed came out and escorted us from the waiting room to his office. "I have a contract for you to sign, and you guys can stay in the building. My attorney wrote it up," he said on the walk as he led us to his office. Once inside, he pointed to the two chairs sitting across from his desk. DeMarco and I sat down, facing Ed across his rather cluttered desk.

We discussed paying off Big Larry's debt to him, but now Ed had increased the amount that Big Larry owed him by an additional ten thousand dollars. He also informed us that the rent was an additional eight hundred dollars per month over the old figure. Fumbling through the pile of papers on his desk, he located the document he was looking for. "Here you go. All you two need to do, is sign by the 'x,'" he said while handing the paper to DeMarco.

DeMarco took the paper extended to him. I scooted my chair closer to his, and he did the same. The contract was held up in front of both of us.

"Oh, no, you don't have to read it," Ed said shaking his head. "All you need to do is sign it." *Yeah,* I thought, *like DeMarco or I would actually sign something like this without reading it first.* Ed must have been tripping. Ignoring him, we continued to read.

"Give me my copy so we can review it with our attorney tonight over dinner," DeMarco said noncommittally after we looked over the contract.

Ed got up and left the room for the copier down the hall, looking miffed for going through the trouble.

"Look Haley, you know what I think we should do," DeMarco said quietly, eyeing Ed bent down over the copier twenty feet down the hall. "I think we should take whatever it is that we are even thinking about giving him, the sixty thousand, and just come new with our own shit and our own building. Fuck paying off Big Larry's debts. Fuck paying off another nigguh's debts. Ed is full of shit with that contract. I'm gone save my breath when he comes back. We just take the contract and leave. I'll use it for scratch paper. Fuck explaining anything to him."

DeMarco made a good point. I really couldn't argue with what he said. He was right. Although I wanted to keep Eastside West around, I realized it would be better to move on and come anew. Importantly, we would still put the West Coast music scene back on the on the map with another company. Plus, I was digging the name, Life, Inc. Records. "I'm with you on that."

Ed returned with a big grin on his face. "Boy, that Larry really knows how to screw things up. You know I gave him so many chances. I guess he was just a loser," he said. DeMarco and I looked at each other; a look of disbelief covered our faces. Ed continued, "Haley, ever since you stopped being in charge and Big Larry moved up to take on more of a leadership role about a year and a half ago, things just went downhill for that company. Tell me something, why did Larry stop you from being in charge?" I didn't answer. I stood up reached for the contract and DeMarco followed my lead. Ed gave it to me and we left. "We'll be in touch if were interested," I said. I guess it was in my voice that Ed shouldn't be holding his breath.

No, DeMarco and I would not save Eastside West. The next day I went ahead to proceed with closing down the Entertainment Company and giving it a decent burial. I called the telephone company and have the telephone turned off. I notified PG&E, the pool table, vending machine vendors, and the leasing company from where Big Larry had leased some of the recording equipment. The equipment went up for sale at auction, which apparently was not well-advertised, for there were few bidders. DeMarco actually ended up purchasing eighty percent of the Eastside West's recording equipment, at bargain prices.

After our initial hunt for office space, DeMarco and I started spending more and more time together looking for more office space, going to recording studios, breakfast, lunch, dinner, and the movies. You name it, we did it. As I got to know DeMarco better, I realized that we were so much alike. Like me, he was ambitious, had the same "go get it" attitude, and knew how to create opportunities even when they did not exist. He knew what he wanted out of life, and he knew how to make things happen. You read about people like us who had already made it. The Berry Gordys, Russell Simmons', Suge Knights, P Diddys, Damian Dashs, Sylvia Rhones, and the Tracy Edmonds'. A lot of underground rappers and producers used to say that we were them in the making, and that we were in at the same place at which these entrepreneurs were, before they made it. I guess this was reason why a lot of them sought us out. They figured DeMarco and I were the perfect representatives for them on their route to super-stardom.

He was good for me. Seems like when I wasn't with him, I was sulking and finding comfort in bottles of Remy Martin, Hennessy, and glasses of Apple Martinis. I guess Eastside West's closing affected me more than I thought. I could feel myself slipping into a depression. I began to lose interest in my entrepreneurial endeavors. DeMarco took notice of my depression. I could tell he was concerned. My days would start and end with telephone calls from him. DeMarco and I had grown closer.

One morning I woke up to my telephone ringing. I looked over at the gold clock on my dresser; it was 3:30 a.m.

"Hello?"

"Hey, Haley, its me, DeMarco. I was thinking. Why don't you talk about your goals and your dreams of being an entrepreneur anymore? What's up with the magazine girl? It's a damn good idea. The West Coast, we need a magazine like that. A lot of people gone love you for it," DeMarco said.

"I'm gone do it."

"When?"

"I'm just taking some time for myself right now."

"Yeah, I mean you gotta do what you gotta do, but don't lose sight of your dreams.

"I know, I know, I know," I said sucking in a deep breath and releasing it.

"What's the matter?"

"Nothing."

"Hmmm."

"'Hmmm' what, DeMarco?"

"I was just thinking, that's all."

"DeMarco, to tell you the truth I'm not feeling it. The whole 'be your own boss' entrepreneur thing. I am just thinking that maybe I should just go out and get a job. I'm sure I can get one at any of the major record labels here in Los Angeles."

"Hmmm, that's interesting."

"Why you say that?"

"I mean you are always talking about how people should give meaning to their degrees and put them to use working for themselves. You're always consulting with people, helping them launch their own businesses. When you talk about owning your own business, it's obvious that it's your passion, and now you're contradicting yourself and talking about working for somebody else."

"DeMarco, I don't know. I'm just not feeling it anymore. It's like I've lost the desire. My enthusiasm just isn't there anymore."

"Well, you better get it back."

"I know, but I'm just not feeling it anymore. Besides. I have an interview tomorrow at Interscope for a VP of marketing position. I need the money."

DeMarco was unmoved. I could sense the bulldog in him staking out a position with a determination that would not be budged. "First of all, you are not going to make nearly as much money working for somebody else as you are going to working for yourself." He sighed. "You know that. If you sell only fifty thousand records owning a record label versus selling a million records as the VP of marketing for Interscope, you still gonna come out ahead. Second, I can pay you. Just tell me how much your bills come to each month and I will give you the money and then some."

I guess I didn't catch the significance of that last sentence; it was the middle of the night and I wasn't truly awake yet. "I mean, yeah, that's true, but starting my own label and a magazine is going to take a lot of money and I don't have it. I mean, I guess I could sell some real estate, one of the two houses my grandmother, my fathers mother, left me before she died. But, its too risky and I ain't willing to take that risk." Although I have four other siblings, I was the only child that my father had, and my father was his mother's only child. My grandmother elected to split her four properties between my father and I. She also paid for my undergraduate and graduate education. I was her pride and joy. It was through me that she lived a lot of her dreams. If I achieved success she internalized it as though she, too, had accomplished it.

"Haley, remember around the first time that I met you and we talked at the studio about the business of music, and I loaned you that book and you told me about your magazine?"

"Yeah, I remember."

"Man, the things that you were saying inspired me. As you talked, I was thinking 'this woman really has what it takes to make it.' You have the intelligence, education and the drive. Haley, I'm not easily impressed, but you impressed me. You're so smart and you don't even realize it. I mean, I believe in you. So, never stop believing in yourself."

I couldn't help but be taken aback. Okay, so it was only talk, but it was good talk and I was really in a funk. Or had been, until that moment. "Wow, DeMarco. Is that what you think of me?"

"I do. Haley, you got what it takes. I mean you already did the hard part, obtaining your degrees and all that. The rest is easy. I already told you I can front you the money to start your magazine, and we got the record label Life Inc. Lets just do it."

Now DeMarco's offer sunk in. "Wow, thanks." I didn't know what else to say, there with sleepiness still in my eyes.

"Well, let me let you go. You were just on my mind, that's all, and I wanted to give you a call. I'll see you in the morning for breakfast, if you're feeling up to it. There's this cool little restaurant on Sunset Boulevard I'd like to take you to, or if you want, we can have lunch at this restaurant in Malibu." It's on the beach, sits on the water. It's your choice."

"The restaurant on Sunset sounds good. What time should I expect you, or do you want me to meet you there?"

"You know what? Let's go to Malibu. I'll pick you up say at eight in the morning. We can go for a walk on the beach or something before breakfast. They say it's gone be hot tomorrow so you might wanna dress light."

"Alright."

"Bye, Haley."

It was a turning point. Our relationship moved up a notch.

Eight

With DeMarco's encouragement, I began to accompany him to the recording studio. The rap group, The Divided Souls, signed to his record label and were working on their debut album, *In The Game*. They were from L.A.'s South Central neighborhood. South Central was much like other inner-city low-income neighborhoods, where drugs and violence are rampant. The Crips and the Bloods each lived on different sides of the neighborhood, and made their presence known by the color of the clothes they wore, by spraying paint on walls, and, at times, by spraying bullets at each other. A lot of young people who resided in the neighborhood's housing projects saw music and rapping or even producing if they made beats- as their way of getting out of that dispirited and dangerous environment. They looked up to others who had used music to escape South Central, such as Ice Cube.

DeMarco had a lot of contacts in the music industry. The next thing I knew, he was setting up interviews for *Rage* and I at the recording studio with the different rappers that arrived to record. When popular artists like Snoop, Nate Dogg, and Badd Azz came through the recording studio, DeMarco would set up an interview for me. Sometimes I was at home when he'd call to tell me to come to the studio to conduct an interview. If, for some reason, I couldn't make it to the studio, he'd provide me with their contact information so I could reschedule the interview to a later point.

DeMarco re-motivated me to launch *Rage* and persuaded me to do a rap compilation. We named it *Rage* Magazine & Life Inc. Presents Underground Bosses. He said that the CD and the magazine would promote each other. Thanks to DeMarco, I was rejuvenated and ready to get rolling with my entrepreneurial endeavors. I went out in search of talented and creative people to help get Rage Magazine off the ground. I posted the following ad on *www.craigslist.com.*

"New Urban Culture Magazine Similar to Vibe and The Source Seeking Writers, Graphic Designers, Art Director's and Photographers. At this time, the position is unpaid; however, if we meet and vibe and we agree to work together, I will include you in my business plan by name, title, and salary. If you are looking for a unique opportunity to get in on the ground-up of an exciting opportunity, please respond. Only those who are serious and immediately ready to go to work need to inquire."

Rage Magazine became my passion again. I dreamed, breathed, and lived Rage. In the end, that ad proved to be most beneficial. I was overwhelmed with resumes. Once *Rage's* doors finally opened, this is from where I found and hired a lot of my staff.

Nine

DeMarco was serious most of the time.
He could have more playful moments, but these were brief exceptions to
the rule. His boys capped and told jokes on each other, but never included
DeMarco in such humor. Now, DeMarco sometimes humiliated and spoke
in a condescending manner to them. But his boys continued to respect him,
never responding in kind. When his boys told jokes and he was around, he
didn't laugh or acknowledge them in any way. He was above that. He always
seemed to be in his own world, thinking.

DeMarco was what you'd call a real nigguh. He didn't talk behind your
back. If he had something to say about you, he said it *to* you—straight to
your face, never using gossip to send his message. People who knew DeMarco
knew the way he conducted business; they knew never to buy into the "he
said, she said" bullshit. If someone was set to start confusion between another
person and DeMarco, they were just wasting time, because DeMarco's reputation preceded him. He told it like it was, no more and no less. There were
a lot of stories out there about what he'd done for those who respected him.
There were just as many stories about what he'd done *to* those who had not.

Men and women catered to DeMarco's whims. They showed him affec-
tion and respect. The women knew his status as a rich drug dealer and wanted
to profit off his trade, although his good looks didn't hurt. They also knew

67

that if you were one of his women, he spent money on you.

The guys knew of his power. They knew that DeMarco was big in the drug trade, and was running things. They knew the respect commanded by other equally as respected drug dealers in the game. They knew his status as a rich thug, a multi-millionaire. If DeMarco wanted, he could make one phone call and have you dealt with: they knew that he had so much love from people in the game that if he wanted you killed, he didn't have to do it. Someone else would do it for him.

DeMarco was hard. He had a different kind of relationship with women than he had with men. He didn't have a reputation for putting his hands on females. That's not to say he wouldn't hit a bitch, because if she disrespected him in a manner that called for it, I am sure he would slap her. However, he usually walked away from arguments with women. He wouldn't argue with us. He was always kind to women, even when he ended his relationships with them. When he got tired of seeing a woman, he simply stopped calling or seeing her. For instance, when she would call him, he'd talk to her shortly before hanging up, always telling her that he would call her back… but he never did. So, eventually she would stop calling. This is how he ended all of his relationships when he grew tired of someone If he ran into her, he acknowledged her and was cool. He'd even stop and chop it up with the woman for a minute. Sometimes, he'd call late at night for sex, but that was it. He didn't spend any more time with her. He had the ability to control women like no other man could, like the character of an Ice Burg Slim or that found in a Donald Goins novel.

If you were a man, DeMarco respected you until you displayed a sign of weakness. If he ever see this, he'd look at you with disdain, and dislike you. Sometimes his hit-or-miss style became brutal, depending on how he felt at the time.

Those regularly around DeMarco, especially his boys, were preoccupied with making sure he felt comfortable. For instance, If he entered a crowded room, they'd give up their chair to him or they would always ensure that plenty of weed was kept in his presence. He had plenty of his own weed, but it was a respect thing. On the other hand, if you were his friend, DeMarco looked out for you and took care of you.

DeMarco had a humble spirit. He was known as a cool brother…most of the time. He smoked a lot of chronic, but his personality was calm even before that. The chronic made him placid. But this led some to make the mistake of believing that DeMarco was so mellow, they could disrespect him and get away with it. Boy, were they wrong. Once disrespected, DeMarco's mood changed, and his volatile temper surfaced. People found out that DeMarco could fight, and quite well at that. As a child, he used to box at the local gym and later for the Golden Gloves. When DeMarco was disrespected, his retribution was nothing nice. So, both his good and bad reputations preceded him. People who knew him either liked him or despised him, men and women alike. However, more people liked him than hated him; he was a straight shooter. Utopia would comment, "DeMarco would rock a bye someone in a minute." It took me a while to see DeMarco's other side, the dark side. But I began to see it over time.

Ten

In the beginning, conversations between DeMarco and I centered mostly on discussions about the business of music. However, as time went on, our discussions became more personal, more intimate. As our platonic relationship progressed, our ties strengthened. We became inseparable friends. Through conversations and spending time with me, DeMarco helped me get sober and overcome my brief depression. He'd take me to lunch, dinner, the movies, plays at the Lorraine Hansberry Theatre, and the spa at the Beverly Hills Hotel and Hotel Bel Air. Sometimes we'd even drive to a spa resort two hours away in La Jolla or head to Las Vegas for a few days. Once we even went to Catalina Island for a weekend. He would never let me pay for anything.

Along the way, I saw how DeMarco had game. He was a smooth talker. The women he went out with knew he was married, and each one knew about other women in his life. They accepted their relationship with him on his terms. If they didn't, he simply stopped calling them and cut them out of his life.

The women in his life was a hot topic. The stories he'd tell me about his sex life was interesting at times. He always talked about it. Like most of us, he loved sex. Often he'd ask me for advice or he'd want to know what I thought about a particular situation pertaining to his sex life and a woman he was sleeping with. He'd say he wanted a woman's perspective. I gave him mine. But sometimes the sex stories were too vivid. I'd have to tell him to leave out the details. When he talked about us sisters in an overly condescending manner, I'd have to remind him that I *was* a woman he was talking to. When he patronized us, I'd ask, "what woman broke your heart?"

"I ain't never had a bitch break my heart," he'd retort.

But even while our relationship was still strictly business, I did things for him I'd never have pictured myself doing for a man. One evening, he called and asked me to ring the doorbell of some married woman he wanted to see and had been sleeping with. *He must be tripping*, I thought, but for whatever reason I still did this for him. I guess it was the excitement...it was a little like a sorority prank. When the woman's husband would come to the door, I asked for her. Once she appeared I'd inform her that DeMarco wanted to see her and that he was around the corner waiting in the car. She'd follow me out. I did this on several occasions.

Sometimes his mistresses would even end up at the same restaurant or movie theatre he'd be at with another woman. He'd acknowledge them with a simply hello to them and they'd speak back to him. If they were jealous they'd roll their eyes at the woman he was with, but they never said anything to her. They never attempted to disrespect him or front him off. When they saw him again alone, sometimes they'd let their jealousy show with a remark., "Who was *that* ugly bitch you was with," or "that bitch I saw you with the other day need a new weave or something," were typical comments.

He'd respond to them. "She ain't worrying about you, so why you worrying about her?" But none of the women really tried to push the issue. They knew where they stood right from the get-go.

DeMarco's affairs never went home with him. As bold as he was, I wondered at times how he pulled that off, but he did. Like I said, the brother had game. Unless his wife snooped, that's the only way she would ever found out about DeMarco's affairs. And if she did snoop, she'd have to be Mrs. Colombo because DeMarco didn't leave himself freely exposed.

In his cell phone address book, he stored the telephone numbers of the women he messed around with. He had two categories: Bitches and Hoes. I guess the Bitches were better than the Hoes, near as I could tell. On one occasion, we were in the car when he picked up his cell phone and said, "let me call my hoe."

When the woman answered, he said, "What's happening, hoe," I heard her voice, and astonishingly, she was laughing! After hanging up with her he casually scrolled through the "Bitches" category and said, "Now, let me call my bitch."

I looked at him. He did *not* just say that, I thought. But he had. I heard the sound of a different woman's voice greeting and DeMarco, not missing a beat, said, 'What's happening, bitch?' Just like the other woman, she laughed and chatted with him. When he hung up, I demanded to see his phone.

"Why," he asked.

"Because I want to see what you got me labeled under." I suppose that was always lurking at the back of my mind: that someday in DeMarco's mind I'd inevitably become just another woman in his eyes.

"Oh now come on, Haley, I wouldn't do that to you."

"Let me see your phone, DeMarco?" He hesitated, but I locked him in a stare; after a moment, he handed it over to me.

I scrolled through the numbers, through the Hoes and the Bitches' categories. Once again, DeMarco was true to his word; I did not see my name. Then I got to business contacts. There I was: Haley Jones. With attitude, I handed him back the cell phone. A look of surprise covered DeMarco's face. "Haley," he paused, "I would never put you in either of those categories. I don't think of you in that way."

"You better not," I responded. I could be serious, too…and I was. And DeMarco knew it. "You just better not."

He fixed his eyes back on the road and drove quietly. He didn't say a word until we pulled up in front of my house and said, "I'll see you tomorrow."

As he became more comfortable with me, he began divulging even more personal things to me about him and his life. With the exception of his hustle, and his wife who he didn't talk about, there were no limits to what we discussed . DeMarco kept his other business separate from our business dealings. One thing's for sure, he's a smooth and shrewd businessman.

We were at a recording studio in Pasadena where some of his artists were recording. Rumor had it that some of the more popular rappers in town and celebrities, including the rockers, were DeMarco's best spending customers —buying pounds of weed, coke, and other drugs from him at a time.

DeMarco and I were sitting on the couch at the recording studio talking, when a well-known rapper—with a top-played video on MTV and BET-walked in. He had a prearranged meeting with DeMarco to purchase two pounds of chronic. He came in and handed DeMarco a brown paper bag. DeMarco opened the bag and pulled out the money.

"Hey, Big A, come and count this with me," DeMarco said. Big A was DeMarco's brother. He was kind of like DeMarco's personal assistant and bodyguard. He was built for the job. About the same height as DeMarco at 6'2" and about fifty pounds heavier than DeMarco's lean 195 pounds. Big A must have weighed about 250 pounds, all of it muscle with the exception of a bit of a stomach. He and DeMarco counted the money together.

"It's all there," the rapper said.

"Hold on, partner," DeMarco said.

"Nigguh, its all there! Give me my chronic."

"Nigguh, hold on. Business is business. It's my policy to count my money," DeMarco said. The rapper leaned against the wall and waited for them to finish counting the money.

"Go on, nigguh, do you thang then." He paused for a minute and then continued talking. "DeMarco man, I heard yo bitch doing pornos now, like your other bitch Tina Cherry."

"Tina ain't my bitch."

"She ain't? Nigguh?! Damn I wish I'd known that. I just saw her the other day and I was gone get at her, but I was like, 'naw that's DeMarco's bitch, I'm gone leave it alone'."

DeMarco laughed. Money smoothly continued to flow through his fingers. "Man, get at her even if you think she my bitch. I don't give a fuck. I don't give a fuck about a bitch. You'll know if she really my bitch cause, she wouldn't get back at you if she is. If she get back at you she ain't my bitch, or at least not one of the bitches that I care a little bit about. Tina, she use to be my bitch, but she ain't anymore. She need to write a book, *A Hundred and Two Ways To Suck Dick*."

"Damn like that, now I know the next time I see her I'm gone get her number. She making money doing that porn shit though. She in a few of my nigguh's videos. I might put her in my next video."

"Yeah, I was watching BET the other morning when I was on the treadmill at home. I seen her slutted-out ass."

"Nigguh, you still doing your porno film?"

DeMarco looked at me with an unwavering eye while keeping his hands on the stack. "Yeah, I'm finished filming it. It's being edited right now."

"Who distributing it?"

"I don't know. I'm gone put it on the Internet. Snoop said he got a hook-up with *Hustler* for me. So, me and that nigguh gone both be the executive producers. You know the porn industry, they love Snoop. He came out and sold like a hundred and fifty thousand of his porno in like less than two months. That's good for the porn industry. Hell, *Porno Queens* was everyone's talk, everybody was buzzing about how popular that was, and it only sold like fifteen or twenty thousand."

"What's your film gone be called?

"*Hoes Wanna Have Fun*. I'm gone do a remake of Cindy Lauper's *Girls Wanna Have Fun*, but instead of saying girls wanna have fun, I'm gone bring in some hoes and have them say hoes wanna have fun."

"You crazy DeMarco. Anybody I know in the porno?"

"I don't know. Latecia, Cookie, Mary...them bitches up in it. Some of my nigguhs is in it, too. My other brother, that nigguh in there fucking two bitches. Cookie and Latecia, man them nymphos got a lesbian scene together. I got some new bitches though up in it, too."

"What about that other porno bitch you use to fuck with."

A smile covers DeMarco's face. "You talking about Hits From the Back?"

"Yeah, Hits From the Back, that's her name. Baby, she got ass. Man I heard she got her clit pieced and her pussy is good."

"Yeah, her shit right. I still hit it from the back, sometimes." DeMarco giggled. "She in Hoes Wanna Have Fun."

"Nigguh, you put your girl up in the porno?"

"She just my bitch. She ain't like my wife or one of my wives or like my main girl or nothing. She just my bitch. I don't give a fuck."

"Well all I know is, I want a copy of *Hoes Wanna Have Fun* when you done making it."

"You got it."

"DeMarco, you are off the motherfucking hook! I hope you using condoms, dude."

"You got it. Haven't you heard of AIDS? Ass in deep shit. If you don't cover up before you go in that's what you get your ass into. I ain't going up in a bitch raw. Only my wife, that's about it. I mean I then slipped up before. Everybody fucking has at some point, but I'm pretty much on it. I had an AIDS test three months ago I'm straight. Nigguh, you had your AIDS test?"

"Yeah, I just took one of them motherfuckers, too, and I'm straight. Hey DeMarco, where this weed from?"

DeMarco was almost done; he ignored the rapper's question until he had finished. He looked at the rapper, then at Big A. DeMarco nodded his head at the latter.

"Humboldt County," DeMarco said. "You asked where the weed from, it's from Humboldt." As DeMarco spoke, Big A produced a fat bag of chronic from somewhere on his person, like a magician performing a trick, and handed it to the rapper.

A huge smile appeared across the rapper's face. He made the bag disappear somewhere on his own person as well, and turned to walk away. DeMarco looked at him. "Next time you need something, call one of my affiliates. I don't sell this shit like this no more. I just did this one for you." The rapper stopped in his tracks and spun back around.

"Nigguh, I remember you when you use to be on the block selling this shit."

DeMarco smiled. "Yeah that was a long time ago, about 7 or 8 years ago, but yeah, nigguh, next time you need something go through one of my associates."

"Alright, baby."

Before the rapper could leave the building for good, he came back inside the studio.

"Hey DeMarco, I know what you said about going through one of your associates, but just then one time for me, please? You got some Sherm?"

DeMarco looked a little surprised. "You want Sherm?"

"Yeah."

DeMarco was all business now, giving the rapper a look of appraisal. "Nigguh, what you spending?"

"Two more pounds worth."

"You got the money now?"

"I gotta run back home to get it. Five G's, right?"

DeMarco's gaze was like that of a spider regarding some insect caught in its web. "Nigguh, you crazy. We're talkin' eight, and that's just 'cause I'm in a good mood."

"Man, I'm your best customer. You ain't gone give me no discount?"

"Hell, naw, nigguh. I'm a baller. We don't give discounts. This ain't Ross, motherfucker. And by the way, for the record, you ain't my best customer. Even if I gave out punch cards, you'd still have some spots to fill, nigguh. Some of your boys spend twice, three times as much with me regularly. To be honest with you, nigguh, what you spend with me in a week, I spend in a day on clothes, jewelry, and shit and paying my kids' daycare and private school tuition and supporting my mama and my grandmama."

"Ah, my nigguh why you trying to clown me?!" They started laughing. It was all part of the game.

"But really, blood, let me get a deal on two pounds of sherm."

"Alright. Look, cousin, since you just cop two from me already and you want to cop two more, I let it go for sixty five hun. Now, nigguh, that's a deal."

"Alright, but nigguh, what if I also cop a kick from you? How much you charge me?"

"Now, nigguh, you know a kick gone cost you sixteen. Come on now."

"Damn, nigguh, no discount?"

DeMarco shook his head at the same time the word "no" came out of his mouth, and continued. "So do you want the two and a kick, or just the two?"

Begrudgingly, the rapper accepted the Sherm and the kick.

"So you got the 16 and the sixty five hun?"

The rapper nodded. "Yeah, nigguh."

"So what, you selling now, nigguh, or something?" The rapper ignored him. "That's fine, you don't wanna say, you wanna keep your biz to yourself, that's cool."

"Hold on. Let me go outside and find a pay phone. I'll just have my boy bring it to your house if it's cool."

"Yeah it's cool." They both left. Not even five minutes later, DeMarco returned inside the studio. Handing his rapper, who was probably no more than 16, a large Ziploc bag full of Chronic he pulled from under his coat, he ordered, "here, roll some of this up for us."

"You got a blunt?" he asked DeMarco. DeMarco tossed him one.

I just sat there quietly.

Eleven

It was Friday. I was hanging out with DeMarco so much lately, I'd missed the last couple of Clique sleepover socials at Krystal's, so I knew I had to go to her place tonight or I wouldn't hear the end of it. I grabbed my clothes that I was going to wear the next day with my red satin Victoria Secret Pajamas, and packed the garments in my dark brown leather Moschino overnight bag. I headed out the door to Krystal's. As soon as I walked into the weekly girls' night get-together, Krystal started.

"Girl, you and DeMarco, y'all spending way too much time together. What is that about?"

"We got a lot of the same goals and we get along perfect. We have just been out looking for office space. Besides we enjoy each others' company, that's all." I already felt like I was on the defensive, and I didn't much care for it.

"I know, but DeMarco's married. I hear that his wife is a trip, too. She lin drug rehab now, but she ain't gone be gone forever. She be out in a minute."

"Oh, so that's what he meant when he said to me she was away," I voiced.

Camille spoke up. "He told you she was in rehab. Right?"

"The way he said it is that she was 'away.' I didn't push the issue. I figured when the time was right, if he wanted to, he'd tell me what he meant by 'away.' I figured she was in jail or something, but I wasn't sure," I said.

Utopia continued, "Y'all shouldn't be spending that much time together. All the late night hanging out, talking on the phone all day and all hours of the night. It ain't good. Haley, you need to keep it business with that *married* man. Besides what do y'all be talking about for all of those hours when you are out with him until two, three and four in the morning? What y'all be doing? The other night I called you at 3 a.m. and you and this man was together. What's up with that?"

"Girl, I went to Kinko's on Wilshire downtown around midnight 'cause my printer is broken and I had to print some papers. Around one in the morning, DeMarco called my cell. I was still at Kinkos. He asked me if I would print him out the event list at reggae.com. He said he had some business to take care of in the city and he'd come and get it. When you called, we were just sitting in my car talking in front of Kinkos. He parked his truck behind mines and got in my car."

"Yeah, but it was three in the morning when I called you, you should not be out with him at that time."

"Girl, you are making something out of nothing!"

"I don't know about that," Utopia contended.

"Haley, I've said it before and I'll say it again, messing with a married man is dangerous. There is no telling what a person might do if they feel they are losing their family," Krystal contended.

"Haley, you have got to think about all of this stuff this with his wife," Utopia interjects.

"Haley, really, take a look at this picture," Krystal began to add.

Cutting Krystal off, I rose to my rebuttal. "You guys, there is nothing going on between me and DeMarco. I know better. I don't believe this. You're making something out of nothing. Everybody's making something out of nothing, including my family. For the record, DeMarco and I enjoy each other, that's why we hang around together. Ain't nothing gonna happen between us. Don't you know that I know that there is no future with a married man? This is a business relationship that will be a profitable one."

"Yeah, girl, that's what you say now. All I'm saying is just be careful, girl. Watch those feelings and those emotions, they'll slip up on you. Plus DeMarco is a smooth brother, the kind you don't want to fall in love with, 'cause he'll just break your heart," Camille interjected. Utopia nodded her head and then maintained, "Please, not him. Do not fall in love with him."

"Like I said," Krystal leaned back on her couch. "Don't forget I've been there done that too, but in my case I didn't know when I started dating the guy he was married. I found out later, and I cut his ass loose without hesitation once I found out". She continued, "Also DeMarco's a man with a swing-ing dick, so trust me if you give it up he ain't turning nothing down."

"I mean, I am not stupid. I know how men are, and I know how DeMarco is. Yeah sometimes DeMarco flirts and sometimes I flirt, but it's nothing. Men and women who are friends flirt. You guys know that, but nothing ever has to happen. Y'all know what I'm talking about 'cause y'all got a lot of male friends and y'all know how it is with them. We are the ones that has to keep things in perspective."

"Haley, that might be true but we aren't spending the kind of time with them like you and DeMarco are spending together."

"I know you guys are right and that I got to be careful. The other day me and DeMarco were driving in Riverside. We had gone there to drop off some promotional flyers and posters to these reggae artists—DeMarco's really into reggae—who live there who are performing in the upcoming New Year's Reggae Bash DeMarco is giving at The House of Blues Downtown L.A. They're helping to promote the event. Anyway, so we driving, right, and DeMarco starts talking about how much less expensive apartments are to rent there than in L.A. He was like, 'in Riverside you can get a two-bedroom apartment for like eight hundred dollars a month. You can get a one bedroom for like only like six fifty or seven hundred and fifty dollars.' He kept looking in my direction, right, I guess he wanted to see my reaction to what he was saying. With excitement and this big smile on his face he said, 'Haley, we should get an apartment here!'"

"See what I'm talking about?" Krystal said with a triumphant look in her eyes.

"Uh-huh," Utopia said, "that's how it starts."

I went on. "So I ask him 'For what? What do we need an apartment for?' He says, 'So we can do promotions out of it. It would be a good base for us. We'd be between Los Angeles and San Diego. San Diego has some of the big-gest reggae shows. We could go to all of the reggae shows there and you could do interviews with all the reggae artists for your magazine.'"

"'But you already have an office in Beverly Hills,' I told him. Then he said, 'I know, but we need to be in Riverside. If we are in Riverside, we are in the middle of everything.' And I tell him, 'If we got an apartment together, do you know what that would look like, DeMarco?' Then Demarco said, 'No one has to know.' And I tell him, 'DeMarco, your wife will find out about that apartment.' He told me she wouldn't. Then he went on to say that to be honest, he really didn't care."

"Shit, wives always find out," Utopia interjected.

"That's what I told him! I said, 'DeMarco, your wife will find out about that apartment, trust me. It's not a good idea.' I mean, Krystal and Camille, talk to me. What do you guys think about what I am telling y'all?"

"Girl, you already know what I think. I ain't got nothing else to say bout y'all two," Krystal replied.

"Me either," Utopia said. Both Krystal and Utopia ran their fingers across their lips and sealed them.

Camille really didn't have much to say. She mostly laid back on the chase with her eyes closed and listened. When the night ended, Krystal retreated to her bedroom, while I took the downstairs guest room. I guess that Camille and Utopia slept right there in the living room, for the next morning when I arose, they were laying in the same places watching television. Krystal was in the kitchen making breakfast. After we ate, we all showered, got dressed, and lounged around Krystal's house for most of the afternoon and into the early evening.

I asked, "Hey what time is it?"

"It's 4:00," Utopia responded.

"Hey, y'all come take a ride with me to the Jordan Downs. I need to find No Love to let him know he has studio tomorrow night. Did I tell y'all that me and DeMarco working on a comp together?"

"Is that right, what's it gone be called," Camille asked.

"Underground Bosses."

"Alright, girl, give me five minutes and I'll be ready," Krystal said.

"We'll be in the car. Come on Camille and Utopia, let's wait for her in the car," I said.

Camille sat in the front passenger seat of my silver Range Rover. Utopia got in the back.

"So you working with No Love," Utopia asked from the back seat.

"Yeah, we putting him on our comp."

"He tight, but these local rappers, they need to quit playing and do it. They need to get serious about what they doing."

"It's a few of them who are serious about what they do, and they doing the best that they can. I mean you gotta give them credit. They going into the recording studio, making music, pressing they CDs, and distributing them."

"Yeah, but Haley, they staying local."

"Well yeah, they don't know how to take their music to the next level."

"I didn't take long, did I," Krystal asked as she got into the back seat of the Range.

"Naw, you cool, " I started the engine and drove off.

Utopia continued, "Now, Haley, what were you saying about these rappers advancing to the next level, you know from being underground rappers to mainstream rappers you hear on the radio?"

"Yeah, Haley, why do you think these rappers don't take their music to the next level," Camille asked.

I began to explain. "From what I've observed, it's either because they do not have the money to take their music mainstream, or they don't understand marketing. They do not understand marketing and promotions, how to implement an effective marketing plan to get them the sales to get noticed and get major distribution. These local rappers are releasing album after album every year, and in some cases twice a year, with no real success, because of this. If the money was there, along with a tight marketing plan, more of them would experience success on the mainstream level, or at least blow up on the underground."

"That makes sense," Krystal said.

"Sounds 'bout right," Utopia said. Camille nodded.

"That's a good thing about working with DeMarco. He has the money and I understand marketing and promotions. He also understands radio and working with the DJs and the DJ pools and all of that. A lot of the local talent is bypassing the DJ pools, and they need those DJs to get exposure. All DJs from the radio stations to the clubs belong to a DJ pool. The DJ pool provides them with free records to play at clubs and in their mix shows. Man, those pools are what they need to make their music more popular and break. The DJs around the country play the songs in all the clubs. The partygoers around the country going to the clubs, they hear that and like it, and start asking the DJ 'who is that?' Next thing you know, they buying it. Next thing you know, the radio stations are playing it."

"Damn, Haley, you know your shit," Utopia said.

"If I were a rapper, I'd wanna work with you," Krystal agreed.

"That's why I want this woman to be my business partner in my adult entertainment company," Camille said. "Damn she is bad, and well-read. Haley, that's why DeMarco sought you out and wants you to be his business partner, 'cause he knows you're smart," Camille said.

"Yeah, DeMarco knows what he got in Haley," Krystal said. "Haley, I'd like to be your attorney at your entertainment company. Don't forget me when you make it!"

I just smiled.

Twelve

I turned the corner into the Jordan Downs Housing Projects in Compton. It was off the freeway and seemed like a whole other country outside of the glamour of L.A. There were no movie stars or beaches here. This is where we were all raised. Jordan Downs was like any other inner-city community. Drugs and violence were common. Youth emulated as role models those that lead a life of crime. The clique and I were fortunate to have survived that environment with our ambitions and faculties intact. Many did not.

Immediately upon turning into the projects, I spotted Lil Rob, Scherzo, Riff Raff, Dollar Bill, and Quincy. I pulled up to the curb a few feet from where they were standing, and rolled down the passenger window. "What's up everybody?" Riff Raff raised his head and chin up, motioning a reply.

"Me and you," Dollar Bill shouted at me.

"Yeah, whatever, nigguh," I mumbled beneath my breath. The clique laughed.

"I know he ain't flirting," Krystal said.

"Yeah, he flirting."

Quincy walked over to the truck and placed both hands on top of the roof, over the passenger door. "What's up, Haley and Camille," Quincy said.

"Hey, Quincy," they responded.

"All you see is Haley and Camille," Utopia asked him from the back seat.

"Who dat back there," Quincy asked. He leaned into the truck to see who the voice belonged to. "Oh, what's up Utopia, and Krystal how y'all doing? I didn't see y'all sitting back there. You know I would have spoke to y'all had I seen you guys."

"We good," Krystal replied.

I looked up at Quincy. "You seen No Love?"

Quincy stepped back from the truck and looked around. "That nigguh was just out here a minute ago. I don't know where he went. He probably in somebody house or something. Hold on, let me ask this nigguh if he seen No Love." He turned to a man across the street, also a rapper, who was bent over working on the engine of a tired-looking Cadillac Seville. "Hey, hey, hey, Yuseff! You seen No Love?" Yuseff turned around to look at us, his blue mechanic's jumpsuit stained with oil, socket wrench in hand. "He left with them hoes he was talking to a few minutes ago. Is that Haley? What up, girl."

"Yeah, it's me. Hey, Yuseff, how you doing?"

"Shoots, I'm good." He gestured at the car, half pointing and half shaking the wrench at it. "Just trying to get this old piece of shit running, that's all. I'll holla at you later. Maybe take you to dinner or something. Hey, bring your cousin Kim with you. I wanna get with that. We can all go to dinner together."

"Alright."

Quincy looked back into the truck at me, "He gone, but he'll probably be back in a minute. You want me to give him a message or something?"

"Yeah. Tell him he has studio tomorrow night at eight o'clock, if you see him."

"Alright," Quincy said, tapping the door of the Range and walking away as a car pulled up nearby. "Hey, let me get this sale from these Filipinos right here. They wanna buy some rocks." With a practiced gait, Quincy sidled up towards the driver-side window. "Hey what y'all need," Quincy said. Damon, another block hog, rushed the car, flowing smoothly up to the window, making the sale before Quincy could get there. *Okay*, I thought, *here come some fireworks*.

Sure enough, Quincy and Damon started arguing even before the car pulled away. "Motherfucker, you don't take my sale. I got 'em!" Just as he said that, the Filipinos drove away. Damon had made the sale. "Hey nigguh," Quincy yelled behind the car with the two Filipinos in it, "that wasn't cool, y'all know y'all always cop from me, but it's cool. I'll see y'all next time."

Another car took the Filipino's place, a blue Lexus driven by a Caucasian wearing a shirt and tie. Krystal gave a wry grin. "Damn, look at that white boy who just pulled up in the Lex, he look like he must be a businessman or something. He out here buying crack like he buy a burger at the drive-through. Man, white America needs to see this."

I looked at her. "Girl, I know this ain't yo first time seeing white boys and Filipinos and shit rolling up buying crack in the hood?"

"Naw, I was just saying."

"Oh, 'cause I was about to say," I said.

Leaving Quincy to his clientele—this time he made damn sure he got to the car before Damon- I drove down the street slowly, still hoping to see No Love.

"Haley, you driving too fast, you gone drive right by him! Slow down," Krystal said.

"Girl, I'm driving less than ten miles per hour. Look at the speedometer," I said, pointing at the needle that was hitching just below the "10" mark.

"I think that's No Love right there sitting in that car."

I stopped, and we looked inside the car. I shook my head. "Girl, that ain't No Love, that's Michael, Tony and… well, I don't know who that other nig-guh is," Utopia said. Michael and Tony got out and walked up to the driver's side of the truck.

"Haley, I got to get me one of these," Michael said, tapping the door of the Range. "This is very nice."

"Hey Haley, you guys," Tony spoke. He stood back as Michael and I talked.

"What's up with you, Haley?"

"Just working, that's all."

"When you gone let me take you to dinner, one of those nice restaurants you be liking to go to?"

"What nice restaurant I be liking to go to?"

"You know the one on the beach and shit in Beverly Hills."

"What's the name of it?"

"Hell, I don't know. I don't really be going there and shit. I ain't gone even lie, but I'll take you to one."

"Is that right? And what would make you do something like that?"

"Cause you good people." Michael looked back at Tony, they both chuck-led. I looked over at Camille; we both rolled our eyes instead.

Tony stepped up to my window. "DeMarco let me hear this song that you guys recorded the other day, the one called 'Hoes Wanna Have Fun' or something like that."

"Really?"

"Yeah, it's tight as fuck. You oughta hear it. Hey, DeMarco out here now.

There's his truck right there." He pointed to the familiar black Range Rover with DeMarco's trademark LIFEINC license plate. We hadn't even noticed it, which was unusual 'cause we notice everything. Or damn close to it."

Michael regarded the black truck curiously. "Where he at?"

Tony chuckled. "He in some bitch's house. I'm gone go and let him know you out here. I'll be right back."

"You like DeMarco, Haley?" I wondered why Michael wanted to know. Camille, who was looking out of the passenger's window, turned and swung her head looking at me, then looked in the backseat eyeing Utopia and Krystal as if to say 'we are not the only ones with this idea that Haley and DeMarco like one another.'

"DeMarco is my business partner."

"But do you *like* the nigguh?"

"Why you wanna know?"

"Cause Tony going to get the nigguh, and if you his woman or anything like that I don't want him to come out here and see me all up on you."

I had been annoyed at him asking my business, but I could see his point. I couldn't fault anyone for simple self-interest; trying to grab anything out from DeMarco could be bad for one's health. "Like I said, DeMarco is my business partner."

"Haley, let's go and get something to eat after we leave here, I'm starved," Utopia said.

"Me too," Krystal said.

"Me three," Camille chimed.

"Haley, stop by the ATM at Wells Fargo before we go to the restaurant. Me and Krystal gotta get some money," Utopia said.

"Alright."

Tony came running back down the street. "I told DeMarco you out here. He coming out to see you, Haley."

"So, can I take you to dinner?"

Getting involved in Haley and Michael's conversation and intentionally putting him on the spot, Camille asked, "Michael, what's up with yo girl?"

"What girl?"

"The one that's like five months pregnant." Camille gave him a look. "You know, *that* one."

"Me and her? We broke up."

"Y'all broke up?"

"Yeah. She said that she didn't want me to see her no more and that I couldn't see the baby. She told me don't even try and see it."

"Damn, like that," Camille shouted.

Ignoring her, Michael said, "So Haley, what about me and you. You could be my girl, what you think." I didn't really even have to think; I shook my head.

"Why won't you give me a chance?"

"'Cause I don't trust you."

I heard footsteps coming out from one of the buildings. So did Michael; his head turned. It was DeMarco. I got out of the truck and met him just in front of the driver-side door. "Hey. what's up Haley," DeMarco said, approaching the truck. As usual, he was dressed to impress: nice black slacks, black crewneck pullover with a black t-shirt beneath it, and dress shoes. His hands were down by his sides. I was going to shake his hand, but noticed that he was playing with his silver meditation balls, rolling them around in his hand.

"Hey, DeMarco, how you doing?"

He tilted his head and peeked inside the truck behind me. "Camille, Krystal, Utopia how y'all doing?" They spoke.

"What's up with you, Haley," DeMarco repeated to me, not taking his eyes off of Michael.

"Man, just driving around the projects looking for No Love, we got studio tomorrow night and I wanted to let him know, but he's nowhere to be found." My shoulders slumped in exasperation. Maybe the rusted-out environment here was already getting to me. "DeMarco, sometimes I think that I am wasting my time working with rappers. I think the problem is, I want it for them more than they want it for themselves. I mean, where is their dedication? All of them say they want to rap, but they always faking. Faking about showing up at the studio, making it to photo shoots, faking about they tried to call me or they left me a message or something. Why do these rappers be playing? I mean, don't say you want to do something, and then don't or don't half-ass do something."

"Haley, these nigguhs ain't being paid, so you can't expect them to follow through on a lot of shit. If they was being paid they'd be there, trust me. Plus, these nigguhs is like babies, you gotta baby sit 'em. Also, you gotta remember that most of them only rapping cause they friends rapping or because they think it's the thing to do on the block. Haley, if you go to any inner city community in the U.S., you gone find a rapper on every block and you know what else? Most rappers want the fame and not the fortune."

"You think Tupac wanted the fame or the fortune, DeMarco?"

"'Pac wanted the fame."

"You think Puffy wanted the fame or the fortune?"

"Both, that's why he in nigguhs' videos and that's why he is a business-man."

"DeMarco… what do you want?"

"The fortune. Fuck the fame."

"Hmmm."

"Look, Haley, all you got to do is listen to these rappers talk and it is obvious by listening to them whether they want the fame or the fortune."

I thought about all the rappers I had known who swore to me that they wanted the fortune in spite of their attitudes, and then I clearly saw DeMarco's point.

"Yeah, I don't see Dubb, so I guess I should be leaving now."

"Man, that's how it is with these nigguhs, you got to baby-sit them. I keep on telling you that. Man, like I said, these nigguh's ain't being paid right now, they don't understand that you gone pay them when you get paid and that y'all coming up together. "

"Yeah, DeMarco, but they say they want to do this. They say they want to rap. They all say it. Obviously, they ain't too serious. If they were, they'd show up. I am getting real tired of dealing with these rappers."

"It's not that they don't want to rap and make music, it's like I said, it's just that these nigguhs ain't getting paid so it ain't a priority for them."

I saw someone else walking in our direction: OG Ben. He strolled toward us, looking like he was on a mission looking for that early-morning high. Ben is about sixty-two. He lived in Jordan Downs before I was born. I can't even remember the first time I saw him. He was just always there. Everybody in the 'jects knew Ben, and was cool with him. He was strung out on heroin, and had been strung out on drugs since I was a little girl. He'd get off, get clean, only to fall back on, get off, and eventually get back on. Despite this, Ben was the closest thing to a mayor our little city within a city had. Nothing went on around here without him knowing. I yelled, "Hey Ben, you seen No Love?"

"Not since this morning!" The man slowed down a bit as he passed by. He crossed the street and walked in front of my truck. As I watched him, I thought about how this old man had been living in the projects, in the same apartment, for fifty years, and about all of he changes he must have seen occur. When Ben first moved there, he was without addiction, young, vibrant and full of energy, and the Projects were brand spanking new. But over the years, like these buildings, Ben's condition declined and he grew old, tired, and depressed. Now, Ben was worn, barely moving. He was a good brother and it hurt me to see him on that shit, as it was really taking him down. Sometimes when I'd come through the 'jects, Ben would be tweaking. I knew he was bad off when he asked me for a dollar, worse when he hit me up for a quarter. Sometimes I'd give him money, and sometimes I'd turn him down. The last time I saw him he asked, "You got a dime Haley? Now come on, I know you got a dime, Haley."

DeMarco spoke; I moved my eyes off of Ben as he scuttled into one of the buildings. "Haley, I was in Chinatown yesterday and I picked you up a pair of meditation balls. They're in the glove compartment of my Range. Let me go and get them." DeMarco turned and walked away. I watched his back as he ambled to his car. It was not an unpleasant sight, I'm here to tell you.

"He got you some of those things he be rolling around in his hand?" Utopia looked intrigued.

"Meditation balls, that's what they're called," Camille interjected.

"I want some," Krystal said. "This lady I work with have some on her desk at work, and I be picking them up playing with them. They are so relaxing, mind-soothing."

DeMarco returned and handed me the balls. Wherever he had gotten them from, it sure as hell wasn't WalMart. The metallic spheres were in an ornate red box with Oriental characters embossed into the wood itself. The motif was definitely Chinese to the core. I undid a gold catch on the front of the box, and the lid drifted open. Two shiny, smooth silver Meditation balls sat inside atop black velvet.

I didn't know quite what to say, so I settled on "Thank you so much, DeMarco!" I removed them from the box.

"Here, let me show you how to exercise with the balls," DeMarco said, removing them from my hand. In the process, his finger brushed my palm, and I felt a tingle. The balls at work? DeMarco demonstrated. "Put two of them in your palm and bend and stretch your fingers in sequence. You can rotate and revolve them either clockwise or counter-clockwise, like this." He returned the balls to my hand.

"Damn, this does feel good," I exclaimed after maneuvering the Oriental orbs in the manner which DeMarco had described. As they moved around, the silver balls produced a contented melody that sounded like bells ringing far away.

Camille had been watching; I noticed the back window rolled down and her head sticking out. "Listen to the bell sounds they are making. They sound so peaceful. Let me see," Camille said, reaching for the meditation balls. I reached out and handed them to her. She rolled them around, after apparently having watched for a while. "Bend your fingers like this," DeMarco said bending down into the truck. He bent his fingers and rolled his meditation balls around in his hand. But she really didn't need the second lesson. She rolled the balls around as he did. A full minute must have gone by. She was smiling. She closed her eyes, opened them and still smiling said, "I want me a pair too, DeMarco."

"Let me see them," Utopia said reaching her hand from the back seat. Camille handed them to her. Utopia played with the balls. Like Camille had done before, she closed her eyes and rolled the balls around. "Damn, this is relaxing." She opened her eyes, "DeMarco, I want a pair too."

"I'm putting in my order," Krystal yelled. They sounded a little like kids gathered in front of Santa Claus. DeMarco started laughing.

"You know they also have the stone ones and the jade ones. They are soundless. I wasn't quite sure which ones to get you, Haley, so I just got you the ones that I have, that you saw. I also have the stone ones. I use them when I want to meditate in silence." He returned his pair to his pocket. "So what y'all about to get into?"

"Nothing really, they hungry," I said, pointing in the direction of the back seat. "I'll probably take them to go get something to eat and go back to Krystal's."

"Where y'all going to eat?"

"I don't know, probably Crustacean's."

"Well hold on, I'll go with y'all. Just give me a minute. My boy, D, should be here shortly,. He on his way and when he get here we'll go with y'all."

"Alright."

"Hey, I'm outta here," Michael said, extending his handshake to DeMarco. DeMarco just looked at him warily. I sensed something there, and it wasn't good. Michael put his hand down and walked away with Tony, who was smiling. DeMarco's cell rang. After listening to the caller, he pushed the cell's "Off" button. "D is exiting the freeway now, his wife dropping him off. We'll follow you."

"Okay," I agreed. DeMarco walked away and got into his truck. I followed him, not realizing it until I was at the front of my truck.

"Alright, was it just me, or did y'all just feel the strong chemistry between Haley and DeMarco," Krystal asked in a low voice intended only for the other girls.

"Ooh, I felt it! Haley and DeMarco feeling each other," Utopia teased.

"Did you see the look of love in DeMarco's eyes," Krystal asked.

"No, but I saw it in Haley's eyes," Utopia responded.

"All I know is, I ain't saying nothing. These lips are sealed," Camille said as she ran her fingers across her lips motioning as if she was zipping them.

"Yeah, but Haley don't need to get caught up with him. He's a married man. Even if his bitch is locked up, he's still a married man. Plus don't forget DeMarco is a gamer. Always been one, always will be. But they do like each other, it's obvious, so save your breath and don't try and convince them otherwise."

I got back to the truck, hearing that last sentence. I shook my head. I hadn't heard the whole conversation, but I could pretty much fill in the blanks for myself. "DeMarco is my business partner. Nothing more." The clique laughed. "Fuck y'all," I said. I started the car.

Krystal looked me in the eye. "Let me ask you this, Haley: Do you find him attractive?"

"Yeah, he's handsome, but I'm celibate and plan to stay that way until God sends me a good man, someone I'm compatible with and have a lot in common with. Someone who is supportive of me and who is dedicated to helping me get where I want to, and I will help him. Plus, DeMarco's married and like I said, I'm celibate. Nothing would ever happen between us."

"Haley, you my girl and I don't wanna see you get hurt. Just be careful and stop spending so much time with the man," Krystal added.

D's dark blue Lincoln Navigator pulled up next to DeMarco's Range. His wife was driving. He got out and came around to her side, leaned over, kissed her on the lips, and got into DeMarco's Range. She drove off, looking at us as she passed us by. I started to pull out, and DeMarco followed. Then, almost by accident I spotted No Love, who was standing in the cuts with Ridah and another guy.

"Hey, hey, hey," No Love called out, running into the streets; I saw him coming up in my rear-view mirror, waving his arm to get my attention, gesturing for me to come back. I stopped, and he ran up to the truck. DeMarco's Range Rover idled behind mine.

"Haley, what's up? I hear you real busy and that the magazine and label and the comp you working on is coming out tight. I hear you got some major features on that motherfucker. Can I get on it?"

"I want you on it. That's why I was here looking for you. Can you come to the studio tomorrow night at eight?"

"I'll be there." He was panting from chasing my car. "Damn Haley, I should've fucked with you a long time ago. I really wanna work with you. I think it would be good for me to work with a female." No Love was excited. "Haley, I got my album done. Shit, I'm in the studio now working on my next album. You know my cousin supposed to be putting my album out. He with me now, let me call him over here. I'm gone introduce you to him and you can ask him when my shit coming out."

"Alright, I gotta hurry up though, DeMarco behind me, he following me. We going to get something to eat."

"Alright, it'll only take a minute." No Love ducked past two abandoned cars and approached a man leaning against what was left of a lamppost. "Hey Spence, come here, I want you to meet the lady I been telling you about that be doing the PR, marketing, and management shit." No Love walked back, with Spence in tow. "Here he comes. Hey, Haley, when he come over here I'm gone walk away and leave you to talk with him. Ask him when my shit coming out and tell me what he say." Spence walked over. He was holding a black organizer in his hand. No Love introduced us and walked away.

"Yeah, No Love talk about you all the time, said you was helping him to understand the business of music and you was helping him join Ascap and copyright his song lyrics."

"Yeah, No Love got some mad skills. He's a very talented rap artist. In my opinion, him and Tupac were some of the best rap artists ever to exist. No Love just need the right financing behind him and good music and he can make it big. I'm convinced of that. So he says that his album is done and you're putting it out. When is it coming out?"

"Well, No Love gotta go back inside the studio and redo some of those songs you know, and he not ready."

The last thing No Love needed was another delay. "He played the CD for me, it sounds good. Don't anything need to be redone in my opinion. Man, them songs are hitting, he need to get it out there."

"No Love, he ain't ready," Spence said.

I don't have time to waste with Spence. I decided to approach No Love later, tell him that he was ready, and ask him what the hell were we waiting for, thereby removing Spence and any other naysayer out of the loop. "Alright, well, it was nice meeting you, Spence. I gotta go. Here, take my number and give me yours," I said, handing him one of my business cards. "What's your number?" I asked, picking up my cell in order to store it in the address book. He gave it to me.

"Alright, I'll talk to you later Spence. Call me."

"Nice meeting you, too, Haley. I'll be in touch." Spence walked away.

My cell rang. I looked at the caller ID, and saw that DeMarco was calling. I figured he was getting hungry; I knew I was. "Sorry about that, I'm hurrying up," I answered.

"It's cool. I was just calling you 'cause a few of my other boys wanna go with us to the restaurant. They just pulled up behind me. It's like, ten of them. I called the restaurant and they say they can accommodate all of us."

"Oh alright, that's cool."

"My boy, he gone follow us to Crustacean's. He in the white Range like ours, behind me. My other boy, he in the black and silver Hummer."

I saw both vehicles coming up the street. "Alright." I hung up. No Love was re-appearing.

"Haley, you outta here?"

"Yeah, I'm out."

"Oh yeah, you going to dinner with DeMarco and all the ballers," he asked and started laughing. "Them nigguh's Insane and Creature Man just pulled up. He going with y'all to the restaurant?"

"Whose Insane and Creature Man? I heard DeMarco mention that name Creature Man before."

"Fucking kingpins like your boy DeMarco. That's Creature Man driving the black and silver Hummer. Insane's in the passenger seat. They work for DeMarco. They from east Oakland 6-9 Ville too. When Demarco moved down here from the bay, he brought several of his boys with him, including D and Kameron. DeMarco likes you, Haley," No Love said pointing his finger at me. "He ain't gone never let you leave, you good for business. That nigguh see an opportunity in you 'cause you smart. He sees it like you gone help him get out the game. He smart in the streets and shit, but he don't know how to deal with white folks. That's where you come in. Haley, I love you like a sister. Hell, you are my sister that's why I'm telling you what I'm telling you. Hell, he can invest in my music, that nigguh balling! He got some real money. You know how nigguhs be around here talking about this nigguh and that nigguh and how they got two and three hun put away, that nigguh he made millions in this game. I hear he be talking about you all the time." A smile appeared across No Love's face, but was erased with the words, "Haley, be careful with DeMarco." Now a stern and serious look replaced the smile. "I don't think that nigguh gone ever disrespect you or nothing, 'cause you different than most of those females he use to being around and be fucking with, but be careful. Never make that nigguh feel like his back is against the wall with you. I ain't trying to scare you or nothing, I mean you always be yourself with the nigguh, but DeMarco he got a street mentality and that's how he handle things. Then I saw how that nigguh gets down. Don't be fooled by his calm demeanor, his kindness and his charm. Now Creature Man is his sickest hit man. He ain't nothin' nice. You know what that nigguh did? He killed this guy in retaliation of his brother's murder and he went to jail for four years for it. Anyway, it turns out Creature Man killed the wrong guy, so when he gets out of jail he goes and kills the right one. He went to trial and everything, but with his good lawyers paid for by yours truly, Demarco, he beat the case. Yeah, him and DeMarco, they partners in crime." No Love kept on speaking. "Creature Man and DeMarco and them nigguhs' had funk with some gang members and Creature Man cut one of the gangs members arm off and sent it to his gang in box. The nigguh had wrapped it up in gift-wrap and all, even put a bow on it. Man, that nigguh is sick. If he feel that somebody's disrespected, him he always talking about violating them, whatever that means."

"Damn like that," I quietly responded as a worried look showed my face.

"Creature Man wants to sign me to his record label, but I ain't signing with him. It's not that I'm scared or nothing, but I know in the end I will either end up having to kill that nigguh or he'd end up killing me. That fat motherfucker be slapping his artists around and shit, whooping on them. That shit ain't cool. Signing a contract with him would be like making a deal with the devil. I just rather not deal with the nigguh, you know what I'm saying?"

"I feel you."

"I'd fuck with DeMarco, though, 'cause although DeMarco a thug nigguh too, he got understanding and reasoning. That nigguh Creature Man, he ain't got no understanding or reasoning. Only with DeMarco it seems he does."

"So Creature Man got his own record label."

"Yeah, Insane Records, and that nigguh is insane. A perfect name for a demented motherfucker." I sucked in a deep breath and released it.

No Love tapped me on the shoulder, "But, at the same time, shit handle you business Haley use that nigguh for his money though, it's all good. Just be diplomatic about it. DeMarco ain't gone ever let you see his other side Haley. You might see a little bit of it, but he ain't gone never show you how sick he really is. Truth is I don't think there is nothing you could do to make that nigguh disrespect you, so, don't even trip. I got love for you, Haley, and I just wanted to put this in yo ear though so at the same time you know what you dealing with. Feel me?" I nodded. No Love leaned in the window, "What that nigguh say?" No Love gestured subtly in Spence's direction.

"He said that you weren't ready, that you had to go back in the studio and do some things over."

No Love sighed. "Is that what he said?" I nodded.

No Love stepped back from the truck. I could see wheels were turning in his head. He tapped on the doorframe of the Range, looking into my eyes.

Somewhere inside No Love's head, a switch flipped. He looked me right in the eye. "You wanna manage me?"

"Yes." *Yes*, I thought, *and I'll get you out from under Spence's dead hand.*

"Then do it," He closed the door and walked away angry. In his eyes I had seen a fire lit, like I hadn't seen in awhile.

I turned to the clique. "That was DeMarco who just called me. He said that his boys wanted to go with us to the restaurant, they behind him in the white Range and the Hummer," I said looking into the side mirror on my door. Krystal, Camille and Utopia all turned around to get a look at who was behind us. It was more than just brothers in vehicles, now. Apparently the growing entourage of high-end rides was attracting a following of its own. The hood rats were out now, surrounding the cars with DeMarco and his boys.

"Look at them hoes, they like vultures, got they cars surrounded and shit," Utopia said.

"Damn! Looks like them hoes them came out of their houses and shit to see these brothers on dubs and shit and in nice cars," Camille said.

Utopia watched. "Now, I know there's some ballers in those cars, damn I'm getting me one of 'em. Haley, I'm going to pick one of them out after I size him up You check out what he has on his jewelry and shit, and then I want you to have DeMarco introduce me to him, alright?

Camille shook her head as if to say, *I can't believe this.*

"I'm done with the brothers," Krystal said.

I could see where Camille and Krystal were coming from. Still, if that's what Utopia really wanted, I wasn't going to deny her. "Alright, Utopia, let me know the one you wanna get with, and I'll mention it to DeMarco to introduce y'all." I looked in the mirror; the hood rats now nearly numbered a dozen. "Damn, being that them girls got them trapped, I better call DeMarco and see if he ready to roll before he's covered in 'em."

"Yeah," DeMarco answered.

"Damn, y'all alright back there them females all over y'all."

"Ahhh," DeMarco laughed. He clearly enjoyed the attention…and knew it for what it was.

"Y'all ready to go?"

"Let's do it."

Like a caravan, my silver Range, DeMarco's black Range, the white Range, and the silver-and-black Hummer left the hood rats behind, rolled out of the Jordan Downs projects. We reached the freeway and voyaged to another planet called Beverly Hills, where the trendy restaurant, Crustacean's, was located. This was where Los Angeles' elite dined, and some of the biggest names in Hollywood hung out.

"Where did they go," Utopia said, looking back and not seeing the other cars as I exited the freeway.

"I don't know, but they somewhere behind us," I said, looking at the passenger-side mirror. I pulled into the restaurant-parking garage and parked. We got out. "Let's go inside, you guys. We can wait for them in there. It's cold out here." We walked inside of the restaurant and sat down on the leather seat in the lounge, waiting for DeMarco and his boys' arrival.

I stared into the mirror before us. We looked like million-dollar sisters in our clothes. Krystal sported a sheer cabbage rose, brown, cream Prada blouse with a solid cabbage rose tank top underneath. She wore pair of cabbage rose linen wide-legged drawstring pants, all from the same designer, and a pair of brown Prada's donned her feet. She had just gotten her weave done. The black French refined hair cascaded down past her shoulders, sprawling onto her back. She looked tight. On her face she sported a pair of Prada sport rose-colored glasses with the rose colored frames.

Utopia sported a long, wide-wing collar, pink rayon Moschino halter dress with a ruffled hem. A pair of pink Moschino thong sandals with a wedge heel donned her feet. On her face was a pair of cherry-colored Moschino shades, with heart-shaped color lens that sat inside a cherry frame. She was the epitome of feminity in that outfit.

Camille had on a simple sleeveless red Dolce & Gabbana print dress, with a side slit. On her feet she also wore a red pair of Dolce's.

I was dressed in Gucci. I wore a pair of dark blue wide-legged cuffed linen pants, a dark blue spaghetti strap tank, and a pair of dark blue Gucci sandals. A silver chain with rhinestone ornaments ran clockwise across the sandals. Finally, a silver G Face Gucci watch was worn upon my wrist. I sported a pair of $500 Gucci shades with the blue lens color.

"Here they come," Utopia announced pointing in the direction of the door. DeMarco was in the lead, with his boys walking in behind him. Spotting me, he strolled over to me. "Hey, Haley."

"Hey, DeMarco."

"You remember my boy D, "he asked, pointing behind him.

"Yeah, I remember him. How you doing, D?"

"I'm cool." He reached for my hand and kissed it.

DeMarco introduced the rest of his crew. "This is Insane, Eric, Kameron, Raysean, Antoine, Kevin, Ronald, Santos, Money, Big Mike, and Creature Man." I took notice of the long scar on Santos neck. Although he was well-dressed, he was a real grimy, light-skinned-looking brother. Creature Man was a well-dressed, light-brown-skinned, handsome big man, who briefly reminded me of Big Larry. He had a baby face, and was younger than Big Larry. If I were to guess, I would say he was around 31 or 32. He stood six feet four inches at well over three hundred pounds. Creature Man was an amiable giant. He had a soft-spoken voice. "Hello, Haley, it's nice to meet you. My boy DeMarco always be talking about you. It's finally nice to put a name to a beautiful face." With DeMarco looking on, Creature man took my hand inside his and kissed it. The gentle giant, appearing to be every bit a gentlemen, was smiling and looking down upon me. DeMarco continued his introductions. "Everybody, this is my business partner, Haley, and that's Krystal, Camille and Utopia. Haley was the president of Eastside West. That's where I met her."

"You worked for Big Larry," Kameron asked me.

"Yeah. You know him?"

"I know the fat motherfucker." DeMarco and Insane laughed. *Whatever*, I thought.

DeMarco's crew was not your average set of drug dealers; they were all ballers. Flossing, some were in suits, the rest in casual wear. The maitre'd came to seat us. As we reached the table, another of DeMarco's boys who had been in the washroom came up to our table.

"Who is baby right there, that's what I'm talking about," Greg said, pointing at me. He stepped up to me, trying to get his mack on. "You got a boyfriend?"

"That's DeMarco's," D stepped up to him and whispered in his ear. He didn't do a good job at whispering because I heard him.

Greg had already started to backpedal, but DeMarco touched his shoulder. "Hold on, back up. That's my business partner, don't be disrespecting her," he said curtly.

Greg tried to recover his composure. "Hey, man, baby look good, I didn't know she belonged to you DeMarco, my bad." He extended his handshake to DeMarco. They shook hands. He turned to me. "Well it's nice to meet you." Krystal, Utopia and Camille looked at each other. Then Utopia whispered in my ear, pointing under the table at one of DeMarco's boys.

"Haley, that's who I want to meet," Utopia said.

"Who, that one right there?" I had dropped my voice to a confidential whisper while the men talked. "That's Kameron. He was the one driving the Hummer. I'll tell DeMarco, so he can introduce y'all."

"Wait a minute, Haley, don't look now, but he's staring at us. Uh-oh, here he comes!"

"You wearing the hell outta that pink halter dress," he said, approaching Utopia and striking up a conversation with her. Inwardly, I was grateful he'd saved me the trouble of introducing himself to Utopia. They ended up side-by-side, indulging in their own private conversation during dinner. I found out later that they had exchanged phone numbers.

I sat with DeMarco. Krystal sat next to me and Camille next to her. Krystal enjoyed herself at the restaurant by mostly talking to DeMarco's friend, Greg. Camille kept to herself most of the night, being antisocial.

After dinner, we all walked back to the parking garage. All of the guys except DeMarco piled into their respective Range Rovers and Hummer. DeMarco walked the clique and I back to my SUV, which the valet had just brought around from the back. DeMarco opened the front passenger door and the back door on the passenger's side, then proceeded to the driver's side, opening my door. He was ever the perfect gentleman. After I got in, he closed it, and leaned in through the window. "So what you doing tomorrow?"

"I'm not quite sure. It's Krystal's birthday. I gotta find something for us to get into."

"Happy birthday, Krystal," DeMarco said further sticking his head through the window on my side of the door.

"Thanks, DeMarco."

"You gone call me later?" DeMarco's whisper was to me, and for us alone.

I looked at him. "Yeah," I whispered back.

"Tonight?"

"Yeah, tonight," I replied.

Still speaking softly: "I gotta drop D off at home, I should be home in about forty minutes. If you want you can call me on my cell," DeMarco said.

"Alright, talk to you in forty minutes." I put the key in the ignition and started the SUV.

DeMarco stuck his head through the window and planted a kiss on my left cheek. He looked at Camille in the front seat and at Utopia and Krystal in the back seat. "Ladies, have a good night," he said.

"Good night," Utopia and Camille said. Krystal instead waved.

Even before I finished rolling the electric window up, I just *knew* I would never hear the end of it from the clique. And I was right…

Utopia beat the others to the punch. "Everybody be saying yo boy DeMarco is a kingpin. I wouldn't be surprised if it were true, the brother deep in the game and he only sell to the balling drug dealers that are like fucking mini-kingpins themselves. Before they were married, DeMarco's wife Nakeesha sold for him I hear. I hear she ain't the first of his women to sell for him. I hear they all do."

"DeMarco is a sav." Camille interjected. "I heard that when his boy Sherm set him up to be robbed a while back, by the time DeMarco got finished with him, he had him begging and pleading for his life. They say he kept telling DeMarco 'I ain't even trying to see you like this man. Man, I know what you capable of. I know how you get down. Please just give me another chance.' They say DeMarco's loyal soldiers were positioned around the room, watching their boss at work. I hear they were all there: D, Kameron, Prophet, Ceedric, Lil Rob, Antoine, Michael, Quincy, and Scherzo. They were loyal to him. The thing is about it, man, DeMarco has much love in the streets that he's only one of a handful of guys who can go on any set in all of not only Los Angeles, but also Southern California, and not have any problems. This is the kind of respect he commands. DeMarco distributed drugs to his soldiers and they distributed theirs and so on. It was a long line to DeMarco."

Utopia chimed in again. "People got so much love for DeMarco that if somebody did something to him, they'd take care of it for him just on the strength of that alone. Mumbles was his number one boy. He actually is the one who brought DeMarco into the game along with his brother they called B Stone… well, at least that's one of the rumors. They all from East Oakland's 6-9 Ville. Rumor has it Mumbles kept catching cases doing time, B Stone got strung out on dope, and DeMarco was right there and took over his customers," Utopia mouthed. Krystal and I just sat there listening to the dialogue between the two of them.

Krystal weighed in. "Five years ago, the Feds busted down the door to DeMarco's grandmama's house and raided it. They didn't find any drugs in the house, but they did find three hundred thousand dollars in a wall safe that was behind a picture in the living room. DeMarco went to trial for that one, but he prevailed. His money and good lawyers got him off. However, he never got that three hundred G's back.

"I remember also when he used to date Tracy. She had just moved to the Bay from Louisiana. She was one of those light-skinned, green-eyed, Creole women. She was living with her brother who was on drugs in this house in Lakewood along with his girlfriend. She thought that her brother was out in California living the good life 'cause this is what he had told his family. Tracy didn't know that he brother was on drugs until she moved in with him. It didn't take her long to figure it out.

"She met DeMarco one day at the supermarket in Inglewood. She was in love with him. DeMarco just used her. He used to use the apartment she shared with her brother and his girl to keep the weight he was carrying. He would supply her brother and his girl who was also on drugs with coke. Tracy didn't do drugs. DeMarco never brought drugs into his home, it was too risky. Anyway, the Feds, they watching DeMarco, and they busted into the house one day when DeMarco wasn't there and found 10 kicks. Of course, DeMarco didn't claim that shit. Tracy's brother and his girlfriend got fucked. Because the apartment was in there name, they caught the case and ain't gonna see the light of day for a minute. DeMarco paid for a lawyer for her brother and his girl, but they still got fucked."

I was tired of all the DeMarco tales; with these girls, he was almost an urban legend. "What do you have, a fucking dossier on him?"

"Hey, I'm just telling what I've heard," Krystal said. "Tracy continued to kick it with DeMarco even after her brother went to jail until he got tired of her and ended their relationship. I saw her once in passing and she said that DeMarco put her out of the apartment and that he just stopped calling her. She said that she would call him in the beginning, but he never returned her phone calls. She use to come through the 'jects looking for him right after they broke up. The thing is that was the last place she would have found him because DeMarco did not hang out like that. She should have known that he didn't hang on the block. The days of DeMarco being on the block had been over with for several years now. She would have done better looking for him at the Beverly Hills Spa Resort and Hotel, where he would take the women. Usually the brothers only took the women there that they really liked. It was a special privilege for them. DeMarco was different than a lot of the brothers in this regard. He had a different way of thinking. If you hung out with DeMarco, he was going to spend money on you. If he bought something than he also bought it for you, so him taking a woman to the Beverly Hills Spa Resort or spending money on her did not make her all that special. It's just what he did on a regular basis, and if you happen to be with him at the time than you were going to reap the benefits."

Yeah, I knew this part of what Krystal was saying about DeMarco was true. Money was no object to him. If you were one of his girls, you benefited from his trade. He spent money on the women he wanted to keep for even a minute. There actually were a few of them who were more than a one-night stand.

Krystal was still talking, "I remember he had this other girlfriend. Tegra was her name. She was beautiful. She looked like Tyra Banks' twin. Her dyed brownish-blonde hair matched her caramel skin color. She was tall and thin. She resembled a model in one of those Victoria's Secret catalogs. DeMarco always dated beautiful women. Even the girls from the block he fooled around with were real pretty. Tegra had a rep for dating ballers. She ended up in a two-year courtship with DeMarco, and while that was going on, she never worked. She was completely dependent upon him the whole time that they were together.

"DeMarco had put her up in this nice apartment in Riverside. He didn't keep the mistresses he had long term affairs with too close to home cause he didn't want that shit to come home. He used to encourage Tegra to start a business, even told her that he would give her the money to launch it, but she never took him up on the offer. Tegra's job was spending DeMarco's money. The two years they were together, she purchased brand new furniture twice for the whole house and furnished every room. DeMarco never complained about her spending.

"Over time, DeMarco grew tired of Tegra, and as always, he never offered the women an excuse to why they were breaking up. He just moved on and didn't return their phone calls. Yeah, DeMarco, he's a smooth motherfucker. He doesn't have a reputation for hitting on women. That is not to say he will not choke a bitch out if she disrespected him, cause he will."

"Haley, are you in love with DeMarco," Utopia asked?

"What?"

"Are you in love with DeMarco? It's written all over your face."

I sighed. "I said it before and I'll say it again: DeMarco is just my business partner. If he acts jealous, that's his lookout. There's nothing more between us." I looked and sounded convincing…which was good, because for the first time when I issued my standard denial, I felt like maybe I just needed a little convincing—just a little!- for myself…

Thirteen

"A Black man can have any black woman he wants in the world if he plays his cards right. She can have a degree, be a professional and he doesn't have to have a degree or be a professional and he can have her, all according to the way he approaches her. He can work a blue-collar job, be a drug dealer or abuser, or drive a fucking taxi, and she'll take him as her lover. Looking back on it now and knowing what I know now, I wish that I had pursued the college brothers more when I was at UCLA, or even when I was in law school at USC, and married one of them. "

"Hmmm hum," I said.

Krystal was lying on the chase ranting. Utopia and Camille were asleep at the top of the Krystal's black cast iron king-sized Canopy bed and I was at the foot. The canopy bed was beautiful, with the burgundy, gold and white fabric that draped the top of the canopy matching the comforter set, and burgundy and white pillows thrown around Krystal's bedroom. It was breathtaking. I always wanted a king-sized canopy bed. After seeing how good Krystal's bed looked with all of its decorations, I had vowed to redecorate my bedroom next Christmas and purchase a king-sized iron canopy bed similar to her own.

It was 2 a.m. on Saturday morning. We were in Krystal's master bedroom with the fireplace, lounging. A log sat in the fireplace, but it wasn't burning. It was Krystal's birthday. We spent the entire day together, starting with break-fast at 8 a.m. at Roscoe's Chicken and Waffles on north gower and Sunset boulevard in Hollywood. From there, we went to Krystal's mom's house so she could pick up her birthday gift from her, and then we went back to the Crenshaw Mall to go shopping. When we finished our shopping, the bags were piled into the back of my Silver Range Rover with the black leather seats, and then we were off to the Magic Theatre inside the mall to see a 3 p.m. matinee, *The Barbershop*, starring Ice Cube, Cedric the Entertainer, and Eve. The movie was so funny. We laughed like crazy.

After the movie, we went to dinner at a seafood restaurant on Malibu Beach. Upon finishing, we strolled along the sand on the beach and just talked about life, men, and how much we enjoyed our friendships with one another. We got back to Krystal's sometime around midnight. Tired and tipsy from the wine we'd been drinking, we retreated to her bedroom. At din-ner, Camille kept the wine coming. Once the first bottle was finished, she requested another one, and one more after that from the waiter. When we got back to Krystal's she retrieved yet another bottle from the wine rack in the kitchen.

As I was too tired to engage in a conversation with Krystal, she had the floor to herself. Krystal talked to herself further, affirming who she was and reiterating her feelings and opinions about black men. I half-listened to her monologue. Before dozing off to sleep, I threw in some "hmmm hum's", "ain't that the truth's", "I heard that's," and "I feel you's."

Krystal proceeded, "College-educated black men, it seems, ain't inter-ested in dating a sister at all. Hell, we can have a BA, MA, Ph.D., or in my case, a JD, and they still don't want us. No, their preference is Caucasian or Asian women. I heard a well-known black NBA basketball player offer an excuse why he doesn't date black women. He said, 'I don't like nappy hair on my woman's pussy.' Motherfucker. I have heard other brothers say they prefer dating Caucasian women because they don't put them through changes like sisters do and they don't have attitudes. I contend if we have attitudes, it's because they gave us one with the bullshit they put us through. The lying, the cheating, and all the games they play, so when brother says to me that sisters got attitudes, I respond 'its cause y'all gave us one'. Haley, are you listening to me?!"

"Hmmm hum."

She went ahead speaking, "Then there are the brothers who date Asian women because they say Asian women are submissive and bow down to them. Then there is the double-standard issue. The brothers date a white woman, but sisters can't date a white man. If we do, they got something to say, and don't go out in public with a white man cause the brothers gone stare and just might say something sarcastic to you."

"Ain't that the truth."

Krystal continued with her speech. "In the case of the clique, we are all professional black women that have just simply refused to date anything other than a black man. The clique is so representative of the saying that you can take the lion out of the jungle, but not the jungle out of the lion. Well, you can take the clique out of the ghetto, but you could not take the ghetto out of us. I guess the bottom line is this is why we were so attracted to the guys in the hood. We were all clocking dollars and we even all have postgraduate degrees, but it's something about them brothers that we just can't seem to let go of them. I don't even think it 's so much about the sex cause then we all dated men with little dicks. Haley, remember Camille used to complain about the brother she had gone out with whose dick was the size of her pinky, and you and Utopia told me about the small dick men y'all been out with?"

"Hmm huh."

"I don't know why we love them so much. Maybe it's the mentality, the strength that these brothers had displays that keep us wanting them. The truth is, looking back at the situation now and being older and wiser, I feel that we have been settling when it comes to having a man. We should definitely stop limiting ourselves, especially when it comes to making a life-long choice and commitment and when it comes to being happy. Simply put, all we got either is a man who has a drug problem, is a drug dealer, or in the case of Camille and you, Haley, married."

"Umm hmm."

"There is no real future with these kind of guys. Now, I am thinking we deserve better. I deserve better. If I have to get any old kind of man just to say I got a man, I'd rather be alone."

"I heard that," I sleepily agreed.

"It's the same old thing every week. Restaurants, parties, plays, movies, vacations, ski trips, cruises, book club meetings, I attend as part of a crew with y'all," Krystal said pointing at the canopy bed. She continued, "Oh, yeah, then there are the lawyers' conventions that I attend like once or twice a year, the Gavin and Black Radio Exclusive music conventions with you. It seems as if I am not at work, I am kicking it with y'all," she frowned and pointed at the bed. "Now don't get me wrong, I love y'all, but I am getting sick and tired of spending my Fridays and weekends with y'all week after week. That's why I'm gone stop limiting myself to only dating black men and start dating white men, especially since the brothers don't seem to be interested in us and don't know how to treat us.

"I want me a Jean Claude Van Dam, Brad Pitt kind of fine white man. Not a Woody Allen look-alike. Yuck, just to think about him sexually is so repulsive. Poor Mia, she had to look at his shit for umpteen years. If I'm gone have to look at a white man's dick, his face is going to look as good as his dick feels inside of me. They say white men are kinder than black men, and another thing, they really know how to appreciate a woman. I even heard that when the lights are off you really don't know the difference. Plus, white guys are freaky and will go down on a woman real quick. They invented that shit here in America. Sometimes, brothers be perpetrating like they don't go down. If the situation were right, they would probably do it to. Yeah, brothers will go down, too, but it takes more work to get them to do it. The brothers in Africa wasn't doing that shit. But, then again, maybe Cleopatra was getting her pussy ate by some king that is well known in history.

"A white guy is really is not my first choice in men, particularly because our cultures are so different. Also, don't let me lie there is the issue that when we fucking he is going to be off rhythm. Damn! This was the complaint the black women I knew had who had slept with white men. I guess we can work through that rhythm thing, but the bottom line is I want to come. If I come off rhythm, that'll work, I guess. Moreover, a black man, well, besides them not wanting us, there is too much shit surrounding them. It's as though they come with a package deal or something. A combination of either wanting a woman to be like their mother, them being broke, on drugs, ex cons, on parole, liars, cheaters, or abusers. I guess weighing the issues surrounding black men and black women relationships with those that plague black women and white men, outweighs me ever dating another brother. "

I sat straight up in the bed, "I feel you, but naw, Krystal, I love my black men, and I can't stop fucking with 'em. Don't want to," I mumbled. I laid back down. Within a minute, I was snoring lightly while Krystal spoke to four walls.

"The last guy I dated, his name was Flip. I broke up with him eight months ago. Flip was known to create petty arguments. Whenever I would suggest that we go to a nice restaurant like Crustacean's or Aqua's, he'd get an attitude and say something negative, like, 'why you trying to be white and eat like those white folks. Just cause you went to college with them folks doesn't mean that you have to act like them. Girl, don't you know that in the '60s you couldn't go in them white folks' restaurants. Girl, don't forget where you from, you grew up in the hood and that's that, so stop trying to be something you are not. I don't care if you went to the black college or the ghetto and graduated Cum Laud, you still from the hood. Man, you better try and roll on over to Roscoe's Chicken and Waffles or El Pollo Loco or Mama's Place.' This was his regular line whenever I'd suggest we go to a nice restaurant. When we would go to a nice restaurant, it would be a struggle just to get there. Instead of having a beautiful romantic evening followed by hot passionate lovemaking, we would just go our separate ways after dinner. The thing that disappointed me most about Flip is that he would take my joy. Once we arrived at the restaurant, he'd enjoy himself, chatting and laughing with the waiter or waitress. He always seemed to order the most expensive thing on the goddamn menu, and I would always end up footing the entire bill. He would always say that he was going to pay me back on payday. I guess payday never came around because I never was paid.

"That night, I sat across from Flip at the restaurant and realized this would be our last time out together. A moment of sadness overcame me and I fought back the tears. When I felt like my feelings were going to get the best of me, I excused myself to the ladies room. We had been together in the dead-end relationship for three years. I got to the point that the only time he ever satisfied me in the relationship is when we fucked, and the pleasure didn't last all that long. He came and went too fast. After that, the thrill was gone. Yeah, sitting at that table in the restaurant I realized that the 'oomph' was gone from the relationship and that there was no future for him and me. I saw all Black men in this way because of my experiences with them. I figured for all it was worth, I'd try this love thing with a white man. White men had always been attracted to me, but determined to not date outside of my race, I always ignored their advances.

"When I first graduated from college, I got this job at Deloitte and Touché. My co-worker who was white was attracted to me. He use to make all kinds of sexual advances. I was a new employee and he was a manager. I didn't work for him, but he was a good friend with my boss. For my birthday, he sent me a dozen of red roses with an ethnic birthday card attached. It read, 'Happy birthday to a beautiful black woman.' Inside the card were two movie certificates and a note that said, 'Will you have dinner with me tonight? Check the appropriate box, yes, or no. If you check yes, please place this note in the in box in my office.' I checked 'yes' and placed it in his in box. Tim was a cute white boy, but could not see myself abandoning the brothers to date a white man at the time. I accepted his dinner invitation because he was nice to me on my birthday and I thought I would have seemed mean and unappreciative if I had declined his offer. Therefore, that night he took me to Julius' Castle Restaurant. Julius's castle was at the end of a cul-de-sac street in North Hollywood. Adjacent to the restaurant was a dramatic view of the Los Angeles Skyline. At the restaurant, women wore their best. Beaded dresses, minks and diamonds flattered the bodies of many women. Our waiter was friendly. I didn't see any black people in the restaurant until we were leaving. Then I noticed this sister dressed in a beautiful black long evening gown wearing a red satin jacket. She was holding onto the arm of this distinguished looking older white gentleman. I noticed her observing me and Tim from across the way. My eyes and her eyes met, she nodded her head as if to say right on. I wanted to take the time and explain to her that he was not my boyfriend, and that unlike her I had not abandoned the brothers, but oh what the hell, home girl looked happy for me, so I just returned her smile with a smile. I nodded my head in the direction of her date and smiled.

"The next morning at work Tim stopped by my office. He wanted to know if I'd have dinner with him again after work. As an excuse, I told him that I was having dinner at my parents' house after work. 'Then how about lunch,'" he asked.

"I'm going to work out at Club One at lunch time."

'How about a rain check on lunch or dinner,' he wanted to know.

"Maybe," I responded. He left my office with a puzzled look on his face.

"For weeks, Tim continued to pursue me. I never accepted any more of his invitations. After turning him down so many times, he stopped asking me out and eventually left me alone. He even stopped speaking to me when he saw me in passing. That was four years ago. In turning him down, I didn't mean to hurt him.

"Last year I ran into him at The Beverly Center. I was standing in line at the concession stand Hot Dog on A Stick when he walked by me. Our eyes met. He was holding the hand of this attractive sister. He made it a point to walk over to the line that I was standing in. 'Oh my God Krystal, is that you?' He gave me a hug and introduced me to the woman whose hand he was holding. 'Honey, this is Krystal, Krystal and I use to work together. Krystal this is my wife Victoria.' We shook hands. They seemed so happy. She seemed so happy, as did Tim. At that point, I envied her. She had a good man who cherishes her and adores her. This was obvious by the look in Tim's eyes. Plus, I knew Tim, and he was a gentlemen. Something every woman wants. Oh well, my loss.

"Being older and wiser now and realizing all that I have been through with men, if I had a chance to date Tim again I would. I wouldn't let my pettiness and insecurities get involved, and I especially could care less about what the brothers would think. Now, I realize how stupid I was not to go for him back then.

"Now, I am almost thirty and I realize that love has no color and when love calls you better answer. The truth is the color of the man's skin doesn't even really matter because in God's eyes we are all human beings. I tell any sister, 'Don't miss a good guy just cause he's not black.' Date and marry a guy 'cause he appreciates you, makes you happy and treats you better than your mama did. Hell, with a white man I might finally find the happiness I have been searching for.

"With a white man, I would no longer have to have the restaurant argument like I often had with Flip. He too, would like fancy restaurants. Also, I love art: Picasso, Divincci, Van Gough. He would love art, too. Well, the package deal that surrounded the white guy looked better than the one that surrounded the brother. Fuck it, I'm going to get me a white man. I'm gone fuck him and them I am gone have him put a ring on this finger, have a plush-ass wedding, invite all of the Bay Area black socialites, get a nice big house, have kids and live happily ever after. Maybe we could settle in Malibu or somewhere in the valley, and buy a home that's nestled in the hills with a scenic view. On the other hand, maybe we could buy our dream home in Beverly Hills with a view of the Los Angeles skyline in the distance. With Flip, I had no future. Haley, what do you think about what I'm saying?

"Haley?!

"Haley...? The girl then dosed off to sleep. Hell I don't even know why I'm asking you your opinion or why I'm asking any of y'all y'all's opinion. Hell y'all too having men problems. Talking about men week after week. The blind leading the blind, that's what we've been."

Fourteen

At Eastside West, I had been more or less confined to the administrative offices and running the day-to-day operations of the record label. Among my duties were obtaining song sample clearances through the Harry Fox Agency or the publisher, doing the accounting, payroll, and banking. I also handled all of the marketing and public relations. I hadn't been directly involved in the studio production part of things. The few rap compilations that had come out of the studio were executive-produced by Big Larry's cousin, Jerry, who was also the manager of the studio. DeMarco and I decided to split our partnership, with me handling the business side of things, and him running the studio. He also said that I'd set the rules and he'd enforce them.

DeMarco was a shrewd businessman. Although my education came from behind the walls of a university and his from the life of hard knocks and the streets, I learned a lot from him. We worked closely together, and I even became a better negotiator.

Malik, a local filmmaker and owner of Tranquility Recording Studios, already produced some film and wanted to obtain funding from Master P. He knew I had an amicable relationship with Master P. Because he was on tour, Master P was unable to attend the funeral service of a Los Angeles rapper with whom he'd once worked. So, I was asked to read a speech at the rapper's funeral service. I agreed. Master P had also sent a huge, beautiful flower arrangement to the church, which now sat next to the brown wooden casket. The ribbon across the huge flower arrangement read his motto, *From a No-Limit Family to No A Limit Soldier* .

After the funeral service Malik enthusiastically approached me to introduce himself. He told me that he had heard about *Rage* and I, and inquired about my contact with Master P, which he also wanted. He then asked if I would get a copy of a film that he had produced into Master P's hands, seeing as how he was a filmmaker himself. I told DeMarco about my encounter with Malik, and what he had asked of me. DeMarco told me to make sure I was getting something out of the deal.

"What do you propose I ask for?"

"You said that this guy Malik is a producer and has his own recording studio. Right?"

"Yeah."

"Well, we got that compilation coming out. Tell him to give you four songs and let you record an additional four songs at his recording studio. In exchange, you will put his film in the hands of Master P. You will talk him up to P. If he tries to get you to lower what you are asking for, remind him that P is a major contact and that you are only a cell telephone call away from him. Tell him you can put his film in P's hand. This is your bargaining power. Also, make it clear you cannot make him any promises as to if P will contact him or not, but that you can promise him that you can put it in P's hand. Come on, let's hit him on the three-way now, and remember what I told you. Remember, Haley, you are giving him a major plug. Don't let him goad you into lowering what it is that you are asking for. If he can't accommodate you as you are willing to accommodate him, end the conversation and hang up the phone."

"Alright."

I called Malik and did just as DeMarco had instructed me with DeMarco on the three-way, per DeMarco's request. He said that since we were going to be business partners, he wanted to see the way I negotiated in case some constructive criticism could be offered. So, I called Malik with DeMarco on the phone. As DeMarco had predicted, he tried to get me to lower what I was asking for in exchange for the plug to P. As DeMarco had instructed me to do, I politely ended the conversation. After I hung up, DeMarco gave me his thoughts and constructive criticism on the conversation.

"He'll call back. You've already said all that you have to say, and don't renegotiate. Only restate when you feel it is necessary to do so. If he becomes quiet on the phone don't feel the need to speak, you remain quiet also. When negotiating, Haley, you have to be honest with yourself and recognize who has the upper hand in negotiation. If you have it, never accommodate. If you don't, then you can switch up, but only a little. You never want a mother-fucker to walk away with way more than you're getting. " DeMarco said.

Sure enough, not even two minutes later, the phone rung. I looked at the caller ID. It was Malik.

"Go ahead and answer it, and remember what I told you," DeMarco said. He hung up.

Three minutes later, I had my four songs. And his word that I could record an additional four at his studio at no cost. Elated—but not showing it!- I hung up and called DeMarco back.

"DeMarco, its Haley. We're on for Saturday at Malik's studio."

"Cool. Damn, girl, you negotiated the hell out of that one. You cut a sweet deal. Now did you make it clear that you can put it in P's hand, but you can't guarantee that he will call him?"

"Yes, I did."

"Good. If it don't go his way in the end, remind him of this if there is a need to."

"Alright."

With DeMarco's new teachings on negotiating, I got my way with Malik and I began contacting the local rappers, asking them if they wanted to be on the forthcoming *Rage* magazine rap compilation. Next thing I knew, I was overwhelmed with rappers' responses.

DeMarco was very private about his affairs; not wanting people in his business, especially the haters, he made it clear that he did not want anybody to know about his involvement with *Rage* or the Compilation. "When they come out, then they can know," he said.

That Saturday, we began recording the *Rage* Magazine & Life Inc. compi-lation at Tranquility. Working with DeMarco on the rap compilation meant that he and I would continue to spend a great a deal of time together.

Fifteen

The closer DeMarco and I got, I noticed that we showed our feelings for one another more than usual. He became more protective of me, and I of him. It got to the point that if another man tried to get at me or even looked at me for too long, DeMarco would check him. The first occurrence happened at Planet Studios in Orange County. Scott, this White guy who owns the studio, embraced me and gave me a kiss on the cheek. DeMarco who was engaged in a conversation with someone several feet away looked in our direction and shouted roughly to Scott. "Hey, don't be grabbing on Haley, and kissing on her like that," ruffling Scott's feathers.

Scott looked at DeMarco, but didn't say anything. At first, I thought DeMarco was kidding, but soon realized he wasn't. I didn't quite know how to respond, so I didn't.

"Hey, don't be ignoring me man, did you hear me? I said don't be grabbing on Haley, and kissing on her and shit." Scott trembled with fear.

"Alright, DeMarco, I heard you man! It won't happen again, man, alright? Forgive me?"

DeMarco continued, "Man, it better not happen again. Grabbing on Haley like that kissing on her and shit… perverted motherfucker." The whole room was silent. I stared at DeMarco. He looked around the room at every-

110

body but me.

Then came that time when DeMarco's friend Donell and I had just finished eating lunch at this French restaurant, LuLu's, in Westwood. His friend, Jerry, called him on his cell as we were leaving. He wanted to borrow two hundred dollars from DeMarco.

We were parked on the parking lot at Normandy and Fifth Avenue. Jerry and DeMarco had arranged to meet in fifteen minutes. We walked to the car. DeMarco and I got in the front, and Donell in the back. He was in the back seat of the Range playing Grand Theft Auto on the Nintendo game system DeMarco had installed in the SUV. He was staring into the small TV screen that was located on the ceiling. "Hey, DeMarco, why don't you come back here and let me jack yo ass." They both laughed. "I'm tired, man. I am going to lay back and take a nap until this nigguh gets here."

DeMarco was already losing patience. "It's 6:30 now. If he not here by 6:45, we gone roll." He rolled the window all the way down on the driver's side. I was tired, too, so I reclined my seat back about midway. I could here Donell talking to the game, getting mad, yelling when he made a mistake. "Hey DeMarco," I heard a voice say, coming from his side of the car. I opened my eyes and looked: it was Jerry. He was bending down peering into the car. "Hi, Haley, remember me?"

Trying to place him, I stared hard at him. "I let you use my cell phone the day the battery went out on your cell and we were at the radio station. Remember, it was the same day you interviewed Busta Rhymes for your magazine? I was in the Range with DeMarco."

"That was you! Oh yeah, I remember you. How you doing?"

"Good. How you been, Haley?"

"Man, I'm good. You know it wouldn't do me any good to complain."

DeMarco was still reclined all the way back, but he wasn't asleep. Most people looking at him would have thought he was asleep, but I knew he was awake and listening to everything.

"So, how the magazine coming?"

"Good. I've just been real busy with it."

"If you ever need my help with anything, just let me know."

"Thanks."

"Where do you live, Haley?"

"Near Santa Monica," I answered evasively.

"Way over there, I know where that is. So, Haley, you got a number?"

Yeah, DeMarco was awake. He sat bolt upright in the seat, put his key in the ignition, and started the engine. He looked at Jerry and said, "I knew you was going somewhere with that, with all your questions. I knew you wasn't just being nice to Haley and you was trying to get at her. Man, back the fuck up. Move, so I can go!" DeMarco put the car in drive.

"Where you going?"

"I am going to take Haley home!"

"Wait a minute, I'm going with you," Jerry said, running back to the old, green, beat-up, rusty Malibu parked behind us. Or, had been parked behind us. DeMarco had already gunned the engine and started to pull out into traffic.

"You better not follow me," DeMarco yelled through the rolled-down window back at Jerry.

Donell was laughing in the back seat. He turned around to look through the rear window. "He following you, DeMarco," he said.

"I know that punk ain't following me." DeMarco said as he looked in his rear-view mirror to see the green car gaining. He was about to punch the gas when a traffic light ahead turned red, as if to stymie him. We sat there waiting for it to turn green again. Jerry pulled up behind him. Cursing under his breath, DeMarco opened the door and stepped outside. Catching Jerry's gaze and meeting it with his own, he yelled. "If you follow me I am going to fuck you up! Do not follow me."

"Man, you forgot to give me the money you was suppose to loan me," Jerry indignantly yelled back.

"I ain't forgot shit," DeMarco shouted back, "and I ain't giving you shit." Just as the light turned green again, DeMarco got back in the car and slammed the door. "I knew that nigguh was up to something. He wasn't just making conversation with Haley, he just wanted to get at her and ask her for her number. That's why I was sitting there quiet cause I knew he was gone do some shit like that." I sat there quietly. DeMarco's behavior and his reaction to Jerry surprised me. No, it did more than surprise me; it left me speechless. I didn't know how to respond to his behavior. Why was he acting so overprotective? It almost seemed as though he were jealous. Hell, he *was* jealous —that was obvious by the way he reacted. I think DeMarco was falling in love with me.

"DeMarco, what you say you knew he was gone try and get at Haley," Donell said still laughing from the back seat.

"Hell, yeah, I knew that nigguh was gone act like that." I was flabbergasted. Yeah it was obvious DeMarco was feeling me. And you like what likes you. Truth be told, I was feeling him also; I had been for a few minutes now.

Another day, we had some downtime at the studio, as a monitor went down and the engineer went to The Guitar Center for a replacement. DeMarco and I chilled in the engineer's booth. My feminine nature and the boredom- got the better of me.

I sat back and stared at DeMarco. He had a look to die for. He was handsome and smart. It was easy to see how a woman would fall for him. He was the epitome of the saying, "tall dark and handsome." He stood six feet two and a half inches tall. He had a nice, medium build. His dark skin was flawless. His long black dreads cascaded past his shoulders, not stopping until the middle of his back. Those dreads embodied the strength of his character and made him, *him*. I hadn't known DeMarco that long, but already I couldn't imagine him without them. That hair was his trademark.

More than just a style, I noticed over time that the dreads were an indicator of DeMarco's personality. Sometimes he let them hang down his back. Sometimes, he wore them tied back, bound by a black rubber band or black scrunge. When he wore his hair like this, you could really see his features and you knew he meant business. His dark brown, medium size eyes, his full lips—not too big or too small, just the perfect size for kissing…

DeMarco was a well-dressed man. Today, he was wearing a soft black Versace leather jacket with two front pockets, beneath it a black T-shirt and black jeans, all also Versace. *I'll be damned*, I thought when I first noticed a Versace watch donning his wrist. Downright meticulous about the way he dressed, he carefully chose his accessories to match the outfit he was wearing. I looked down at his feet. He wore a nice pear of leather lace-ups. If I were a betting woman, I'd guess they, too, were Versace.

Something about a confident and well-dressed man who wears nice shoes was so enchanting to me, and captured my attention. Mostly, DeMarco stayed suited. He dressed up like an athlete you'd see on television walking to the parking lot after a game, or some rich celebrity out on the town. He wore a lot of dark colors, shades of black, and blues. However, any color could look good on him, and did—he didn't limit himself. No, that man never seemed to repeat an outfit, not even a mere jacket for that matter. DeMarco obviously took his wardrobe seriously, and spent a lot of time and money on his styles. He purchased clothes off the rack at expensive department stores, or from stores in the cuts; sometimes he would have them tailored. He had the identical four thousand dollar gray suit that Michael Jordan wore on Larry King Live, and that Emmitt Smith once wore in a television interview, down to same designer. I imagined that the guy's closet had to be the size of your average apartment just to hold it all.

DeMarco kept his mustache and beard trimmed low. However, the thug in him didn't let him get his nails manicured when he'd take a female to the spa. His usual was a deep tissue Shiatsu massage. He didn't put lotions on his hands. He said he liked the roughness, and lotion would soften them too much.

Yeah, it's hard to hide emotions when you are a woman and have feelings for a man, or a man with feelings for a woman to whom you are close. It is very difficult. To make those feelings go away, especially when the man is your best friend and someone with whom you spend a great deal of time, is damn near impossible. Your lustful stares, googol-eyes, your flirting and playful come-ons, or simply the way you act around him and your attitude is what gives you away and communicates your true feelings despite your best intentions.

Truth be told, I found myself first intrigued by DeMarco's masculinity, the strength of his character he so casually displayed without seeming to realize it, his take-charge attitude and confidence, and the keen intellect that co-existed alongside the thug in him. That intrigue evolved into attraction. Attraction turned into infatuation… infatuation gave way to love.

Sixteen

At DeMarco's encouragement, I moved into his Beverly Hills office, and had the lease transferred from one of DeMarco's former girlfriends into my name. In addition to Life Inc. and *Rage*, the offices also housed my entertainment public relations company, The Press Release Factory. It was actually at DeMarco's encouragement and support that I decided to launch the company. He proclaimed that I was a damn good writer, and since I'd done PR for Eastside West and many rap artists, I should start my own company. Through my contacts and DeMarco's, I landed some popular clients in the music and film industry, including Warner Brothers music and Miramax films. And through a friend with whom I'd attended college and now works for Spike Lee in New York, I landed an PR contract with his film company, Forty Acres and A Mule Film works. With my new company, I stayed busy creating press kits, writing press releases, feature articles, providing media coaching and better interviewing tips to rappers and singers, and booking them on talk shows and press interviews. Starting that PR company was one of the best things I'd ever done. I was bringing in twenty G's a month from that venture alone.

I was getting ready to leave the office and head home when DeMarco called. Man, he was so supportive of what I was doing. He was becoming or had become, I should say- my other half. Not that I ever said anything about it to the clique, mind you.

"Hello?"

"Haley, what you doing?"

"Typing."

"Hey, you ready for your Seff Tha Gaffla interview?"

"When?"

"Right now. He ready to do it. I just got off the phone with him." "What, you serious?" I did and interview with Too Short earlier today over the phone."

"Is that right."

"Yep." I guess to day was my lucky day.

"Well Seff Tha Gaffla, he ready to do the interview right now and he gone get on our comp. I already worked it out with him. I'm coming to get you from the office so you can do your interview. We going to his office."

"Alright. How long are you going to be?"

"I'm about ten minutes away from you."

"Aiight. I'll meet you out front."

" Hey, Haley, wait a minute. Did you ever set up that interview with Dre?"

"No, I haven't done it yet."

"I think you better go on and get that interview with Dre, Haley, before he get real busy. When that nigguh get busy, he ain't gone have time."

"You're right. I am going to call Lisa first thing in the morning and set it up."

"See you in a minute."

Seff Tha Gaffla was a popular underground rapper I had wanted to interview. He was the king of the underground.   Remarkably,   without radio play, Seff Tha Gaffla had successfully managed to establish a loyal and devoted fan base around the country. His followers flocked to their local record stores year after year to purchase his new releases. During his career, Seff Tha Gaffla had recorded nine albums. Each of them had sold no less than a 100 thousand copies, and sales averaged between 250-300 thousand records, all sold independently. His interview was going to be a good one for *Rage*.

Riding high on my recent success as the founder and CEO of *Rage* and the Press Release Factory, I couldn't wait to share the news with the clique. I was getting interviews with some of the biggest names in music and entertainment. I was excited to tell my friends who I'd signed as a PR client or who I'd just finished interviewing for *Rage*.

My interview with Seff Tha Gaffla went well. DeMarco dropped me off at our offices so I could get my truck, and then I headed to Krystal's.

I gave the news before I'd even kicked off my shoes and sat on the couch. "Krystal and Utopia, I interviewed Too Short and Seff Tha Gaffla today."

"Wow, girl," Utopia said, "I didn't think that guy Short talked to anyone!" How did your interview go with Short?" I knew Utopia was a fan of Too Short's. She liked it when he rapped about sex in his music.

"Good. You know, he's such an interesting person, a real smart guy. Did you guys know that he went to Catholic school his entire life until he moved to Oakland from South Central Los Angeles?" Utopia's jaw almost hit the floor. "Catholic school? Short went to Catholic school?"

"I didn't know he was from South Central. I thought he was from Oakland," Krystal exclaimed.

"Naw, he from South Central and he went to Catholic school."

"Who would have ever thought Short went to Catholic school," Utopia expressed.

Krystal had a mischievous look on her face. "I know, Short in Catholic school. Maybe he raps about bitches and hoes and getting his dick sucked because Catholic school inhibited him."

"I don't know, but anyway, he is a really smart guy. I am not easily impressed, but he impressed me in his interview. He was also a straight-A student."

"Damn who would have thought. Short wasn't no joke, huh?"

"Naw, Krystal he wasn't. His parents are professionals though. Both are accountants. His father graduated from Yale and his mother from Pepperdine. They had dreams of him becoming a doctor."

"What?" Utopia and Krystal said at the same time.

Krystal still had that sly, intrigued grin. "The only kind of doctor I could have seen him being was a gynecologist. You know, a pussy doctor."

I rolled my eyes at her. "Anyway, he was even homeless at one time on the streets of Oakland after his friend evicted him. To get out of his situation, he said he resorted to his business skills and sold tapes. Next thing you know, Jive was knocking at his door and the rest is history. Interestingly, you know how we all are trying to make it make our goals and dreams come true? Too Short said that his route to success wasn't one that was a struggle. His story is different than a lot of people, 'cause success just fell in his lap. Now, people in the music industry, like rappers and the entrepreneurs are struggling to do what he did, selling his music independently. Yeah, the story of Too Short is a remarkable one. *Rage* readers are going to love this interview. I have never seen him give one like it. There is so much in that interview that the readers and his fans are going to learn about him that they never knew, and *Rage* is bringing it to them."

"You go, girl," Utopia exclaimed.

"How did your interview with Seff Tha Gaffla go," Kyrstal inquired.

"Cool. He's a real entrepreneur. I mean he is so successful as an independent rap artist and businessman. As an independent artist with his own record label he be selling like 1100-200 thousand copies of his CD's—all of the major record labels want him. They have offered him recording contracts, but he chooses to stay independent and not sign with them. Says he will make more money as an independent artist."

"You know who you should try and get an interview with, Haley?" Krystal asked.

"Who?"

"Suge Knight, I think that this would make for a good interview. Haley, you said something the other day that made so much sense to me and I actually thought about it a lot since you said it," Utopia chimed in.

"No fucking way you should talk to that gangster," Krystal said.

"Oh come on," Utopia said, "stop hatin', Krystal. Haley, you said that Suge was no different than all of the other music executives and that a lot of them were mob-connected, and had done some pretty bad things to people, but because of Suge's status as being a rich black man and gang-affiliated that the media negatively propagandized him and his story. They made Suge look like he is the worst executive of all times. Well, I happen to agree with you, Haley. I think that you should put the rumors about Suge aside and interview him sincerely. Ask him about how he feels about the media's portrayal of him."

"Hmmm. You make a good point," I agreed

"Plus, I have listened to you talk about *Rage*'s vision. *Rage* is more than a rap magazine. *Rage* is about educating and informing its readers. *Rage* is about being a platform to celebrities or those in the public eye. When they are inaccurately portrayed or misquoted by mainstream media they can come to *you* and tell their story correctly. Haley, I think that you are onto something good with your magazine! Fans and celebrities alike are going to love it."

"Haley, girl, if I were you I would stay the fuck away from Suge. I wouldn't even want that motherfucker to know my name or that I exist," Krystal again warned.

"Krystal, you are putting way to much on it," Utopia responded.

"I know," I said.

"Whateva," Krystal replied.

"You know what, Utopia, thanks for saying that. I am going to work on that Suge interview and I am going to give him a fair and unbiased interview."

"You should," Utopia said. "You know what would make for another good interview that would be informative to your readers and that they would like?"

"What? With who?"

"You know the rapper Half Pint right?"

"Of course I do."

"Well he might make for an interesting interview as well. Just recently, he was put in prison because of his song lyrics. I heard on the news something about him violating his parole with violent lyrics. Anyway, I think his fans and *Rage* readers would be interested in Half Pint."

"Wow, Utopia, you want to work for *Rage*? You have some good ideas! I will get on both the Suge and Half Pint interviews. By the way, DeMarco knows Half Pint personally. He can make that interview happen for me. I will ask him to arrange it. Thanks for the interview idea."

"You're quite welcome. I just want to see you make it. Just don't forget about me. I take a new Corvette when you do."

"You so crazy."

Krystal joined in again. "Hey, Haley, Utopia ain't the only one with ideas for your magazine. The six-year anniversary of Tupac's death is coming up. Why don't you interview those who were closest to him and ask them some questions about him… do an article on that?"

"You know, I was actually thinking about doing just that. It came to me the other day when I was working on the editorial calendar, outlining what articles would appear in *Rage* over the next year. I could call the article *Remembering Tupac*.

"I would even interview some white people and make the magazine more universal," Utopia added.

"Dang, y'all got some good ideas." This was a great evening. The clique was at its brainstorming best, and thankfully not once did the issue of DeMarco and I arise.

Seventeen

"*Hello.*"

"What's going on, Squeaky?"

"Squeaky?"

"Yeah, Squeaky." It was DeMarco. His speech was slurred, as if he'd been drinking.

"DeMarco?"

"Yeah."

"Who you trying to call?"

"You."

"DeMarco, do you know who this is?"

"Come on now."

"Who?"

"Come on now," DeMarco said, laughing.

"Who am I? What's my name?"

"Man, I know who I'm talkin to."

"Who?"

"Man, come on."

"Who?"

"Man come on. Haley, if you don't quit with that…"

"What did you call me?"

"Squeaky."

"Squeaky?"

"Squeaky, I called you Squeaky. Why you trippin'?"

Because you drunk off your ass, I wanted to say. "You just never called me that before, that's all."

"Squeaky? I call everybody Squeaky."

"I have never heard you call anybody 'Squeaky.'"

"Haley, what's the matter? You don't want me to call you Squeaky?"

"I didn't say that, I'm just saying I never heard you use the word." DeMarco laughed again.

Flirtatiously, he asked, "Haley, so what's up with you?"

"What you mean, what's up with me?"

"You know, what's up with you? You ain't seeing nobody?"

"No!"

"Why?"

"I'm just not."

"Oh, what, you don't want to be in a relationship right now?"

"Naw."

"Why?"

"I just don't."

"What you just want, a booty call?"

"Not even that."

"What then?"

"I just want to be alone right now, that's all. Is that a crime?" I was getting irritated at the direction the conversation was going. I had half a mind to tell him to call back when he was sober and not one minute before, then hang up.

"No, no crime committed. Hey, let me get another round of Remy," DeMarco shouted to someone in the background.

"Where you at?"

"With my homies at a bar around the corner from my boy's house."

"Yeah, I could tell you drinking. Sounds like y'all having fun."

"So, Haley, when you gone let me touch you?"

"What?"

"When you gone let me touch you?"

My voice got stern. "Quit playing with me, DeMarco."

"I ain't playing with you. Me and you, we could really have something together beyond a business partnership. Plus, you need someone like me on your side permanently. You smart and all, but you a female in a vicious game, the entertainment industry. You need somebody with muscle, like me. Our arrangement: you deal with the business side of things and I deal with the nigguhs. You set the rules, I'll enforce 'em."

I had to admit the booze hadn't totally K.O.'d his brain. DeMarco made sense in a way because the music business was a challenging business for a female to work in, especially in a management position. It was an all-male network, where male presence in business negotiations seemed to be respected to some degree by the other males in the business. I had a side conversation with Master P once during an interview. He commented that I was a strong black sister, and that he respected me as a businesswoman. "However, when it comes to negotiating with the majors, you need a male presence. Even if you don't have a male business partner, make sure you have a male presence with you in your meetings. He doesn't even really need to say anything, but he needs to be there."

He went on about how he negotiated with the white men at the major record labels, and how they still gave him a hard time. "And I'm a man," he had remarked. Another time, I was talking to Suge Knight after an interview I'd conducted with him. Suge, like Master P, commented that he admired me as a woman in the music business. He asked what I would do if a rapper took a song from me. I can't remember what I said at the time, but he shook his head at my response, as if to say, *you really think that would work?* When I asked him why he was laughing, he just kept smiling and shaking his head, but said nothing.

Later, I learned what Suge's laugh was about when a rapper finally took a song. He had recorded for a project on which I was working, when he came in the studio and took the master recording from the engineer. I told DeMarco about the incident. The next thing I knew, the guy personally apologized to me and gave back the CD master recording. With this said, I knew DeMarco's suggestion was a good thing: I handle the business, he handles the rappers and the subsequent problems. Furthermore, we did work well together. He totally supported me; in turn, I was also his support base. We understood each other even when our closest friends didn't. However, I'd have to pass on being his mistress. One day I want to be married, and there's no future with a married man.

"So, you not fucking nobody," DeMarco asked.

He must be drunk. He had never been so direct with me before.

"DeMarco!"

"What?"

"That's personal."

He said it again. "You not fucking nobody?"

I was speechless; I had been celibate for three years. I didn't know exactly how to respond to what he'd just said. He'd never come at me like that before.

Stunned, I became quiet.

He continued, "I don't know how you do it, 'cause once you start fucking, you can't stop."

"Yes, you can stop, DeMarco. Anybody can stop if they put their mind to it."

"Shit, no you can't."

"Well, since you want to get personal, I have been celibate for three years. I haven't slept with a guy in that long."

"Huh?!"

"Yep." I heard him drop his cell in astonishment, as it slipped out of his hand and clattered onto the bar. Cursing, he picked it up.

"Get the fuck outta here," he exclaimed as he brought it back up to his face.

I suppressed a giggle. Well, almost. "Believe it or not, it's the truth."

"Three years!? Wait a minute, you mean to tell me you ain't had no dick for three years, Haley?"

"That's right, if you want to put it so crudely."

"Well, then, you overdue. You way overdue."

"Whatever."

"So, why did you say you decided to go celibate in the first place, and why aren't you in a relationship? Are you afraid? A lot of women don't know what they want. Do you know what you want?"

"To answer your question, DeMarco, I know what I want, and no, I'm not afraid. I've chosen celibacy because I'm tired of the games that come with relationships, the games men play. Of course I want to get married and have children one day. However, I've learned that a woman does not need a man to define who she is. You know, sometimes you just need to be alone, you don't always need a man in your life. You need a break from them and that's what I'm on right now. Plus you guys are just into pleasing yourself especially in the bedroom. I am not threatened by my sexuality. When I'm having sex, I don't just want sex in the physical experience. I don't want military sex: you get on top, hump, and get off. I don't like to lay there like a fucking vegetable and not have an orgasm, and you are having one without me. Like my friend Camille always say, when you are having sex your partner is suppose to be able to take you into another realm, the fucking Star trek Enterprise. I feel her on that. She's right. You need to be able to escape and relax in sex. A lot of guys I've been with don't take me into that realm, so for now I'm cool. Also, the last thing I need is for a guy to be all fucking nervous and say, 'no, I don't want to do that in the bedroom.'"

"Well, damn, what is it that you want to do?"

"Now, your getting way too personal, DeMarco. I've already told you too much."

"Well, I don't mean to get way too personal. I just wanna know!"

"Like I said, you are getting way too personal, DeMarco."

"Alright."

"I will add this, though: I'm verbal and I like to talk while having sex. Man, you guys are so fucking quiet."

"Hey, Haley, I'm not quiet."

"And to answer your question about what I want to do in the bedroom, I'm talking about things like blindfolding your mate, or playing games with your mate like Monopoly sex games, or putting handcuffs on your mate and other things. DeMarco, I had this friend, and you know what she would do for her husband? She would get naked, put on a trench coat and then go and stand on the corner and he would drive by in the car and pick her up as if she were was a prostitute. Sometimes she'd even dress up like a policewoman, a nurse, you know, and it's cool. She was fulfilling his fantasy. And that's what men and women need to do in relationships, is fulfill the other's fantasy. But Black men, most of y'all act like you can't do that for a woman, yet we always fulfilling yours. "

"Haley, you can blindfold me. I'll play games with you, sex monopoly or whatever. I'll even let you dress up like a police woman or a nurse for me. I might even let you stand on the corner nude or in some sexy lingerie and pick you up. I don't have a problem with that, but you can't be putting handcuffs on me."

"Yeah, but I mean than there's other stuff, too, that I like to do."

"What other stuff," DeMarco inquired.

"I mean I'd like for my guy to do my nails, bathe me, shave my pussy, you know. I'm a sensuous type of person, you know? I don't have a problem pleasing my mate, whatever his fetish or fantasy may be." DeMarco was dead silent. I thought he must have hung up or something. "Hello, DeMarco you there?" I called out. I guess he was taking in all that I had said, because I'd said a lot. I was venting to him about my frustrations with men. At the start of the conversation I didn't want to go there, but he got me all worked up, so I let loose. Perhaps I told him way too much? "DeMarco?"

"Yeah, I'm right here. I'm just taking in everything you've said. Damn, Haley, I didn't know you was a freak like that."

"Oh, here we go. So, what are you saying? You not a freak?"

"Hell, yeah, I'm one. Shit, even my mama and grandmamma know that. It's just that I didn't know you was one. Not the way you be acting."

"What is that suppose to mean."

"You know the way you are, all conservative. Just answer me this, Haley, since you celibate and ain't having sex, what you do when you want some?"

"I read my Bible."

"Bullshit, you probably got one of those vibrators or dildos or somethin'," DeMarco said. "Probably a big black one." I laughed despite myself.

"No, I don't."

"Yes, you do."

"DeMarco, I don't have to lie to you. I don't own nothing like that."

"Let me come over and look in your closet then, right now. I bet you I find one."

"What? You crazy."

"Let me come and see, look in your closet. The only way I ain't gone find one in your closet or your bedroom somewhere is because you gone go and hide it before I get there. Don't be running trying to hide it before I get there, Haley."

"DeMarco, you crazy."

"I'm on my way!"

"What?"

"I'm on my way."

"DeMarco, its midnight! I am going to bed."

"Good. That's all I want to do."

"You can't come over here, not tonight."

"Why?"

"Because you are a married man."

"My bitch is in the pen."

"DeMarco, let me ask you this. Did you marry for love?"

"No."

"You didn't?"

"No, I didn't. I married for other reasons, and actually, I ain't feelin' the whole sanctioned-by-the-state marriage thing. To be husband and wife you don't need no papers by no city and county authorities. All it requires is for two people to say they're married, and they're married."

"What? I don't agree with that."

"Look, man, if two people took it upon themselves to be husband and wife and lived as such, then that's all that matters and they are husband and wife."

"Well, one day, I want to be married, but I'm going to be the kind of wife with papers. A marriage license by the City and County of Los Angeles."

"Man, I still say that you don't need no state agency to tell you, 'you married.'"

"Now, I got another question. Tell me this, DeMarco: why do all men cheat? And why y'all always got to call us bitches? Answer the first question first."

"Why do all men cheat? Hell, I don't know, we just do. It's in our nature. Women cheat, too."

"Yeah, but not as much as men."

"That's not true. If a man cheat, it gotta be with a woman?"

"Not necessarily."

"Come on, Haley, you know what I'm saying."

"I know. I'm just playing with you, DeMarco."

"Not all men cheat, it's some who don't. Most of them do cheat, though, you right, but by that same token women cheat equally."

"Why do you cheat, DeMarco?"

"Cause."

"Cause what?"

"For different reasons. I like sex. I mess around because I just want something different, a variety. You get tired of old pussy, but my wife knows what I do, so I'm really not cheating. I just don't let the shit come home."

"So if you cheating and your wife finds out about it, what happens?"

"She tell me I can't do that. That I can't see the woman no more."

"When she says that, what do you do?"

"I stop."

"So why do y'all always have to refer to women as bitches?"

"Because that's what y'all are."

"DeMarco, what is a bitch?"

"A female. Hell, but some nigguhs is bitches, too."

"DeMarco, all women are not bitches."

"Yes they are, pretty much. Haley, would you stop being so sensitive? Y'all women got names for us too. Y'all call us 'punk-ass nigguhs' and shit. That's worse."

"I agree that ain't cool, and I don't refer to men in that way."

"Naw, I ain't never heard you refer to a man like that. But, Haley, you different. A lot of females do call us punk-ass nigguhs."

"DeMarco you a trip. I'm going to write a book about you. I bet it even makes the New York Times Best Sellers List."

"What you gone call it?"

"*Pimp*, or *Games People Play*," I said. We both laughed.

"Ah, listen at you. You couldn't wait to get that out, but I ain't no pimp."

"Are you kidding? All those stories you tell?

"Ah, man, come on now."

"I'm just fucking with you. I don't know… maybe I'll call it, *Game Tight* or *He Got Game* or *Block Hog* or something." We both laughed again. I kept talking. "I know you ain't no pimp DeMarco, but you got game like one, though. I can't believe women buy into some of those stories you tell. Man, I can't believe that women let you get away with the shit you get away with. Where do you meet them?"

"Y'all all like that. A man can only get away with what a woman lets him get away with," DeMarco said.

"You can be broken though."

DeMarco's eyes widened; although I couldn't see it, I could tell. "Can't no bitch break me," he said, sounding as if he were up to a challenge.

"DeMarco, you can be broken."

"Man, like I said, can't no bitch break me."

"You can be broke," I repeated. "I know some women who can break you."

"Man, you go out and find a woman you think can break me, and bring her to me and you'll see who breaks who. Now, don't just bring me any woman. You bring me the baddest bitch you can find. You better do some tough recruiting!

You see, Haley, I don't get emotionally involved with women. I just use them for sex, and sometimes not even that. I might just let her go down on me and leave her broke ass where I found her. From time to time, I might be nice and take a bitch to a movie or dinner. If I'm feeling it, I might even take her to a spa or something. Now, back to what we were talking about: can't no bitch break me."

"Man, my friend Camille would break you."

"Is that what you think?" DeMarco sounded surprised. "Well, I'll be dammed. She couldn't break my boy Jonathan, and he ain't even as hard as me. She let that nigguh get inside her head, so if she couldn't break that nigguh, what makes you think she'd break me? Look, Haley, I would have that bitch crying. I don't wanna do your friend like that. Now, is that the baddest bitch you know? The one that's suppose to be able to break me? Moi?" He emphasized the last part of his sentence with a French accent. "Who else you got for me?"

"Man, it's a few more. Hell, that female you was telling me about that you met and said her aunt wanted to know where you lived and you told her, 'Long Beach,' and Auntie was like, 'that nigguh ain't from Long Beach, he from Los Angeles.'"

"Damn, Auntie sho did. She said I was turning the channels too quick to not know them. She was like my Auntie, say, 'you ain't from Long Beach cause you was laid back on the couch, turning them channels on the remote too quick like you knew them.' She said, 'you were from Los Angeles, ain't you?' I was like, 'goddamn, Auntie blowing my cover!' Yeah, Auntie was a bad bitch. But I bet you even in her day that bitch wouldn't have broke me.

I'll admit it though, Auntie had game. She would have probably broke some nigguhs, but Auntie wouldn't break me."

"Man, Auntie would still break your ass to this day, DeMarco. I am convinced."

"Hell, naw."

"Man, if Auntie wasn't old and she was to go for you, you'd see."

"Man, I'd fuck with Auntie now, I ain't tripping, she cool. I don't give a fuck."

I couldn't help but giggle; I had a picture of DeMarco and Auntie and… well, it was the best laugh I'd had in a while. "You stupid! You are so hilarious."

"Shit, I'll hit Auntie shit. I like them all shapes and sizes. So, Haley, let me ask you a question?"

"What?"

"Now, tell the truth and shame the devil."

"What?"

"Do you think you can break me?"

"Oh without a doubt. If I wanted to."

DeMarco gave out a boisterous laugh. "You wanna try?"

"Uh-uh, I'll pass. You're my friend and that's the way I want to keep it. Plus, I'm one of those people unlike you. I work with emotions in a relationship. I grew out of my days of fucking them and leaving them, you know what I mean?"

"I feel you."

"So what do you say? Can I write a book about your life, DeMarco? So much has happened to you and you have been through so much. Your life is a novel." Realizing I was serious, he became quiet. I could feel him thinking. We'd both read Sister Souljah's novel, *The Coldest Winter Ever,* and loved it. We agreed that pretty much any black person living in the inner city could have written that story, or a similar one. I told him that his life story would make a good urban novel, like Sister Souljah's novel, or one of those IceBerg Slim or Donald Goins novels.

"My boy, D, he got five books for you. Write one about that nigguh's life. I'm gone set it up for you to interview him."

"No, I wanna write one about your life. I'll start it off, 'DeMarco.' No, I'm not going to call you DeMarco in the book. Let's see… hmmm… what would be a good name for you? Bryan. Yeah, that's a good name. I'll call you Bryan in the book."

"Bryan," he shouted it. "Man, don't call me no Bryan, that name sounds like a white boy from the suburbs! I don't even know a black guy named Bryan. I know a Bryant, but not a Bryan."

"I'll start the book off saying, 'Bryan had more game than anybody I know did. He kept the phone numbers of the women he knew in his cell phone address book under two categories: Bitches and Hoes. The women he slept with saw him on his terms. Whenever that became a problem for them, he'd end the relationship…' Let's see, what else have you told me… oh, yeah!"

"I don't want my name to be Bryan. Call me 'Twon' or something."

"Oh, and if it becomes a movie, Wesley Snipes could play you."

DeMarco shook his head. "I don't want that nigguh to play me."

"What? He's a good actor."

"Man, I don't want that nigguh to play me. He ain't no rough nigguh in real life. I want somebody real to play me. Somebody like Ice T or Busta Rhymes. Those are the only two nigguhs that could play me. Them some real nigguhs, especially Ice T. Busta, he real, too, plus everybody I know like the way them two nigguhs be acting."

"Hey, not to be changing the subject or anything, but… DeMarco, you won't believe this. My friend Camille asked me to go into business with her and start an adult entertainment film company, along with a porn web site."

"You should do it. I wouldn't mind going into that business with y'all."

"What? I ain't getting into no porn industry."

"Why not? You gone just be in the office, right?"

"Of course, if I were to do the business with her, but I am not. I would be handling the paperwork and she would actually handle the day-to-day operations. She'd hire and supervise staff and get the actors and actresses. I'd just handle money and paper, not that I'm gonna."

"You need to start that business with her. I'd give y'all the money to start it."

I shook my head. Here we were, back to his original topic, just in through a back door. "I ain't getting into no porn industry."

"Let me meet with her. I want to talk to her. I will start one with her. You know I already got a porno I did. It's called, 'Hoes Wanna Have Fun.'"

"Why doesn't that surprise me? Let me talk to her first. She might not want anyone to know what she is doing. I think she's going to do the business undercover.

DeMarco chuckled. "Yeah, I always thought Camille was a freak. Matter of fact some of my boys other than Jonathan then hit it. She another one who can write a book, 102 ways to suck dick, with her skinny ass."

"DeMarco?"

"What?"

"That's my friend you're talking about. Cool it." I was getting tired of all the sex talk and I did not appreciate his comments about Camille.

Changing the subject, "DeMarco, you know we got to pay the engineer a G next week?"

"I thought we owed him like five hun. How you figure a whole G? I thought we paid the haters Malik and Walter like 5 hundred two weeks ago."

"Oh, yeah, we did, but that was from another bill. I am talking about a whole new bill."

"Oh, alright, we'll pay him next time we got studio. When we got studio?"

"Next Wednesday at seven."

"Alright. Haley, late Friday night, I'm driving down to Humboldt County to handle some business. Why don't you take the ride with me?"

"How long will it take to get to Humboldt?"

"About fifteen hours."

"It don't bother me; I like taking long drives. They are so relaxing to me. How long you going for?"

"I'm staying over Saturday night and coming back Sunday. You wanna go?"

"Yeah, I'll ride with you. But I ain't driving. I just want to be a passenger."

"I'll drive there and back, no problem."

We kept chatting for a couple more minutes. He kept it clean.

Humboldt County is an historic area 250 miles north of San Francisco, and 110 miles south of the Oregon border. The county is popular for its redwood trees, located in the Humboldt Redwoods State Park, and are among the largest remaining forest of virgin redwoods in the world. Hell, some of those trees up near Eureka could get as tall as a 36-story building. But somehow I didn't think DeMarco wanted to go there to become a lumberjack or a park ranger: Humboldt County is also known to harvest among the best cannabis in the world.

Eighteen

That Friday I went with DeMarco to Humboldt. We left at 11p.m. When he arrived in front of my house to pick me up, he called me from his cell.

"Hello?"

"Hey Haley, it's me, DeMarco. Come on out I'm out front." Immediately after stepping outside, I took notice of the silver H2 Hummer. It was brand new. The tags wasn't even on it yet. In the license plate frame holder was the logo of the Beverly Hills Hummer dealer. I wondered, *Is that DeMarco?* DeMarco now had the window on the passenger side rolled down. "Come on," he yelled. He'd obviously taken notice of my hesitancy in approaching the truck.

"DeMarco," I asked.

"Yeah, come on," he repeated.

I opened the door, tossed my Gucci overnight bag in the back seat, and got in.

"Wow. Is this you?" He nodded. "This is really nice," I said, while running my hand across the black leather seats and admiring the Hummer. It's the same color as my Range Rover. He nodded again. "This is really nice and spacious. Is that a navigation system," I asked, pointing to the screen that resembled a mall television screen.

"Yeah."

"If you don't mind my asking DeMarco, how much did this cost?"

"Eighty five."

"Dang! That's a lot of money."

"You can drive it, Haley, whenever you want."

The fifteen-hour drive went by fast after we crossed the Golden Gate Bridge and the bustle, lights, and traffic of the San Francisco Bay Area gradually faded into forest. I looked out the window; I could actually see stars. We talked the whole way there, and we learned even more about one another. DeMarco had commented about his sister who was in an abusive relationship with her boyfriend. He had slapped her around and she went running to DeMarco. DeMarco said he told her he'd deal with him when he saw him. His sister had then begun to backpedal, saying "don't kill him or hurt him too bad."

DeMarco said he then asked her if she was leaving him, and she said no. He asked her why, and she proclaimed because she still loved him. DeMarco judged from her concerns about his safety when he checked him, that he wasn't going to get involved. I wondered about it. "You're not going to help your sister?"

"Look, my sister will get me caught up in some shit and still be with the nigguh, so I say 'hell, naw.' If he don't hurt her too bad, I ain't getting involved. She must like him slapping her around if she staying with him. Fuck it. I mean don't get me wrong, when I bump into him, I am going to let him know I don't like it and to stop, but I ain't gone pay his punk ass no special trip like I started to plan on doing."

"Hmmm."

"We control our emotions and our emotions don't control us."

"Is that what you believe, DeMarco?"

"Yeah."

I shook my head. It was a male-female thing. "When you are in love, DeMarco, it's not so easy."

"How come it's not?"

"Because it's just not. Emotions, are uninvited, they just happen. They develop inside of us. You look up one day and they are just there."

DeMarco shook his head. "That's one of the world's big problems. Too many people lack control over their emotions. Look, Haley. Emotions don't just happen. Emotions are habits. They are created. They are behaviors we produce. They develop over time and we have to be aware and maybe even careful about how we create them and allow them to develop. And, we have to know how to keep 'em from developing when they are not going to really benefit us, but even if we do develop them we can control them. We can direct our behaviors simply by doing and not doing something. You say when you're in love, you don't control your emotions. But we fall in love because that's what we want. If a sister finds herself with some punk ass nigguh that beats her ass, she can control her emotions, none of this 'I'm in love and I can't help it' shit. She can put her foot in *his* ass and move him out the door… or if she can't do the moving part herself, she can call her kinfolk who'll be more than happy to. We can control our emotions if we want to. Yeah, Haley, I can see why you say that we can't control our emotions, but really we can."

We arrived in Humboldt around 2 p.m. on Saturday. DeMarco and I ended up sharing the driving. It was fun driving the Hummer. With all of the twists and turns in the hills, he commented that we should have driven his Lamborghini. Next time, if we were to drive up there, we'd take the other car.

By the time we arrived in Humboldt County, we were starved. We checked into the Best Western Bayshore Inn in Eureka, and ate at the Marie Calendar's restaurant on the premise. After we ate, we headed to our room with the double twin beds.

We weren't in the room five minutes when DeMarco announced, "Haley, I gotta go and handle some business. I'll be back in a few." It was around 4:30 p.m. The long drive had me exhausted. I laid down to take a nap, figuring I'd catch some rest before going to dinner later.

Next thing I knew, it was dark outside. I rolled over to look at the clock:12:02! I had slept right through the evening. I sat up and looked around the small motel room. DeMarco hadn't yet made it back. I turned on the television. An episode of *Good Times* was on, with Lou Gossett Jr. He was dating Thelma, and they had become engaged. He expressed his love for her, but Thelma was unable to reciprocate the expression. So, she returned the engagement ring back to him, thereby breaking off the engagement. With a broken heart, he left the Evans house.

With the television on, I dozed back to sleep. I woke up later to see light streaming in the window. It was 7:30 a.m. A new day. The television was turned off. DeMarco lay fast asleep on his side, on top of the covers of his twin bed, fully clothed. I got up showered and got dressed. I was hungry.

Calling out his name, I tapped DeMarco on the shoulder to inform him that I was going to have breakfast at Marie Calendar's. He acknowledged me, still half asleep, saying "alright," before switching to lay on his other side. As he turned around, I noticed the black butt of a gun under his pillow. Surprised, I stood there staring at him and the gun. He must have sensed my watchful eye on him, for he rolled back over to the other side, sat straight up in bed, and asked, "What?"

"Do you want me to bring you some breakfast back?"

"Naw, I'm cool." I turned and walked through the door headed to the restaurant. I finished eating around 8:30. Utopia called me on my cell. We talked for about an hour and a half. I didn't even bother to mention to her that I was out of town in northern California with DeMarco. She would have made too big a deal out of it, and I was enjoying the outing. So, why bother ruining a good thing? She was going to read more into it than it was.

I headed back to the room after hanging up with her. When I got there, DeMarco was in the shower. He was rapping in the shower *Macavelli's* song lyrics, *Another Day.* When I closed the door he stopped rapping, "Haley, is that you?"

"Yes, who else would it be?" My thoughts went back to the gun I had seen earlier. He continued rapping.

When I lay down at night
before I close my eyes and go to sleep
I thank God for the day
days in the ghetto are short
a place where the sun rarely shines
when I awake in the morning the first thing I do
is thank God for another day
I realize that someone lost their soul and didn't awake to another day
As boys in the hood we lead a life where tomorrow ain't promised to us
In the street life we get caught up and
With all the bullshit that goes on
At times life seems impossible
We go into the world outside of ours and try to make it
But society rejects us so we return back to our world
Where we know how to survive
And do what we gotta do to make it to another day
From street corners we hang, bang and slang,
To the white boys and Asians that drive through our blocks
to buy rocks uncertain about there safety, yet determined to get high
they remain on our block and circle it until they get the rock
this thought society doesn't want to entertain
only to be used by us they wanted drugs to remain
And placed the problems of drugs exclusively on the black community
And Because there's know unity they get away with this shit

Growing up in the streets do little black boys really have a chance
There's gotta be a better way a better plan for us

something tells me that one day Black males growing up
In the inner city are going to see another day

When I wake up in the morning
With all the bullshit that goes on in the hood
sometimes I wonder if I will make it through the day
and if another day I'll see…

I was sitting on the bed with the remote in hand, flicking through the channels on the TV that sat in front of me, when DeMarco came out of the bathroom. He had a white towel wrapped around him, his body still wet. "Haley, you can look or you can turn your head, its up to you," he professed. "I'm 'bout to get dressed." In my presence, he removed the towel from around his waist.

I caught a glimpse of his naked body before quickly turning my body around. I stared at the wall.

"DeMarco you stupid," I remarked while laughing. I couldn't believe he did that. "Let me know when you have clothes on so I can turn around."

"Yeah, whateva," he replied. "Alright, I got my boxers and my pants on. You can turn around now."

I turned around, looked at him. As promised, he was clothed. I pointed the remote in the direction of the TV and continued surfing the channels. Intentionally, I didn't look at DeMarco, with the exception of the peek when I first turned around.

"You bring me something back to eat," he asked.

"What?"

"Did you bring me something back to eat?"

"DeMarco, before I left out I asked you if you wanted me to get you some breakfast and you distinctly said you didn't want any."

"I did?"

"Yes, you did."

"Damn, I don't remember you asking me that."

"Well, I did."

"It's cool. I can grab something from the Marie Calendar's here." Before I could reply —yes, I had asked him, damn it!- DeMarco's cell phone rang. He looked at the caller ID. "It's my boy, D," he said looking at the caller ID display on the phone. "What's happening, D," he answered. I listened to his monologue. "I'm about to get something to eat that's all and head back to LA after that. Is that right? Naw, its cool. Haley with me. Yeah, whatevea, nigguh," DeMarco said looking over in my direction. "It's cool. Naw, I don't need Kameron to ride back with me. See you in a minute." DeMarco hung up the cell.

"D. and Kameron out here too," I asked.

"Yeah, but they just got on the freeway. They gone now."

"I didn't know they were out here."

"I told you I had to take care of some business."

"When did they get here?"

"They got here last night, a couple of hours before we did."

"Hey, DeMarco, you know I was just sitting here thinking. You know No love has a great deal of potential as a rap artist. I think he could get with the best of the rappers including 'Pac and DMX." DeMarco stared down at the burgundy carpeted floor, thinking. He nodded.

"Yeah, I could see why you say that."

"I mean, the talent is there, but he needs a lot of money dropped into his promotions, and he could blow up. If we got him some tight beats, shot a nice video, and put something like a half mil or a million into him, we could saturate the market with promotions and marketing and he'd blow up."

"You know he wants to be on our team. He asked me to manage him."

"That's what you said. I can see No Love's potential and I think you're right, Haley. Let's sign him to our label and do the damn thing. Also, Haley, I'm telling you, we need to sign that motherfucker *Macavelli* to our record label. He like the next 'Pac also. Could you imagine having him and No Love on the same record label?! We'd be like Death Row use to be with them motherfuckers! That motherfucker *Macavelli* is bad. Have you heard his new underground CD he just dropped, *Confessions of A Thug Nigguh?*"

"No, I haven't."

"Have you heard the mix tape that nigguh put out last year?" I shook my head.

"I got them at home. When we get back to L.A., I'll let you hear it."

"Isn't *Macavelli* from Oakland also?"

"He sure is. Born and raised in 6-9 Ville, where life is brutal and only the strong survive. Man, he's been dropping underground tapes for the last five years, and, actually, before that 'cause he been on others rappers' shit before he started doing his own thang, and he ain't even 20 years old yet. Seems like every time he drops one, he gets better and better, and he already good." DeMarco was staring at me, looking straight through me. He was in deep thought, and then continued. "Yeah, we need to get that nigguh on our team. We'd do big things with an artist like him, and we'd all come up. And that nigguh a real nigguh, too. Yeah, Haley, we need to find him and holler at him. I'll get a number on him from my boy."

"Alright."

After DeMarco ate, we got on the road and headed back to L.A. DeMarco asked me if I wanted to stop at Lavender Hill Spa in Calistoga and get a massage. It was on our route back to L.A. I accepted his invite.

Calistoga is a beautiful, peaceful town ninety miles outside of San Francisco. Its residents are mostly Caucasian. The town is popular for its world-acclaimed wineries, beauty treatments, and spas.

Lavender Hill was one of the most popular spas on the entire West Coast. The spa was dedicated to maintaining a serene environment and to enhance relaxation of the body, mind, and spirit. So, the atmosphere there was rather tranquil.

The spa consisted of five small cozy cottages with wood-burning stoves, which were nestled into a terraced hillside and covered in lavender bushes. Beyond the garden was the main house, where massages and facials were offered. The lightly-stained hardwood floors and the white French glass doors that the generous sunlight poured through created a comfortable, warm environment. For Krystal's birthday two years ago, Camille, Utopia and I brought her to the spa. We had driven up to the Bay Area to go shopping and spend the weekend. I promised myself that the next time I went back, I was going to have the seaweed bath.

DeMarco picked up the purple brochure with gardenias on the cover, which outlined the spa's services. I looked over his shoulder and read the brochure. I was intrigued by a paragraph that said "Foot Reflexology Treatment." I asked DeMarco about it. He explained that it's an ancient Chinese technique designed to help increase deep organ circulation and strengthen the immune system by applying pressure to the nerves in the feet. Seems like the Foot Reflexology Treatment was the perfect remedy for a high stress life. The one-hour treatment included an herbal footbath, and a neck and shoulder massage. I also decided to have the Aromatherapy Facial. DeMarco decided on the one-hour Anti-stress Aromatherapy Deep Tissue Massage Treatment.

To start us off, before our individual spa treatments, DeMarco suggested trying the Aromatherapy Mineral Salt Bath. The fluid was composed of white sea kelp, therapy salt, Dead Sea salt, and essential oils. The bath was said to relieve stressed-out muscles, and uplift the mind with the purest essential oils imported from around the world.

After seeing a picture of the small and intimate cottages designed to accommodate two people, and realizing just how close the quarters there would be, I told DeMarco that I didn't think it would be a good idea for us to do the bath. I suggested that perhaps we should skip it, reminding him that he was married.

"Haley, if I ain't worrying about my wife, you shouldn't be worrying about her either. Now what's the matter? You don't trust yourself," DeMarco responded rather seriously.

"No, I don't trust you."

"Don't worry about me. Worry about yourself. I got me. Obviously you don't trust yourself. I ain't got no problem with it, you do… you keep talking about it."

Still standing in the spa's lounge, I opened the personal services brochure again that I held in my hand. I decided to go for it. *Fuck it*, I thought.

"Alright, DeMarco, let's go for it. But if I go with you in that cottage, you got to promise to behave yourself."

"Man, all I want to do is go in there and relax. We can talk a little bit about our goals and shit. Look, Haley, I promise to behave as long as you promise to behave," he said. With the attendant in the lead, we headed for the bath cottages for our treatment and bath.

The spa attendant walked us to the cottages, helped us settle in, and went her way, leaving us in the cottage together. Inside the cottage, two huge brown wooden Jacuzzi bathtubs sat side by side in the middle of the floor. "Turn around DeMarco, and don't peek while I undress and get in."

"Okay," he said. He turned around.

"No peeking, negro," I said jokingly.

"Haley, would you just take your clothes off and get in?"

"Okay, I'm in now. You can look."

"Haley, I don't care if you watch me when I undress," he said pulling his shirt over his head and dropping his Fubu jeans to the floor. He stood before me with only his blue boxers on. He began removing them, revealing some of his pubic hair, which I only saw a flash of; by then, I had already turned my head.

"Ahhhh, shit," DeMarco sighed contentedly as he sat down in the tub of hot, soothing water.

In the wooden tubs, DeMarco and I sat facing each other. We reflected on our goals, constructing tactics to make them a reality. "Haley, I am so grateful that I met you. We have a lot of the same goals in life. You know, the entertainment business, being entrepreneurs." I agreed.

"Yeah, it's not every day you really meet someone with your passion, and it's not every day you meet someone who has the same goals as you. That's what I appreciate about you"

"We should move to Atlanta, Haley. We could buy a house there together. Hell, we could buy a warehouse and renovate it into a recording studio. Atlanta real estate is a lot less expensive than California real estate. It wouldn't cost all that much."

"yeah and I love Atlanta—been there three times."

The bath warmed and invigorated me, right down to my bones. At times like this, I really liked talking to DeMarco. "DeMarco, we need to build a recording studio of our own. That's real talk. I am tired of being on other people's time, you know, in the studio."

"Let's look into it. I mean, you know I already got most of the recording equipment. I just need to get a spot."

"Sounds good."

"You know what, Haley?"

"What?"

DeMarco reclined back in the tub. "I'm tired of being in the game. I want out. There is so much conflict in the streets and your life when you're in the game. You don't know who to trust, you can't trust anyone. I'm tired. Whoever wants this life, they can have it. I'm done with it. I really don't like conflict. It brings misbalance. As long as I am in the game I am going to be misbalanced. I got to get out," DeMarco sighed.

"So why don't you?"

"I'm working on it. Working on becoming a legit businessman. Working on finding my other half. I'm working on a lot of things right now, Haley."

"Your other half? You've already found that. You already have a wife."

"Did I ever tell you why I married my wife?"

"Cause you love her."

DeMarco nodded. "No." I married my wife because she got pregnant and I felt it was the right thing to do. Then she got pregnant again and we had a second child together. I fucked up. I mean don't get me wrong I love my kids, and I thank God for them. I'll always be there for them. But I'm going to divorce her. I'm going to see an attorney next week and have him draw up the divorce papers."

I didn't say anything. The bath was what I was thinking about, inasmuch as I was thinking about anything. I just wanted to enjoy it; thoughts of the game and DeMarco and I and all of the drama receded. I rested my head against the back of the tub and closed my eyes. When I looked up, DeMarco also had his own head resting against the back of the tub, with his eyes closed. We apparently both dozed off to sleep. The bath was an hour long. I was the first one up, and looked at the clock; it was 6:30 p.m. We must have been asleep for at least thirty minutes, as it was 5:40 p.m. when had gone inside the small cottage.

"Hey, DeMarco! It's time for our massages," I called out.

DeMarco opened his eyes. " What time is it?"

" 6:30."

DeMarco stood straight up in the Jacuzzi. I'm sure he would have sworn up and down that he had still been half asleep, not thinking about the fact he had no clothes on. Hell, I was still a little dreamy myself. The water in the Jacuzzi only came up to his lower thigh…

My eyes grew big. I pointed, "Damn, DeMarco! I didn't know you had it like that."

He grinned. He picked up the white terry cloth towel from the edge of the Jacuzzi where it rested, and stepped out of the tub. His naked ass was exposed, and he blushed as he wrapped the towel around his waist.

I didn't remove my eyes from him.

"Not bad." I liked the site of his dark, glistening wet body, and wondered what it would be like to be with him. From that day forward, I have never really seemed unable to get such thoughts out of my mind. Right there in that cozy little cottage made for two, I was feeling DeMarco and DeMarco was feeling me.

"Your turn," DeMarco said, motioning for me to get out of the tub.

"Turn around," I instructed him.

"Oh, come on now. We are both adults."

"DeMarco, turn around."

"I ain't turning around," he joked. "I'll cover my eyes."

We were flirting. "DeMarco, turn around!" I was now laughing.

"Would you just get out of the tub, woman? I ain't gone peek."

"DeMarco, you are full of shit." The smile was still across my face. I grabbed the white towel from the edge of the tub and stood up and got out of the tub. Still covering his eyes, DeMarco spread his fingers apart peeked through them.

"Not bad."

"You asshole," I giggled.

DeMarco walked over to where I was standing and planted a kiss on my lip. Before abruptly turning my head away, I kissed him back. Not looking at him, I warned, "Don't do that, DeMarco."

"Okay," DeMarco mumbled beneath his breath.

We went inside to the main house for our individual spa treatments. As always, the treatment at Lavender Hill was incredible. Once we were finished there, I felt tired and relaxed. I climbed into the back seat of the Hummer so I could stretch out and chill. DeMarco was reclined way back in the driver's seat. He always drove this way, especially on long trips. It was now 7:45 p.m., and would nearly be 2 a.m. by the time we made it back to L.A.

"DeMarco, when you get tired, let me know and I'll drive," I said.

"Alright, but I got the drive back. I like taking long drives, they're therapeutic to me. They give me time to clear my head and think, to figure shit out."

In the Hummer, I sat catty-corner to DeMarco. I tried to take my mind off him, to get those moments at the spa out of my mind. Well, maybe I didn't try too hard. He was my fantasy for the entire drive back to the Los Angeles.

Starting at the top of his head, I stared at his long black dreads. I think about all those years he took to grow them, and how it would feel if I were to hold them in my hands. Moving my eyes slowly down his long, well-built body, I focused them on his crotch. I thought about my kiss with DeMarco. I wanted to kiss him back slowly and passionately. However, I respected his marriage. His commitment was with his wife.

I have had my share of dead-end relationships, and promised myself—when I took my vow of celibacy three years ago that I would never enter another one of those going-nowhere situations.

I thought about the fact that if DeMarco wasn't married, we would have been the perfect couple. As the saying goes: behind every good man, there's a good woman, and I sincerely believe that I could have been that woman for DeMarco. After all, I had enjoyed looking at his behind. Yeah, if DeMarco wasn't married, I would not have had a problem giving into all of his wants and desires.

We finally returned back to Los Angeles and stopped at a red light. I stared at the side of DeMarco's face, studying it intently, moving my eyes down his body until I got to his crotch for like the umpteenth time. I had a conversation with myself, debating about how many inches I'd seen when he dropped his towel in the cottage. Damn, he could be in a porno. *Is he a good fuck*, I wondered.

Where had that thought come from? Suddenly, I was smiling! With that smile fixed on my face, I lifted my head and eyes, and looked into the mirror attached to the windshield. I found DeMarco's eyes fixed on me. My heart started pounding fast. *Oh shit, did he see the lust I had for him in my eyes?* I began to worry. *Did he see me sizing up his package?* I'd been caught. I thought I was going to die.

Then it hit me. All the while I had been staring at him fantasizing, he'd been staring at me, also fantasizing. We both had that look of seduction in our eyes. We both had experienced a sexual fantasy about the other at the same time.

Nineteen

"**911,** Haley this is Blade call me," the message in the numeric pager read.

"Blade, I just got your message what's up?"

"Man, it's all bad. It's all bad. No Love he dead," he cried uncontrollably into the phone.

"What?"

"He got killed last night—early this morning in a car accident."

"Are you sure. How do you know this for sure?" But I knew I was grasping at straws. Blade didn't sound at all unsure of what he was saying; he wasn't the type to lay something like that on someone unless he knew for sure.

"First my boy call me with the news right?"

"Um hum."

"Then I call over to his girl's house and she just picked up the phone screaming and hollering. It's true, he dead."

"He died in a car accident?"

"He was driving, two more rappers was in the car with him. They all dead. They was going fishing. The left at midnight last night. You knew how No Love liked to fish. Anyway they say he hit one of those cement dividers."

"Ah man!" *Shit!*

"Who were the other rappers in the car?"

"I don't know. Don't nobody know them. They wasn't even his boys. One of them is from Texas and the other from Milwaukee. They had been working with him doing some recording over at Planet Studios. I figured you hadn't heard the news yet so I called you."

"Man, I can't believe it, No Love dead. Let me make a few phone calls. Thank you Blade for calling me and letting me know.

I called DeMarco to tell him the news. This wasn't going to be easy; he used to be tight with No Love. And sure enough, it wasn't. DeMarco settled into a brooding silence as soon as I told him.

After hanging up, all I could think about was all that No Love had to live for. In my opinion, he could have competed with the best of them—Pac, DMX, any of them. He never really got his chance though, because no one ever put the money into that was needed for him to blow up. He just never met the right people, I guess.

Me, him and No Love had just started working together. There was so much that we wanted to do with him professionally. Realizing his talents and capabilities for years I wanted to work with No Love, but contracts he was in prohibited us from working together. Now, he was free of them and for the past 3 months since he had been emancipated, we had been working together in the recording studio. It started with me doing public relations for him. He appointed me as his manager after a series of discussions that we had and he saw where I wanted to take his career.

He had just told me the other day, "I should have fucked with you along time ago."

I spoke at his funeral. I hadn't planned on speaking, but somehow I go the strength to walked to the pulpit and speak. "To the family of Randy Sims a.k.a. No Love. No Love and I both started in the music industry at a young age. He started as a rap artist and I as an entertainment manager. We were both novices in an agonizing game. However, as the years passed we became veterans and were able to lace the boots of upcoming talent. Recently, No Love and I discussed our support of each other's endeavors and we decided to form an alliance. He brought me on his team in a key role as an advisor and public relations person. We made a vow to each other that whichever one reached our goal first; we'd bring along the other.

The death of No Love disturbs me greatly. He is perfect examples of inner city males who are products of their environments. The inner city does not discriminate. Any child, regardless of race, can know to well what it means to live in the inner city. No Love knew this, relayed through his music, and his ethnically diverse fans reciprocated it to him with nothing but love.

Twenty

"*If you speak* up you are a problem, you're a bitch. If you do what they want you to do and they can control you and manipulate you, then you're okay. You know what these men want? They don't want a woman who can think for herself, they want a fucking puppet, that's what they want."

It was Friday night. The clique was at Krystal's for our regular Friday night girls' dinner sleepover. We were listening to Utopia expressing herself about men and relationships. She sat on the leather sofa in the living room venting, expressing her feelings about Antoine, her dirty work (a.k.a. sex partner) who she was developing feelings for. She hadn't entered into the relationship with the intent of it not turning into anything, of course, but now it seemed Antoine had the potential to become more than her dirty work. She could see a real relationship with him. However, he was playing games with her, telling her that he loved her and wanted her to commit to him.

However, he didn't want to commit to a relationship. *He* wanted a one-sided open relationship in his favor. To get her to buy into his philosophy, he argued that a man can sleep with one hundred women and that it made him a man, but if a woman slept with a hundred men, it made her a slut.

Utopia was one short step from being totally livid about it all. "Haley, Krystal and Camille, let me tell you what that motherfucker Antoine gone say to me. 'A man can lay in the gutter and be a drunk, and go and clean himself up and put on a suit and he's Mr. So and So. A woman on the other hand if she is a drunk and lays in the gutter she is a disgrace.' So I told him, 'Look, a hoe is a hoe, be it a female kind or a male kind' and would you believe the asshole had the nerve to argue with me about this. Seeing we wasn't going to get anywhere with him and the conversation, I ended it. You know what the problem is?"

"What?" We all spoke at the same time.

"There's two. One, a black man doesn't know how to be a man 'cause no one has taught them how to be men. Two, the problem is I fell in love with the motherfucker."

"That's been all of our problems, falling in love with these men," I said.

"That's been the world's problems," Krystal added.

Utopia went on. "Yeah, but love sucks—seems like relationships don't last."

"Girl, you know what I say, we be getting into the way a brother looks and he gotta be fine and all that, but I say to hell with the fine brothers. Maybe we should get us a ugly motherfucker who's nice and good in the bedroom—to hell with the looks. And you know what I bet he'll appreciate us," Camille said.

"Huh," Krystal nodded.

"You make a good point Camille. Y'all remember Peter?"

"That was the dude from Panama right? The brother that was majoring in Biology at UCLA," Krystal probed.

"No," Utopia said, "Peter was the Sigma brother that lived on campus, and was Tim's roommate."

"Tim who played football, right," I asked.

"No, ladies, Peter was the one from Nigeria. I dated him for two years. He was the engineering major. Remember?"

"Oh Peter, yeah, I remember him," Krystal said. Then, nonchalantly: "He was the one you said was a good fuck."

"Exactly, anyway, he was not attractive at all. He was a nice guy, a geek, but a nice guy. He was extremely smart. He made the dean's list the four consecutive years he was at UCLA. Anyway, my point is I should have married him, but I was so into the way a guy had to look in order for me to get serious with him. Plus he had this softness about him—something I never liked in a man.

"Yeah, he was a soft brother. I can't be with a soft brother," I responded.

"I concur," Krystal said.

Utopia continued, "Yeah, if it wasn't for his softness I could've married him.

Married him? "Girl are you outta yo mind? He was ugly!"

"Girl, looks ain't' got nothing to do with a man's performance in the bedroom," Utopia said.

"Sho don't," Krystal agreed.

Utopia kept on talking. She was really getting into this now. "Hell, sometimes it seems like the uglier they are the better they fuck. Hell, for most of the relationship, I put up with his geeky ass because the sex was good. After our relationship got old, when we had sex, he was only interested in pleasing himself. Many nights I just lay on my back in the bed with him on top of me enjoying himself. Once his joy ended, he would roll over to his side of bed with his back facing mine wanting to be left alone. He left me feeling used. I hated that feeling.

"What put the icing on the cake and ended our relationship was when he stopped fulfilling me sexually. He switched up on me. He went home—back to Africa—and came back telling me his newfound do's and don'ts in bed and he stopped going down on me. He came back from his trip talking about 'I don't do that no more'. Something happened down there in Africa, I don't know what, but *something* happened. Then he started becoming too possessive."

Camille nodded. "Girl, I am feeling you on that shit you said about the sex not being good and men just wanting to please themselves in bed. Tony does that shit—on me and off me in two minutes—making me feel like a hooker and shit. 'If you are going to roll on me and roll off I can't fuck with you', I told him. 'Hell, I can go and get me a two hundred dollar stripper, and get myself off. I don't need you'. Then he's rough. 'Quit fucking me so roughly' I told him, 'I don't know who in the fuck you been fucking, you been fucking a man or something, but be more gentle with me motherfucker.' I'm going to write down a list of shit for Tony. Number one, don't fuck me like a prostitute, number two, don't fuck me in two minutes. If you're tired lay down and go to bed we ain't doing no fucking how-to video on coming as quick as you can." We were dying laughing, holding our stomachs.

With a serious look across her face, Camille continued, "No really, the shit is insulting to me. In the bedroom you and your mate is suppose to be relaxed and you're both suppose to be taking each other to the next level, like the *Enterprise* on Star Trek. I ain't suppose to be in the bed with a goddam attitude 'cause you ain't fucking me right—hello? Hell, I understand that you may be stressed out and you wanna be happy, but damn, make me happy too. She shook her head. "Man, Tony could be a whole lot better," she said. "I told him 'damn, go look at my web site and get some tips—shit'."

"Let me tell y'all a story," Utopia said, "With Peter, early in our relationship, the sex was good. I will never forget the first time we had sex. He had came over to my off-campus apartment to tutor me in statistics. When he arrived, he carried a pepperoni pizza in his hand and videotape of the movie *Patriot Games*. Utopia closed her eyes and inhaled, and then exhaled. "I still remember the smell of the pepperoni pizza. This had been his third time tutoring me. Instead of immediately leaving and going home after our tutoring session had ended like he always did, he stayed to watch the movie. The only television that was in the tiny apartment was in my bedroom so we retreated there to watch the movie.

"I was a couple of paces in front of him as we walked down the short and narrow white painted hallway that led to my bedroom. A silver oval mirror hung on the wall at the end of the hallway. When I looked up into it, I saw the both of us. I caught his eyes fixed on my ass. He was smiling."

We sat in rapt attention to Utopia's tale. "After we had entered my bedroom, it occurred to me that I did not have a chair in there for him to sit on. I stopped at the door abruptly. He was following close behind and my sudden stopping caused him to walk into my ass. 'Let me get you a chair', I said walking around him.

"When I returned with the chair, he was sitting at the foot of my bed on top of the white down comforter. I put the chair down. He rose from the bed and sat in it. I put the tape in the VCR, propped some pillows up against the headboard and rested my back on the pillows between my back and the headboard. I kept my eyes focused on the television. I did not look in his direction because I could feel his eyes on me. It felt a little uncomfortable. As the movie progressed and we really got into it, I began to feel more comfortable. An hour into the movie Peter announces he is tired. 'Do you mind if I sit rest my back on the headboard with you,' he asked.

"'As long as you don't give me any problems', I said."

"'As long as I don't give you any problems, no come on I wouldn't do that'."

"Things were cool. Me and Peter were sitting on my bed watching *Patriot Games*. Mother Nature called, so I excused myself and went to the restroom. I sat on the toilet seat and stared into the vanity mirror that hung on the wall directly in front of me and I thought about Peter. It was clear that he liked me, and although I was not physically attracted to him, I thought about the pleasure that he could bring me. Plus, I hadn't done it in a long time. Three months to be exact and my body needed it. Realizing that he would not turn down the opportunity to get his jollies on I wondered whether or not if I should sleep with him.

"Sitting on the toilet, in my mind, I pictured the two of us having sex. I went over the idea in my head of sleeping with him. 'Maybe I shouldn't', I concluded. Between my legs, I felt something. It was that feeling that made me say fuck it and in the words of R Kelly, 'I'm fucking him tonight.' I knew that I did not want to get serious with Peter, but that he would be a cool fuck when I needed it. He was a black motherfucker and from experience, I know that they fucked the best. Besides, I didn't want to make love. I just wanted to fuck.

"I decided to take a quick shower. I exited the shower and looked at my nude dripping wet body in the mirror. I was pleased with the way I looked. My stomach was as flat as Janet Jackson's," Utopia said throwing her hand up in the air—raising the roof.

"Go on Ms. Jackson if ya nasty," Krystal shouted from the couch she was sitting on.

Utopia kept on telling the story. "For the past six months, I had been working out four days a week at the gym. I looked tight. I was pleased with the way my body looked. I reached for the towel that was beneath my robe that hung on a hook on the bathroom door and dried off. After lotioning my skin with Victoria Secret Pear, I sprayed the Pear Fragrant Body Splash over my entire body. I reached for the Arid Extra Dry deodorant that sat in the medicine cabinet. Suddenly, I realized that my underarms could use shaving. Although you could barely see the new hair growth, I shaved. I could not let my new lover see me even a slight bit not together. I put my white terrycloth robe on that I took from my hotel room when I visited to the Claremont Spa and walked back to my bedroom. Peter was lying on his back on top of my bed with his clothes on. He was asleep. I guess I took too long and he dosed off. I climbed on top of him. My hair was wet. 'You took a shower'?" he asked.

"Yes."

"'You smell so good. What kind of perfume are you wearing'?"

"Covering my mouth with my index finger, 'Shhh'. I said. I planted small kisses all over his face. Between the kisses, we stared intently into each other's eyes. Holding my ass, he pulled me closer to him. He was kissing my neck. The next thing I knew he was pulling his blue Fubu shirt off and then his white T-shirt followed. For two minutes, we kissed hard and passionately. When the kissing got old Peter began taking off my robe. He pulled the white belt that held my robe closed from out of its loop. I instructed him to get up and I unbuttoned his pants—sliding them all the way down to his ankles. He bent down undid his red Converse tennis shoes…"

"Not the Converse," I interjected laughingly.

"Shhh, let me finishing telling y'all the story," Utopia said. Holding one finger over her lip, "now where was I, oh yeah, I will never forget this— before Peter slid his pants off he reached inside the front pocket and pulled out a condom. I push him back onto the bed and get on top of him. He inserted his finger inside of me, sliding them in the opposite direction that my body moved. "I want you to go down on me," I whispered in his ear. He said nothing. He scooted downward, I scooted upward, and he fulfilled my request, bringing me to ecstasy. Handing me the condom, 'here put this on,' he said."

"'I ain't ever done this before'," I told him.

"'I'll help you', he said taking the condom out of my hand. He opened it with his teeth, took it out of the package, and rolled the condom onto his erect penis. The he, directed me back on top of him.' He slid inside of me. He held my hips and we bumped and grind for about thirty minutes."

"Can you spare us the details," I shouted.

Utopia ignored me. "I saw Peter again that next night and the night after that and the night after that. In a two-week period, we had sex about twenty times.

"But then he goes to Africa and visits and comes back talking about he don't go down no more. Shortly after he returned from his trip, one night while we were in bed, Peter said to me in his thick Nigerian accent, 'in my culture oral sex is forbidden, a taboo.'

"I responded, 'not in my country'."

She continued mimicking his accent. "'Utopia, if I can't please you with my dick baby then I can't please you at all. These lips don't eat a woman's poontang again'."

"'What's the matter with you Peter? You're acting as if I have asked you to commit an unpardonable sin,' I said to him and he said, 'that is very much what I have been doing with you, Utopia, and I can't do it anymore. We just have regular sex from now on'."

"As the months went on, I began to see less and less of Peter. It was a new semester and our schedules had changed. When we did see each other we'd sleep together and immediately after sex he would either leave or roll over and go to sleep. If he stayed, as soon as daylight came he'd leave. Unfulfilled in my relationship with him 'cause this motherfucker stopped going down on me, I started seeing other men. Eventually, we broke up. The truth is if a man ain't gone use his mouth on me, he can get the fuck on. In my opinion, oral sex is better than the physical act."

"Never go with a guy who don't go down on you, Krystal voiced.

"That's real though, but the worst thing is a guy who does not know how to go down correctly. I had this one guy he was just slobbering on me and shit. I was like what and the fuck are you doing having a seizure or something? I told his ass to do it right or I was going to go down the street to the club and find me a female and have her go down on me correctly," Camille said.

"They gotta know how to go down right though, I had a brother and this man use to use his teeth. Can you imagine somebody crunching you down there. I slapped the fuck out of his ass all in his head, and he had the nerves to ask me what the fuck I was doing.

"I hate guys with mustaches that's the real drawback on getting satisfaction," Camille said. Camille looked at me. "Girl, I'm about to be like you—celibate." Krystal and Utopia laughed. "No, guys I'm serious—dead serious. If I'm not getting it correctly, I don't need it. Toney is so fucking rough in the bed. You know what last night I really had to ask the motherfucker I'm like what you been doing fucking men? I wasn't playing when I said that. I have to teach this motherfucker Toney how to be in the bed."

Krystal contended, "I had this one brother he was an A plus, plus in bed. He was Sensuous, massaged me. The only thing about that is that he had mental issues and I had to let him go. However, I fucked his ass one more time after he got out of the psych ward."

"You are a fool girl, Camille said.

"I don't mind teaching a man how to be in bed, but he has to listen. To keep it real with I figured cause Tony's an OG, he's 42, you'd think he'd have the bedroom shit down. Plus he's stacked, he's like twelve inches. He could be a whole lot better. It's not about a man hitting your shit. I don't want military sex you get on top hump and get off. Where I will sit there an lay like a vegetable and not have an orgasm and your partner has one and you don't. You need to be able to escape and relax in sex. There are different levels of sex. When you are having sex, you go outside yourself to another experience. I don't want my mate to just make me come, but rather to bring me to that orgasm where I can be free and I'm going to bring him to an orgasm where he can be free.

For me I have to have the joy of the mind and not just the physical experience when I am having sex. I need to be taken into another realm. Tony is not taking me into that that realm.

Then there's the whole other issue. I'm verbal Tony is quiet. I really like to talk . He's quiet in bed. When I tell him to talk he gets nervous and says some dumb shit like What do you want me to say. I tell him say whatever comes to mind. Respond verbally to the way I'm making you fell. I ask him what you scared of Tony what's the matter

"You girl stop lying," Krystal said.

"I know huh Camille responded, but really he is thick and long. He got it going on. He could be in a porno—really. Anyway, it's a god dam shame to have all that equipment and can't use it. You know what I had to tell that motherfucker the other night, What the fuck are you doing? You fired, Get the fuck up get up."

"Ooh girl know you didn't," Krystal said. Utopia was rolling laughing.

Turning her head to the side looking dead serious, without blinking and eye, "you thought I didn't Camille said. Hell, I will tell a man a heartbeat, get your ass up off of me. I m not going to school for theatre what the fuck is this? If you can't handle me in the bed, get the fuck up. Camille kept ranting, "My last boy friend had a little dick the size of a pinky, but he could fuck. Oh yeah and one more thing about Tony, he comes to fucking quick. Next time he does that shit I am leaving him a fucking quarter on the fucking pillow. I am going to fuck his head up.

"Girl you tripping," Utopia said.

"Naw, she talking some real shit," Krystal added.

"Hey not to be changing the subject or anything, but I was I was just sitting here thinking—do you know who I think is probably a real good fuck, Camille stated?"

"Who," Haley, Utopia and Camille inquired.

"Bobby Brown." We all agreed unanimously. It had to be the sex that had Whitney sprung.

"You know who else I think can fuck?

"Who," the clique collectively said.

"Dam y'all sound like a bunch of owls, who."

"Camille would you please stop, I said.

"Who girl," Krystal explored.

"Samuel L. Jackson. He look like he a rough motherfucker though."

"Umm, I don't know, maybe," I said raising my eyebrows. She went on, "I know he's a hell of an actor."

Utopia frowned. " I been having a crush on that man for a long time. Now, Haley, that's one married man I'd sleep with. I am sorry Latanya, "Krystal smiled and said.

"Now, his wife Latanya, looks like she'd kick a woman's ass behind her man. I wouldn't fuck Samuel if I were you. Latanya will fuck you up and she from the hood. By the way, they was on the cover of last month's Essence. I read the interview and Latanya she a strong sister I think she running thangs."

"Latanya ain't' running shit with Samuel—trust me—Samuel ain't no joke. Krystal said."

"On the female side I think Foxy Brown can fuck, "Camille said.

"Denzel Washington now I bet you he is off the motherfucking hook in the bedroom, Krystal said.

Oh you guys before I forget, I put an ad on craigslist for actors and actresses to be in the porno I'm shooting and I got a huge response. Hand me my briefcase on the other side of you Utopia," Camille said. Utopia handed it to her. Camille opened it. She removed the white 8.5 x 11 envelope from the briefcase. It was so stuffed full with papers that it was busting at the sides. "Look at all the responses I got from my posting on the Internet Camille said, dumping the e-mails she'd printed out onto the coffee table in front of her. Girl I got every thing from actors, actresses, filmmakers and writers responding.

"Dang, like that? Maybe I'm in the wrong business and I should get into the Adult Entertainment business myself," Utopia said responding to the huge pile of papers in front of her.

"Girl at first I thought people was going to want to get paid a lot of money to be in a porno. When I replied to the inquires I received from people showing an interest in being in the porno I asked them point blank what they wanted to be paid. They wrote me back. One guy said he wanted $100 and another $200 bucks and a few of them said that they are willing to help me get started as an entrepreneur and would do it based on the contingency of the sales. Can you believe it.

"That's all they want," Krystal questioned?

"Listen to some of these e-mails," Camille said picking one up from the coffee table. 'Hi my name is Paul. I'm five feet ten inches and Mediterranean. I'm good-looking—not buff. I will only do straight videos.' Anyway, this is the guy I responded to his e-mail—asking him how much he wants to be paid to shoot a twenty-minute scene and he said $100."

"Here's another one. "Well, if you decide you use me a lot I would need some pay up front for the session. If you just want to do a few sessions then for now I will work for free and take the what we agree on if the video sales. I am very easy to work with and be around. I understand you are just starting out and I hope you can do well in your adventures. I would love to help. I am also in a local punk band and I am an art grad from the East Coast that majored in film and music production. Please let me know what I can do to help. Call me any time. Sure, I'll even do it for free. The experience alone will be worth the price of admission. Will send pictures on Monday. So who will I co-star with? Thanks Larry.

Camille was all excited. Here's another one. Listen to this. I am a 24-year-old Filipino/Pakistani female. I am five feet four inches and petite. I have done a few shoots since moving out here last summer. What is the pay scale, what sorts of scenes are you planning on shooting, and is this mostly gay, straight, mixed, etc. I have a few photos upon request, and some stills up on a preview of another porn site (name). Please call me regarding your offer ASAP

She kept on reading. Hi I saw your ad on Craig's List and may be interested. Please tell me where the finished product will end up? Internet, video?

The pay scale and the type of health testing you require. I can send a picture if necessary. Best regards Kim.

I'm a 40s white bi-male, good looking, hung, and interested. I am interested in making a porno movie. Please e-mail me the details. Where are you guys located? What do you pay? Tell me a little about the scenes. What kind of sex? I want to be in porn! 22/6 feet/180 pounds.

Now here is one from a filmmaker. I'm interested in helping you with your project. I have a lot of digital video equipment: VX 2000, non-linear editing computer, etc. Give me a call. And he leaves his number.

Now here's one from a writer, Camille aid. I'm a Los Angeles black writer and like to write a few XXX scenes. I always have some ideas. Let me know if you're interested in hearing my ideas. Sharon.

Here's another, Would you need any still photo work during your adult video shoot? If so I would like to offer my services.

I saw your ad on craigslist and thought that starting Pornography Company would be a good idea for a business. I have had ideas bout shooting my own porno, but what I always laced was the contacts to distribute or market the video. It seems like you are just the guy to work with. I am a young filmmaker, who just graduated from college with a film production degree and who is seeking other mean so of income. I f you want to produce a low budget, but high quality porn I would suggest working with me. We should get together and talk about the ideas you have and other ideas we could come up with to get this project rolling. Please contact me.

"So when do you plan to have your company up and going, Utopia asked?

The Internet web site will be up and working in two more weeks. I met with the web guy today and he is pretty much complete with the site. I just need to call up I Bill, which is the credit card company that I am going to be using and its on. I plan to be done shooting the porno in three months. I plan to releasing it, marketing and promoting it about a month after that—by the way Haley I'm going to need your help. " Haley nodded her head in agreement.

"Girl, you are really doing it," Krystal said."

"Yep. I'm actually going to be shooting the porno's. I'll probably bring in one or two more filmmakers also.

"So you have to go out and get office space," Utopia asked.

"No for now, I'm going to work out of my home. The Internet stuff is so easy to do from home. With the film stuff that stuff is going to be filmed on location, so I'm cool for now working out of my home. As my company grows, I will look for office space. Everybody, you're looking at the CEO-slash-filmmaker of Uninhibited Films," Camille said.

Twenty-one

"*Here ladies DeMarco* sent you all a gift," I said—placing the three red Chinese material covered boxes with the silver meditation balls inside on the table.

"That was nice of him, "Utopia said.

"Sure was Krystal blurted out.

"That was a nice gesture. You know another name for these meditation balls are Ben Wa Balls a.k.a. sex balls. My friend Sicily uses them," Camille said.

"Uses them where?" Krystal inquired."

"She inserts them in her vagina before sex."

"Camille, your friend puts these in her vagina?" Krystal asked.

"Sure do."

"What?" Utopia and I were both amazed. "How do you get them out?"

"You squeeze them out," Camille responded.

"Camille how come you so for sure?" Krystal had a sly grin. "You used them things before?"

"No." Camille laughed. "But I've used other similar kind of sex toys."

Krystal looked over at me. "Tell DeMarco we said thanks. Utopia and

Camille said likewise. I nodded.

I dropped down onto the soft white leather sofa in Krystal's living room when, no surprise here, she brought up me and DeMarco. "So what's up with you and DeMarco? The two of you are spending a great deal of time together. Seems like everyday y'all two be together."

Camille was trying out the meditation balls—in her hand. "Girl you better be careful with that *married* man."

Utopia also had silver balls in her hand. "Girl, you know the two of you are actually dating? Right?"

"Sho is," Krystal added.

"What, how could we be actually dating and we haven't even kissed— let alone slept together—that doesn't make sense. You guys are worse than my parents. Damn!"

Utopia just smiled coyly. "Girl, like my mama says, if it walks like a duck and it quacks like a duck, then it's a duck. Y'all dating, just admit it Haley."

"Haley, I gotta agree with Utopia, you and DeMarco, the two of you are dating,"

"How you figure?"

"Girl, as much time as you too spend together, on the phone, in restaurants and at recording studios, out late night to like 2 and 3 a.m. Y'all dating, D-A-T-I-N-G, dating."

I felt irritated. Part of me was fed up with the whole topic, DeMarco and me, DeMarco and our relationship, what was I doing with him. I didn't like anyone up in my business, even the clique. But at the back of my mind, I knew the clique had a point…and that was perhaps most annoying of all. "Hello, again, how could y'all say that I have never slept with the man or kissed him," I repeated.

Camille leaned forward, and put her two silver balls back in the Oriental box. "But y'all in a relationship together—all the same. Y'all fraternize and you getting together all the time—regularly and y'all laugh and flirting with one another on the phone, in each other's face—everybody sees it. Haley, the man isn't stupid, come on now, and neither are you. I am sure that he knows that you like him and vice versa."

"Right," Krystal said, "I mean maybe it ain't physical, but y'all in an emotional relationship," Krystal said. "You've gotta admit that much, Haley."

"I concur," Utopia proclaimed.

My voice slipped a notch. I suppose the whole issue was like a sore spot, and that spot had been rubbed just a little too often. "DeMarco is my business partner and that's it. Believe it, or not. He's totally supportive of what

I'm doing and me and I am totally supportive of him and what he is doing. We are there for each other. Yeah, we enjoy each other's company and all, we go places together and we are even out late nights together, but we are only just friends—that's it—trust me."

Krystal responded to my speech. "Calm down Haley, damn! Are you trying to convince us or yourself," she asked.

"Wow you guys, I don't believe you—you guys are making something out of nothing."

"Now what's this wife business Haley?" Krystal asked?

"DeMarco mentioned to me that his wife is 12 years older than him," I answered.

"How old is she," Krystal queried.

"Forty-four."

"And how old is DeMarco? That would make him right around 32."

"He recently turned thirty."

"Oh so he got him an OG bitch."

"I heard they got three kids," Utopia inquired.

"Yeah, they do between the both of them. DeMarco had one before they met and they have two together.

"How old are these kids," Krystal asked.

"DeMarco also has a 12 year old that he had with another woman before he met his wife. The two kids he has with his wife are six and eight."

"Where are the kids while she's in rehab? I know they ain't with DeMarco 'cause the brother ain't got any time for kids. He got both feet in the game, and from time to time, he takes one of them out to work and to kick it with you Haley.

"They are too with DeMarco," I said. This much was true: DeMarco did look after his kids…as much as his line of work would allow. "DeMarco has a live-in housekeeper named Maria. She prepares their breakfast and gets them ready for school on the mornings DeMarco's not there. When DeMarco's home, he does this. While they're at school, Maria cleans house, wash—you know, she does all the household stuff. She also prepares their dinner. She doesn't take off 'til around 5 or 6 in the evening.

"DeMarco's sister Yvette and her five year-old son Brandon live with him also. She lost her Section 8 and didn't have nowhere to go, so DeMarco let her move in with him. She's been staying with him for the last year and a half. Her son goes to the same school as DeMarco's two younger sons; DeMarco pays his tuition at the private school. Yvette doesn't have a job, she lives with him rent-free, drives one of his cars and he gives her money." Whether I realized it or not my voice was full of pride for DeMarco—they could say what they wanted about his life in the "game" and how he used women, but the man looked after his kids, and that was a boast many men the rest of the clique had hung out couldn't make. Not by a long shot. "She takes them to school. On the weekends, they're with DeMarco's mother. His children, they don't want for anything. He compensates, you know, for the time he doesn't spend with them buying them things—expensive gifts. PlayStations, X-Boxes, Nintendo's—video game discs—whatever his children ask for, he buys them. Without a doubt, he wants the best for them."

Utopia nodded; the look on the other girl's faces showed I'd scored a point they couldn't diss DeMarco on. "His wife Nakeesha, I hear is real ghetto, she suppose to be home soon, what you gone do Haley," she turned to me and asked. Krystal and Camille also wanted to know.

"I never met her." I figured they were right on this point. "From what I hear, she put the 'g', the 'h' the 'e' the two 't's and the 'o' in the word 'ghetto'."

Utopia seemed to have mastered the meditation balls. "She from Long Beach, grew up in the projects. That bitch is a real hood rat. Her running mates are females in their early to mid twenties all from the 'jects. If you ain't hip that's the projects," she said, giggling. I knew she must be getting tipsy; we all knew what the "'jects" were.

"Girl, all I know is his wife is getting out soon from what I hear. You better listen to us and stay away from DeMarco. I hear she is crazy and she has been known to fight women over him. I have heard that she will cut your tires, and even show up at your job and doorstep."

"What?"

"Yeah, keep your distance," Utopia made it clear.

"From what I see all DeMarco is going to do in the end is hurt you Haley, leave him alone," Krystal said.

"Well, all joking aside, I don't think he is going to hurt her, Krystal I think he really likes Haley," Camille said.

"Wow the dead has risen," Krystal said. Utopia belted out a loud laugh. She went on. "Camille, it's so good to see you coming out of silence."

Camille gave Krystal the middle finger and continued talking. "He is not going to intentionally hurt her. But because the man is married, she is bound to get hurt. It's bound to happen. Plus, DeMarco has a dark side to him anyway and Haley when you go places with him you taking a chance—really you are. The bottom line is you don't know what he's done to who or who's looking for him. Really when you are with you are putting your life at risk. Bottom line Haley—you're going to do what you want to do. It doesn't matter what I say or what Krystal say or what Utopia say—bottom line Haley's going to do what Haley wants to do. Haley it's your life. I'm here for you." Camille said looking at Krystal and Utopia.

Thank you Camille. Now that I could deal with. "Will you all stop talking about me as if I am not here. Thank you Camille. Now about men and their dark side, what's your point Krystal? All of our men have a dark side to them. In case you've forgotten, they're in the game. Krystal I know you ain't got no man right now, but you got dirty work for the nights you want some, and he in the game too, so let's not go there."

"Dam Haley, you sure touchy."

"I am just not for you guys' bullshit tonight Krystal. I already know how you feel about DeMarco and me. For you to say some shit about his dark side, that doesn't make sense. Hell, you out with yo nigguh, yo dirty work or the nigguhs in the past. You don't think they need to be lookin' over they shoulder? The same holds true for you and them, so y'all putting y'all's life at risk too. I don't want to hear yo shit Krystal. Not tonight!"

Sometimes the wine chilled out the clique socials. But sometimes it could give us all an edge to our tempers. Tonight, the edge was there, most definitely. "So what's up with y'all then—you and DeMarco, yeah right y'all ain't seeing each other, looking at each other all lovie-dubie, huh. I'm surprised you ain't with the nigguh now," Krystal shouted.

"We need our space," I retorted.

"I have never heard you say that before."

"You ain't heard me say a lot of things before. All of y'all just stay the fuck out of my business. Man, y'all must think I am stupid or something and I'm not. I am not stupid. Yeah there's and attraction between me and DeMarco you're right, but I ain't ever going to act on it. I am the one keeping things in perspective, not DeMarco. I'll admit it. He's been trying to get the pussy. If I wanted to give him some pussy, hell yeah, you damn right he'd take it. He's a man with a swinging dick. I mean yeah…"

Krystal cut me off, voice stern, a little like a mother. And that was the wrong tone to take with me, especially at that moment in time. "Girl, quit fooling yourself."

Abruptly and angrily, I stood up from the white leather sofa and picked up my black leather collarless short waist Fendi jacket that matched the Black Fendi boots beneath the Levi jeans I wore. "I knew I should have kept my black ass home tonight. I ain't for all this shit." Utopia laid her meditation balls on the table, rather abruptly. "Now you guys just let it go. Stop arguing. You two are like sisters."

"Well, sisters argue sometimes," Krystal said.

"Krystal! Ooh, I want to say something to you, but I can't. Utopia, Camille I'm outta here. Talk to you later," I said as I stood up from the leather sofa in Krystal's living room.

"You leaving, girl? You tripping."

"Whateva, I am tired of the accusations from you guys and my parents that's all," I said. Quickly. I headed for the door.

"Wait a minute, Haley. Before you leave let me share this story with you," Krystal said.

"Fine, whatever," I said. I stood there and listened.

Krystal took a breath. So did I. "I had this friend. Monique was her name. She was dealing with this married man for thirteen years. He was cheating on his wife and my friend, she had two kids for him. She was so unhappy. She reminds me so much of you and DeMarco. Her nigguh was a lot like DeMarco, you know, his character. Girl, you know what she did one night cause she hadn't seen him in a while? I don't know—it was for something like two or three weeks. She broke in his house with him and his wife—crawling through a window and into his bedroom on her stomach. Girl, he was in the bed with his wife asleep and she tapped him on the shoulder and told him she wanted to talk to him. He was pissed. She was obsessed with him. Anyway, she wound up really hurt and caught up with this man. He never left his wife and she continued to stay with him. Her and his wife, they knew about each other Haley. This man he had his cake and ice cream at the same time. My friend, she was miserable. For thirteen years, she was with this man as his mistress.

"Then you know what ended up happening? She ended up getting breast cancer and she died. She died Haley. She was sad. Her whole life centered on this man. She gave him all that he wanted, but he couldn't give her what she truly wanted. The man was married. He loved her, but he also loved his wife. He was committed to another woman. His commitment to his wife was deeper than his commitment to her. Haley all I'm saying is I don't want to see you end up like Monique—miserable, looking up and seeing 13 years or your whole life has passed you by, leaving you nothing to show for it, nada, zilch." She made a circle with thumb and forefinger. "I don't want the same thing happen to you that happened to Traci to happen to you. Like you, she was beautiful. She was so beautiful and she was smart. Like with you, the problem was she fell in love with a married man."

I felt my eyes getting puffy. "Look, I'm just going to go. No hard feelings, okay? I just—I just want to be alone. Okay?" I proceeded to the door and left, closing it gently behind me.

But, as I learned later, the discussion went on even after I was on my way home.

Krystal waited until she heard my car engine start. "I guess Haley and DeMarco are having relationship problems. I heard through the grapevine that she and DeMarco were arguing in front of the studio the other night. Something about she was complaining to him that he was too selfish and only thought of himself and didn't communicate with her. She even told him that she picked the wrong business partner." Krystal said.

"Girl, who told you that?"

"A little birdie."

"Come on now Krystal, quit playing. Who told you that?"

"Alright, alright, alright, Ronnie T."

"The rapper that's signed to DeMarco's label," Utopia questioned.

"Yeah."

"What? Why didn't you tell us this before?"

"I'm telling you now. He also told me that DeMarco is sprung on Haley from what he sees and that all the guys in DeMarco's clique see it and are talking about it, D, Kameron, Ceedric all of them. He says that DeMarco is always talking about Haley, how smart she is how she knows how to talk to people no matter their background, how she is making things happen and how focused she is."

"Is that right?"

"Yeah, he says DeMarco is really impressed with Haley."

"Well it's obvious that they have eyes for each other. The truth is I don't think it started this way. I think that their feelings for one another evolved over time. I think DeMarco was looking to use Haley in the beginning—when they first connected, but ended up developing feelings."

Krystal poured herself another glass of wine. "Oh and check this out, Ronnie T. said that one day they were all driving in the Range with DeMarco right. Him, Raymond, Keith, and Eric and you know how the brothers always calling females bitches right?"

Utopia rolled her eyes, "Yeah, they all do."

"Well, Raymond was saying something about Haley, you know just talking, and he said to DeMarco 'you know that bitch Haley', and before Raymond could finish his sentence DeMarco snapped and said 'hey don't be calling her no bitch—that's my business partner'. He said that everyone in the car had a surprised look over their face and that that's when they all realized that DeMarco really did have feelings for Haley. No one called her a bitch again, I guarantee that. He said that the only time he ever saw DeMarco react that way over someone calling a woman a bitch was when Tyrone had disrespected him one day when they were playing basketball and had called his wife a bitch. DeMarco snapped on him and beat his ass," Krystal said.

"What so DeMarco really does have feelings for Haley," Utopia mouthed.

"Yeah he does, but he also has them for his wife," Krystal quickly retorted.

"I'm sitting here listening to you guys talk about Haley and DeMarco and really questioning DeMarco's motives. I mean I had questions to. I mean you guys the truth is Haley is gorgeous, Camille said. "She always looks her best even when she's not dressed up in her usual Fendi, Jones Inc or Tomatsu suits. Looking at her beauty and her intelligence, I see why DeMarco has fallen for her. Not only is she pretty, she's smart and sophisticated. A lot of women only have one or the other, but not Haley, she has them both the good looks and the intelligence. Not to mention the fact that she has the kind of body that no matter what she wears looks good on her. I see why DeMarco's attracted to her and struggling with the issue of unfaithfulness to his wife.

The bottom line is if Haley was willing, so is he. I have to admire her strength thus far. I mean Haley's been celibate for three years and not even DeMarco has hit it as much as she is around him and as much as she is attracted to him. DeMarco knows about her celibacy, she told him and this probably made her that much more attractive to him. Most of the women he deals with are hoes, not Haley. Maybe he's the guy to bring her out of celibacy. She says they haven't slept together and I believe her. Haley's a woman who keeps it real, just like she admitted that she did like DeMarco. We know Haley has a good heart. If you ask her for something, anything, she'll give it to you. She will do anything to make someone she liked life easier. Haley is a good person, a good woman who would never intentionally harm any one. With DeMarco I guess it's just one of those things where she found herself caught up. You guys can say that I am selfish, wrong or stupid—but I do wish that things could work between DeMarco and Haley. They seem to bring out the best in one another.

"You know about what you were saying," Utopia pointed at Krystal, "With regard to your ideas on Haley and DeMarco being soul mates, if DeMarco were not married I would think that he and Haley are soul mates."

"Huh, yeah I have to agree with that one. Man, they do have a lot in common and they get along so well. Them two, they can go far together. They can make a lot of money together. They both smart," Krystal said.

"You know Krystal, I think DeMarco feels stuck in the relationship with his wife," Utopia said.

"Yeah now that I'm looking closer at the picture, I agree, but he ain't leaving her."

"He will if Haley offers him more."

"Umm, I don't know?"

"Krystal, I think DeMarco is thinking a lot of things right now, you know? I can see him leaving Nakeesha for Haley. DeMarco wants out of the game and he knows that if he stays with Nakeesha, he will never get out."

"Maybe you're right. I know one thing for sure, Haley better be careful cause Nakeesha ain't no joke. April from Jordan Downs told me that when she catches DeMarco cheating on her, she goes crazy. She said that Nakeesha is a lot to contend with. You know, whenever it come down to his wife or a mistress, in the end, DeMarco gets rid of the woman he was having the affair with," Utopia said.

"Yeah, and that is when Haley is going to end up hurt," Krystal said.

Twenty-two

DeMarco and I decided to go to Lawry's Restaurant in Beverly Hills for dinner. Lawry's is popular for their herbs and spices and its seasoning salt of the same name in particular. Lawry's has some of the best steak and prime rib in all of Los Angeles. They also have chicken on the menu. Whenever we'd go there, DeMarco always got the five-spice chicken. It was delicious. Over dinner, DeMarco and I made small talk.

"Did I mention to you that I was flying into Oakland next week?"

"No you didn't. What you going to Oakland for?"

"Business… I need to see a few people." DeMarco chuckled to himself. "I might stop by and visit some of my family while I'm there—I don't know."

"What?"

He shook his head. "I was just thinking about something. Did I ever tell you about this female back home in East Oakland named Diamond?"

"No you never mentioned her. Who's that? Somebody you been seeing?"

"No, nothing like that. Diamond is like nine years younger than I am. She's a kid to me. She's my first cousin Chyna's best friend. We all from the same neighborhood; East Oakland's 6-9 Ville. Chyna lives in New York now. She's a model. Her career brought her to New York. She's doing quite well actually."

"Are you talking about the supermodel and fashion mogul—Chyna Azzino-Milano," I asked. DeMarco nodded. "That's your cousin," I said sounding surprised.

"Yeah," he replied. He went on, "but to make a long story short, Diamond, she a sav. She like the toughest female I know. She a strong sister like you, Haley. She has a strong mind and real leadership about her. Diamond actually works for me. She got hustle in her. She making more money than all of the nigguhs I got working for me."

"Is that right?"

"Well maybe not D, Kameron, or Creature Man, but other than them, yeah, she clocking."

Any female except perhaps in the bedroom rarely could impress DeMarco. "Dang like that?" DeMarco stared me in the eye and nodded his head up and down.

"Yeah Haley you gotta meet Diamond, she good people. Maybe you could be a positive influence in her life and give her some direction. She's smart and she growing tired of being in the game, and trust me I know how it feels to want out of something, but the money keeps you there. You know what happens to those who the money keeps there?"

I knew all too well. "Yeah, they either end up one or two places, in jail or dead." I looked him square in the eye.

"You got it." But not me Haley, I'm done. I'm tired of looking over my shoulder. Not knowing who to trust. The shit can make you paranoid. I'm giving the street back to the dogs. They can fight over the title kingpin."

"So when you leaving for Oakland?"

"Thursday, I'll be gone for a week. You wanna go? You can meet my family. My aunt, uncles, cousins and shit."

"I'll go, but you already got your airline ticket right?"

"Yeah, but I'm sure I can get you on the same flight. I'll call my travel agent in the morning."

"Alright sounds good."

"Oh yeah just so you know D and Kameron coming to. They leaving a few days before me. They staying at some hotel in San Francisco."

"Alright."

"I'm staying at the Marriott Hotel in downtown Oakland."

"Just wondering, how come you ain't staying with your family peoples out there?"

"Because I need my space and to keep my anonymity. If I stay with my relatives, I wouldn't have any control over who visits. Plus, I got some enemies back home and I wouldn't feel comfortable doing that, staying with my family that is."

I thought about that time when Krystal had warned me about being around DeMarco for fear of me catching a bullet with his name on it. I smiled uneasily. "Oh, I see, I was just wondering."

"Should I get a one or a two bedroom suite." I held up two fingers.

"Haley, why don't you give me a chance?"

I shook my head no.

"How come?"

"Because DeMarco you're married and it's wrong to be with a married man."

"Haley, I see the way you look at me."

"And I see the way you look at me DeMarco, but it doesn't mean we have to go there."

"Why not, oh I know because I'm married," DeMarco said sarcastically.

"Exactly," I responded. "Plus we have a great friendship, we've become best friends and I don't want to lose that. If we were to date and it didn't work, then we'd probably develop ill feelings for one another and I don't want that to happen. I would hate to lose what we have."

"Man, you worry more about my wife than I do." I hunched my shoulders. "Haley, me and my wife we not gone make it. I married her for the wrong reason. It wasn't love, trust me, and I knew it when I married her. But I married her anyway. Truth is, I felt obligated."

"Show me your divorce papers and then we'll talk." DeMarco stared at me from across the table. He started to say something, but refrained.

"Not to be changing the subject, but this prime rib is really good. But you don't know anything about that, huh DeMarco, Mr. Vegetarian." I lifted a piece of the prime rib up in the air on my fork waving it in the air and then putting it into my mouth. I managed to get a smile out of him.

"I'm going to stop you from eating meat. I don't let my women eat meat."

"Whateva. And remember, I'm not *your* woman."

Demarco pushed back in his chair. The waiter came over to our table before DeMarco could respond. "Would you like dessert, Ma'am? Mr.?"

"I'm cool. You want dessert," DeMarco asked.

"No, I'm cool." He looked at the waiter and said, "I'll take the check."

When the waiter returned with the check, "I got it this time," I announced. As if he hadn't heard me, DeMarco opened the large leather looking burgundy wallet the waiter left behind, placing a crisp $100 bill in it. He closed it.

"DeMarco, you're always paying for everything, let me get the check this time?"

"Its cool."

"DeMarco," I said with raised eyebrows.

"What? You get it next time. Don't worry about it."

"Alright, thanks, but you said that last time, remember."

"Did you enjoy," the waiter asked picking up the wallet from the table.

"Every thing was great." And that was the truth; it had been good.

We walked back to the Range Rover, which we had had to park in the three-story parking garage that serviced Lawry's and the nearby mall. The mall itself had closed as we were at dinner, so the cars had thinned out considerably from the time we had parked. It was also dark. About a third of the mercury-sodium lights were burned out or flickering fitfully, casting an annoying pink-orange light.

As we rounded a corner, I heard footsteps. Something about them didn't seem right. DeMarco heard them too, and grabbed my hand, beginning to turn around. But it was already too late. Two men wearing black ski masks and dressed in all black flowed out from behind a parked van. One was tall and thin, and he had a .45. The other was short and stocky, with a nine aimed at me. The tall guy pressed the tip of the .45 against DeMarco's rib.

"Break yourself fool," he warned DeMarco. The short stocky guy put the gun in my face. "Don't scream bitch, or I'll shoot you," he said.

"Ah man," DeMarco responded. But he kept his cool. As my heart raced, I took some comfort in the fact that, given his "career", this probably wasn't the first time DeMarco had been jumped. He'd know what to do.

The men escorted us behind the van. Next to the van was a panel truck. The two vehicles were parked close together, and between them and the concrete wall of the parking garage was about five feet of space. Five feet of space, I realized, that was out of sight of practically everything else. Even if the garage had any security cameras, and those cameras were maintained better than the lighting in the place, they wouldn't see what went down here.

The men sized DeMarco up. He was cool under the pressure. "Here man, you want my wallet, it's in my coat pocket, 'kay." Keeping the .45 at the ready, the tall man reached in and grabbed it. Then attention shifted to me.

"Let me get a better look at you," the tall guy said, removing my long royal blue Jones New York wool coat, along with my purse. "Damn, keep your gun on him," the guy said to his short henchman, pointing at DeMarco, "and if he moves shoot him."

"Man what are you going to do? You got his wallet."

"I'm gone fuck this bitch." I suddenly felt cold. I began to shiver.

"What? Nigguh we ain't got any time for you to be fucking this bitch. Let's take this nigguh to his shit and rob his ass. Then let's kill this motherfucker and the bitch too and get it over with, before someone comes," the short stocky guy said.

"Man just wait a minute and shut the fuck up. I'm gone get me some pussy."

The short guy shook his head emphatically. "Nigguh you crazy. We got a job to do and it ain't got nothing to do with you fucking a bitch. Now let's just get the d what we came for."

"Nigguh shut the fuck up and hold your gun on that motherfucker and like I said if he moves shoot him."

The taller guy looked at DeMarco. "I ain't gone kill you. Not yet anyway. I want you to watch me fuck yo bitch first. Come here bitch," he said. Not waiting for me to make a move, he grabbed me by the neck, choking me. I gasped for breath as he flung me to the cold cement ground. I landed on my knees, next to some loose pages out of the LA Times. I was down there coughing, with one hand around my neck trying to soothe the pain. When I felt the tip of the gun touch my temple. I burst out crying. "No please don't do this, you got our money," I pleaded.

DeMarco's face remained impassive, but I detected the first hint of emotion. "Man, look, you need to let her go," he said slowly. "It's me you want. She ain't got more than thirty, maybe fifty, and it's all in her purse, which you already got."

"Shut up," the tall guy said to DeMarco. With the short guy holding the gun on DeMarco, the tall guy got down on his knees on the ground where I was. He was in front of me. My legs were pulled together. He put his hand between my tightly held together knees and attempted to pull them apart. I struggled to keep them together. Frustrated, he yelled, "open your legs bitch." Next thing I knew he slapped me. Immediately, my lip began bleeding. I stuck my tongue out and licked the blood. I was crying and scared.

Again, he put his hand between my legs. He set his gun down so he could devote both hands to overcome me. I struggled to keep my legs together, but with leverage and both hands, he won the struggle. That's when I slapped him and he slapped me again on the other side of my face. I looked at DeMarco. His eyes were fixed on the man who was holding the gun on him.

"Man this is business, it's not personal," the guy said. DeMarco fixed him with a gaze that had gone from impassive to angry to downright feral. The guy was trembling. The gun was shaking in his hand. He tried to keep DeMarco in a staring match, but he lowered his eyes. By now the tall guy had my legs pulled apart and had pulled his pants down to his thighs. He had placed his gun on the ground next to him. I was still doing my best to fight the bastard off me, but he had me on the ground.

Somewhere in the garage, a car backfired. The short guy turned to look, probably thinking it was a gunshot. His .45 wandered off DeMarco's ribs. The distraction only lasted a second or so, but for the gunman it was one second too long. DeMarco swiftly brought his knee up into the gunman's crotch while his right hand grabbed the piece in a single fluid motion. Now, the gunman was staggering back, while DeMarco grasped the hand that held the weapon. The gunman was strong. DeMarco was stronger. As his henchman kept struggling with me, the gunman found the .45 turned on him and pointed into his abdomen.

"No, fool," DeMarco said as tears welled up in the man's eyes. I heard the unmistakable sound of a bone breaking in the man's wrist as his piece was turned in his immobilized hand at an impossible angle. "When y'all wanted my money, it was business. When you tried to fuck her, it became personal, asshole."

The man whimpered. He knew what was coming. His eyes went wide as he became consumed by the knowledge. Then DeMarco squeezed. The gun went off. Twice. The short man crumpled, leaving the gun in DeMarco's bloodied hand. The tall man lost all interest in me, diving for his gun. DeMarco stepped on the nine, holding it under his shoe. The man started to reach for it, then stopped. He looked like a fly caught in flypaper, fingers about six inches from his piece.

The man, on his knees, looked up at DeMarco. DeMarco had the .45 aimed squarely at his head. "Want something, asshole?" DeMarco asked casually.

"I—I—hey, look man, you win, okay." His eyes turned to his henchman, now in his death throes in a spreading pool of blood. "I got money. Nine hun, in my van. I got rocks, too, and, and two gold rings." He was blubbering as the barrel of the .45 ended about a foot from his head, held in DeMarco's steady hand. He kept looking back and forth between DeMarco and his dying henchman. Looking at those six inches between his fingers and the gun, inches that may as well have been miles.

"Good," DeMarco said. The man began to smile, thinking perhaps he was going to be able to get out of this after all. "Even a sack of shit like you probably has some next-of-kin."

The smile melted away. The man comprehended, thought the last thoughts he would ever think. Two more shots rang out in the parking garage. With an almost melodic tinkling, two more shell casings hit the concrete floor of the parking garage. DeMarco casually did an ammo check on the .45, and extended his hand to help me to my feet.

"You okay?" he asked. "Come we gotta get outta here. We walked to his truck that was up another level in the parking garage and exited the building. Of course, it didn't end there; DeMarco had blood on him, and a couple spots were on my outfit as well. We stopped at a house out on the outskirts of town. A man welcomed DeMarco. Inside, we each stepped into a large shower stall and removed all our clothing. Even my purse went, the contents carefully emptied onto a countertop.

We left ten minutes later in another set of clothes. I never asked DeMarco what the stop or the change in clothing was for; I didn't have to. I had heard DeMarco talk about the man in the house before, and the purpose he served in DeMarco's organization. I knew that before we even reached the freeway, the clothes we had worn in the parking garage—the clothes splattered with the thugs' blood would cease to exist.

Inside the car, I thanked DeMarco for saving me from being raped, and for saving my life. There is no telling what would have happened had the guy succeeded in his attack on me. He probably would have killed me. Maybe, he would have even killed DeMarco too. I just thank God that DeMarco acted smart and quickly.

Twenty-three

When we arrived at Oakland's International Airport, we headed straight to Hertz car rental. A big attorneys convention going on in town had drained the motor pool there, so Hertz had a limited number of cars available—and DeMarco hadn't reserved one. "I got a Geo Metro or a Geo Storm," the sales associate said, with his eyes fixed on the computer monitor. I gave DeMarco a sidelong glance staring at his dark blue Sea Jean suit, black Cole Haans shoes, gold Huguenot watch and gold chained around his wrist. I knew he was not driving a Geo anything. He wouldn't be caught dead in a car like that.

"That's all you got?" A puzzled look rested on DeMarco's face.

"That's it."

"Alright thanks," DeMarco said. "Come on Haley, let's go over here to Avis and see what they got."

The salesman appeared perplexed. "None of those cars won't do for you sir?" DeMarco nodded.

"Well wait a minute, give me a second. Let me check something else." Staring into the computer screen the sales associate typed onto the keypad. DeMarco's cell rung.

"Yeah," he answered. "What's up Kameron?" He shook his head. "I don't know. Let me think about it and I'll get back at you…I'm renting a car right

170

now let me hit you back when I get to the hotel…Yeah I'm gone call you and D back and then I'll let y'all know."

The salesman looked at the screen, typing in keystrokes as he talked. "You know we have like two big conventions going on in town right now so things are kinda tight." He kept his eyes fixed on the screen while talking. "Oh, I have a black Mercedes 500 SL and a dark blue Jag, but those cars rent for nearly $300 a day sir. Well, we also have a smoke-gray Cherokee Jeep. That rents for $80 a day. What do ya say? That may be a little better on your pocket."

In the middle of his conversation with Kameron on his cell DeMarco tilted the cell away from his mouth, and casually said to the salesman, "I'll take the Mercedes."

The sales associate's eyes grew big. He stuttered, "OK. sir, ok sir. You need to leave a deposit on your credit card that totals the price of the rental for one week."

"What?" DeMarco shouted. "No, not you Kameron." He fixed the sales associate with a level gaze.

"That's our policy, sir."

"Man I ain't never heard of no shit like that. But fuck it, whatever. I don't even feel like arguing with you." DeMarco placed the Visa on the counter along with his driver's license. He continued his conversation, "Yeah, naw let's go to Humboldt tomorrow afternoon that's when I told him we'd come through. Alright, see you in a minute." DeMarco hung up his cell.

"How many days will you be needing the car, sir?"

"A week, he responded. "I'll just pay you now also for the weekly rental."

Apparently DeMarco's fiery look had accomplished what words could not. "You can wait until you return the car to pay, sir."

"So now you telling me I don't have to pay up front. Fuck it, I prefer to pay it in full now just to be done with you."

"Alright sir, would you like to take out the additional insurance at $18.95 per day?"

"No thanks. I am already insured—for a lot less than that."

"Alright, sir it'll be just a second let me total this for you." He typed in some keystroke. "The total is $2,220.95." He placed the bill on top the counter. DeMarco looked over the bill and signed the paperwork. With an exaggerated gesture, he snatched back his Visa card. "Y'all accept cash, right?" The salesman nodded. DeMarco reached into his suit pocket, pulling out a well-stuffed money clip. From it, he counted out $2,300 in crisp one hundred dollar bills. The sales associate recounted it and handed DeMarco his change. A subordinate who had been watching the transaction fished a set of keys out from a locker under the counter.

"Okay sir, just give me a few minutes, someone is bringing your car down now. "

"Come on Haley lets get out of here." DeMarco turned and walked outside.

"Thank you sir," the sales associate said as we left through the glass door.

The black Mercedes 500 SL was beautiful. I admired it as the Hertz employee drove it down the ramp. He popped the trunk and got out, handing DeMarco the keys. "Have a good day," he said and walked away. We put our luggage in the trunk and drove off to the Marriott.

I was still admiring the Mercedes. "Isn't this like the one you got at home?"

"Uh huh sure is. Same year and everything."

"How come you don't drive it all that much?"

"I do drive it. It just seems when you see me I'm in the Range. You really like this car," DeMarco asked as if he were surprised.

"Heck yeah. You can drive mines if you want or I'll buy you one."

"Don't write a check your mouth can't cash."

"Oh is that challenge?"

"Maybe, maybe not. I'm just saying don't write a check that your mouth can't cash. Anyway, how much a car like this cost? About seventy?" DeMarco shook his head, "Ninety."

"What, that's like twice as much as I paid for my Range and I got it used. It was two and a half years old when I purchased it. But you don't know nothing about that huh DeMarco, 'cause you brought your Range brand new at a price tag of about seventy huh?"

"Seventy five," he corrected me.

"Anyhow like I was saying don't write a check your butt can't cash."

"No way. Never that. If I buy you one, what you gone do for me."

"What you want me to do for you?"

"I take the fifth."

"Why?"

"'Cause I don't wanna incriminate myself," he joked.

I rolled my eyes and laughing said, "You stupid DeMarco." He smiled and then became quiet. He was thinking. The attraction from both of us was in the air. *Damn if only he were not married* I thought, knowing there was no future with a married man. Quickly the thought entered my mind that he could make for good dirty work, but as quick as that thought entered my mind I dismissed it. Dirty work is not what I needed. I needed a husband to love and to cherish and to spend the rest of my life with and to grow old with.

The ride through the city reminded me of the civil rights movement. Once the home of the Black Panther Party of Self-Defense and other black revolutionaries, Oakland had a lot of history. It had been more than eight years since I'd been to Oakland. Although the Bay Area was only a six-hour drive from LA on I-5, I rarely went there. Many of the well-to-do and professional Blacks that lived in the Bay Area resided in Oakland Hills. Below the Hills was a different world—the world inside the veil, where the dregs of society dwelled, urban America. Below the Hills sat East Oakland. DeMarco's former home.

"I'm hungry, you hungry," DeMarco asked.

"I'm starving."

"What you wanna eat? Jamaican, Creole, seafood, Thai, Indonesian, what?"

"Creole."

"OK, that sounds good. We can go to the Gingerbread House. It's near Jack London Square. Not too far from downtown. Let's just check in our suite and put our luggage away and then we can go to the Gingerbread House."

"Cool."

Our two-bedroom suite at the Marriott was breathtaking. You could look out of the living room straight into San Francisco. You could even see the skyscrapers in the distance beyond the Bay Bridge. It was beautiful. I admired the view.

"You ready," DeMarco asked.

"Yeah." We headed out, got into the Mercedes.

"Is that my boy Frank Nitti?" DeMarco said, staring hard at the guy behind the drivers seat in the black Lexus stopped next to us at the red light. We could both recognize Tupac Shakur booming out of the car, singing "Me and My Girlfriend."

"That is my boy," DeMarco said, excited. He blew his horn, but the guy couldn't hear him over Tupac. He kept on driving passing us. Speeding, DeMarco caught up with him. Finally the guy looked over at us. He took a double take, recognized DeMarco, and pulled over to the curb. DeMarco pulled up behind him. Frank Nitti got out of his car and ran over to our car. DeMarco stepped out.

"DeMarco, is that you nigguh," the guy called out approaching him with a huge smile on his face. "Nigguh, me and Capone was just talking about yo ass on the phone this morning." The two greeted each other with a hug.

"What's happening, when you get in town nigguh?"

"I just got here."

"How long you here for?"

"A couple of days."

"You should have let a nigguh know you was coming and I would have through a big party for you and had you some hoes, nigguh." Frank Nitti said. Then he looked into the car and let out a little shriek. I chuckled; I knew what had happened. He figured I was DeMarco's girl and he'd fucked up.

"You a fool," DeMarco said. Then he introduced us. "Frank Nitti this is Haley, my business partner. Haley this is Frank Nitti." He reached his hand through the window frame and extended his handshake. "Damn you fine. This is yo what DeMarco?"

"That's my business partner."

"Nice to meet you Haley. Me and this nigguh go way back since we was kids," he said. Man, DeMarco where y'all off to."

"We going to the Gingerbread House to get something to eat. You wanna come?"

"Yeah, I'll go. I wanna talk to you about some things. I'll follow you."

DeMarco got back in the car. "Damn, I thought that was that nigguh. I ain't seen him in a minute. He good people."

"So y'all grew up together?"

"Yeah in 6-9 Ville."

"Ain't Yukmouth and the Luniz's from there also."

"Yeah, Yuk my nigguh. He live in LA," DeMarco said sounding surprised as if I should have known that. "I see that nigguh all the time. Yuk know Frank Nitti."

"Is that right?" DeMarco shook his head. We parked right in front of the Gingerbread House and waited until Frank Nitti pulled up. He caught up with us outside the restaurant. He opened his mouth to greet us, but his cell phone rang.

"Hello," he answered. Then he pulled the cell away from his mouth. "Hey, DeMarco," he whispered, "it's Capone. You want me to tell him you here?"

"It's cool," DeMarco said.

"Nigguh guess who I'm with," Frank Nitti said all thrilled, returning the cell phone to the side of his face. "DeMarco. Naw, I ain't bullshitting. We standing right here in front of the Gingerbread House." DeMarco winced at what he had just said. Handing DeMarco the phone he said, "Capone wanna holler at you." DeMarco took the phone.

"What's happening wit ya?… Naw, I'm only here for a couple of days… You coming?… Well come on then… Yeah, nigguh I wanna see you. Aiight. Hey Capone, just you I don't wanna see them other nigguhs. Aiight see you in a minute." DeMarco handed Frank Nitti back the cell.

"That nigguh on his way here. Come on let's go and order. He can order when he get here." DeMarco walked ahead of Frank Nitti and me. He held the door for us. I entered the restaurant first, followed by Frank Nitti.

"Welcome to the Gingerbread House," the light skinned Creole lady with a French accent greeted us. "Is this your first time here?" DeMarco shook his head indicating he'd been there before. He pointed at me and said, "but its her first time here."

"It's your first time here? Well, you are going to love our food, it's made especially for you," she said. "Since you have never been here before I would like to point out something to you about our menus. Here, let me seat you and get your menus and I'll show you."

"We expecting some more people so could you give us a big enough table," DeMarco asked.

"Is seven chairs enough for you?"

"Yeah, that's fine."

At the round table, DeMarco pulled the chair out for me. I sat down in it. He sat next to me, across from Frank Nitti. The waitress returned with our menus handing, one to each of us. Looking at me, she said. "The dishes with the asterisk next to them have to be ordered two days in advance. Other than that you can order anything else on the menu."

"Ok."

Frank Nitti sat the menu down next to him on the table. "Yeah, nigguh I really need to talk to you, holler at you about some things," he said.

DeMarco ignored him for now, staring at the menu. "I think I'm going to have the grilled Fillet of Sole with the vegetables. What about you Haley, what you having?"

I smiled. "DeMarco, every time we go to a restaurant you always seem to order the best thing on the menu. I'll have the same thing your having."

Frank Nitti picked the menu up. "I know what I want I want: the red beans and rice with diced green onions and tomatoes, cornbread and the smoke sausage." The waitress came back to the table and we gave her our order. By the time our food came to the table, Capone had arrived. He came walking through the door with as huge a smile as the one Frank Nitti had greeted DeMarco with. Upon seeing him, DeMarco stood up from the table, welcoming him warmly. He then pointed at me and introduced us. "Haley this is Capone, Capone this is Haley, she my business partner." I stood up. Capone extended his handshake. We shook hands.

"Nice to meet you," he said. With my hand in his hand, he planted a simple kiss on my cheek. I glanced at DeMarco, unsurprised to see the storm clouds in his eyes.

"Hey watch that, don't be kissing on my business partner like that disrespecting her and shit," DeMarco said.

"I ain't disrespecting her man. Am I disrespecting you, Ms.?" I didn't say anything.

"Nice to meet you, man," he asserted.

"Nice to meet you," I replied and sat back down. Capone took the seat on the other side of Frank Nitti.

"DeMarco, I didn't mean any disrespect, man."

"Its cool," DeMarco responded.

"No man really, I ain't even trying to go there with you. I ain't even trying to see you like that."

"Nigguh I said it's cool now drop it."

"Nigguh he said forget about it," Frank Nitti threw in his words.

"Alright, nigguh I just wanna be sure."

"So Capone you gone order or what nigguh," DeMarco asked. He waved the waitress over to our table. "I want what he got," Capone said, pointing at Frank Nitti's plate. "That looks good."

"Ok it'll be about fifteen minutes."

"Hey nigguh Diamond hit me on my cell when I was driving over here. I told her I was coming to see you, and she said she wanted to see you, so she gone be here in a minute."

DeMarco frowned. "Yeah, I was gone call her, but I guess you beat me to it. Who else you tell I was here, at the Gingerbread House? Shit, with this public an itinerary, if somebody wanted to assassinate my ass I damn sho wouldn't be hard to find."

"I thought it was cool."

"Diamond folks. I wanted to see her. But not necessarily right now…"

"I'm sorry about that." DeMarco shook his head. "So what's been up wit ya Capone?"

"Shoots me and Frank Nitti been wanting to holler at you about a few things," he said rubbing his two palms together while eyeing Frank Nitti. "We was thinking that you could supply us with more coke and heroin."

"Hold on, DeMarco hissed, looking around, cutting Capone off in mid sentence. He looked at me. He looked pissed. No, scratch that—he *was* pissed. "It ain't cool to talk about this right now. And y'all know how I get down. You wanna talk business, bring it to D or Kameron, what you think I'm paying them nigguhs for to hold my dick," DeMarco said, looking into their eyes. "Now, if y'all wanna have dinner with me, that's one thing, but if y'all wanna negotiate, I ain't bargaining right now and I ain't talking business. This ain't exactly a private place, you know. If that's what y'all wanna do, then y'all can bounce.

"Besides if y'all wanna talk business, there's a hierarchy here. You need to bring it to Diamond first. Then, if she knows I'd like your terms, she can bring it to D or Kameron." And as quick as DeMarco snapped, he became nice again and everything was cool. His transformation astonished me as did the respect he got from these thugs, who went back to eating as if nothing happened.

DeMarco's cell rung. He looked at the caller ID. "It was D," he announced. "Damn, I forgot to call him and Kameron back. Yeah," DeMarco answered. "I'm at the Gingerbread House, eating with Frank Nitti and Capone, why don't y'all come through. Diamond on her way here too, we can have a fucking party," DeMarco said, sarcastically staring at Capone. DeMarco hung up. Looked over at me sitting at his side and smiled and winked at me. "You alright," he asked?

"I'm fine."

"Here comes Diamond," Frank Nitti announced.

"DeMarco, how you gone come to the "O" and not let me know," Diamond declared as she approached our table.

"Actually, I was going to call you." DeMarco stood up and embraced her. "I got somebody I want you to meet. Haley this is Diamond, Diamond this is Haley. Remember I was telling you about Diamond, Haley?"

"Oh, so this is Diamond," I said extending my handshake. "Nice to meet you."

Shaking my hand she said, "It's nice to finally meet you. DeMarco talks about you all the time. Says that you are real smart and been to college and shit. He glad to have you on his team, he ain't never letting you leave."

"Is that what he said?" I looked at DeMarco.

"Yep, sure is." Diamond sat down in the empty chair next to Capone. Diamond was a pretty chocolate girl. With long silken jet black hair, but she was without class, real ghetto. Ghetto fabulous though, I must admit. She had on some bad-ass cocoa brown leather Fendi boots that matched her brown Gucci cocoa brown leather pants and the matching leather shirt. I liked it so much I asked her where she had purchased her outfit. She told me she got it from the Gucci shop in San Francisco. Said she paid a G for the pants and 12 for the shirt. Then she went on giving me the price to everything, she was wearing. I paid fourteen for the boots and another twelve for the purse and the glasses cost me four. Diamond really knew her clothes though cause sister girl looked at my black dress and asked, "Gucci?" She was on point. Said she had the same identical dress and paid a nice grip for it, also.

"DeMarco how is your brother Michael doing. I haven't seen him in years," Frank Nitti said.

"He good, real good," Demarco said – shaking his head.

"He still selling real estate?" DeMarco nodded.

"So he married?"

"Naw nigguh. What's up with the million questions."

"I was just asking—that's all." DeMarco looked through Frank Nitti.

"Anybody seen or heard from Ghetto," DeMarco wanted to know.

"That motherfucker tried to play me," Diamond responded. "You know what he did to me? He tried to take my dope, and I had to put The Commission on his ass. That's what I wanted to tell you about, DeMarco."

I later learned that Diamond was a queen pin that worked for DeMarco. They say she was worth 7 million. Rumor had it DeMarco was worth 4 or 5 times that amount. Through DeMarco, Diamond was elevated to that status. Because she was associated with him and he was well respected in the streets, she got her respect. Everyone knew Diamond worked for DeMarco. The Commission was put together by her, all of its members handpicked and given their pseudonym by her. The Commission consisted of her boys that were on her team that worked for her; Frank Nitti and Capone were a part of The Commission. They handled her problems whenever they arose and they distributed drugs for her. And, from the sounds of things, Ghetto was now a "problem" to be "handled."

DeMarco looked at me. "Diamond, we can talk about that later. Rest assured, I'll help you with your problem. Right now I am just asking if anybody seen or heard from Ghetto?"

"We ain't' heard from or seen the nigguh in about a week," Diamond said. Frank Nitti and Capone agreed.

"That's all I was asking and you've answered my question," DeMarco said. Man he was sure snappy. For the first time I saw the leader at work. Yeah, I guess at work we act different than we do when we just kicking it with people. The waitress brought out Capone's order. She asked Diamond if she wanted to order anything, but she didn't. She said that she had just eaten. D and Kameron came through the door. I hadn't even noticed when the walked in; they sat in the two empty chairs next to Diamond. They acknowledged everyone with a simple hello. Now all seven seats at the table had people sitting in them.

"Y'all eating," DeMarco asked looking over at D and Kameron.

"Naw, I'm cool," D said. DeMarco looked at Kameron. "I'm cool," he said. Then he looked at me. "You like the food?"

"Yeah it was excellent."

"You ready?"

"Yeah."

"Let's go."

DeMarco placed a $100 bill on the table to cover the cost of everyone's meal. He announced that he was leaving. He reached for my hand and as if under a trance I gave it to him. "Diamond, I gotta go, but I'm gone see you tomorrow. I want you to have dinner with me and Haley."

"Aiight, cool."

"Hit me on my cell around four and we'll hook up sometime around then."

"Where you want me to meet you at?"

"I'll let you know tomorrow when you call me."

"Aiight. Bye Haley. It was nice putting a face to the mystery woman that DeMarco always be talking about." I smiled.

"Frank Nitti, and Capone it was good seeing y'all man. I'll be in touch," DeMarco said. DeMarco and I left the restaurant hand in hand with D and Kameron in tow. Outside the restaurant, Kameron called DeMarco off to the side. DeMarco released my hand from his grip saying, "I'll be right back. Kameron and DeMarco was talking a few feet away from where me and D were standing. D and I stood there in silence. I caught D's stare. "DeMarco likes you Haley. I have never seen him treat a woman like he treats you. I ain't never seen him treat too many people like he treats you."

In the car, DeMarco commented that Frank Nitti and Capone had their own hidden agenda. He predicted that they would soon be breaking way from Diamond. Said it was about a power thing. However, he was going to make it clear to them that she was not to be harmed in the process. He also said something about if they wanted to branch out on their own it was cool, but they had to pay him and Diamond an honorarium to do so. I guess it was a respect thing or something. DeMarco contended that he believed they were the two behind the resistance Diamond was beginning to receive from The Commission and from some of the round the way brothers on the block.

"Haley you know Diamond is good people and she's like a little sister to me. I want the best for her. There's a lot of things she hasn't learned because she never had a mother or a father to teach her. I 'm hoping that she can make a connection with you and some of you would rub off on her. 'Cause she's really lost right now. She wants out of the game. I see it in her eyes. But she doesn't know what else to do. Somehow, she needs to network with you. You can be that mother for her that she never had. You can teach her. I think she can take her leadership skills in the game and apply them outside the game. Yeah Haley, it would be good for you and her to be friends. You can give her the direction and guidance she needs because behind the attitude and the money, she hurting, she's unhappy. Also maybe you could teach her how to be more selective about the kinds of guys she chooses to go out with."

I reflected on what D had told me, how DeMarco never treated a woman the way he treated me. I supposed it was true. Somehow, I just couldn't picture DeMarco showing a soft side to anyone…it's not like he would rub shoulders with, say, Kameron and ask him if he was happy and contented with his work.

The next day me, DeMarco and Diamond had dinner at the restaurant inside the Marriott. Later that night DeMarco went to go to Humboldt with D and Kameron. He wasn't coming back until the next day. I invited Diamond to spend the night with me at the hotel. I told her that she could sleep in DeMarco's bed.

The next day we went shopping in San Francisco. The way that started was a story in and of itself, I'm here to tell you. DeMarco broke me off ten G's—that's right, *ten*—and told me to get whatever I wanted. He gave me the money in front of Diamond. Her eyes grew big. "You can go and buy you a leather fit like the one Diamond had on and you liked and some other shit," he said to me, handing me all those crisp $100 bills. Shit, all that hardly even fit in my wallet. If my clique had been with me, sheesh, I would have *never* heard the end of that one.

Now, don't get me wrong, the clique, we always wore expensive clothes. But we purchased one or two pieces at a time. We ain't never went on a ten thousand dollar shopping spree. Off to San Francisco me and Diamond went. We took the BART, to downtown San Francisco. The 12th Street BART Station was located across the street from the Marriott. We exited the train at Powell Street Station, in San Francisco. It was located in the heart of downtown among its trendy shops and restaurants. Diamond and I shopped until our hearts were content. As we liberally supported the local economy, we got better acquainted with one another. All of that shopping caused us to work up an appetite. We ate at the Equinox Restaurant in the Hyatt Regency Hotel. After that we headed back to the Marriott. On BART, we talked.

"You know Haley, DeMarco really likes you, don't break his heart cause if you do your gonna see me," Diamond said.

"First of all, I don't think that DeMarco needs you to handle his affairs and secondly, DeMarco and I are business partners."

"Why don't both of you just quit with the 'that's just my business partner'," Diamond said sounding like a baby. "DeMarco feeling you and you feeling him."

I cut her off saying, "DeMarco's a married man."

"And….?"

"In other words nothing can happen between us and nothing is going to happen between us."

Diamond sighed; she seemed like a teacher trying to teach a particularly difficult lesson to a slow child. "Haley, I saw DeMarco break you off ten Gs, he brought you with him here, y'all staying in the same hotel suite together, he's kind to you—trust me, he wants more than a business partnership from you. Girl, stop denying it. You know what I think? I think that you both use this 'he's just my business partner and she's just my business partner' thing as an excuse to be around each other, knowing y'all feeling each other especially you Haley. If you gave up the pussy, I bet you DeMarco will stop with that 'Haley's just my business partner' real quick. But he respecting you until your ready. Personally, I think he already got you and all he needs to do is reel you in and when he did he wouldn't get any resistance. He just doesn't realize it yet. Like you Haley, I'm a woman and I know."

"Yeah whateva."

"Yeah whateva. Truth is Haley you good people and I want to see things work with yo and my boy. He's not happy in his marriage. Neither is his wife. DeMarco deserves to be happy and I want to see him happy more than anything. Truth is Haley you the right bitch for him."

No, she did not just nonchalantly call me a bitch, I was sitting here thinking. I could have got upset, but I didn't. The truth was I couldn't blame Diamond for keeping it real. Really, that's what she was doing.

When we arrived back at the hotel DeMarco was there, with D and Kameron. They were all sitting on the couch in the living room. Seeing all the bags, he asked "What you get me?"

"What?"

"Ah you wasn't even thinking about me, it's cool," he smiled. Although he joked about it, momentarily there was tension in the air, he seemed somewhat offended. I was actually taken aback by his attitude, but I excused it. Me, Diamond, DeMarco, D and Kameron ended up driving back over to San Francisco 'cause DeMarco wanted to eat at the Cheesecake Factory. San Francisco had the only Cheesecake Factory in the entire Bay Area. We all piled in the dark blue Chevy Suburban D had rented and headed back across the Bay Bridge into San Francisco, the city by the bay. By now it was nighttime and the San Francisco skyline looked incredible. While riding across the bridge if you looked to the left you could clearly see Pac Bell Park. The stadium was full. The Giants had a game and were entertaining their guests. With some opera glasses we could have read the score.

After dinner, D dropped me, DeMarco and Diamond back off at the Marriott. DeMarco had invited Diamond to spend the night with us. We all sat up in my bed watching *A Thin Line Between Love and Hate*. Diamond was on one side, DeMarco was on the other, and I was in the middle. Last I remember, it was one in the morning and we went from sitting up in the bed with a pillow between our backs and the headboard, to laying down in the bed watching the movie. We all fell asleep with our clothes on. One by one we got up and showered. DeMarco, ever the early bird, must have gotten up around six and showered and got dressed. Then I showered, and then

Diamond. Both of us sported one of our new outfits. It was a hot day so I put on my $220 brown Gucci linen pants, with my brown $90 Gucci tank top that I got on sale at the Gucci store in San Francisco. I also sported a pair of dark brown slip-on sandals, also happening to be Gucci. Diamond was dressed in all Gucci too. She wore the white Gucci linen pants identical to my brown ones and a white tank top that was also Gucci. Like me, she said that Gucci was her favorite designer. I went back and forth between Gucci and Jones New York. DeMarco had on red Michael Jordan sweat pants, with a white long sleeve Jordan T-shirt. On his feet he sported a pair of red and white Jordans. He turned to us. "So where we off to, ladies?"

"Let's go have breakfast downstairs in the restaurant and then DeMarco you can show me your old neighborhood," I said.

DeMarco gave me a cockeyed stare. "6-9 Ville, you wanna go to the Ville?"

"Yeah you seen the 'jects, I'm from and now I wanna see the 'jects you from."

"Damn, like that," DeMarco said.

"Haley when DeMarco be coming to town he stay clear of the Ville," Diamond said.

"Naw its cool, I ain't been through there in a minute let's go to breakfast and roll through the Ville." After breakfast, we headed over to the Ville, DeMarco drove.

"Diamond you don't be coming over here no more either do you," DeMarco inquired.

"Uh-uh, not since them nigguhs shot at me and tried to kill me. I stay clear of the Ville."

"Diamond, where you live."

"I live out in the boonies in San Francisco with my son Zaire I was telling you about."

The Ville was a typical inner city community, filled with drugs and violence. I guess you've seen one inner-city housing project in America, you've seen them all. DeMarco rode through slowly, but he didn't stop. He pointed out to me where he used to live. *Man, he sure came up*, I couldn't help but think. I came from a similar environment in Jordan Downs in Compton. I couldn't tell you which was worse—Jordan Downs or 6-9 Ville. As we left 6-9 Ville, my eyes caught a group of little black boys playing. They were holding little toy guns, shooting at each other. I saw their future, wondered how many short years it would be before they had guns in their hands shooting real bullets and whoever lost the fight didn't just get up and come back to play again. Looking them over, I wondered who the next kingpin would be.

Then I thought about the group of girls I saw hanging on the block. They must have been no more than 11 and 12 or so I imagine. I thought about their futures, one of them possibly the next Diamond, a queen pin. I sunk down in the front seat. My mood was somber. I remembered my pain growing up in the projects. Then I thought about an old Indian proverb, "Do not judge a man until you've walked two days in his moccasins."

We left the Ville, and the late morning sunlight coupled with the beauty of the rest of San Francisco Bay lifted my spirits. Feeling the need to put on some lipstick, I pulled down the sun visor on my side to stare into the mirror. My eyes caught Diamond. I fixed them upon her. My thoughts on Diamond, she real ghetto, but nice. She was also pretty and intelligent. She was a good debater, strategizer and rationalizer. *If she went to college, it would refine her,* I thought, *and she could be anything.* I saw it in her. Yeah, I could see what DeMarco was saying. She was good people but needed direction. Behind her tough attitude that was her defense mechanism was a gentle soul. If she wanted it I had no problem giving it to her. Looking at her in that mirror I realized she had it in her to be somebody other than the queen pin she was. I imagined that if she took the game she had from the d game and applied it to a career, there would be no stopping her.

Closing the mirror and the pushing the sun visor back up, I said, "Diamond, you would make a good lawyer."

"It's funny you say that because that's what I want to be. But I got a felony conviction so that's out."

I shook my head. "Not necessarily. Actually, my friend Krystal is an attorney and I recall her saying something about California being the only state that allows someone with a felony to practice law." I turned around and looked at her. Her eyes lit up.

"Really?"

"That's what my friend Krystal says. Here write this number down and call her. Tell her you met me and I told you to call her and let her know that you DeMarco's folks. She'll be glad to answer any questions you might have." I gave her Krystal's number. Diamond thanked me. "So to be a lawyer all I got to do is go to law school?"

"First you gotta go and get your BA degree from a university and then you transfer to law school."

"How long does it take to get a BA?"

"About four years."

"How long is law school?"

"Three years."

Some of Diamond's enthusiasm drained away. "Damn that's a lot of years. It takes way too long to become an attorney."

"Yeah, you can look at it that way. But the years are going to pass anyway, so why not make those years that are going to pass anyway productive?"

"That's a good point, Haley." DeMarco drove quietly listening to our conversations.

I liked Diamond. She and I clicked from the gate despite our conversation on the BART train about my feelings for DeMarco and his feelings for me. In all honesty, she was speaking the truth. I invited her to come visit me and spend sometime with me in LA. I told her she had an open invitation and that any friend of DeMarco's was a friend of mines. DeMarco and I spent the rest of our time in the San Francisco Bay Area, being tourists. We went to Fisherman's Wharf, Pier 39, Alcatraz, The Wax Museum and Ripley's Believe It or Not. On that trip to the City by the Bay, DeMarco and I got to know each other even better, including our likes and dislikes. We got to know each other's personalities. DeMarco could be moody as I could be. We were two confident people who found solace in being alone. We didn't always need people around us. In fact, we enjoyed well the time we spent by ourselves. We were both thinkers.

That last night in the Bay Area, we sat in our hotel room, watching the sun set behind the San Francisco skyline. DeMarco looked into my eyes, "Haley, when you gone give me a chance?" DeMarco asked.

I looked away off into the distance. I was speechless. DeMarco had no idea how bad I wanted to give him a chance. He was unaware of the daily struggle I had with my conscience about being with him, and sleeping with him—a married man.

Just as I was about to share these thoughts with him, he sighed. "Take your time, I got all the patience in the world." He watched a seagull as it did a lazy loop.

And for the time being, I kept my thoughts to myself.

Twenty-four

It was Wednesday. My 32nd birthday. I had a recording session at Tranquility. To my amazement when I entered through the door I was welcomed by Utopia, Krystal, Camille, Skerz, D., Eric, Kameron, Dollar Bill, Malik, Walter, some of DeMarco's other boys and DeMarco's voices yelling "Surprise." I was speechless. The surprise party had definitely taken me by surprise.

On a table set up in the studio was a cake box. DeMarco observed the look on my face when Malik lifted the top off the cake box. Wherever they'd gotten the cake, it sure as hell hadn't been the Hallmark bakery down the street. The cake had a picture of two black women going down on a brother—I couldn't believe my eyes. Seeing me blush and my brown skin turning red, DeMarco laughed. "Damn Haley—you can't even look at the cake."

I tried to regain my composure. "Who brought the cake?" No one responded.

"Who's the guy," I asked?

"I don't know, but he don't have dreads," DeMarco answered. Laughter filled the room. "Somebody hand Haley a knife so she can cut the cake," DeMarco said aloud. Malik went upstairs and came back with a knife, giving it to me. I approached the X-rated pastry, debating over which section to cut first. I made my decision, but with exaggerated deliberation, I shifted the knife around from hand to hand. Then, with a wicked grin, I karate-chopped the knife into the cake, neatly slicing through the cake, and, obviously not by accident, the penis. It came off with one chop. The bananas fell out. "How did DeMarco know banana cake was my favorite," I wondered.

DeMarco gave a wince. "Ouch—Damn Haley you did that like you meant it," Everyone snickered, including me. My face felt hot, but what the hell—I had stepped right up and played along with the dirty joke.

Krystal was standing next to me, holding the small purple plastic plates. She leaned over and whispered, "DeMarco got the cake, and planned the surprise party" in my ear.

DeMarco was now sitting on the futon across the room eating cake. When he looked up and noticed me and Krystal huddle talking, he raised the white plastic spoon in the air, pointed it in our direction and yelled out to us, "Hey you two cut out all that whispering,"

I nodded slightly. Then, after a moment, I turned to DeMarco. Innocently, I remarked, "DeMarco how did you know that Banana cake was my favorite?"

"I didn't, its my favorite. Who told you I brought the cake—alright who was the snitch," DeMarco joked.

Dollar Bill enjoyed the cake more than anyone there. He had five slices. Every time he'd come back for another slice he would do this little gyrating hip dance. He had everyone laughing. Dollar Bill had personality.

"Here Haley, read your card," Krystal said handing me the card. It had a cat with sunglasses driving a little red sports car. Everybody gathered around. I read the card aloud:

It's Your Birthday. I wish I had enough money to buy you a fine Italian Sports car," the front of the card read. *I opened it, read the inside: "Not that I'd buy you one. I just wish I had the money. Oh well, Happy Birthday, Anyway."* Everyone burst out laughing.

Looking around the room at everyone, "Wow, Thank you so much you guys, this was totally unexpected."

"DeMarco brought you that too—he had us all sign it before you got here," Krystal whispered into my ear again.

For my birthday, Utopia gave me a pair of Gucci tennis shoes, a Gucci T shirt and a Michael perfume gift set from Saks Fifth Avenue that included perfume, a body lotion and dusting powder. Camille gave me a red Gucci sweat suit that matched the Gucci tennis shoes Utopia had given me, and Krystal gave me a $300 certificate to The Spa at the Beverly Hills Hotel. The Clique always went all-out for our birthdays and Christmas presents.

My birthday present from DeMarco was a $2,176.00 Black Versace Briefcase portfolio. It had a one silver button with a number lock on it. A dust bag that said, made in Italy was included. He purchased the Versace Briefcase from the Gianni Versace store on Rodeo Drive in Beverly Hills. He also gave me a $209.00 1.2" wide, Versace black leather belt that also included a dust bag and was made in Italy. Krystal had tipped him off about what to get me. Earlier that week she and I had gone to the store and she saw me eyeing the briefcase and the leather belt.

The birthday party at the recording studio took me by surprise as did my gifts. It was one of the best birthday parties I ever had, and my first surprise party. I'd always wanted a surprise party. Thanks to DeMarco my wish had finally came true in all those years.

Twenty-five

My phone rang. It was Friday. The clique was calling, reminding me that tonight was Girl's Night Out at Krystal's. At first, I started not to go to Krystal's for our Friday night girls' dinner sleepover ritual. However, I went because I was spending way too much time with DeMarco, and had I not gone I would have been with him. At least, those were my thoughts.

When I arrived Krystal's house door was unlocked, so I walked in. When I walked through the door Krystal, Camille's, and Utopia who were sitting on the couch in the living room with their heads turned in my direction. They all looked like deer caught in the headlights of an oncoming car. "What you mean to tell me you got away from DeMarco tonight," Krystal teased with a look of amazement on her face.

"Damn, I know," Camille said.

"I told y'all I was coming," I replied.

"Haley you look good. Love the hair. Did you get it cut again?" Camille asked.

"Yeah… I just left the salon. Do you think its too short?" I asked—touching the back of my short sassy black hair.

"No its cool."

"I'm actually thinking about letting my hairstylist Bobby give me one

188

of those long Janet Jackson weaves, you know. I just hate to come up off 15 hun."

"What and get rid of the Halle Berry look," Krystal said jokingly.

Camille went on, "Every time I see you Haley—you glowing more and more."

"Maybe, I need to get me a married man, so I can glow like Haley," Utopia said facetiously.

"Carry on, continue talking about what you guys were talking about before I came." I said.

"What? Camille voiced.

"I said 'you guys can finish what you were talking about before I got here'."

"Girl, I thought that you was going to be here at seven, it's 8:30," Camille said.

"Yeah, I got caught up, sorry I'm late!"

Krystal turned to Camille. "So Camille, what do you think of the "M" word?"

"Masturbate?"

"No, the other "M" word."

"Motherfucker?" Camille giggled.

"You're really being facetious."

"I know what you're talking about. Marriage. I'm just messing with you. I think that if a man and a woman love each other, get along with each other, and can see a future together, then marriage is for them."

"I feel the same way," Krystal asserted.

"I feel that marriage is an excellent outward manifestation of one's love for another," Utopia said. I nodded my head in agreement.

"Krystal, what would your family and friends think about it if you married a white man? My family would be accepting. Most of my female friends would also be accepting. However, my male black friends would probably have a problem with it. They'd feel like I turned my back on the brothers completely."

"You know, I think its going to happen," Camille said.

"What?"

"You marrying a white man. Check this out," Camille said changing the subject. I took this survey on my web site, asking white men if they'd want to sleep with a black woman and a lot of them admitted that their fantasy is to sleep with a black woman. About 60 percent of them said that they would act on it one day. 25 percent said they probably wouldn't and the other fifteen said they don't know if they'd act on it or not."

Krystal gave a miffed look, and changed the subject back to me. "Damn

Haley, girl you glowing. You look good. What's your secret?"

"Her secret, Haley's in love with a married man and his wife Nakeesha gone kick her ass when she get out," Utopia said teasingly.

"Girl, I got yo back.," Camille said.

I smiled. "Right, whateva."

Krystal leaned back in her chair. "Girl, I heard that Malik was offended by that birthday cake DeMarco gave you the other night."

"What? Why would he be offended."

"He said that DeMarco disrespected you."

"Nah, I didn't find the cake offensive at all. It was funny actually."

"I was a little taken aback by it."

"Really Krystal—that's surprising coming from you, 'cause you are about the most liberal person I know. I never would have guessed 'cause you seemed to enjoy the cake as much as I did. Everyone did."

"Girl, you better hope that Nakeesha don't get wind of that cake, that'll be the reason for it to be on, Utopia alleged."

"Fuck you, Utopia," I said, grinning.

Krystal gave Utopia a look, then turned back to me "You know what's gone happen? DeMarco is going to be there when Nakeesha kicks your ass and he is going to side with her. I'll bet you anything he is going to leave with her after she finishes whooping on you, Haley You watch and see." Utopia burst into loud laughter.

I loved the clique, but sometimes they just got on my nerves. "You know what you guys, I'm leaving. I am in a good mood and I am not going to let y'all take my joy. I'll see you guys later. Utopia, Krystal, I really thought y'all was my girls and all y'all doing is giving me a hard time about DeMarco— with whom I have nothing going on—and y'all chopping me up behind my back like I am a hoe or something. If you have anything you want to say about me—say it to me—not behind my back to each other. Furthermore, if you want to know anything about me just ask."

Krystal stood akimbo. "Alright Haley, just ask?"

"Yeah just ask."

"How come you always leaving when we try to talk to you about DeMarco. Haley sit down," Utopia voiced.

"No, I don't want to sit down and hear y'all out." My cell rung.

"Damn, she ain't been here all of five minutes and the man calling her already," Krystal said. I looked at the caller ID—sure enough, it was DeMarco. Smiling I answered, "Yeah?" A huge grin sprawled across my face. Not wanting the clique in my conversation, I stood up from the couch and walked into the kitchen. It was adjacent to the living room.

"No, she didn't," Krystal said—looking around the room at Camille and

Utopia.

"Uummm," Utopia expressed.

"We can still hear you," Camille humorously shouted from the couch in the living room. I laughed loudly. Aw, hell with it, I thought, walking back into the living room with my cell growing out of my ear like some kind of plant, and I sat back down, resting my head on the back of the couch.

It wasn't like I wouldn't have told the clique about it later anyway.

"Yeah you can see me tonight? In a minute? No, meet me at my house in an hour."

Krystal walked over to me, bent down and spoke into the cell, "DeMarco don't be taking Haley from us we don't see her that much these days. Now we gotta find another single lonely, depressed woman to join our Friday night dinner sleepovers!"

" Yeah, DeMarco don't take her from us, let her spend some time with us," Utopia added.

"Yeah, you hogging her," Camille said. The girls giggled.

I spoke to DeMarco. "You hear what they said?"

Yeah, I heard them. They're too funny. Tell them I love them too."

"DeMarco says he loves you guys."

"Love you DeMarco," the clique shouted.

"Haley, ask DeMarco if he got a friend for me," Utopia said.

"DeMarco, Utopia wants to know if you have a friend for her?"

"Tell her she don't want to date many of my friends."

"He said you wouldn't want to date any of his friends."

"Ask DeMarco why he hating on me like that."

"Did you hear her ?"

"Yeah. Tell her that I wouldn't introduce her to any of them because when it don't work out or they disrespect her I don't want her blaming me."

"He said no, Utopia, and I ain't passing no more messages. Alright, see you at my house," I told DeMarco.

"See you in a minute." He hung up. I placed the cell phone on the coffee table in front of me.

"I knew it was too good to be true that you were here, now you leaving us to go and be with DeMarco," Krystal asserted. "Since you've met him you've put us down. We hardly see you these days."

"Ooh I know what y'all gone do tonight," Utopia said. Camille sat down next to me. "Just answer me this: does DeMarco have a big dick?".

I was speechless.

"I ain't gone ask you y'all business but I bet that motherfucker can fuck," Krystal said.

"You know who I bet he can fuck that's why Haley's in love with a married man," Utopia mouthed off. The clique teasing me, it was all fun and games, but when Utopia threw the words "married man" out like she did, my smile turned into a serious look. What, did they think I could ever forget the man was married? "Fuck you Utopia, and Krystal" I said.

"I know, but you still love me," Utopia said.

"Of course she does," Krystal said.

"Yeah, I love y'all asses."

My cell rung again. I reached for it, but Krystal's hand shot out and grabbed it up from the table and she looked at the caller ID. "Well surprise, surprise. It's DeMarco," she announced. "Damn Haley, you must have some good pussy to get a brother like DeMarco whose been used to loving them and leaving them to be hounding yo ass. You got the brother changing and shit over you. You gone have to let me know how you did it."

The phone trilled again. I wasn't much for those custom rings some people put into their cell phones—it didn't play Beethoven's Fifth or any shit like that. To fuck with the clique's head, "Hey baby," I answered. DeMarco didn't say anything right away. I guess I even startled him. "You at my place already? Alright, I'm leaving now. Alright, by…you know I do." I hung up.

"Girl, why didn't you tell that man you loved him back, Utopia wanted to know."

"Haley, you gave him a key to your house," Krystal asked.

Oh brother, here we go. "Yes I did, and I have a key to his apartment and the studio."

"He gave you a key to his house," Krystal shouted.

"You are not listening, I said his apartment. He also has an apartment."

"Oh yeah I forgot about that. So when's the divorce and when's the wedding?" Krystal asked.

"Y'all stay out of my business. I'll see you guys later.". I winked. "I got a date. " I got up to leave.

What's really up with you and DeMarco?"

"He's my business partner."

"Let me rephrase the question: Do you like DeMarco?"

"For the record Krystal I am not in a courtroom, but I respond to your questioning anyway."

"Just answer the question Haley."

I looked around the room at Utopia first, Camille and then Krystal. Alright y'all wanna know the truth? Yes, I am starting to develop some feelings for him—Yes."

"Ah ha—bingo!" Here was Krystal the attorney, exultant in the point she just scored. "Does DeMarco like you?"

"You guys know DeMarco be flirting his ass off with me—like he just was a minute ago on the phone." I looked at the phone.

"Ok she's telling the truth," Krystal said. She continued. "Have you two ever kissed?" I was silent. I could see the look in Krystal's eyes. She would roll on like a tank now that she was started…

"Do I need to repeat the question. Let me repeat it for you."

I sighed. "No, you don't need to repeat the question." After a moment's pause, I continued. "Yes, we have."

Looking over at Camille and Utopia.

"Oh boy, Utopia and Camille said at the same time."

"Basically, I got caught up with DeMarco. None of this shit was supposed to happen. I wasn't supposed to fall in love with him. He was only supposed to be my business partner. We were going to make lots of money together. That's all that was suppose to happen. When I first met him, I wasn't attracted to him. He wore dreads, I hated dreads. You guys know I hate dreads," I said looking around. "But I accepted his dreadlocks and liked them. I even found myself touching them—admiring them. Now, I love dreads—even thought about getting some myself.

"Nor did I care for DeMarco's attitude about women or his sexist attitude. I don't like sexism, I don't like sexist men, but I accepted his sometimes-sexist attitude, because there was more to it than that. DeMarco liked to be in control—over men as well. To him, it was just business—you know, the idea that if you want something done right you'd better do it yourself. I like to be in control, but I backed off some and let him lead—not over everything, but on a lot of things. When we first met, DeMarco probably didn't have eyes for me either."

"I wouldn't say that," Krystal interjected.

"Maybe not. Who can know for sure what's in another's mind? I can only guess. I can only speak for myself. All I know is we became friends, he'd confide in me, I listened to him and offered him advice. I confided in him, he listened to me and offered me advice. We hung out together. We became best friends. Went to the movies, lunch, dinner, and the recording studio, out promoting. I sometimes kicked it with him at his brother's house, his house, and alone. We did this for two years and we were strictly platonic.

"One day I was staring at him and found myself saying to myself—this brother is not bad looking. Next thing you know I'm talking about how handsome he is, and sizing up his dick in the car, or just wherever. Then he's asking me to get an apartment with him. Next thing you know we kissing, next thing you know I am in love. I know that we can't help who we fall in love with, but we can help who we choose to date. Bottom line: DeMarco is married and I know its wrong for me to love a married man. But I am where I am."

I looked at Camille. I could tell by the look in her eyes what she was probably thinking. "I am so sorry Camille for condemning you and thinking less of you when you dated Jonathan. I am sorry I didn't understand your dilemma—or even try to understand. I am sorry that I condemned you. When you was going out with Jonathan, I lost respect for you, but I was wrong. I am so sorry. I had no idea what you were going through."

"Haley don't even worry about it. I forgive you. I am your friend and I am here for you in good times and bad times."

"I know you guys think that I have not been listening to you. I have, but it's not easy to just turn your emotions off when you love somebody. Especially when your emotions run so deep. You know what DeMarco told me last night when I told him that we were seeing to much of each other and we should spend less time together because he's married and my conscious is bothering me. He told me that he was never letting me go. A while back he asked me if I would marry him if things didn't work out with his wife and we haven't even slept together. Well there you have it," I said throwing my hands up into the air and then letting them them fall down onto my lap.

Krystal was speechless. "Wow." Utopia said.

"You said a lot," Camille said.

"So you two haven't had sex," Utopia queried further. I shook my head no and then added, "not yet, but I want to and he's been ready. I told him that as long as he was married there could never be anything between us.

His response was 'I had a relationship that lasted four years and my wife never found out about it'. I told that negro that I was not about to be someone's mistress for four years or any period of time, and that motherfucker kept on saying, 'I ain't letting you go ever.' I'm thinking 'what the fuck does that mean?'. If I want to go, I am gone. You know what? When I sit here and I tell y'all that I am through with DeMarco I really mean it when I say it, but I've said it before a million times then he calls and when I hear his voice I forget about what I said. But l I really do mean it when I say it."

"That's deep. Yeah girl you are in love and I am worried about you, we all are," Krystal said. She went on. "Pray to God about this."

"Yeah girl that's what I would do," Camille said. Utopia nodded in agreement.

"Well I know what I gotta do. I just gotta do it. I have to distance myself from him."

"Well girl, you know we here for you right?" Krystal said?"

"That's right girl," Utopia chimed in. "Girl let me give you a hug you need it." After Utopia hugged me, Camille and Krystal followed, kissing me on the cheek. "We are here for you," Krystal said, "sorry for coming down on you the way I did. I really didn't mean any harm."

"Yeah, I know. "It's nothing. I love y'all. I thank God for putting all of you in my life. You are the best friends a woman could ever have," I expressed. And I meant it, every word of it. For this moment, all the strife was gone, we were the clique again, strong sisters who had each other's backs, come whatever the rest of the world threw at us. And over the years, that cruel world of cheating and feckless men, bills, family drama, and misfortune had thrown a lot our way, but it had bounced off of us, 'cause we hung together.

"I love you too Haley," Krystal said.

"I love you too Haley, "Utopia said.

"I love you too Haley, Camille said.

We were strong. I left Krystal's, headed home.

I called out DeMarco's name as I entered the house. "DeMarco".

"I'm in the living room." I walked into the living room. DeMarco was sitting on the couch reading Marcus Garvey's book, *Life and Lessons.* He held the book up in the air. "I read this book along time ago. Mind if I borrow it to read again?'"

"Not at all," I said, sitting down next to him. I sat my keys down on the coffee table. I noticed the glass Chess set on the table as he so often did—DeMarco had been playing himself. Captured game pieces lay on the table—at the side of the board. A lot of times when he couldn't sleep he played chess. Seems like the more stress he had going on in his life the more he played. He also played Chess II. DeMarco said it was designed by a French publishing company that had published numerous books about the subject. Chess players around the world were surveyed about their ideas about the game and based off of that survey Chess II was created. DeMarco said the advantage was more pieces and more action. He said Chess II came out in 1998. He started playing it when he first learned about it in 1997.

In Chess II you could build your own terrains. DeMarco's love for chess was obvious. Once I asked him what he liked so much about that game. He said, Chess just makes him more aware about life, where he's at, where he needs to be and how he's going to get there. To get there you got to strategize, he said. "Basically, chess teaches you insight. How to be a keen observer, how to advance and fend off, how to, rescue and destroy. The strategies you learn in chess can be applied to life and your battles with your adversaries, which is what the tiles on the chess board represent. It's the battle field and the pieces represent life's adversities," he went on.

"I remember one day he was playing this new chess. That doesn't look like a regular Chessboard and there more pieces looks like," I commented.

"That's cause 'm playing Chess II," DeMarco said. "Chess II is the same as regular chess there are just some new pieces like the Squire and the Cannon." He explained Chess II to me. " The Squire, moves two tiles at a time in a forward position, sits in the rear rank between the knight and the bishop. The piece was specifically designed to address the imbalance between the knight and the bishop." The company who makes Chess Ii discovered, Chess players don't think twice about exchanging their knights for their bishop that are counterparts of the other. Therefore losing one presents a problem. The Cannon is like the pawn. They need to add a few more pieces, pawns to the game to fill the front rank. There needs to be a piece added that feels the void between the rook and the knight. The piece should be similar to the king; but can move and attack or strike up to two tiles away in any direction."

And that's how DeMarco explained Chess and Chess II to me. He loved to play chess. The game of tactics and conquest . He'd play alone or with someone. He'd even log on to the Internet and play people from around the globe on the Internet. From as faraway places as Amsterdam, London and Sydney. Sometimes his games in person or via the Internet would last for 2 to 3 days. When he played alone sometimes those games went on for a week or two. He use to even sit there with a note pad when he played alone mapping out moves 10 and 12 steps ahead. Sometimes, I think he took the game too serious. I don't know what that was about. He also played Chess II. On the Internet.

"This was a deep motherfucker. Man, Garvey had it all planned for us. His ideas, philosophies and opinions are remarkable—DeMarco said staring at Garvey's book. Especially his ideas about entrepreneurship and how black people need to own their own businesses. Haley, you know it was reading Garvey—this book as a matter of fact," he said, pointing to it, "that made me want to own my own company. That's how he's affected my life. I heard Spike Lee once say that *The Autobiography of Malcolm X* changed his life. After reading it, he saw the world and things totally different. Well, that is what reading Garvey and studying his 21 lessons that he once taught his students in secrecy did to me. Garvey changed me and made me see the world in a new light. Garvey helped to shape my way of thinking. W.E.B. Dubois was another one. Ever read, *The Souls of Black Folks?*"

I stared at Demarco in amazement. "You read Dubois too?"

"Yeah, why you looking at me like that, brothers do read you know."

"I'm knowing, but I didn't know thugs did."

"Well this one does. I also read Machiavelli. You read Machiavelli?"

"Yeah, in college. I read all of those books with the exception of Garvey at UCLA. I read Garvey after college. A friend—actually this guy I was dating at the time— turned me on to Garvey."

"So Haley, what do you think about *The Souls of Black Folks?*"

"That's a deep essay."

"What you think about it Demarco?"

"Dubois spoke some real shit in that essay. The shit he said about Black people coming from two worlds. The World Inside the Veil and the World Outside the Veil and about how Black people, we come from the world inside the veil, but have to interact in both worlds to be successful."

"Yeah, Dubois wrote that essay must have been over 80 years ago and what he said is still practical today.

When I think about the world inside the veil, inner city communities infested with drugs and violence, and the world outside the veil, the suburbs, where we go to work, school, and just how Black people gotta interact with both worlds, I think about Tupac."

"Why is that?"

Because he is so representative of the urban black male and the urban male period, no matter what color he is. He was from the world within the veil; however, he had to interact with the world outside the veil. When he did this, he brought all that he learned with him into the world outside the veil. His belief system, his ideas, his philosophies and opinions and he applied them to his New World—Hollywood and the two just didn't mix."

"Hmmm I see what you're saying, it's like what's right in one world is not necessarily right in the other?"

"Exactly."

"DeMarco, have you ever read the book *Invisible Man* by Ralph Ellison?"

"No, but I heard about that book. I hear it is a must-read."

"It is. I got it in my bookshelf in the hall if you ever want to read it."

"Haley, have you ever read this book called, *They Came Before Columbus?*"

"Yeah, by Ivan VanSertima."

"It's about how Africans came to the New World before Columbus. VanSertima says that the people who sailed with Columbus saw remains of Africans at Indian Burial sites in the New World."

"Damn, Demarco, you are up on your reading."

"Of course, one day I'm gone go to college to and get me a degree in business."

"Well I'll say, what college you gone go to?"

"UCLA—like you did." DeMarco smiled. "Well excuse me. After that, I might go to law school. That is, if I am successful in getting my record expunged."

"Krystal told me that California is the only state that you can practice law with a record—I ain't got no felony convictions though—Just some county jail time—I've been lucky. I just say that to say that you can still practice in the state of California with a felony.

"I been talking to my boy, and he supposed to take me down to the county and show me how to get it expunged. Krystal could probably help me with that, huh."

"Yeah she can and she'd be glad to. Maybe me you and her could go to dinner our something and we could talk about it."

"Let's do that."

"Haley, what you looking for in a husband?"

"DeMarco?"

"What?"

"You don't have to do that."

"Do what?"

"You know what I'm talking about."

"Oh, you think that I'm just making small talk." I rolled my eyes.

"Baby, if I didn't care I wouldn't ask. Besides I'm wondering if I got the qualifications."

"Alright you wanna know, I tell you."

"Get some paper and write them all down." I went into my office and raided the paper tray of my printer and my pen collection, coming back with two sheets of paper and two ink pens. "This is mines," I said, holding one sheet, and I gave one to DeMarco. "This is yours. You write down what you are looking for in a woman also, DeMarco."

"What I Want In A Man," I wrote across the top of my sheet of paper. I started making my list, even as I heard DeMarco making his. I didn't look at his. I focused on mine. Ever the businesswoman, I numbered the entries on mine. Then he saw what I was doing and copied me, also numbering his, I took notice.

We finished at about the same time. "Here it is," DeMarco said triumphantly. "What I Want In A Woman."

"How many things you got on your list, Demarco?" Demarco looked at his paper, "eleven, I got eleven on my list. How many you got?"

"Seventeen." I could see DeMarco's eyebrow go up. "Alright let's exchange our lists and read each other's."

I read his list.

1.   Strength
2.   Self Respect
3.   Confidence
4.   Loyalty
5.   Supportiveness
6.   Smart and intelligent

7.   Believes in me—puts her confidence in me
        Not challenge my authority and listens to me cause I
        am not going to guide her wrong and she needs to trust
        me to do that.
8.   Follows her own mind
9.   Attractive
10.   Good lover
11.   Keeps people out of her business

As I read his list, he read mine.

1.   Compassion
2.   Trust
3.   Friendship
4.   Communicator
5.   Respect
6.   Support no matter what
7.   Loyalty
8.   A man who instills trust and confidence in me
9.   Someone who really makes and honest attempt at
        understanding me
10.   A man who doesn't argue
11.   Spends time with me
12.   Leadership
13.   He has to have his own money
14.   A good listener
15.   Who sincerely loves me and cares about me
16.   Who thinks about me and is considerate of me
17.   Handsome

"I've got half of the stuff on the list, and could work on the other half," DeMarco said tossing the sheet of paper onto the coffee table in front of him. He leaned back on the couch.

"What half you got?"

"Spending time, respect, loyalty, confidence, not two faced, leadership, I definitely got that, good listener—although you don't think so. Let's see, oh I have my own money. Unselfish, humorous, enjoys sex—I definitely enjoy sex. Oh and I sincerely love you and care about you. I'm handsome, The thing I got to work on not cheating. You know what? Looking at the list again, Haley I realize I have all the qualities you are looking for in a man, with the exception of not being a cheater. However,

I could see myself being committed to you."

"Huh."

"What about my list, what you think?"

I meet all of your qualifications," I said, tossing the paper on the coffee table and falling back on the sofa.

"All of them?"

"All of them."

"What about the good lover one?" I just shook my head. My body and my heart was thinking why don't you come closer and find out. But my mind told me not to take it there. I followed my mind. Although the struggle was killing me. I stared off into the distance.

"What you thinking about Haley," DeMarco asked.

"Oh just about a lot of things." His question threw me off guard. I hadn't expected him to ask me my thoughts. I guess the look on my face showed me in deep thought. And yeah DeMarco was right, I sure was thinking deeply, rationalizing with myself about why its not ok to be with a married guy; however, he was the exception. Besides he wasn't happy with his marriage anyway, he was forced into it. It was the best thing for him to do at the time. DeMarco persisted. "What's on your mind?"

"Listen at you, you want me to tell you what my thoughts are. My thoughts are personal. They're between me and God," I replied. DeMarco kissed my forehead. We both dozed off to sleep on the couch. We didn't wake up until the next morning.

Twenty-six

Today went by fast. I spent it with the clique. We had lunch at Aunt Kizzy's Kitchen. After we went to Krystal's and hung out. She cooked dinner. Next thing you know it was midnight and then 3 a.m. As soon as I walked through the door at my parent's house my mother was all over me. I was staying there for a minute while I was having some remodeling done at my house.

"Where have you been, with that married man," she asked.

"What?"

"Yeah, I know that's who you've been with."

"Mama, I've been at Krystal's. If you don't believe me you can call her and ask her." Next thing I knew the cordless phone was staring me in the face. I dialed Krystal's number. Her phone rang. She answered.

"Krystal, hey girl this is Haley, my mother doesn't believe that I was at your house tonight. She thinks that I've been out with DeMarco fornicating. She's standing right here for you to confirm where I've been." Inside I was wincing at having to go through this charade, at having to play these childish games.

"Alright, put her on the telephone, Haley." My mom got on the phone.

"Hello."

"Hi Mrs. Jones, how are you?"

"Good, and you Krystal?"

"Fine, Haley just left my house—about twenty minutes ago. I cooked dinner and we all had dinner, and after dinner we sat around talking. We didn't realize how late it was until somebody looked at their watch and said it was three in the morning."

"So, Haley was at your house."

"Yes, Mrs. Jones."

"Thank you. Sorry for bothering you, Krystal." *Not as sorry as I was.*

"No problem Mrs. Jones."

"She said you were at her house," my mother said, hanging up the phone. She walked out of the room.

"Mama, Mama?" She kept walking. Trailing behind her down the hall, "Mama, I am not going to stand for you embarrassing me in front of my friends. I am a grown woman."

"As long as you are in my home you will abide by my rules."

"Mama, I am only here because my house is being painted and my kitchen remodeled over the next two weeks. I haven't been here two days and you are starting this with me already. Would you please stay out of my life? I am grown. I take care of myself. I don't ask you for anything. You can't stop me from seeing DeMarco and if I want to be with him tomorrow or anytime I will be with him."

"Stop your back talk to me Haley."

"No Mama, I am tired of you interfering with my life. I'm tired of you being suspicious about me and DeMarco."

"What's going on out there," my father yelled from behind his bedroom door?" "Nothing," I protested.

The white door to the bedroom opened. Wearing a striped blue robe with a white cotton Fruit of the Loom T-shirt and a pair of navy blue socks pushed down to his ankles, my father appeared in the hallway with us women. He was puffing on his dark brown wooden pipe. The smell of cherry tobacco filled the air.

"What in the hell is going on out here? Y'all done interfered with me trying to read the newspaper," he said between puffs.

'Nothing."

"Nothing, that's what y'all always say when y'all arguing and I ask what is going on, nothing."

"Mama," I said to my father, gesturing at my mother, "she always in my business, embarrassing me in front of my friends. Calling them, confirming that I was at their house and not with DeMarco. I'm a grown woman, I can do what I wanna do."

Removing the pipe from his mouth and holding it in his hand, "Now,

Haley I'm with your mama on that one. We will not condone your going out with a married man. We didn't raise you like that and we won't have it. Now, we raised you right in the church and you know what the Bible says about adultery. "

My temper started to slip. Having to do PR with the clique for my "relationship" with DeMarco was bad enough. But in my own parents' home? *No, I'm only going there once.* "First of all, again, for the record, I am not dating DeMarco." I enunciated my words with exaggerated care. "I am not sleeping with DeMarco. He is not my boyfriend. I am not his mistress. He is my business partner. When will you guys ever see it. I am tired of being accused of something that I am not guilty of. Furthermore, if I *were* dating him it would be nobody's business. I have my own money, he has his own money. Ain't nobody giving us nothing."

"Well it don't look right you running around with that married man like you do, and you stop talking to your mom and me that way. If you don't like our rules than leave."

Not a problem! "Okay." I took a deep breath. "I'm out. I will leave tomorrow. I will go and stay at a hotel or a motel or something."

"Haley we will not have you running around with that married man," My mother voiced."

"You know what, I don't even need this. I'm leaving." I stormed into my old bedroom. It was now the guestroom. When I spent nights at my parent's house this is where I stayed. When I got to the room, I headed for the closet. I placed my hand on the small round gold doorknobs, I swung open the double shutter white closet doors. One of the doors came off its track, as they often did because they were lightweight. I guided it back on track, and grabbed my large Brown Luis Vuitton Duffel bag that I purchased for two thousand dollars last summer while I was vacationing in Paris. Without taking the few clothes I'd packed off their white plastic hangers, I stuffed them in the duffel bag, hefted the bag, and left the room.

I walked down the stairs, past my mother and out the door at the bottom of the stairs.

"Haley, where are you going, come back," my mother called out.

"She going with that man," my father replied. "You going with that man. You taking food out of that man's kids mouth," he went on.

Stopping in my tracks I sighed. The duffel bag thumped to the driveway pavement. I turned around, running both hands through my hair. "You guys are really stressing me out. Accusing me of things that ain't true—like going with a married man. You are my parents—how could you even go there with me? You guys raised me better than that. For the millionth time, I am not going out with DeMarco. I am not sleeping with DeMarco."

They did not appear convinced; they still had that same old accusing look in their eyes. I threw my hands up in the air. "I give up. You guys think whatever you wanna think; you will anyway. Okay, I'm sleeping with DeMarco, a married man. I'm taking food out of his children's mouth 'cause he's so poor," I laughed; I couldn't help myself. DeMarco, poor..."and he spend all his money on me. I wasn't at Krystal's house tonight I lied, she lied I was really with DeMarco at his place. Is that what you want to hear? Mom? Dad? I am tired of your suspicions. I am tired of everyone's suspicions. I don't care anymore, I really don't," I turned and walked away. I pushed the alarm on the key ring to the Range, the black electric locks popped up. I opened the door, threw the dark brown Luis Vuitton bag on the seat next to me, and climbed up in the truck, closing the door behind me. It was cold inside the Range Rover. I was shivering. I'd left the window rolled down midway. My finger went to the button to roll the window up, but before I could do so, my mother appeared at my window like a carhop in a vintage drive-in diner.

"Haley, let me talk to you baby." My finger toyed with that button. A little more push, and... But my mother's tone was conciliatory, too much so. My finger drew back from the power window control. "Haley don't hate me."

I took in a deep breath and released it. "Mother, I could never hate you. However, for the record I am not sleeping with DeMarco, he is my business partner. I am tired of the accusations from everybody, you, Dad, Krystal, Camille Utopia, the rappers, DeMarco's friends, his family, everybody, they are not fair. Everyone doesn't know how to mind...their...business."

"Haley, can I say something?"

"What Mama?"

"Be careful baby. If you say you are not sleeping with DeMarco, I believe you. I am looking in your eyes and I see the truth, I see genuineness in you right now. Haley, I'm a woman—just be careful that's all I'm saying. Haley, I know your true feelings for DeMarco I see it as plain as day. The way you talk about him, the way your conversations go with him when I hear you on the phone with him and the flirting. Baby, I know that sometimes flirting with men is fun in games. Baby, I know that male and females can have platonic friendships, but they have to keep things in perspective—especially the flirting. "Haley, don't be angry with me. I love you and I don't want to see you hurt. DeMarco is not the guy for you. He's too street, he sells drugs, and he's a thug. You are an educated woman with morals and values. Me and your daddy raised you to be with a guy who is deserving of you. A guy who when you are with you do not have to worry about your safety. Besides, guys who do what he does end up in one off two places: dead or in jail. You don't wanna be around when that happens."

"Not always mama," I interrupted.

"Haley, I want you to be honest with me."

"Yes, mama."

"Are you in love with him."

"No way."

"Do you like him."

A slight smile appeared on my face. I shook my head no. But my smile, like a breach in a dam, grew bigger and bigger and bigger. Covering my face with my open palms, "Mama, I think I'm falling in love." I lowered my head. There, it was out. I dropped my hands to my lap and stared back at her mother, feeling as if the window was in a confessional rather than a car. She stared back.

"I know. He's falling in love with you too and that's a problem. That's both of y'all problems—falling in love. It really wouldn't be a big issue if he wasn't married. However, he still wouldn't be the guy for you—not him. Haley stay strong, don't give into him, don't sleep with him, don't let it happen. Haley he is just going to break your heart. Even if he doesn't set out that way, he will. The man is married. He has a wife. Have you considered that? There's no telling what she will do if you go with her husband." Damn, my mom was sounding like Krystal. That's exactly what she had said to Camille and me.

"Thanks Mama." And I meant it; I now felt like I was talking to my mother again, rather than an accuser. We exchanged a hug through the window. I turned on the engine. It was 3 a.m.

My mom looked around me at the duffel bag sitting next to me on the passenger seat. "Baby, where are you going?"

"To a motel."

"Haley, come back in the house, please?"

"Uh uh, I'm cool with that."

"I love you Haley."

"I love you too Ma." My mother put her hands on my shoulder—leaned into the car and planted a kiss on my cheek. Then my cell phone rang

"Who's calling you at this hour?" I looked at the caller ID.

"It's DeMarco." My mother stepped back from the car, shaking her head. I could tell it was more from sorrow than anger, however.

With a big smile on my face, I flipped open my cell.

"Hello?"

"Where you at?"

"I'm in front of my parents house talking to my mom. I'm about to leave. Where you at?"

"Shit, in the city waiting on my boy. He just got out of jail and he suppose to be meeting me." *One of two places*, my mother had said.

"Oh."

"Haley, I need yo friend Krystal to write me up a contract for this rapper I wanna sign to our record label, and I need her to look into this case for me. Actually, for my boy. Can you make it happen, for me to meet with her?"

"Sure, when you wanna meet with her?"

Sometime next week."

"Hey DeMarco, let me call you right back, I wanna finish talking to my mother."

"When you calling me back?"

"In like ten minutes."

"Aiiight, see you in a minute." I hung up the phone and sat it in on the passenger seat.

My mother said gently, "That was a late call." I nodded yes.

"What he want, calling you this late?"

"He was just calling, it's really not a big deal. He's a 24/7 kind of guy when it comes to business. Why you acting like that?"

"Haley, a man does not call a woman at 3 a.m. unless he got something on his mind."

"Bye Mom, I love you." I started the engine.

"I love you too baby. Let's have lunch or something tomorrow, alright?"

"Yeah, alright. Go on Mama, I'll wait until you get in the house." She went inside and closed the door behind her. I drove off. After driving around for forty-five minutes in a circle in Westwood, I spotted the Motor Lodge Motel. I parked and went inside.

"How much are the rooms here for the night?"

"One hundred thirty dollars a night, the middle aged stout blond haired woman said.

"How much for the week?"

"Nine hundred."

"If I stay for two weeks can you give me a discount?"

"No mam, I'm sorry, I can't."

"Alright, well, let me pay you for the week. If I decide to stay longer, I'll just pay you by the day," I handed the woman my Diner's Club card.

"I am sorry ma'am, we do not take Diner's Club."

"What you don't take Diner's Club? How come?"

Shaking her head, the woman said, "We just don't. Some kind of policy thing. I am sorry. We do take American Express, Visa and MasterCard. Would you like to put your charge on one of those cards, ma'am?"

"Yeah, you said you take American Express," I said, fumbling through my wallet full of credit cards before finding the one with the classic Roman centurion logo.

"Yes ma'am."

"Give me a room on an upper floor please."

"Do you want a room on the end—cause I have one or..."

"That's fine give me an end room thanks."

After I settled in the motel room, I called DeMarco. It was about 4 a.m. "Yeah? He answered the cell on the first ring

"What you doing?"

"Who is this?" DeMarco actually sounded a bit upset.

"DeMarco?"

"Yeah?"

"It's Haley!"

"Oh. Your voice sounds different, deeper. At first, I thought you was my baby's mama. I was about to be like 'what the fuck she doing calling me?' What's up with you."

"You," I replied.

"Is that right?"

"Yeah."

"How so."

"Come by and I'll show you."

"Where you at?"

Looking around the motel room, "some motel in Westwood. Come, I'm going to make you an offer you can't refuse," I flirted.

"Hmmm, an offer I can't refuse?"

"Yep."

"You horny Haley? You sure sound like it. You ready to let me touch you?"

"Yeah, I think so," I said biting down on my lip.

"Haley, you been drinking?"

"No, well a lil bit." That was earlier today.

"What was you drinking?"

"Krystal made Apple Martinis. I had three."

"Three Apple Martinis?"

"Well, more like two and a half—cause I didn't quite finish the third glass."

"Oh, so what you want me to come over there or something?"

"Yeah, or something?" We both let out a silly laugh.

"Is that right? What's the address to the motel where you at?" I gave it to him.

"You would wanna hurry up before I change my mind and stay in celibacy."

"I'll be right there. I got to make a quick stop first. Give me an hour."

Aiight, I'll see you then. I'm in room 25, its upstairs. Hey DeMarco, I need to talk to you about something."

"What?"

"We'll talk when you get here."

I figured—correctly—that this was one time DeMarco would not be late. An hour later, almost to the minute, DeMarco knocked at the door. I opened it. "Hello?"

"Hi DeMarco?"

"Hey baby?" I gestured for him to come in side. He walked in—making his way to the queen size bed and sitting down at the foot. The door closed behind him, locking itself. I followed him and sat down next to him. Sitting on the bed, we stared into the mirror attached to the brown wooden dresser in front of us. Temptation was in our eyes.

"So what you doing in a motel, I thought you were staying at your parents' house for a minute," DeMarco said.

"That's a whole other thing. That's what I wanted to talk to you about. Would you believe my parents accused me of sleeping with you. Then they came at me with all these demands and shit. Can you believe that. I'm grown."

"What they say?"

"It really doesn't matter. Hell, Krystal, Camille and Utopia think we sleeping together also."

"Yeah, I already vibe that one. "

"So it ain't just my family and friends, it's yours too," DeMarco voiced. "Haley, I had no idea that we were going through the same things. Last week I was eating lunch with my mama and my grandmother they questioned me hard about you and our relationship. They complained that you and I spend way too much time together and that I liked you and you liked me. They accused me of sleeping with you. Actually they been saying this for the last year and a half now. You know what my grandma asked me?"

"What?"

"She asked me if I was planning on leaving my wife for you. She said that's what she believed. I told her that I found you very attractive and smart and I was like 'I ain't gone lie I been trying to hit it, but Haley, she won't take to any of my advances.' Anyway, I went on assuring her that you were my business partner and friend. I'm just glad to know that I am not the only one going through this. How about that.

So I'm Just sitting there thinking as my family had cornered me about my relationship with DeMarco, so DeMarco's confronted him about his feelings for me.

"My grandmother asked me if I was in love with you. I told her I had feelings for you. She asked me if my feelings was love? Before I could answer she said, "Yep, you're in love. I asked her how do you know when you are love?"

"If she is the first thing you think about when you wake up, and the last thing you think about when you go to sleep, you're in love, son—that's what she said.

"Am I the first thing you think about when you wake up and the last thing you think about when you go to sleep," I asked Demarco. He stared at me for a long time and then told me I was. He went on speaking. "I told her that I was feeling things for you that I have never had never felt for a woman before. I told her that each day I am with you makes me want to get out of the game and settle down. I told her that I was glad I met her at a time in my life where I could really appreciate you for the woman you are. I even told her that I feel like God put you in my life and me in your life cause it was meant for us to be together and support each other. It's like you fill in the gap in my life that I don't. We are a perfect team in more ways than one . When I married Nakeesha I wasn't in love. Divorcing her has nothing to do with me hating her or even disliking her, she is the mother of my children. I could never hate her. I got love for her, but I'm not in love with her. I wish her the best that's one of the reason why I'm letting her keep the house and everything in it when I leave. Nakeesha benefited greatly from being with me. I'm just not happy with her. I felt like she never completed me. I wish that she finds a good man and marry him. Maybe he can give her what I can't. Then I told my grandmother about that time you asked me if I was happily married. I told her that I think you knew the answer before you asked me that question that you knew the truth." I just sat there listening to DeMarco go on. He continued speaking. "What attracted me to you are your looks, your attitude and the fact that you are so smart and a go getter like me. In addition to being fine as hell, you was a different kind of woman than the ones I'd been use to dating, you're educated. And that's what got my attention about you. Wow, and I thought and she even likes a thug like me. I would have thought that a woman like you would be out of my league Haley. That you would have wanted a college-educated black man or something or even a white man. Right before I met you Haley, I became completely disenfranchised with the street life. For the first time I realized I had to make a serious decision concerning my life. It was either roll with it or pump my brakes. I decided to pump my brakes. I started cutting my profit and expanded my game cause the game is sold and it never will be told. I mean I'm still hustling and doing my thang on the low but at the same time I'm staying focused on my goals with you as the woman in my life. I'm tired of living life on the edge. I want to make a change. With Nakeesha I ain't gone ever get out the game. With you I will, I have a future. Plus, you know what Haley?"

"What?"

"I love you."

Wow DeMarco said a lot. That was the deepest conversation he ever had with me. He later told me that after he told his mother he loved me, his mother just started crying and hugged him…

"I love you too DeMarco."

"Yeah, Haley, I ain't even gone lie my boys think we fucking too."

"That's crazy."

"You know what I'm thinking Haley?"

"What?" But I could see it in his eyes.

"I am thinking that sense everybody already has already put us together and are accusing us, we might as well fuck."

"That's how I'm feeling."

"Let's do the damn thing, been wanting to do it for a long time."

"Me to."

Sitting next to each other at the foot of the bed, me and DeMarco stared into the each other's eyes. Feeling awkward, I looked away. But that long-standing barrier was crumbling, and no one, no last-minute reluctance, could stop it from coming down. I looked back into the mirror in front of us. I stared at DeMarco again. I imagined being with him. I wanted him badly. I wanted to feel him inside me. He was staring into the mirror looking at me. After our stare down, he looked around the small dingy room, with the dim lights. "This is the kind of room you could do some serious fucking in," he said.

I laughed out loud. "Funny you said that cause those were just my thoughts." I said.

And so it began.

DeMarco leaned over and planted soft light kisses all over my face and my lip. I turned my head to the side. Slowly, he planted kisses on my cheek, neck and behind my ear. I turned my body into DeMarco's. Embracing his face in my hands, I closed my eyes, and returned his soft kisses on his lip. Our kissing became intense. Our breathing changed. It became heavy. In the two years, we had known one another it was happening for the first time between us and for me the first time in three years. DeMarco stood up from the bed and reached for my hand, taking it inside his. He pulled me up from the bed. Now I was standing in front of him. He placed his hand on my waist—pulling me closer. He caressed my ass in his hands and planted more small kisses over my face and lip. I felt him rising against me.

I whispered into his ear. "I'm taking a shower, you coming?" I turned and walked away. I caught his eyes fixed on my ass as I walked past the mirror. DeMarco followed me into the small white bathroom. I turned on the shower, and fiddled with the hot and cold faucet knobs—going back and forth between the two until I found the right temperature. I began undressing. DeMarco watched my strip act. It was hot that day, ninety-eight degrees. I was dressed light. I pulled my red Dona Karan tank top over my head uncovering my bared breasts, my hardened nipples were sticking straight up. I dropped the matching red Donna Karen shorts to the floor, stepped out of them, and kicked them off to the side. Now, I stood before him with only a red thong on and the medium size gold hoop earrings in my ear that Krystal had given me two years ago as a gift when I got my MBA degree. I was sexy and seductive. Like a new car owner inspecting their new vehicle DeMarco stared at me as if he were looking me over for inspection. With raised eyebrows, he looked me over. He walked up to me and peeked inside my thong—sticking a finger inside and pulling it back.

"You shave," he inquired?

"Always, do you have a preference cause if you don't want me to shave I won't," I said.

"It's cool." However, I do have one request?"

"What's that" I flirted as he moved in closer.

"From now on I want to be the one who shaves it."

"Request granted."

"Let me see what you working with," DeMarco said stepping back from me to get a better look at my body. I flaunted it, turning around with attitude like Naomi Campbell on the runway.

He looked at my body, curved hips and my protruding behind. Then he began his strip tease act. First, he removed his red puff jacket—letting it slide down his shoulder and pulling it off—dropping it to the floor. He slid the red T-shirt and the white T-shirt he wore beneath it, with the Sean Jean logo over his head simultaneously taking them both off at the same time. He followed by pulling off his white socks, his white Sean Jean Jeans followed. Dam he's Sean Jean out I thought to myself as he undressed. But, boy did he look sexy in those jeans that were hanging off his ass. He wore the hell out of them. Now he was standing before me with his white Sean John Boxers on. His dick peeked through the slit in the boxers. I found my eyes fixed on his dick, holy cow, I've found the "fucking beef, USDA beef," I muttered.

"You say something."

"No."

DeMarco's had a black rubber band tied around his dreads. They were pulled back from his face. I touched his face with the tip of my fingers, admiring his features. His nice full lips and his beautiful dark hard body. His muscles outlined his masculine six-foot two-inch frame. His stomach was flat. The result of working out five times a week at the gym. I knew it took a lot of work to get his stomach like that cause it took me a lot of work to get mines like that.

At first, I was going to attack him like a wild animal. I reasoned with myself. First, I could kiss him passionately, and then just fuck him right here and have some serious hardcore sex, I thought.

"Come closer," DeMarco whispered. I walked closer to him—stopping just a few inches shy of him. We were standing so close that I felt his breath on me. He kissed my neck.

"Umm, you smell good. What kind of perfume are you wearing?"

"Issey Miyake."

He continued kissing my neck. "See anything you like," he whispered.

"I sure do," I said taking a step backwards, staring down between his legs. I took a deep breath. Then I spotted his tattoo and he spotted mines. Butt naked, we checked out each other's tattoos.

"Haley, is that a new tattoo?" DeMarco was pointing to the small purple keyboard, with the white and black keys that was tattooed on the small of my back. "Rage" was written across it. "I never noticed it before—you know when you wear you tank tops or your t shirts."

"I been had it. Had it for a while now. "

"Huh, that's nice."

I looked him over. I saw three letters tattooed on his forearm. "What's this?" "Gang literature from when I was a youngsta in Oakland."

"What gang you belonged to?" DeMarco ignored my question.

"And what's this?" I ran my fingernails over a female's name—Victoria—tattooed next to his heart.

"That's my sister. She died when I was twelve. She got shot."

"Oh I'm sorry to hear that, what happened?"

"Some crazy shit—her murderer was never caught. A lot of people said that it was her boyfriend. I never met him. Well, I did see him once after she died. Anyway, he was a new guy she'd been dating. She actually was murdered in Iowa. She had been living there for about a year. I hadn't seen her in about a year and a half."

"Oh well being that that's your sister, its cool for you to have her name on you, I guess." I expected my words to bring a smile to DeMarco's face, but he didn't smile. He acted as if he didn't hear my comment.

"What's this I said pointing to the scar on his right shoulder then at the other one just beneath his right nipple."

"Gunshot wounds from a 22."

I touched the wounds with the tips of my fingers. "How did these happen," I asked.

"It's nothing." he responded. "This one," he said, pointing at his shoulder, "was just in and out." Pointing to the one right below his nipple he said, " I ain't gone lie, now this one hurt like a motherfucker, I still remember the pain and that was more than ten years ago."

"How many times have you been shot?"

"Five."

"DeMarco you have got to be careful. I looked at him and in that moment sensed what it would be like to lose him. I felt saddened. "We gotta hurry up and get you outta the game. I can't wait until all of our business ventures take off and we make lots of money. I kissed the gunshot wound beneath his nipple. Then worked my way up to his lips kissing his neck and then his lips again. DeMarco hesitated before kissing me back. I removed my red thong. I pulled his boxers down. His dick sprang up. He stepped out of his boxers. I stepped into the shower. DeMarco followed me into the shower. I lathered the small white washcloth and washed his back. After I finished, he washed mines. After another passionate kissing session in the shower, we got out. I reached for the towel on the towel rack wrapped the white towel around my body. DeMarco followed. He wrapped his around his waist. DeMarco headed to the king-size bed. He sat down on it. I walked over to my overnight Louis Vuitton bag and took out the baby lotion and Johnson's gel out of it. Then I walked over to the bed and handed them to DeMarco.

"Here, put this lotion on my body." DeMarco stood up from the bed.

"Baby lotion," he asked. He looked puzzled."

"I always use baby lotion."

"Is that right," DeMarco said putting the lotion on my stomach, arms, legs and feet.

"Put some on my back and my ass," I said turning around. After DeMarco finished. I snatched the white towel from around his waist, dropping it to the floor. I picked up the pink bottle of Johnson's baby lotion and gel mixing the two together in my palms. I rubbed it all over his hard body.

"Do you want me to fuck the shit out of you or do you want me to make love to you," DeMarco whispered in my ear after I was finished. I rolled my eyes around and thought about it.

"I want you to do a combination of the both. I want you to start gentle though."

"Lay down, here," DeMarco instructed me, pointing to a spot on the bed. I laid on my back.

"How long has it been?"

"Three years."

"Dam!"

"Be gentle, I'm like a virgin."

"You stupid," DeMarco laughed.

"DeMarco put the condom on." I felt him inside me. I pulled back. "Wait a minute—you're skipping the foreplay." I hit him in the chest. "Get up."

"What? We already did that in the shower."

"DeMarco, I want you to eat my pussy."

"What?"

"I want you to go down on me negro, I said. Don't be acting like you do hear me or like you don't eat pussy. Everybody knows all dreadlock brothers go down."

"Man, I really don't be doing this."

"DeMarco, you telling me you don't have oral sex with your wife?"

"Man, I don't be eating bitches pussy."

"Well I ain't no bitch, so eat motherfucker. DeMarco ignored my last comment.

As I was laying on my back with my legs apart, resting my right hand on my right thigh, my other arm folded back behind my head—DeMarco touched the small round earring in my clitoris. With the tips of his finger he played with it.

"You got your clit pierced, he said as he continued fondling the small round gold earring with the tips of his finger. I like that." He smiled.

"Yeah along time ago." Now DeMarco was fondling my hardened nipples. He rolled his tongue around them. I moaned and groaned as they disappeared inside his mouth. DeMarco dropped his head between my knees. I tossed my head back. I held onto the back of his head. I moved to a movement that satisfied my body.

I was moaning and groaning. With DeMarco still between my knees I was walking backwards in bed—running away from him. DeMarco stopped momentarily, and looked at me to see what was up with me. He dropped his head back down "WHAT WAS THAT? I shouted.

DeMarco looked up again, "What?" He looked at my body trembling as if I was having a stroke or a seizure or something. DeMarco laughed.

He dropped his head back down between my knees, involuntarily; I pulled them together—squeezing his head between them. Placing his palms between my inner thighs he pushed them back and held them their. "Wait a minute," I called out." The tiny explosions wouldn't stop coming.

DeMarco stopped and laughed. You're tripping.

"I ain't never felt this shit before," I exclaimed. Look at my body, it's shivering. We stared at the unintentional movement of my chest, arms and legs again.

DeMarco shook his head. "Wait a minute are you telling me you ain't never experienced an orgasm before," he questioned?

"Is that what that was?"

He sat on his knees in the bed. "Haley, don't bullshit me—you ain't never had an orgasm?"

"Is that what that was?" DeMarco looked at me questionably. I went on, "I ain't never felt no multiple intense explosions like that before. DeMarco why are you looking at me like that."

He shook his head. "Are you saying you have never came before?"

"No I've done that many of times, but I ain't never felt that deep intense long feeling that I just experienced. After that, I'm going to want to come like that every time I have sex. Are you capable of that?"

"you stupid" DeMarco laughed.

"Are you."

"Of course I am." A stern look appeared across his face.

Now DeMarco was laying on his back. I took him in without touching him. He moaned and groaned so much he sounded like temptations or some other singing group adlibbing to a song. Next, I straddled my body over his. I guided him inside of me. Slowly, I rode him. Holding my body tightly against his DeMarco leaned into me.

Now, DeMarco was on top of me. Exploring his sexuality, I attempted to stick one of my fingers in his ass. He hit me in the head.

"Ouch, what in the fuck is the matter with you," I yelled—grabbing hold of my head. I was angry.

"Haley, I don't play that gay shit."

"What? I'm just exploring you."

"Well, don't explore my ass, I don't play that gay shit. My ass is off limits."

'Well then fuck me hard motherfucker." DeMarco's a good listener.

"Now my face was all squinted up, so was his. I was biting my lip. All those faces he was making made me laugh. I opened my mouth, letting out a loud scream, I embraced his head. Folding my arms over it, I grasped it tightly. DeMarco and I came slowly. The sex was good. DeMarco held me in his arms the entire night. When daylight came and I rose to get out of bed he tugged me back down. "What are you going? I got to take a shower and get ready for work."

"Play hooky with me today and stay in bed."

"I can't do that I got to go to work and make money, so I can pay my bills."

"But you work for yourself stay here with me. Come on stay in bed with me."

"Man, I got to go to work and make some money so I can pay my bills,"

I said seriously.

" I'll pay you your day's salary."

"DeMarco, DeMarco, DeMarco. You are crazy."

"How about it, you stay with me."

"Let me get this right, if stay here with you—you gone pay me a days work."

"Yes. How much is it?"

"$125 an hour times 8 hours, that would make you owe me a G.

"A G it is then."

"DeMarco."

DeMarco raised his head up from the pillow. He looked at me. "Now, what's the matter?"

"What are we going to do?"

"Stay in bed and fuck all day."

"But, if you paid me that would make me feel like a hoe or something. You know, you 'd be like paying me to let you fuck me."

"What. You're kidding right."

"Well."

"Stop Haley. I don't want to hear it. Are you going to stay with me or what?"

"Yes I'll stay with you." He laid his head back down on the pillow.

I thought about DeMarco and our lovemaking. What impressed me most about DeMarco's lovemaking was that he was interested throughout it how he was doing, how he was making me feel. It was obvious that pleasing me was at the forefront of his mind. This impressed me because this didn't seem to be the case with most black men.

Laying in his arm, I asked, "DeMarco tell me something about your childhood."

"What you wanna know?"

"Ummm, what was it like growing up in East Oakland? What you do for fun when you lived there?"

"Let's see what was it like growing up in East Oakland. What did I do for fun," DeMarco repeated.

Well, I guess I'll start here since you wanna know about me and you try-ing to figure me out and shit."

"DeMarco, I ain't trying to figure you out," I said jokingly.

"Yeah right, whateva."

"Negro, I figured you out a long time ago." I leaned over and kissed him on the lip.

Lying back in his arms, "I'm listening—tell your story," I said.

Haley, where I was born and raised in East Oakland's, 6-9 Ville, you can call it the jungle. It was all about survival of the fittest. Only the strong survived. It was like living in and surviving little Beirut. The drug dealers, users, pimps and others who led a life of crime were my mentors. I wanted to be like the drug dealers 'cause they had money and everything you could ever want in life. In the hood you can be broke, aiight or rich. I wanted to be rich. That's why I chose to be like the successful drug dealers I knew. The dealers, they took me under their wings and looked after me. They raised me on the streets, I learned lessons on how to survive in East Oakland's 6-9 Ville, a.k.a. The "Black Hole, a.k.a. Little Beirut".

They called it by these names 'cause of the all the crime, the violence and the murders that occurred there. You know, some terrorists or whatever could shoot up some shit hole on the other side of the world and the cameras would be all over it, but when the killings went down in Oakland, no one cared. When I was growing up Oakland was the murder capital of the world followed by East Palo Alto, a.k.a. EPA, that was less than 45 minutes away across the Hayward Bridge and Sacramento to the east, about a hour and a half's drive from Oakland.

To survive in an environment like the one I came from, you had to be a thug. Everybody wanna say 'it's bad to be a thug', but they wrong. A thug keeps it real. A thug is what he does, what we gotta do to stay afloat. A thug is highly respected in the streets for his actions in the street. A thug will do what he gotta do to survive even if it's wrong. Just 'cause you a thug don't mean that you are a murderer or a robber. All thugs don't get down like this just like all people don't get down like this, but some do. Seems like that's what my whole life has been about, surviving and searching. When I started living the thug life, I could barely jump off the porch.

"To make money and to survive, I did my "thug thang" on the streets of east Oakland. When most kids were at home sleeping at ten and eleven at night, I would be chilling with the big homies on the block. At nine years old, I sold my first sack and started getting into trouble. Hustling, shooting dice, and experiencing the street life. I was fresh wild in the streets and raised more hell than the devil himself. Before I left East Oakland and moved to Compton, I was running the drug scene in all of East Oakland and West Oakland and in some areas of San Francisco. Drug dealers were buying from me. I was considered a "ghetto mayor", a young tycoon—this is what the real ballers were to the people in our community. The different individuals from the area, they was hustlers. East Oakland use to be popping back in the days. In East Oakland on East 14th and 69th you could do anything you wanted to do. Get your hustle on and do your thug thang. It was like you roll through, and you'd see all your friends and whoever you wanted to see from the area. Basically, if you were looking for someone who was from Oakland and you couldn't find them—roll through East 14th and you'd be sure to find them. About four years ago, East 14th was all paradise. Black men weren't beefing with each other then, and it wasn't all that killing. It was cool.

"In the end, it seems everybody got it how they lived. I mean I have seen family members and friends kill and be killed. Ever since I could remember, ever since I was a little boy, it seems every month I knew someone personally who had died at the hands of violence. Now, as an adult it's every fucking week that someone I know personally dies. I have gone to so many funerals and served as pallbearer that I've stopped counting.

"You know what Haley?"

"What?"

"After moving to Compton is when I made my real money. I balled even harder in the game there than I did at home back in East Oakland and I started moving up even further. People started calling me a kingpin and shit. At first I didn't pay it much attention, but one day it dawned on me I was. I had sets sewn up in California, Washington and Oregon and was even moving my supply into Vancouver up in Canada and even a few cities in the Midwest. I am so deep in the game that I now require the other dealers who buy from me to cop a thirty thousand dollar minimum every time they step to me. My procedure is they pay me upfront and a week later they get it at a designated place. Without fail, I never let them down. This is my reputation.

"Why do I do it? Having a lot of money feels so good. Nobody in my family wants for nothing—not even my mother who truthfully speaking I am still angry with, but fuck it. Next thing I know, a lot of the local rappers was coming up to me asking me to put out their albums and I would turn them down. One day, watching Eazy E in this television interview, I realized that through music I could make a whole lot of money, get rich legally and not have the law on my back so I took some of those rappers up and put out their music for them and started Life Inc. Records.

"In spite of everything I've gone through growing up in East Oakland, I had some of the best times in my life there as a kid playing. I remember I use to cut class at McClymond's High to hang out at the Eastmont Mall with my friends, playing video arcades and shit. You remember River Raid and Donkey Kong? I musta spent a whole month playing those games."

"So, that's why you drive the way you do?" I giggled.

DeMarco grinned. "In middle school, me and my friends use to cut school and visit other schools, getting at the females, and we was doing our thug thang on the block. When you missed too much school, Truancy would come looking for you. Man, they would even show up at your door. If Truancy caught you, they would take you to Oakland Unified School District's main office, downtown on 12th street, and you had to stay there until your parents came for you late in the evening, and if they didn't come you'd be taken to Juvenile Hall. My mom didn't show up this one time, and I went to juvenile. That was a fucked up feeling—you know?"

"Umm."

"Truancy caught me twice, but before they caught me the first time, I must have got away from them at least eight times. I'll never forget the first time Truancy caught me. It seemed like the longest run of my life, I'll tell you."

"What about your mother—your parents? They weren't there for you?'

"Man my mother was fucking hoe—you know there's eight of us. We all got different fathers. Man, she was tossed. She just old now and acts different. She's changed. Even my grandmother use to be off the hook."

He looked in my eyes. "Honestly, Haley I have been searching for a long time for a woman like you."

"Stop it, DeMarco."

"No, really I have."

"Well now that you've found me what are you going to do?"

"Hold you tight and never let you go. I am going to keep you with me always, Haley."

"How long is 'always' going to be for you, DeMarco? Why don't you stop while you are ahead and get out of the game."

"Never that. Anyway after things wasn't happening for us, my grand-mother decided to move our family here—to Los Angeles—Compton— to another disheartened environment in search of a better life. For years before we moved here she owned a home in Compton. She's originally from Compton. When she moved I decided too follow. I was already doing business in south-ern California and my business was doing well. I gathered up some of my boys that I trusted and brought them here with me to LA.

"Now that I am older Haley I think about the consequences of my con-duct, and I have changed. Believe it or not, had you met me five years ago or even four years ago, you would not have liked me and we would have not have got along as good as we do. I was hell. I didn't give a fuck about nothing. I didn't care about nothing or no one—especially females."

"What made you change?"

"Just getting older, seeing things differently, having children—daughters especially. I wouldn't want a guy doing to my daughters some of the shit I did to females. I'd kill them. Remember when females use to wear dookie braids?"

"Yeah, I had some."

"When a female would piss me off—I mean really piss me off—I use to snatch one of her dookie braids out of her hair. Man, I had a whole lot of them on my dresser. Yeah, I think it was my girls that really changed me, and made me start looking at things differently. Anyway, I still do my dirt. I just try and keep on the low. I guess you could say over the years I became more street-savvy about the way I do my thug thang. But Haley, I am tired of being in the game. I'm tired of the hustle and looking over my back and shit. Tired not knowing who to trust. Tired of trying to figure out who the snitch is this month. I am just tired, tired, tired. I just want out of it. Well that's enough about that. Now, you know my life story."

"It's sad, but it's about survival of the fittest, and that you are."

Twenty-seven

"Hello."

"Hey girl."

"Hey girl."

"What you doing Krystal?"

"Just working."

"Camille, something is troubling me. I need to talk to you. Can we meet today for lunch?"

"Yeah, sure. What's on your mind?"

"Haley."

"Haley?"

"Yeah and that DeMarco situation. Her mother called me last night. She's also having issues with Haley and DeMarco's relationship. Anyway, you know Haley's been staying at her parents place while her place is being painted. Well, to make a long story short her mother thought she'd been out all night with DeMarco when she went home last night or early this morning I should say. Haley wanted me to confirm with her mother that she'd been at my house."

"What?"

"Yeah, girl. I am worried about her. She's losing herself in love with DeMarco. You and I both know it's not a good thing, he's married. Girl, we

221

got to talk to her."

"Girl, Haley knows what she's doing."

"Haley has no idea what she is in for as soon as his wife gets home. I don't know when her time's up, but it's soon. She will be home soon. Haley's my girl and I don't want to see her hurt."

"She's my girl too and I also don't want to see her hurt. Look, the two of them are just friends. She hasn't even slept with him."

"That's what she tells us. Let's say it's true though and she has not yet slept with him—how much longer can she hold out as much as they are together?"

"So you think that DeMarco is going to hurt her?"

"Not intentionally, but she is bound to get hurt. Camille, the man is married."

"Girl, I don't know. I think we should just stay silent on this one. I mean we both have already talked to her and told her what we thought about her relationship with DeMarco. We have already stated our case. Let's just leave it alone. In the end no matter what happens, we'll be here for her—like we are for each other always anyway. It's not like Haley didn't have our backs before when we fucked up. If that bitch Nakeesha gets out of place with our girl—we'll just have to kick her ass."

"You don't feel me Camille, forget it. Forget that I even called you. I will talk to Haley by myself."

"Girl, where you wanna meet?"

"Naw, forget it."

"Krystal, where do you want to meet?"

"Forget it."

Look girl, I ain't got time for this. I am at work. Now, where do you want to meet?"

"Let's meet at the Olive Garden, the one near your job."

"When?"

"In an hour."

"Alright, see you there. Bye."

"Bye."

Camille was running about 20 minutes late; the traffic was abominable. When she got to The Olive Garden, it was packed. She looked around; Krystal was already sitting at the bar. Camille sat down on the barstool next to her. "Girl, you drinking this early in the day," Camille asked, pointing to her glass.

"Girl this is water and ice."

"Oh, it looks like gin on the rocks."

"No, that's my Friday and Saturday night special."

"Oh yeah, I almost forgot you are just a weekend drunk." Krystal shook her head. A smirk appeared across her face.

"They're paging us," Krystal said, sticking her hand inside the pocket of her powder-blue trench coat and pulled out the little white pager with the Olive Garden logo. She and Camille made small talk as they walked to the front of the restaurant and approached the guy in charge of the name list and give him back the pager.

"Krystal, I like your coat. Is that new?"

"Girl, I been had this coat. I brought it at Macy's when I lived there like 2 years ago. It was on sale. I got this coat for only thirty bucks. It was originally four hundred dollars and they just marked it on down and down."

"What?"

"Come with me this way ladies," the waiter said.

Camille and Krystal reached the table; the waiter deposited the menus onto it. "Girl go on and sit down, I'll be right back. I gotta go to the restroom. Order for me," Krystal said.

"What do you want to eat?"

"Get me what you get."

"Alrightie."

Camille sat down and picked up the menu. *Everything looks good when you're starving,* she thought. It didn't take her long to choose her order. And Krystal's. She signaled the Italian waiter to come and take the order; he hurried over. He looked like someone right out of the *Godfather* movies.

"Are you ready to order Miss, or do you wish to wait for your friend.

"No, I am ready to order. I will be ordering for the both of us"

"Ok ma'am."

The waiter pulls his order sheet out from the pocket on his green apron.

"What would you like to order ma'am?"

"We'll have the Smoked Ravioli with Portabella Mushrooms, and two Raspberry Lemonades.

"Ok ma'am."

"Would you like soup or salad?"

"What's the soup choice?"

"Zupa Toscana."

"I had that before. It's good, but I think we will have the salad."

Krystal returned to the table, talking on her cell phone. Handing me the cell she says, "Here, Haley wants to talk to you. She called me when I was in the bathroom. I told her the two of us were having lunch."

"So what y'all doing—chopping me up," I asked.

"Girl, no, we are just having lunch."

"Y'all phony as hell; the two of you talking about me doesn't change a thing."

"Girl, it ain't even like that."

"Right and y'all suppose to be my girls."

"That's real girl, but…""I'll talk to you later," I said.

"Girl, wait a minute you got it all wrong. We care about you, and if Nakeesha wanted to throw them with you, we got yo back. But girl, DeMarco is married, and you are supposed to respect that."

"It's not that simple."

"I know. Let's talk. What are you doing after work? Can you stop by?"

"I got studio tonight; we got some rappers coming through."

"You and DeMarco huh. What time is studio?"

"Eight o'clock."

"What time do you get off work?"

"Five."

"So let's get together before you go to the studio."

"I am having dinner with DeMarco before studio. I would ask you to join us, but being that you don't like him I don't think that would be a good idea."

"Girl I ain't never said that I hate DeMarco. For the record, I don't hate DeMarco, Haley. Do I think he's a user? Yes, I do. Anyway, I need to talk to you; me and Krystal need to talk to you." Krystal reached for the phone. "Hold on, Krystal wants to speak with you."

She took the phone. "So I take it you can't stop by Camille's after work?"

"I got a prior engagement."

How about tomorrow after work, it's Friday?

"I am going to the Juvenile concert with DeMarco. I can't."

"How about Saturday."

"Yeah, we could hook up then, but it will have to be before five."

"Alright, see you then."

"Bye."

"See you in a minute." Krystal clicked the cell off, looking miffed. "Damn, that girl has got DeMarco on the brain. She is even starting to sound like him. You know what she just said before hanging up, she said 'see you in a minute.' That's DeMarco's talk."

"Yeah, instead of saying 'goodbye'—he does say 'see you in a minute'."

"Anyway after y'all left my house the other night around two in the morning, Haley called me with her mother, she was like 'Krystal my mother does not believe that I have been at your house, she thinks I was with DeMarco. Anyway, she is standing right here for you to confirm where I've been'. Mrs. Jones got on the phone. I told Haley I left my place about twenty minutes ago and that we had all been hanging out."

"What? You serious, her mom called you."

"Yep."

"Girl, in the end you know who is going to get hurt."

"Who?"

"Two people."

"Haley and DeMarco."

"No, Haley and DeMarco's wife. DeMarco knows how to separate his emotions. He knows how to keep things in perspective and not get lost in love. He ain't gone be hurt in the end, trust me."

"Huh?"

"Camille, I mean look at the whole scenario. While Nakeesha is away her husband is having a ball. He's fucking everybody. "Now, I say all of this to say this about DeMarco the user. He seizes opportunities. DeMarco wanted a better life, and he met a woman who wanted a better life. She had more than any other woman he had ever met and she became his wife, but now he knows Haley, and she is her replacement. With his wife, DeMarco feels stuck. He never truly loved his wife. He only married his wife because she wanted him to and he felt obligated since she took the rap for him. The fact of the matter is DeMarco knows that if he stays with her, he will never get out of the game, and he does want out badly.

"That's why he's investing in music and putting out CDs. His wife has taken him as far as she can. I think that DeMarco sees Haley as the person who could help him advance to the next level. It's not so much that he loves Haley, but she is his ticket that will advance him to the next level. He's seen Haley at work. We have all seen Haley at work. We admire her. She is a go-getter. She is a smart woman. She's got a mouthpiece on her. She can talk her ass off and she's a good negotiator. He knows as well as we do that Haley knows how to create and take advantage of opportunities. Bottom line, the girl knows how to make things happen. Because he is so opportunistic, he does not want to lose Haley. Bottom line: DeMarco only cares about himself. Other than himself, the only people I think he genuinely loves are his children. I'll give him that much. But that's it. That's all.

"We have sat there and listened to Haley talk about him. His whole thing with his mistresses is just not to bring it home. If it gets home then it's a problem and the mistress has to go, and this is when Haley is going to get hurt. Remember what Haley said about what DeMarco said about what happens when his wife finds out about one of his affairs. He tells her 'the bitch was paying me and if you say I can't see them any more, then I'll stop'. So they have an understanding: he can cheat and do his thing, but don't bring it home. He's careful not to do this."

"Damn girl, you are sure speaking the truth, but you know what I think. When Haley needs us, I think that we should just be there for her. Haley is smart. She already knowing. Let's just back up and give her her space. The truth is I am really rooting for Haley and DeMarco. I really hope that DeMarco leaves his wife and I hope that he and Haley make it. I see them going far together. They are both so smart. Both so ambitious. Yeah, you said some stuff on point; however, I do not agree with everything you said. I mean yeah we know DeMarco's history with women. It's pretty much the same as every black man and all the men we've dated."

Krystal interrupted, holding her index finger up in the air as if she was pointing at something. She rolled her head around, and said so seriously and with attitude, "I have *never* dated a man who was married."

"Yeah, but we have had our share of men with DeMarco's personality traits—that's all I am saying."

"So what? Do you not agree with what I said?"

I don't think that DeMarco is using Haley. I think that initially it may have started this way, but I don't think that that is the way it is now. I think that the relationship grew on DeMarco just like it grew on Haley. Their feelings for one another, you know. DeMarco respects Haley. You have to admit respect to women ain't something he's known for, but his respect for Haley is so apparent. I think you're right when you say that he wants her to help him advance to the next level and personally, I don't see anything wrong with that.

"I also think that Haley is a hell of a woman and DeMarco has never met a woman like her. I think that before his wife, DeMarco probably never even got caught up with a woman before. His wife caught him up—that's why he married her. I think that what DeMarco is feeling for Haley right now, he probably himself did not know that he could feel. This is what I see. Now you can agree with me or you don't have to, but just as love crept upon Haley and she fell in love with DeMarco, love also crept up on DeMarco and he fell in love with Haley. It was bound to happen. She's beautiful, he's handsome, they have a lot in common, and they spent a great deal of time together. They confide in one another about personal issues, they are close. If Haley gets hurt in the end, she'll deal with it and she'll get over it. We all do. And it will just be a growing experience for her, a lesson learned."

Twenty-eight

The sex was so good with DeMarco the night before that I called him the following evening and asked him if he wanted to meet and do it again. Readily he agreed. He told me to meet him at his house. In twenty minutes.

With his shirt off, bare feet and only his pants on and the black belt that looped through the loops of his charcoal gray Dolce Gabbana suit pants DeMarco sat on the white leather chase in the bedroom. I entered wearing a shiny black patent leather dominatrix suit. The zipper on the suit was zipped down to the top of my 34 D breast. My hardened nipples pierced through the patent leather leaving and indent. The tightness of the suit accentuated my body curves—my small waist, firm 32-inch stomach, my hips, and protruding ass that black women are known for. A black velvet and patent leather trimmed cat woman mask covered my face. My big round made up eyes with its fake long eyelashes looked through the two holes in the mask. On my feet, I wore a pair of thigh high, black stiletto patent leather boots. I carried a rolled-up black leather whip in hand. The end of the whip was in my mouth; I was biting down on it. My Mac Currant lined—O colored lips covered the tip of the whip. I was sexy, alluring, towering, voluptuous and arousing in the attire.

Aroused, you could see the bulge of DeMarco's raised up dick pressing against the inside of his Dolce's.

DeMarco rose from the chase. "What you gone do with that whip," he asked pointing at it, walking in my direction.

"Oh this thing," I said removing my eyes off DeMarco temporarily glancing at the whip I held in my hand and then back at him. I raised whip in the air. I looked at it again, lowered it back down to my side and stared back at DeMarco. "I'm going to beat yo ass—that's all," I said nonchalantly in a seductive voice. My eyes moved down to the bulge in his pants. I lifted my eyes back up to DeMarco and licked my lips. A smirk appeared across his face. "Naw, it ain't going down like that he said, waving his two hands in the air. He took a step backwards as I approached him.

"What are you scared of DeMarco?"

"I ain't scared of shit, but I ain't into having my ass beat while fuck-ing—that's not my fetish or fantasy. Hell me fighting with a nigguh on the streets is enough. I dam sho don't need to be fighting in the bedroom with my woman while we having sex.

"I dam sho don't need to be fighting in the bedroom with my woman while we having sex," I repeated, mimicking him in a baby voice. "Scaredy cat," I teased as I walked closer to him and kissed him on the lip.

"Yeah, Haley I might let you blow me or something, but you ain't beating my ass," DeMarco said.

"And I might let you blow me," I snapped back abruptly. Bringing him back to the conversation, and the mood, I lowered my voice to a whisper, "So you are not going to let me fulfill my fantasy." I said seductively. I was pouting.

"You can fulfill your fantasy, but choose another one or you can close your

eyes and imagine that you are beating my ass or imagine that you sticking your finger up my ass like you tried to do last time we was in bed and I hit you in yo god dam head. I don't play that shit. Close your eyes and imagine that you are doing whatever with those beads or whatever shit that is you brought from the sex store when we went to get that lubricant that I told you don't get and that you was wasting your money on cause you wasn't using it on me—make that your fantasy."

I rolled my eyes and sighed. "DeMarco you don't choose or create some-one's fantasy for them. It's the one who fantasizes that creates his or her own fantasy.

"Man, Whatever. Look, fuck that shit. I'm experimental in the bedroom. I'm a freak like you. I will do just about anything with you in bed Haley except for what have already told you I won't do. Other than that everything is pretty much cool. Haley I don't even want to have this discussion no more with you." DeMarco was agitated.

"You scared?"

"You can call me whatever you want," DeMarco said undoing his belt buckle, the button on his pants, and the zipper and then sliding them off, "but naw Haley; I can't let you beat my ass. I ain't that kind of man. You must be confusing me with some white boy you fucked in college from the suburbs or something and let you do some crazy manie shit like that to him." Now he was standing before me in white—one hundred dollar Dolce Gabbana boxers with the black trim around the waist.

"I ain't never fucked a white boy. I only been with brothers," I snapped. Dam why did DeMarco always have to be so patronizing.

"Well them some gay motherfuckers." I found myself becoming incensed. Had I not been so horny I would have walked out and left his ass right there where he was standing in the bedroom with his hard on. However, my body longed for the sex.

"So what's up? You gone give me some pussy or we just go stand here and talk," DeMarco said. I shook my head, let his last remark go through one ear and out the other, stepped up to DeMarco and clasped my arms around his neck. I kissed him on the lip passionately. He grabbed me by the waist, pulled me into him as if we were not already close enough and kissed me back passionately. While we were kissing DeMarco reached behind me and removed the leather whip from my hand tossing it across the room.

"Dam baby you look good." he said raising my arm and taking a step backwards. Although, I was petite, a size five, and hundred and twenty pounds, I was towering in the costume. I moved in closer to DeMarco. With his boxers still on I rubbed my body up against his. Standing upright, DeMarco lifted my body onto his. He held my body tight—palming a buttock in each hand. After the storm came and left, I slid to the floor. Now, he was groaning. WHAT WAS THAT, DeMarco shouted. Move, back up, back up back wait a minute Haley." I leaned back on my knees. He held his pointing finger up in the air, "Haley wait a minute hold on. I stared at him.

"Ah shit, DeMarco kept saying over and over again. It must have been one of those thirty-minute orgasms.

"What was that?"

"What was what, I asked?"

"That? Feeling."

I shook my head unbelievingly. "DeMarco, are you saying that you never had an orgasm before?"

"Naw, I had organisms before, but never no shit like that." I smiled, I knew I had him hooked. Yeah, DeMarco was sprung. In all honesty after the first time we made love I knew I had him hooked. I don't care how powerful or how strong a man is, or how much thug he got in him, he always has a weakness for women and inadvertently can be controlled by a woman and her pussy. Pussy makes the world go round. Women, with our pussy's, we control men. I held DeMarco Speed, CEO of Life Inc. Records, executive producer, multimillionaire kingpin, under the control of my pussy. A bad bitch can control a man. It doesn't take rocket science for a woman to become a bad bitch. A woman who's been there and done that can learn from her trials and errors in a relationship how to be a bad bitch. She has to take what she's learned from those lessons and apply it. Most importantly she cannot give in. The right woman can break any man. That was DeMarco's problem. He'd never been caught up with a woman before and he never met a bad bitch—like me—only bitches that thought they were bad. Bitches he reversed the game on cause they really didn't have they game down. Like I said, it's about learning from those mistakes and knowing how just how to get inside a man's head and break his ass down mentally from time to time, you know.

DeMarco let the zipper down on my patent leather jump suit and slid it off my shoulders. It dropped down to the floor. In the bed I laid on my back. He got on top of me.

"I reached up and grabbed a handful of his long black dreads, squeezing them. "Ouch, let up off my hair you pulling too tight. I spread my fingers apart, his dreads released through the openings of my fingers—from my grip as I climaxed. Say my name?" I was commanding.

"Haley."

"Ahhh shit." DeMarco was really into it.

My name say it."

"Haley, Haley, Haley, Haley, he called out."

Now the room was quiet. I lay with my head turned sideways. DeMarco relaxed on top of me. We dosed off to sleep.

The next morning I woke up, showered, and got dressed and left him sleeping in his king size bed I left him a dollar on the nightstand. I didn't call DeMarco for two days, by the time day three rolled around he was blowing up my cell. Finally, I decided to answer.

"Haley, what's up with you, I haven't heard from you? What's the matter? Was the sex good, was I good?"

"You were all right." He was silent on the other end.

Damn, the truth is he was the best fuck of my life, but I didn't want him to know that. Not yet anyway.

Twenty-nine

DeMarco began to display new behaviors. His lateness, no-shows, and disappearing acts were becoming regular occurrences, and I didn't like it. They became my number one pet peeve, and led to our first big disagreement when he failed to pick me up on Christmas Day to see *Ali,* starring Will Smith. For more than two months, I had known that I was going to see *Ali* on Christmas Day. Everybody who knew me knew this. It's all I talked about. On Christmas Eve several of us were at the recording studio, talking. The engineer asked me what my Christmas plans were, and I told him that I was going to see *Ali.* DeMarco was there, too, and asked if he could go. "Sure," I told him.

DeMarco called me at noon on Christmas day. He informed me that he was heading to the theatre to pick up the tickets for the night show. "Some of my artists wanna go with us. I'll get our tickets for all of us for the 9:00 show tonight," he said. He called me again a few hours later to let me know that he had purchased the tickets.

"I'll be at your house at seven thirty to pick you up, Haley." Seven thirty comes, but I don't hear from DeMarco. Eight o'clock comes; I don't hear from DeMarco. Eight fifteen comes; I still don't hear from DeMarco. So, I called him. He didn't answer his cell. Ten minutes later, he called. By now, it was 8:25 p.m. "Haley, I am on my way to get you. I should be there in ten minutes." 8:40 came, and still no DeMarco. The clock moved around to five before nine. No DeMarco. So I called him again, and I have to admit that by now, I was irritated with his delay.

"DeMarco, what's up? Where you at? It's almost nine, the movie starts in like, half an hour, and we got to go all the way to the valley to the theatre! We'll never make it."

"Yes, we will. I am almost at your house."

"Look, DeMarco, if you are not coming now then don't come Fuck it. You keep saying you coming, that you are on your way, but you still not here."

"Look, Haley, I am almost there. I'll be there."

I was out of patience. Just what the hell was the hold-up? "DeMarco, if you are not coming now, don't come. Bye." I hung up.

Now it was a quarter after nine. No fucking way were we going to make that movie without a helicopter. Yes, I was pissed. So I called him on his cell and ask him what was up.

"What do you mean, wassup?! I just got on the bridge, you said that you didn't wanna go."

"I don't fucking believe this! You stood me up. You stood me up!"

"Now come on, Haley, you said don't come and get you."

"No, DeMarco, I said that if you are not on your way, then don't come and get me."

"Oh, now you playing games? You said don't come and get you… that's what you said, Haley." DeMarco was talking. I was yelling.

"I can't believe that you fucking stood me up!" I hung up the cell.

Not even five minutes later, DeMarco called back. "Man, Haley, you said that you didn't want to come. Let me drop these nigguhs off and then I will come and get you."

The phone rang back ten minutes later. "Man, Haley, there is too much traffic out there. I will just take you to see it tomorrow or something."

I hung up the phone on him again, without so much as a response.

The following morning, he called again. "Hey, Haley, I am on my way to see you. We need to talk. I'm going to stop by your house."

"Okay" *I'll believe it when I see it*, I thought. That subtext probably came out in my voice, but I was making no apologies.

Within twenty minutes, DeMarco pulled up in front of my house. I came out and got in his Hummer. Nervously, he looked at me. He reached down and pulled up two movie tickets. Sighing, he said, "Here, these are for you. They're for the show that starts at 3:30 today at Magic Johnson Theatres in the Crenshaw Mall. Look, Haley, about last night… I would have never left you on purpose, but you said that you didn't want to go."

"No, DeMarco, I didn't say that. I said that if you were not coming now, then don't come. You'd been leading me on for hours, saying that you were on your way." DeMarco apologized again. He extended his handshake. "Can we put this behind us and move forward from here?"

DeMarco wasn't the type to apologize. That he did meant a lot to me. I still didn't completely forgive him, but I shook his hand. Unfortunately, his no-shows and his lateness were becoming new patterns.

Next, he stood me up at the studio. I was upset, but I let it go after he explained he had some impromptu business to handle and got caught up. Being stood up while at the studio happened a couple of more times. I avoided the subject for a while and just put up with it, so "sooner or later" became "later." The truth is, I knew what he was into before I got with him. I'm sure he was handling his business. I mean, he was a businessman running a big business. He had a staff to supervise and a lot to oversee. He even told me from the gate that a lot of times he would not be able to attend the recording sessions at the studio because he had his plate full with his business.

DeMarco often expressed how he wanted out of the game, and wanted to be there with me more. I believed him, but at the moment he was deep-in with both feet. From time to time, he'd take one of them out and put it in the music business, as he had been doing with his label company and the other CDs he'd put out; so, periodically, he'd help me. But DeMarco still made his money from the game. Therefore, the game was the most important to him, and not the entertainment business. His goal was to make the entertainment business his exit out of the drug business.

Unfortunately, women like me still existed. Women who thought we could be demanding and change a brother. Like a lot of other women, I learned the hard way that you really can't change a brother from the block until he's ready to change. Taming a guy who is in the game is harder than taming a wild horse. The horse is the easy chore. Eventually, the animal gives in, but brothers like DeMarco who are in the game with big egos and control issues are more than just a simple challenge. You just need to leave them be and work around them and their issues. In time, you hope that they see the light.

So, I kept putting off meeting with him to express how I felt about his disappearing acts and his inability to keep his word as of late. I figured that eventually, I'd talk to him about the way I was feeling. But even "later" comes, and "eventually" soon follows. One day, however, "eventually" arrived. DeMarco was supposed to meet me at the studio at noon to help me run the session. He was complaining that Malik and Walter were overcharging us.

DeMarco had said that he wanted to run the next session, and that he'd be there. "Running a session" basically meant keeping the rappers in line and watching the engineer who always tried to take longer to mix down a song so that he could make that much more money. In short, the job entailed keeping production up and bullshit down. Because he complained about how the studio robbed us, he decided to attend all sessions from here on out to deal with the engineer and the hours. But afternoon came, still no DeMarco, and the rappers were shooting the breeze while the engineer messed around with his dials and levers. I waited for DeMarco to assume his newfound role, but it appeared that he had stood me up again.

Finally, I saw DeMarco. We had dinner at Chevy's, after the long and rather unproductive recording session. He spoke evasively about a lot of bullshit he was currently dealing with. Over chips and salsa, I broke it down to him. "DeMarco, a partnership is suppose to be a fifty-fifty thing. I am tired of all the problems and everything; I am dealing with them alone. I need your help. You say you are going to be there. You always have complaints about this and that, the mix downs, the engineer, everything. You need to be in the studio. You need to be there when the mix downs are happening. You said you were going to be there," I told him.

"First of all… my disapproval or discontent. It's not really complaining, Haley, it's just that I know how the shit is supposed to be. The engineer is not a good engineer. He's lazy, but the mix downs are sounding good now. After I have him remix the song like, five times, and I direct him on what to do, what instruments to bring up, fade in and fade out, they coming out tight." He was about to say something more, but I cut him off.

"But this is about more than what engineer drags out what track. DeMarco, I need you to keep your word with me. If you tell me that you are going to do something, then I expect you to do it. Stop telling me that you are going to do something and you don't."

"Oh, you are talking about Sunday night. I told you my cousin had his baby and I just dropped everything and went to the hospital."

"DeMarco, I was waiting on you. You called me at six and said you were on your

way to the studio. You said you'd be there in twenty minutes."

"I know I was on my way, but then I ended up going to the hospital."

"I called you."

"I turned off my phone. You know you can't keep your phone on in the hospital."

I sighed. "You could have called to let me know you weren't coming. For some reason, I get the picture that you see me asking you to call me if you can't make it to a meeting we have, as me exerting some kind of power over you. You perceive it as me keeping you in check, like I got you reporting to me or something… and it's not even about that. DeMarco, I am your business partner, and we got to be tighter than we are. If we not tight, people see that."

"People see what they wanna see."

"DeMarco, if we not tight people see it. You can't tell me they don't."

"Yeah, you right. We got to be tighter."

"You got to be tighter."

"Alright."

"I was still waiting for you at the studio. I had everybody waiting, 'cause you said you was coming. Do you know how that makes me look? And you suppose to be my business partner? Business partners don't leave their business partners hanging, DeMarco. I mean, think about it: what if I stood you up all the time? If I told you I would be there or that I was doing something and kept you waiting. How would you feel?"

DeMarco stared off into the distance, speechless. I could tell the chronic he was smoking before we met had obviously kicked in. He was stuck.

"What are you doing, DeMarco?"

"I'm just thinking about what you said. Putting myself into your position," he said, staring off into the distance. He continued, "Yeah I see your point. You right, Haley. I won't do that to you again."

"DeMarco, you're confusing me with your bitches and your hoes, and you're making a big mistake."

DeMarco laughed. "No, I have never thought of you in that way."

"Well, when you do shit like ditching me or not showing up when you say you will, that's what you're doing. You're making a mistake. Maybe it's not intentional… all I am saying is, don't treat me like that."

"I would never treat you like that. I don't even see you like that. But you right, I gotta keep my word with you."

"I really hope you mean what you are saying, DeMarco, and you are not doing me like you do your baby's mama when you agree with her just to avoid an argument."

"Oh shit," DeMarco said, and started laughing. "Damn, Haley, I gotta be careful what I share with you."

"DeMarco, I am getting to know you quite well."

"Haley, I am not bullshitting you like I be bullshitting my babies' mamas."

"DeMarco, I really like you and I really want to work with you, but you are not giving me nothing to work with. I'm done."

"What do you mean?"

"I'm done."

"What do you mean?"

"Whateva you think I mean!"

"Well, what do you want me to do?"

"Whateva you think needs to be done." I stood up from the table and headed to the Hummer on the parking lot. DeMarco paid the bill and followed me out of the restaurant. When he exited the restaurant he spotted me next to the Hummer. Approaching the truck, he hit the alarm button on his key chain, unlocking the door. We both got in.

"Look, Haley, if you want to go on and continue the comp without me, and you wanna do your thing without me, that's fine. I am still here for you, though. And if you need anything, let me know. I will give it to you. I keep my word to you. But maybe you should do the comp on your own. I listen to you talk, and your ideas there different from my ideas. You want to drop and promote in the South and the Midwest, and I feel we should drop and promote right here." Reaching into his coat pocket, DeMarco pulled out a roll of cash. The two bills on the outside were hundreds. DeMarco didn't need to play the game of rolling a bunch of ones and fives with a couple hundreds on the outside to make it look fat; with DeMarco, what you saw was what you got, and I knew I was looking at a wad of better than three Gs' worth of green.

He handed me the wad. "Here, Haley, just as I promised. Here's the money for the studio time. If you need anything else, just let me know. I want you to do some PR for my label; I'll pay you for it. Let's try and meet next week and I will let you know what I need." We were not back in front of my house. DeMarco leaned over and kissed me on the cheek. I got out of the truck. Closing the door behind me. He rolled down the window and yelled, "I love you Haley!"

I turned around and called out his name, "DeMarco…"

I could see the surprise in his eyes. They lit up. I walked closer to his truck and looked through the rolled-down window. "I don't want it to end this way . Let's finish what we started. Let's just move forward."

DeMarco extended his handshake; I extended my hand, and shook his. "Haley, I believed you when you said that you really liked me and that you really cared about me. I also like you and really care about you. I promise I will not ever let you down again. So… does this mean I got my job back?"

"Yes."

"Are you going to fire me again?"

"That depends."

"Depends on what?"

"That depends on if you do some shit again that you suppose to be fired for."

DeMarco let out a boisterous laugh. I smiled, turned, and walked away. He drove off. It was the last time that I saw him, and that was twelve days ago.

Something was definitely going on with him. That was the last conversation I had with DeMarco until he called me today to enquire about a bank deposit, also requesting my presence at his place. Previously, it was unusual to not hear from him for one day, maybe even two; I couldn't remember a twelve-day silence since we became friends.

On the drive over to DeMarco's, I had so much planned to say; boy, I couldn't wait to see him. However, I decided that when I got there, I would let him do most of the talking since it was his agenda, and he was the one who called the meeting in the first place. Then, after he would finish, I would let him have it about not returning my phone calls for days and remind him that we are still business partners. For all he knew during his silence from me, we could have had a business dealing to contend with. I was also going to hit him hard about standing me up on a few occasions and for his frustrating disappearing acts.

Thirty

I pulled my Range into the driveway of DeMarco's home, behind the Lamborghini sitting between the well-known Hummer and Range Rover. I got out and walked up the stairs that led to his big, beautiful San Fernando Valley residence. My new black weave cascaded down my back onto the back of my light blue Chanel suit. It was blowing in the wind. The exquisite-looking home with its two huge, white pillars reminded me of one that you'd see on *MTV Cribs* or *Lifestyles of the Rich and Famous*. I rang DeMarco's doorbell. As I waited for him to come to the door, the security camera above the front door caught my attention as it focused in on me. It moved around, capturing all that it could in its tiny lens. I heard the little motor working.

"Hey, Haley, I'll buzz you in. I'm in the living room." DeMarco's voice sounded through the intercom next to the doorbell I'd pushed. I heard a low buzz as the lock was disabled; I turned the doorknob and entered his home. The living room with its two large ivory pillars was just beyond the foyer, and directly in front of me as I entered the house and passed through.

"Hello, Haley," DeMarco said, and then took in a deep breath, releasing it with an *ahhh*. He was sitting on the couch with a gun holster strapped around his upper body. I was taken aback because although it was well-known that DeMarco was a gun enthusiast, I'd never seen him with one. The gold and white gun stuck out of it. Seeing that holster strapped to him brought images of an old Western movie gunslinger that my parents loved. But the image didn't last for long. No one would mistake DeMarco for any cowboy. DeMarco was dressed in black:, wearing a pair of baggy black Fubu Jeans and a black Fubu long-sleeve T-shirt. One of the arms of the T-shirt had two red stripes going around it. A pair of black and red Jordans were on his feet.

In his hands were the trademark silver meditation balls. However, these didn't have the bell sound like the ones with which he usually exercised. They were silent. He was rolling them around in one hand, one over the other. "Have a seat," he instructed me, as he stared into a gaze. I sat next to him on the couch. I watched him as he quietly sat there. DeMarco continued to roll the balls around in his right hand while he massaged the left side of his temple with the other hand. His dreads were hanging down. He ran his fingers through them, pulling them back.

Waiting on him to break the silence seemed like it was going to take forever, so I decided to speak.

"DeMarco, what's up with you?" I asked. He shook his head. He glanced in my direction. "Your hair looks nice. It's long. It grew." He touched it. "How much this cost?" He asked. That brought a smile to my face. Playfully, I punched him in the arm.

So what's up with you?" I repeated.

"Nothing really," he said. "I just got a lot on my mind, that's all. So, what's going on with the studio? We owe Malik any money?"

"Yeah, we do."

"How much?"

"Fifteen hun."

"Alright. Who else we gotta pay?"

"We owe Postcards Express eight for the postcards and posters we ordered, and a thousand to the T-shirt guy, and three to the graphic designer."

"Is that it? Did we pay, uh… what's-his-name, for the box of blank CDs and cassettes we got from him? I wanna make sure we take care of him."

"No, we didn't; that's who else we gotta pay. I think we owe him something like five hundred."

"Alright, I'll give you the money before you leave here so you can pay all of those bills." His fingers kept rotating those silent balls, one over the other.

"Alright."

"Let me see… there was something else I wanted to talk to you about. Damn! What was it… I forgot. Let me see… what was it?"

"DeMarco, what's wrong?" He shook his head and continued speaking, "Oh, yeah, that's what I wanted to talk to you about. I need for you to make an appointment with our attorney and have him to rewrite our artist contracts. See if he can see us sometime next week. I can do any day except Thursday. I was looking over them and I want him to add some clauses in there. Just some shit I want us to be covered on…"

"I thought you wanted Krystal to do that, DeMarco."

"I want her to do some other stuff for us, but not that… and what else was there that I wanted to talk to you about?"

DeMarco kept on rolling the balls around in his hand. From the time I had arrived until now he had not stopped rolling them. He leaned back on the couch, resting his back against the back of the sofa. He stared off again into the distance. He was thinking. Some heavy gears were turning in his head behind that stolid gaze. He was speechless.

Again, I broke the silence. "You never let me in. DeMarco, would you let me help you?"

"Would you please stop asking me that?! Ain't shit wrong with me," he snapped, in a voice that echoed around the living room.

"DeMarco, would you please lower your voice when you are talking to me? I am not screaming at you, so would you please stop screaming at me?"

"Man, this is the way I talk." He said still shouting. "I talk to everybody this way but my grandmother."

"Well, you have never talked to me like that," I snapped back. Angry, I stood up from the couch and headed to the door.

"Where are you going?"

"I'm leaving."

"Oh, my God, I can't believe you're upset because I raised my voice. Haley, you are being way too sensitive."

At the door I fumbled with the lock. For some reason I couldn't open it. That's when DeMarco appeared at my side. He pulled my hands away from the doorknob and the lock. "Would you please just sit down."

"No, I'm leaving." He stood between me and the door. That's when I felt my eyes starting to swell and then a tear rolled down my face. Before he could see it, impetuously, I ran into his bedroom, closed the door behind me and jumped onto the bed. I buried my face in the comforter and let the tears flow out. DeMarco entered the room. He came over to the bed and sat down.

"Haley, what's up with you?" I didn't respond.

He repeated his question, "Haley what's up with you?" Still I said nothing. He got up and walked around the bed to get a closer look at me.

"Oh, my God, you're crying." He seemed unsure what to make of it. "Haley, sometimes we gone have disagreements. I know that I yelled. Come here."

"No, leave me alone."

"No, I ain't leaving you alone. Haley, you spoiled. Now, come here and stop acting like a baby. Come here."

"No."

Sitting on the bed he started speaking in a quiet, tired voice that I had never heard from him before. "Woman. I didn't mean to make you cry. I just got a lot of shit going on, but you haven't done anything to me but be here for me. I'm sorry. And I will be more aware of the way I talk to you. Really, I didn't mean any harm."

Wiping my tears away, I sat up in the bed and looked at him.

"Do you forgive me?" I nodded. DeMarco wiped my tears away. He kissed my forehead. I kissed him back on the lip.

"DeMarco, something's wrong… I feel it. What's going on with you?" He looked away. "DeMarco, please don't do this to me. Don't shut me out. I care about you. Why don't you want to talk about it with me?"

"Cause it's a lot of bullshit that you don't need to deal with, and I ain't gone bring you no bullshit." I shook my head and threw my hands in the air. He began speaking, in that voice, which led me to finally realize just how tapped out DeMarco was.

"Haley, I'm tired of being in the game. Like my brother did, I want out of it. I wanna do just like he did and come up legit. He was smart to get out when he did and start his own real estate business. He flipped his money. I've learned so much from him. You know, Haley, it doesn't matter how much you think you are on top, respected in the game, or that you got people under control—there's always one motherfucker out there who gone challenge you, and then you gotta handle it. When I use to just sell weed, I was a much nicer person. No one gets shot over weed. But if you sell powder… heroin…that's where the money is. But it makes you mean, real mean and I don't like what I'm becoming. Truth is, I'm a nice motherfucker."

Over the next half hour, DeMarco broke it down to me: his life in the game that about which he'd never talked to me, the subject of those conversations that abruptly ended when I walked into the room, that other side of him that had been hinted at which I had always suspected to exist. He had ordered people killed. He had kidnapped and tormented people. He rambled at times, talking about having to deal with a trader that was on his team and something about how he humiliated him with a broom handle and then the guy had lost his mind.

"You know, I really wish I hadn't did to him what I did. I should have handled it differently. I was wrong for that one." There was a part of me that felt cornered, as though there were a monster on the other side of the bed. But DeMarco looked haggard and beaten-down in the soul. Maybe that's why I didn't run from him. Monsters didn't look that way; they didn't appear as though they'd lost their souls when they talked about what they'd accomplished. "Looking back over a lot of things I did, I should have handled it differently."

"So, what do you want to do now, DeMarco?"

"The brothers on the block, they can have this life. I'm done with the thug life. You know what, Haley? I was reading the Bible last night, and you know the part about reaping what you sow?"

I nodded, "I know the scripture well."

"Well, when I die, I know that I am going to die a horrible death 'cause I've done a lot of wrong to people and I'm going to reap what I sow. It's written." And, for just about the first time, I could actually see DeMarco facing something that made him afraid. "It's not death I'm afraid of. You can't be in the game if you're afraid of dying. I'm afraid of being reborn again. You know, reincarnation?" I nodded again. "When I meet my maker… wow! I just hope that he takes into consideration where I was from and it was about survival of the fittest and only the strong survived. I hope he takes into consideration when judging me for the thug life, and how we are created and our mentality is created by society's alienation of us, and how we are made by our environment. You know, I've never been baptized?"

"No?" DeMarco shook his head.

"Me either," I sympathized.

"What, you haven't been baptized either?"

"Nope," I affirmed.

"Maybe one day we can wash away our sins together. We need to find a church."

"Let's do it. Doesn't it say somewhere in the scriptures that if you are not baptized before you die, you can't go to heaven?"

"Naw, not being baptized won't stop you from going to heaven, I don't think. I need to research that one, though, 'cause I wanna be for sure that I'm telling you the right thing. I'm going to get baptized because I feel in my heart I should. I want to show God an outright dedication, you know?"

"Yeah, me too, that's why I wanna get baptized, too."

DeMarco continued, "Man, then I got all this pressure on me. I have to be a million places at one time, it seems like. Every time there's a problem, I'm the one whose gotta deal with it. This is what my disappearing acts are all about. I be taking care of business." I just sat there and listened. DeMarco had so much more to say despite the outpouring. "Also, I want to set up a nonprofit organization. I'll call it the Urban Memorial Fund, that would pay the funeral expenses for inner-city youths and young adults who are killed at the hands of violence if their families cannot afford to pay on their own. That's the other thing I need our attorney to do for us: set up the non-profit, push all the papers. When the time is right, we'll drop a hundred thousand dollars into the fund. In addition to paying the burial costs for their loved ones, the fund would also give each family two thousand dollars."

I saw the seriousness about what he was saying in his eyes. A part of me couldn't believe what I was hearing. But I knew he was sincere. *He really wants to change the course of his life*, I thought to myself.

"Not to be changing the subject, but, DeMarco, a couple of years ago, I read this interesting article in Black Enterprise about independent record labels and the business of music. The article talked about the success of independent record labels, like No Limit, Cash Money, Roca-Fella, and most recently Wreckshop Records outta Houston and how they all received huge multi-million dollar advances from major distributors who wanted to distribute their music after they experienced success as independent record labels. They sold something like fifty to one hundred thousand records. No Limit, Cash Money, Roca Fella, and Wreckshop all got advances in the twenty-million-dollar range from the major distributors once they signed with them for distribution.

"Huh? You think we can sell a hundred thousand?" Skepticism was all over DeMarco's haggard face.

"With a strategic marketing plan and the right marketing budget, of course we can. DeMarco, if our rap compilation sells one hundred thousand copies, you know what that means?"

"Yep."

"What it means?"

"It means we can do like Master P, the Cash Money Millionaires, Wreckshop did, like all of the other independent record labels who were successful and went on to sign with major distributors and got huge advances."

"Exactly. If we sell a hundred thousand copies, it sets us up to negotiate for a twenty million advance from a major distributor. Once any independent record label sells this many records, the major distributors seek them out. I say we follow Master P's marketing plan and drop the comp in the South first, and then in the Midwest. Then we come back to the West Coast in four or five months. We can start promoting here now, though. The South and the Midwest are going to be more receptive to us. Plus, there's more people there and its easier to get radio play there than it is here."

I could see some energy returning to DeMarco. "Let's do it."

"Cool." No, it was far better than "cool." I knew business was in DeMarco's blood. It was a drive of his that he couldn't live without. Putting together a music venture would fulfill his need to be in a "game" of some kind. It would quench his thirst for success. Best of all, he wouldn't have to kill people or spend his life looking over his shoulder.

" Haley, let me ask you something?"

"What?"

"How's your credit?"

"Excellent."

"Good."

"Why you ask?"

"I have been thinking about the future. We are going to have to establish that *Life* and *Rage* were funded independent of me and not funded with drug money. You know the Feds still watching a brother. The last thing I want to do is make it, be a goddamn legit millionaire and they trying to RICO-statute our shit."

"You know, DeMarco, it's funny you mentioned that because that has been on my mind lately, especially being that the target debut date for *Rage* is less than four months away."

DeMarco agreed, "I hear they been snooping around wanting to know what groups I have been working with and going to the studios trying to learn how much money I have been spending. They even went to my distributor who has distributed my past CDs with a lot of questions."

"Is that right?"

"Yeah, but he didn't tell them anything."

"The Feds?"

"Yeah, just some shit from a few years back. They hate a thug for living large, that's what it's about. I just need to cover my steps. Haley, I'm going to trust you, but you better not fuck me, don't let me down," DeMarco said prudently pointing his finger in my face.

A surprised look covered my face. I took his finger in my hand and held on to it before pushing it away. I asked him for clarification.

"All I am saying is, don't leave me standing with my dick in my hand."

"DeMarco, I ain't trying to see you like that! Why you talking crazy to me? Why you coming at me all vile and shit?!"

DeMarco ignored my comments. "Make sure that both of those companies, the record label and the magazine, are in your name only, and make sure that they are incorporated. The Feds may or may not ever make anything out of the success of *Life* and *Rage*, but judging from what my luck has been, more than likely they gone come at us. Did I tell you my boy's girl got arrested and started singing like a fucking bird?"

"What?!"

"Yeah, I went to see my lawyer today 'cause my boy's lawyer had some questions he wanted to ask me. I answered his questions with my attorney present. Anyway, through my attorney I have learned they are inquiring about our relationship and wanted to know if I was your financier in *Rage* and *Life*. In the event that they launch an investigation into the financing behind both companies, I want us to be covered. I… *we*… can't afford to take a loss, Haley. Plus, I don't want them to be able to link me to having given you any money. There are thirty things on the RICO Statute. All a court has to do is find you guilty on one of them, and they can seize everything you own. Clearly, we need to be prepared to be able to identify where the money came from to launch both *Life* and *Rage*. Therefore, we have to create a paper trail that does not lead back to me, and will itemize all purchases made by both companies under your name and line of credit… follow me?" I nodded. DeMarco went on, "You know my real estate and a lot of other shit I own I had put in my brother Michael's name. He's rich. He made his money from real estate. He has his own company. He's a broker, and does mortgage loan brokering. If the feds ever checked him out, he could prove that he has the income to own those things. "Haley, do you trust me?"

"Of course I do." I could hear the clique in the back of my mind, warning me that DeMarco used women and threw them over his shoulder like empty beer cans when he was done with them. But somehow I doubted any of DeMarco's one-night stands had heard what he had told me.

"You are going to have to take out a $100,000 loan against your home, deposit it in a checking account, and write checks from it. We won't touch your money, we will use mines. As you spend yours, I will replace it from sources that can't be traced back to me. It must appear that you are financing the record label and the magazine. We'll need this paper trail. We need to be six or seven steps up on these bastards. On Monday morning, contact our distributor, Northwest, and request a credit application. We can cut a deal with them to press twenty thousand CDs with a eight-page booklet for fourteen five or so. We are going to use the line of credit they extend to you to press our CDs, cassettes, and vinyl. We are also going to lock down advertising on the mainstream radio stations in our target markets with radio commercials introducing the Rage Magazine compilation. I read the marketing plan you wrote. To lock down the South and the Midwest just as you have recommended, and to meet our goal of selling a hundred thousand units is going to take about $100,000 in promotion dollars. We will use the loan from your home and your credit cards to pay for radio promotions, posters, flyers and other promotional material. The Promotions departments at the radio stations take credit cards. With the brilliant marketing plan you came up with, I am confident we can sell 100,000 CDs in less than eight months. This will put us in a good position for a lucrative distribution deal with a major record label and set us up for a huge advance."

Yes, I thought, DeMarco had a keen sense for business. He had the whole thing worked out. What he had said made so much sense. I didn't think of his move to be wrong or even unethical. Hell, the white boys had been doing it forever; in their high circle, one hand washed the other. But this was new knowledge to the smart brothers like DeMarco. The truth is, neither company was funded on drug money because of the loans and lines of credit I had obtained. However, I must admit that I never would have took out the home loans or sought the other lines of credit had DeMarco not promised he'd reimburse. There was just no way I would have been willing to risk all I had in that way.

DeMarco laid back on the bed next to me.

"Come here," he said. I laid in his arms; resting my head on his chest, he embraced me. Next thing I knew, DeMarco was fast asleep snoring. I got the distinct feeling he hadn't slept much the past few nights. I looked up and stared at him for what seemed like forever, and then I also dozed off.

On Monday morning, I called Northwest and requested a credit application. They faxed it to me and I immediately returned it. Within the next hour, they called me back to inform me that I was extended a line of credit for twenty thousand dollars. I called my bank and the credit companies. By the end of business on Tuesday, I had a $100,000 line of credit on my home and about $90,000 in credit on an assortment of plastic.

We were ready to move. And we did, with DeMarco applying the same acumen he'd shown for his old game into this new venture.

Thirty-one

The day before DeMarco's wife got out of rehab, he and I were laughing and talking on the telephone. At the time, I hadn't known it was only one more day. We were talking about everything: about music and *Rage* and good restaurants and gossip, when he laid it on me.

"Did I tell you that my wife gets out tomorrow?" THUMP! My heart dropped. For a second, I thought it had stopped. I didn't want to hear this shit; I was hurt, crushed, speechless. I didn't want him to know that what he had said had twisted me, fucked me up. Quickly, I had to recover from that blow and continue the conversation.

"Oh, really? That's good," I said. "I am so happy for you." Actually, what I thought was different. *That fucking bitch. What nerve! Abandoned your family for three years and then come back expecting things to be the same?* I didn't want DeMarco to know that what he had just said had me all fucked me up. I still felt shaken. During the time I'd known him, that was the longest conversation I ever had with him about his wife, and that was a short conversation in itself. In our discussions, he just simply didn't talk about her, and neither did I. Until DeMarco made the announcement about her homecoming, I had almost forgotten that he was married and had a wife in rehab. With effort, I continued the conversation, amidst everything that the clique had warned me about. These concerns flooded my mind like a tidal wave.

DeMarco took a deep breath and released it into the phone. "Yeah, man, she about to be home," he didn't seem too happy about her arrival. As I listened to his reaction, I wondered if I should feel guilty or pleased that there was still hope for us. But then the businesswoman in me spoke up, cutting right to the chase with the bottom-line question: *Where do I stand now?*

"DeMarco, are you happily married?"

After a long pause: "Why did you ask me?"

"I am just asking."

"Why did you ask me that?"

"I was just asking.'

"But why did you ask me that?"

"If you want to know something, you ask!" On the other end of the phone in the midst of the silence, I felt him thinking. Finally returning to the conversation, he hesitantly decided, "Yeah, I'm happily married."

"So, what happens to us?"

"What do you mean 'what happens to us?'"

Isn't it fucking obvious what I mean? I could feel tears welling up in my eyes; I forced them down. "Your wife's coming home. Where does that leave us?"

"I told you already that I'm divorcing her."

"When?"

"I just need to meet with my attorney and have him draw up the papers."

"*When,* DeMarco?"

"In a few weeks."

"So, your wife's coming back home to you. Y'all staying in the same house, sleeping in the same bed, right?"

"Man, look, Haley… just hold on. We gone be together. You already know that, so why you tripping?"

"DeMarco, you're full of shit."

"Man, whatever. I then already told you what was up. If you don't believe me then I don't know what else to say."

"Whatever, DeMarco."

"Man, Haley, have I ever lied to you? Have I?"

"No."

"Well, then you have no reason not to trust me. All I need for you to do is give me a little time. I need to make my move at the right time. I just need you to stand by my side and be there for me and you'll see."

Somehow, I just wanted something a little more concrete. DeMarco was the one on the phone, but all I heard was the clique...

Thirty-two

To break the monotony of our weekly "girls spend Friday together" ritual at Krystal's house, we had dinner at Utopia's. I couldn't wait to get there so I could pass along yesterday's news from DeMarco to the clique. As soon as I walked in the house, I relayed his wife's homecoming to them.

Camille was the first to speak. Thank God there was no "I told you so." Well, actually there was, but it wasn't like *that*. "I saw it coming a long time ago. Girl, you should have kept it business with that man from the start. Haley, if he were really going to leave his wife, and you were sure of it, I'd say hang in there 'cause y'all really is building something. Plus, y'all do got love for one another, I see it. However, you are too smart and too pretty a woman to let this man make you his mistress, his second family. All he's going to do is keep lying to you, telling you that when the time is right he is going to leave his wife, but he isn't. At least I don't think he is. I know, been there done that, remember? If I were you Haley, I'd move on."

Utopia was more practical. "Haley, she a tall, big bitch. If she comes after you just kick her in her pussy and run. Get the hell out of there, take off running. Fuck that."

"Alright, girl, his wife is coming home… it is time to back up, way up," Krystal said. "Make sure that business stays business with him. Keep it there with him. I heard about his ghetto bitch, Nakeesha. I hear she goes crazy over him when she finds out he's cheating. Be careful."

Krystal went on, "Haley, I swear to God, last night I had dream that DeMarco left his wife for you."

"What?!" Camille exclaimed.

"My dream was a trip. In my dream, you and I were talking, Haley, and you said to me, 'Krystal, today DeMarco asked his wife for a divorce, but she refuses to grant him one. DeMarco said that it could take more than three years for him to get a divorce because she is being stubborn.'

"Then I asked you, 'Did he at least complete the paperwork and submit it to the courts', and then you said, 'No, he hasn't, it's going to take three years.' Then, I said, 'Yeah, but at least he could initiate the paperwork and get it started.'

"Then you said, 'In time, he will divorce her. For now, we are going to live together. His wife is just refusing to sign divorce papers because she thinks that it will keep us apart. I love DeMarco and he loves me, ain't nothing gone keep us apart,… nothing.'

"Then, Haley, in my dream, I said to you, 'Let me ask you this question. How do you feel, dating a man with a wife and family?' And you said, 'I'm okay with it, obviously. If I wasn't, I wouldn't go out with him.'

"'Don't you have thoughts about his wife's feelings or his children's feelings?' I asked you. Then you said, 'His children are going to be okay. We love them. They will spend time with us. I guess I do have some reservations about our relationship, but I love DeMarco.' Then I said, 'Haley, don't you think his wife loves him too?' Then you told me that she did, and that's why she refused to sign the papers. But finally you told me he didn't actually draw up the papers, he just told her about it.

"Then this woman who I never saw before appeared in my dream, and she was talking to you, Haley. She said, 'test him, and see how much he loves you. Tell him to go to Haiti and get one of those quick one-day divorces.' You said, 'I looked into that already. It costs too much. Do you know how much it costs to fly to Haiti, and pay hotel costs? In addition to these costs, you still have to pay the Haitian government a lot of money.' Then the woman said, 'Well, good luck.' Then you called me on the phone and was like, 'Krystal, DeMarco's wife called me.'"

"What did I tell you she said?"

"She was like, 'Hi, my name is Nakeesha and I'm DeMarco's wife. Why are you interfering with our marriage? He's happily married and he has children.'

"And I asked you what you said. Haley, you said that you told her DeMarco wasn't happy with her and that is why he was with you. His wife started crying over the phone, asking you to leave him alone. She had told you that you were not the first woman that he had messed around with that she has had to deal with. Then she hung up. I woke up and that was the end of my dream."

"Did you really have that dream, Krystal?" I asked.

"Yep, sure did."

Utopia piped in. "Just wondering, Haley, did you share with your pastor anything about your relationship with DeMarco?"

"It's funny that you ask, 'cause a while back I did," I answered.

"And what he say?"

"He said what I was doing was a sin and he was gone pray for me, said I needed to get on my knees and repent and ask God for forgiveness. That's what he said, Utopia."

Krystal joined in the conversation again. "Haley, I'm sorry but I do not really feel for you in this relationship. I feel for DeMarco's wife and his children."

"How could you say something like that to me, Krystal? I am your friend."

"Girl, you went into this relationship knowing that the man was married."

"Yeah, but it didn't start that way."

"Haley, his wife is home now. You need to leave him. You are too smart and intelligent to be with a scandalous man like DeMarco. Trust me, if he were to leave his wife for you, he'd do the same thing to you at some point that he's doing to her. And I say 'if' because I do not think he is going to leave her for you. Haley, I love you, girl. Can't you recognize the warning sign: DeMarco has his cake and ice cream at the same time and he's eating it, too. He is never going to leave his wife for you or anybody else."

"You don't know that for sure Krystal," I snapped back.

"And you don't know for sure that he is! He took vows with that woman and no matter what he tells you, he loves her and that is why he is with her. They live together… remember, Haley."

"He says that he loves her, but he is not in love with her." Krystal rolled her eyes. "You don't even know Krystal. I told DeMarco I was going to leave him. He begged me not to leave."

"Haley, that's just game. I got four brothers and I have observed their relationships with women. They have pulled that same shit on their women. 'Oh, baby, don't leave, I love you, I need you' that DeMarco is pulling on you."

"But, I really think he means it. If you had been there, Krystal, you'd know what I'm talking about." I was tired of trying to explain to everyone:

no, I wasn't abandoning my life for DeMarco; and, no, I did not set out to fall in love with a married man. I looked around the table at everyone. "Ladies, I am leaving. Krystal, I don't want to discuss the topic of DeMarco with you anymore. Plus, I am starting to think that you are a wee bit jealous 'cause you ain't got a man." Biting my tongue before I could say more, I headed for the door.

Krystal was unbowed, standing with her arms folded in front of her. "Ain't that a bitch. Wait a minute, Haley, before you walk out of that door. Let me tell you something: I am alone by choice. If I wanted a negro like DeMarco, I could have him. I could have a whole bunch of them. But unlike you, Haley, I know that I deserve to be something other than a man's mistress or some drug dealer's fling. Aren't you tired of dating drug dealers with 'dreams and ambitions?' Do they ever attain them? We then all had our share of men like that, but ask yourself: do any of them ever attain these goals they claim they all have? DeMarco's on a chase now and that's what it's about with him. Haley, you are his ticket out of da ghetto. Don't you see it? Haley, you can get mad at me and you don't ever have to speak to me again if you don't want to, but this is what I see. How long have I known you?"

"Oh, Krystal… since third grade."

"More than twenty five years. Haley, you are like a sister to me. Hell, I'm closer to you than I am to mines. I don't want you to end up hurt, that's all. But if you do, I'm still going to be right here for you, helping you to deal with it. But if I don't speak what's in my heart to you and then DeMarco does the very things that I think he might, I would feel so bad. If DeMarco proves me wrong, Haley that would be great. He just might, but what I told you is just what I see."

I felt tears coming to my eyes. How could I explain what I felt? About how I knew DeMarco was really trying to improve himself, about how he and I just… well, for lack of a better word, just *clicked* together? How I was strong where he was weak, and visa-versa. How we made a team.

I tried, but the words just wouldn't come. Even if they did, I knew Krystal would throw them back in my face. Maybe with the best of intentions, and certainly with no malice. So I had to settle for tears. I just walked over and gave Krystal a hug. She returned the embrace.

"Krystal, sometimes you really piss me off, but I know you mean well. See you tomorrow." I kissed Krystal on the cheek and headed out the door.

As I drove home that night, lots of thoughts were going through my head again. DeMarco wanted to get out of the D game. He knew that if he stayed with his wife, he would never get out of the game. She had helped him advance as far as she could. Now things were at a standstill for him, and would remain as such for as long as he remained with her. Krystal was right:

DeMarco knew that I was the one who could take him to the destination he was trying to get to. Also, I realized that we made a great team and he could also help me advance to the level I wanted to advance to.

The clique just didn't get it. But I couldn't hold it against them. In time, they would understand…

Thirty-three

DeMarco and I were on our way to Mama Mia's, the Italian restaurant in Malibu. "Nakeesha thinks she's pregnant… something like seven weeks," DeMarco said. I took notice of his gold wedding band on his finger as his hand grasped the steering wheel. It was the first time I had ever seen it, but I acted as though I hadn't. He continued. "She gotta go to the doctor, you know, just to be sure. She wants me to pick her up another one of those home pregnancy kits on my way home tonight. The first one she did a couple of weeks ago didn't come out positive, but she says she knows she pregnant."

I slumped back in the seat. Things had been sliding downhill ever since Nakeesha had gotten out Her, pregnant? *Wouldn't that just be some great fucking icing on the cake*, I bitterly thought. The more I ran it through my mind, the more I was coming to a conclusion that I didn't like: my feelings for DeMarco were wrong. He was married, and loving a married man is unjust. I had known it all along and now it was turning around and biting me on the ass, big-time. As much as I wanted to be with DeMarco, I couldn't. My conscience was now getting the most of me.

"DeMarco, your wife is out, she's home now," I said slowly.

"We have to stop seeing each other."

"Not really."

"What are you talking about? Yes, we do."

"Man, you are my business partner and if she can't understand that, then fuck her. Anyway I'm divorcing her, so it really doesn't matter."

The look I gave DeMarco was fire. "Fuck her, you say? Funny you should put it that way, DeMarco. If she think she pregnant, then, yeah, you *been* fucking her. Now you say you divorcing her? Yeah, right!" I rolled my eyes and shook my head.

"Hey, man, you don't have to believe me, but I am."

"Why should I believe you? You having your cake and eating it, too. Well, after you file for your divorce, we can resume our relationship. And if you don't, and damn quick, then its over."

"Man, you trippin'. What's wrong with you? Why you acting like that? I thought that things was cool between us. All the time that we have been spending together growing to know each other. What's up with that, Haley? You gone just walk out on that?"

"DeMarco, I deserve more than to be your mistress."

"And I'm telling you that I am divorcing Nakeesha."

"Well, let me see a copy of the divorce papers, stamped 'Los Angeles Superior Court'. 'Til you got that, it's just talk… it ain't real. Anyway, about your wife's pregnancy. Congratulations! What you hoping for, a boy or a girl?"

DeMarco removed his eyes temporarily from the road, looking at me. "So, what's up with us, Haley? You wanna be with me?"

"Do you wanna be with me? I should be asking that, I'm not the one fucking someone else. DeMarco, you got games. Quit playing."

Getting upset, "Why in the hell you think I'm playing?! I'm not playing with you. Me and you, we really have something, and you need someone like me on your side. Come on, Haley… let's get a spot together?"

"I don't believe you. Your wife is home. You sitting here telling me she might be pregnant and you acting like its nothing, and it is something, and then you want me to move in with you?" My inner voice and rationale of right and wrong was getting the most of me. I was uneasy about our love affair. It didn't feel right. It wasn't right. From the moment I consummated my relationship with DeMarco, taking it from a platonic alliance and friendship to a sexual affair, I couldn't help but think about the way I had came down hard on Camille for having an affair. Now, here I was doing the same thing. It was the start of the New Year, and it was shaping up to be a shitty one. "DeMarco, I don't want to go into the New Year like I spent most of last year: Struggling with my feelings of love for you, between my morality, and righteousness and the beliefs my parents instilled in me about being with a married man.

"I like you and you like me, but we can't be 'cause you can't give me what

I need. You can't give me a commitment, you can't give me loyalty. Maybe you can in a business sense, but not in a relationship sense. The truth is, I knew this from the gate. But I still gave you part of my heart. I was so stupid. So really you're not to blame for the distress that I'm feeling inside. So, you can go back to your wife and your bitches and hoes. I wish you the best that life has to offer. "DeMarco, let's just say goodbye now, so it all ends on a good level. I ain't trying to be a part of your game. I ain't down with this two-family shit. You going back between us and all that. Do you know how humiliating it is for me to be your mistress, and to know that everybody knows it? It's bullshit, and according to the Bible, which I believe in, I am wrong for loving you, and the truth here is the real victim is your wife. If I could have you and not have to share you, then I would see a future with you, DeMarco, but this is not the case."

DeMarco sighed. "Haley, you are complicating things even more. When two people really care about each other and love each other the way we do, love don't have to be that complicated." My eyes started to swell. I tried to fight back the tears, but they rolled out uncontrollably. Not wanting DeMarco to see them, I turned my head and stared out of the passenger window.

I had to get outside. Something inside snapped. The light ahead turned red, and DeMarco brought the Range Rover to a halt. I opened the door and got out.

"Haley, what are you doing?! Come back here!" I could see DeMarco somehow inch the car out of the line of traffic, skirting along the curb. I walked faster. I heard the car screech to a halt, the door open as DeMarco got out. I felt numb as he grabbed my arm. "Oh, my God… you're crying," he said. I finally turned to look at him, saw the hurt look in his eyes. And that made it all the more painful. He embraced my face in his hands and with his thumbs, he wiped away my tears. The more he wiped, the more those tears flowed.

But his embrace was genuine. I couldn't bring myself to leave him again. "I am not going to hurt you. Come here." He beckoned me, and I laid my head on his chest. We hugged.

" Haley, stop focusing on my wife. All you need to do is focus on me, us, and what we got. I'll handle Nakeesha."

"How?"

"I'm divorcing her. I already saw an attorney. I've paid him to draw up the divorce papers. Haley, I need a woman like you on my team and in my life." I was still sniffling, though my eyes no longer leaked as much. DeMarco went on. "I ain't never tripped off a female like this before, not how I'm tripping off you… you're different than the other females I've dated, Haley, and I ain't ever met a woman like you. I mean, look at you. You're smart, educated, confident, classy, and strong. Not that long ago, I wouldn't have known how to appreciate you. I would have done you like all the rest, and fucked you over. When I was younger, I had a couple of females in my life that I fucked over pretty bad. There's a couple of them I wished I hadn't fucked over. If I could go back and change things, I would. There was this one female I dated, she reminds me of you… I fucked her over pretty bad. She was good to me. She loved me, but at the time, I didn't know what it meant to be loved by somebody or to love somebody, but now I do since I've met you. Haley, I have felt things for you that I didn't know I could feel for a woman. We can be together if you would allow me to be in your life."

He kissed my forehead and then pecked me on the lip. I hugged him. I couldn't help myself when he was like this. "DeMarco, I wish we could freeze this moment forever."

"Me too, except for the part of how hungry I am. Are you hungry, Haley?"

"Yeah."

"Lets go." Hand in hand, we walked back to the truck.

Thirty-four

After we left the restaurant, DeMarco asked me to drive with him to San Diego to see Zion, a popular reggae singer who was like the Michael Jackson of reggae… without the weirdness. He was the headliner for a concert there. DeMarco said that he didn't want to be driving back too late, so we should stay up there for the night at the Ritz Carlton. I agreed to go. On the two-hour drive, Al Green's song, *Love & Happiness* came on the radio. Turning the volume up, DeMarco said, "That's my boy, Al."

"Sure is."

"He's my favorite singer."

"Mines to," I said. I was surprised to hear that he was also DeMarco's favorite singer. "You know his song, *Simply Beautiful*, DeMarco?"

"What you know about *Simply Beautiful*?"

"I know about it. You know Mary did a remake, but it don't sound like Al's."

"Naw, it don't."

"When all of my brothers and my sister got married at their wedding reception, they all played Simply Beautiful. It was the first song they danced to. When I get married, I am going to play it, too, and it will be the first song my husband and I dance to. Al is tradition in our family, I guess you could say."

"If I were ever to get married again, I'd play Al at my wedding. Actually, I'd just pay him to come and perform live."

"Damn, I heard that. How much you think it would cost to get Al to do that?"

"You could probably get Al for about ten G's."

DeMarco turned the radio up again louder. We sang along the lyrics to Love & Happiness with Al.

"Have you ever been in love, Haley," DeMarco asked as the song ended.

"Yep. It's like Al says, it can make you come home early. And if you're not really in a good relationship with someone and you are enjoying, maybe, a new person in your life, it can make you stay out all night."

"That's true."

"What about you?"

"What?"

"Have you ever been in love, DeMarco?"

"No, I ain't never been in love with a bitch." DeMarco saw me cringe, shrink back a bit.

"Excuse me, a woman. I meant to say, I have never been in love with a woman." I grinned. Maybe DeMarco was finally learning some manners.

"I met a woman though that I could fall in love with."

"Is that right?"

"Yep."

"What is it about this woman that you like?"

"Ooh, everything. She's ambitious like me, smarter though. She probably doesn't know it. Let's see… she's articulate, confident, just a real go-getter, and she got good people skills. And she's sweet… and beautiful, might I add. Those are the things I like about her."

"Hmmm, does this woman have a name?"

"Of course?"

"What's her name?"

"I ain't telling you that! You might know her or something." DeMarco had a wry grin.

"Where she from?"

"I ain't answering no more of your questions."

"Well?"

I felt DeMarco's impassioned eyes on me, watching my every move.

"You better keep your eyes on the road," I said.

I looked over at him, our eyes met again. I saw his sexual craving for me in his eyes. Eyes don't lie. I vibed his lust, his intimate desire to be with me. The feeling was mutual. I wanted him inside me as much as he wanted to be. I looked at him imagining my arched back in motion like a seesaw, moving up and down on him. I longed to grasp his head in both hands, to squeeze and hold tight his long cotton-soft black dreads, releasing them and letting them slip between my fingers each time I came, and to grasp his head in both hands over and over again. That was my DeMarco fantasy. For lack of a better quote in the words of R Kelly, "I'm fucking DeMarco tonight."

We reached the building. Zion appeared on stage, wearing blue jeans and a dark blue T-shirt. His long, dark-brown dreads were wrapped around his head in that trademark signature style that resembled a king's crown. The crowd went crazy, chanting, "Zion! Zion! Zion!" The smell of marijuana wafted throughout the concert hall; people in the crowd were smoking the stuff and freely passing it around, sharing it with whomever took it.

The concert hall was packed, as Zion was playing to a sold-out crowd. The only source of illumination came from flicking lighters held up in the air by the audience. The flickers gave the whole venue a primeval look. DeMarco and I were arm-in-arm. Before his performance, Zion had a moment of silence and prayer for Bob Marley. Upon speaking of the famed reggae star once on stage, I could tell he'd taken a few hits himself.

"If it were not for Bob Marley, I would not be standing here before you today. Bob Marley does a lot for the business. Bob Marley, he paved the way, he died for the music. He was one of the artist that let you know when you made your album you must tour. We learn a lot from Bob Marley. He made a lot of upcoming artists know that you got to be persistent, tough, and you gotta be there for it, 'cause it's a hard road and it's a tough game, but you just have to keep lifting up your head.

"Bob Marley he suffer a lot. Rastafarian people, we suffer a lot. We always try to find out why we suffer and why people have to suffer. In America, there is luxury. You're suffering here too, but you know what I am saying. It's like Babylon: here you're quicker to be corrupted and earn a dollar. As a Rastafarian, Bob Marley freed the people and opened our eyes. To be Rasta is an act of faith. It is to make a pledge. A lot of people you see wearing dreads, they don't understand. As musicians and artists, we have to help to get the faith international, to open a lot of people's eyes to the faith.

"When I reflect on the environment that nurtured and sustained Bob Marley, I see one of the world's most notorious slums, and I think about a poem from one of yours: Tupac Shakur, 'The Rose That Grew From Concrete.' At first thought, we conclude a rose can't grow from concrete; however, the Bible let it be known that miracle stories do exist, where we observe that while in the womb, a man's life has been predestined. Through fables, we hear the tales of how they grew up against the odds and later succeed. Like the rose that grew from concrete in Tupac's poem about life in the inner city, Bob

Marley is a rose that sprung forth from the dirt roads and monolithic streets of the slums of Kingston. In Jamaica's ghettos, where lost souls are nurtured, sustained, created and depart, reggae's most beloved blossomed and prevailed over obstacles."

Zion then chanted lyrics from his popular song, Babylon Will Fall.

Never hold your breath and put your trust in a politician
For it is written, one-day Babylon will fall
Never hold your breath and put your trust in a politician
For it is written, one-day Babylon will fall
The crowd was chanting along with him,
Never put your trust in a politician
For it is written, one-day Babylon will fall
The music started, Zion continued singing the song.
Never put your trust in a politician
 for it is written, one-day Babylon will fall.
She is corrupted, wicked and depraved like the Africans who loss
their language, Babylon was to blame for all the blood shed the
red, the yellow and the green
That's why I say
Never put your trust in a politician
 for it is written, one-day Babylon will fall...

The concert lasted two and a half hours. DeMarco and I stood in front of the stage the entire time, dancing and singing to the music of Zion. We also noticed that there were more white people in the audience than Black.

When we arrived at the Ritz Carlton Hotel, DeMarco pointed at the white leather sofa in the lounge and told me to have a seat; he'd be right back. Five minutes later, he returned. "I got a suite for us. I wanted to make sure that tonight is special. I wanted to make sure that tonight is right," he said. He reached for my hand, taking it inside of his. We walked to the elevator, and only an old white couple stood within. The woman wore a beautiful black-beaded sequined gown; the man had on a black tuxedo. They were a cute older couple, who appeared to have come from attending an extravagant affair. They exited on the fourth floor, but before stepping off the elevator, the old man planted a kiss on the woman's lips. Outside of the elevator, he also slapped her butt. The woman jumped, giggled, and covered her mouth with her hand, "Oh, Ben!" A wide smile covered her face. Obviously, she was not expecting that.

DeMarco and I quietly witnessed their flirting. DeMarco laughed after the door closed. "Look at freaky-deekie pops! Did you see that shit? Pops is about to get his freak on! All I know is, I am about to be like pops."

DeMarco and I got off on the 20th floor. Stepping off the elevator, DeMarco dropped the electronic key, which resembled a credit card with its black strip, onto the red colored carpet. He bent down to pick it up at the same time I did. We bumped heads.

"Ouch," we said at the same time, even though it had been startling rather than painful. Bending down, holding our heads, we kissed. First there was one kiss, then two kisses, and then more followed, one of us kissing the other slowly and passionately. Our breathing changed. It became heavier. Standing in the hallway in front of the elevator, DeMarco started to undo his belt.

"Wait a minute. Hold on, not here," I said. Looking at the signage on the wall in order to locate the direction of our suite, "What is our room number?" I asked.

DeMarco looked at the white plastic key he held in his hand, then the piece of paper which the reservations agent had given him. "2127. It's to the right," he said, with his eyes fixed on my ass. I led the way with him following closely behind. When we got to the door of our suite, DeMarco slid the key in the slot on the door. The green light came on; he pulled the key out of the slot and opened it.

"Oohhh," I sighed as I entered the luxurious suite. It was breathtakingly beautiful. On a self-guided tour, I walked around the suite, with DeMarco again in tow from room to room. The living room, the bedroom, the bathroom. There was a large Jacuzzi tub that sat in the middle of the bathroom floor. DeMarco peeped inside the bathroom and retreated to the bedroom. "This must have cost a fortune," I mumbled beneath my breath.

"I heard that… you're worth it," DeMarco yelled back.

With his black suit pants and white T-shirt on, he was lying on his back on the brass king size bed with a red and gold comforter. His eyes were closed. I stayed in the bathroom to run the water in the Jacuzzi tub. For a moment, I walked out into the bedroom, and noticed DeMarco asleep on his side. So, I turned around and went back into the bathroom, closing the door behind me. While the Jacuzzi was filling with water, I called Krystal from the bathroom wall phone.

"Hello."

"Hey, girl, what you doing?"

"Washing dishes."

"What you doing?"

"Girl, I am in this beautiful hotel suite in San Diego with DeMarco."

"What, shut up?! Y'all fuck? How was it?"

"Girl, stop! I am in the bathroom and there is a phone in here so I decided to call you."

"Well, everybody ain't able," Krystal mouthed jokingly.

"Well, anyway, I gotta go. I just wanted to say hello. I will come by and see you when I am back in the city tomorrow evening."

"Alright. Bye."

"Bye."

The Jacuzzi was full; I turned off the water and got in.

Relaxed, I closed my eyes. I thought about all good things, and slowly I reflected upon a time when I was a little girl. I saw myself walking down the street with my mother. A slow, cold drizzle fell from a grey sky. My mother was wearing a grey overcoat with two large front pockets. I wore a yellow raincoat. Underneath it is a pair of striped blue overalls with the lace around the collar. My cousin, Robin, also had a pair back when we were kids. Her mom had bought hers first, and I liked them so much that Mom took me to Macy's to buy a set for me. On my feet were a pair of yellow rain boots. We just came from shopping at Macy's for school clothes.

The warmth of the Jacuzzi settled in. Lazily, my mind now drifted to thoughts of DeMarco. I thought about how lucky his wife was to have a strong husband like him, and how if I had a man like DeMarco on my side, I'd do right by him and there would be no stopping me. I thought about his wife. I hope she appreciated him.

Then I imagined her and DeMarco being together forever. Maybe we could do as the Mormons do and have our marriage sealed; that is, if he were to leave her and we were ever to marry thought. My good friend Gail is a Mormon. The only black Mormon I've ever known. In fact, before Gail became one, like a lot of Black people, she believed that Black people couldn't become Mormon. Anyway, through her, I learned that their marriages were sealed in the temple. They believed once a sealing was done, no matter with whom, that was the person they would spend eternity with. It didn't matter how many times that person married; they were bound eternally to the one with whom they had accomplished the sealing.

Resting in the Jacuzzi with my eyes closed, I felt a draft intrude on that easy warmth. I sensed that someone was watching me. I opened my eyes to looked up, and saw DeMarco standing in the doorway staring at me and not saying a word.

"Do you mind if I join you?"

"Come on."

"I bet you would like that, wouldn't you?"

"Uh huh… come on, motherfucker," I teased.

"Why you got to talk to me like that?" DeMarco undressed. First, he removed his T-shirt, and his pants followed. He made his way to the Jacuzzi and pulled the boxers off as he stepped into the water. *Ooh… nice… real nice,* I thought to myself. I was at the top of the Jacuzzi while he got in at the other end. We faced one another as we had in the Calistoga hot tubs, except now the only difference was that we were in the same tub. We stared into each other's eyes. "You know that Al green song we heard tonight on the radio on the drive up here, DeMarco, that you said was your favorite song?"

"Yeah."

DeMarco, if I gave you my heart, tell me: What would you do with it."

"I'd be good to you, and I'll never do anything to hurt you."

"How do I know that you're telling me the truth?"

"You got to trust me. Give me a chance."

"DeMarco?"

"Yeah, Haley?"

"Never mind. Let's just enjoy the moment for what it's worth."

Bracing his hands at his sides inside the Jacuzzi, he scooted upward to me. He lifted both of his legs over mine, placing his on top. His hands were under the water. I felt him touch me.

"Haley, are you ticklish on your clitoris?" He smiled. I grinned back real hard; all you could see were my white teeth. The way he was making me feel caused me to rest my head on the back of the Jacuzzi. I enjoyed the moment.

"Ooh-wee, damn! It's hotter than a motherfucker in here," I shouted. I was fanning myself with one hand. I sat up in the tub, staring DeMarco in the eye.

"Come on, let's dry off," DeMarco said, getting out of the Jacuzzi. He reached for the two white terrycloth towels that were on a gold seashell towel rack on the nearby wall. He handed one to me and wrapped the other one around his waist. He reached back for my towel and began to dry my body off, beginning with my breast. He moved the towel down to my ass and worked his way down to my legs.

I reached for his towel and quickly snatched it off. Then, I returned the gesture and dried him off from head to toe. When I wiped the water away from his dick, DeMarco twitched a few times and laughed. "Haley, would you stop tickling me, please? Haley, would you please stop," he kept repeating between laughs as we made our way to the bed. His dreads were hanging down his back. I gripped his head tightly and grabbed a hand full of his hair in both hands as my body tensed while he was inside me; I tightly squeezed them and released them as I came. "Oh, DeMarco…" became my chant of the night. The lovemaking was over. DeMarco rolled over to the other side and fell asleep.

"DeMarco? DeMarco!" I called out his name a few times to no avail. He doesn't respond. *I don't believe this shit.* I got up and walked around to the other side of the bed. Calling out his name again, I tapped him on the shoulder.

He looked up. "What?"

"DeMarco, I want you to hold me."

Lifting the covers up, "Oh… I'm sorry, baby. Come on." I went underneath the covers with him.

"DeMarco?"

"What? " he asked, half asleep.

"Hold me."

He wrapped his arms around me and stayed in his grasp as he shifted his arms around my waist and my neck throughout the entire night. I didn't feel guilty about fucking him; not one time. My thoughts about his wife: *Fuck her. Hell, what did she expect him to do while she was on lockdown for two years?*

Thirty-five

Nakeesha and I finally met.
It was a Saturday afternoon. DeMarco, the engineer, and I were working on mix downs for our rap compilation. DeMarco and I were still feeling each other after returning from a romantic weekend in Monterey. Sex with him was everything that I had imagined. He was the kind of guy in bed that remained concerned with me and the way he was making me feel. He put a lot of time into conversing while we were having sex.

The Monterey trip was unplanned. We had a business meeting at Julius's Castle, a quaint restaurant located on a cul-de-sac in Bel Air. Actually, the occasion was quite romantic, as DeMarco had reserved a private room for us, which cost $300 in addition to the $175 dinner.

But now, we were back in Los Angeles, and therefore back to reality. At Tranquility studio, we watched the engineer and a rapper work on a track. Ten minutes after our arrival, Nakeesha walked right through the door, looking like a thunderstorm in progress. Either someone had tipped her off that we were here and she had come damn quick, or she had just guessed that we'd be at the studio. Although we'd never met, I automatically knew it was her, and she clearly knew who I was. That deer-in-headlights-pinned-to-the-highway look on DeMarco's face was my confirmation that it was Nakeesha. Her eyes shot lightning at us both.

"So, we finally meet." She extended her hand. I could tell the gesture was purely courtesy, feigned friendliness belied by a glacial stare. "I am Nakeesha, DeMarco's wife. I know you know about me." I just looked at her. She continued, "I wanted to meet you, and see who this woman is my husband does not want me to meet, he spends so much time with, and is always talking about to anyone who will listen. I want to meet the woman my husband is so dazzled by. So, what's going on with you and my husband?"

The engineer and rapper were casting glances in our direction. I noticed the two had pushed their headsets away from their ears even as they kept the appearance of working on the recording. I wondered if one of them had tipped her off, if for no other reason than to watch the fireworks that would surely ensue. I gave them both a glare, but then I turned back to Nakeesha.

"We are business partners, trying to make some money together."

"What kind of partners?"

"Business partners."

"Business partners don't stay out together until 4 a.m., and business partners let their wives meet their partners," she said as she stared long and hard at her husband. "I'm not stupid. I know what the fuck is going on with y'all."

I looked at DeMarco, who was still sitting next to me. He was trying to appear comfortable, but he was overdoing it because now he was slouching down in the chair in which he had previously sat upright before her uninvited entrance. He didn't say anything. *I'll be damned if Krystal wasn't right*, I was thinking. *This motherfucker isn't saying shit. I guess he is just going to let us battle it out.* Sitting there, knowing things are about to get really ugly, I turned over my options in my mind. *Do I kick this tall, big bitch in her pussy? You know, be the first one to throw the punch, be the aggressor so I might come out on top?* Yet I also thought, *I can't be nice to this ghetto bitch, 'cause she gone take my niceness for a weakness… so don't try and explain shit to this bitch.* I looked over at DeMarco again, and he still remained nonchalant and said nothing.

"Bitch, I want you to stay away from my husband."

"Your husband pursued me. I did not pursue him. DeMarco?" I called his name. He didn't respond. He was just sitting there, looking straight ahead. The engineer quietly sat in front of the Mac computer, staring at it as if he were watching a movie.

Nakeesha suddenly threw an uppercut, sending me to the floor. I looked at DeMarco. He acted as if he wasn't even fazed. He *still* sat there, although he slightly repositioned himself in the chair when I fell in his direction. I thought about all that he had said about protecting me and not letting anything happen to me. *That bitch! She hit me, and DeMarco isn't coming to my defense; that motherfucker.* I looked back towards Nakeesha in time to see her fist flying at my face a second time. Then Malik entered.

"Everybody get out," he yelled. The engineer, DeMarco, and Nakeesha, and I moved outside to front of the studio. DeMarco was walking away with Nakeesha, and then climbed into DeMarco's Range Rover. I yelled, "DeMarco, you son of a bitch!"

He turned around and said, "Haley, that is my wife. I love you, but I'm in love with her."

I woke up trembling. That dream had seemed so real…

Thirty-six

Tellis called me on Saturday morning. It was good to hear from him, since we used to be really close. We were always platonic friends, and he was one of my closest confidantes and advisor about many things. Our work and subsequent busy schedules didn't allow us to spend that much time together anymore, as we had in the past. But, we managed to talk a couple of times per month, and periodically got together for dinner.

"Hey, Haley, we are overdue for dinner," the voice on the other end of the phone said.

"Tellis, I thought you had forgot about me! I haven' heard from you in so long."

"For the last three months, I've been out of the country, in Japan. I had business there."

"Is that right? I was wondering what happened to you. I called you and left you a few messages."

"I got them when I got back. You should have sent me an email. I would have gotten it sooner. So, we on for dinner tonight?"

"Sure, you coming to get me?"

"I can come get you. Where you wanna eat at?"

"It doesn't really matter. Somewhere where it's not too noisy, though, so we can talk."

269

"Let's go to Georgia's."

"Alright! Damn, the food is so good there." Georgia's was a popular, upscale soul food restaurant owned by Denzel Washington and Debbie Allen. The "Who's Who" of L.A. frequented the place, as did the ballers and anyone else who wanted to have soul food in a classy atmosphere. Georgia's was similar to a supper club. Throughout dinner, a guy dressed in a black tuxedo would play on the baby grand piano which sat in a corner of the restaurant. Sometimes, there would even be a good jazz band featured at the club. Of course, only the best jazz musicians played at Georgia's.

"See you around six-ish," Tellis said.

"Sounds good. Call me when you get out front, and I'll come out."

I had first met Tellis Mahon, CEO of Mahon & Associates Brokerage Firm, at the UCLA Black Law Student's Association's (BLSA) annual fundraiser dinner about seven years ago. He was genuinely a nice person. Before I met DeMarco a few years ago, Tellis was going to invest in a record label I wanted to start, but I didn't follow through since I was already committed to Eastside West.

Tellis was a brilliant man. He came up, from nothing to something. It is amazing that he was so successful, considering all that he had to overcome in order to make it. His story was so motivating to me. He grew up in Shreveport, Louisiana during a time when racism was rampant in the South. Tellis was the youngest of fourteen kids. Neither of his parents were educated: his mother was a housewife, and his father worked for the local oil company. While in the third grade, it was discovered that he was exceptionally gifted, for he scored so high on his IQ tests. The elementary school which he attended made him take the test five times, doubting that a poor little black boy could score so high. Each time he took the test, his score was higher than the last. This was the story with which Tellis loved to inspire others when he'd give a speech or wanted to point to an example of the importance of one's self-confidence. He graduated from Stanford in the early seventies, earning a degree in political science, and then attended UCLA, where he not only received an MBA but also graduated from law school.

Tellis attended UCLA with L.A.'s mayor, Tom Bradley, back in the seventies. The two were good friends. Tellis helped Bradley get elected as mayor by making a large financial contribution to his mayoral campaign. He also used his power and influence to help some of the liberal politicians get into office. When Maxine Waters ran for City Council, Tellis was right there, supporting her. His money made him arguably the second most influential guy in Los Angeles behind Bradley back in the day.

Earlier that year, he donated $50,000 to the law school. He was asked by the Black law students to deliver the keynote address for he was an excellent speaker. I was impressed.

Tellis was a handsome older man in his late fifties now. He was the kind of man that a very sophisticated, mature woman would fall for. His gray hair made him look quite distinguished, and he bore a resemblance to the retired basketball player Julius Irving, otherwise known as Dr. J.

Tellis was reserved, smart, and confident, and he had style and class. He was a well-dressed man. He had a discriminating taste in clothes, and was one of the few men, if not the only man- I knew who could out-dress DeMarco. He wore two, three, and four-thousand-dollar suits, always looking like a million bucks. If he wore a pair of Levis jeans, he'd top it off with a three-hundred-dollar Cooji or Dolce Gabbana sweater, or a three to five-hundred-dollar pair of shoes like Cole Haans, Ferragamo, or Barrett's. His clothes looked good on his tall, medium-built body, and he topped off with expensive jewelry, usually a Rolex or Bvlgari watch that carried a price tag of ten grand or higher. On occasion, Tellis would wear diamond cufflinks.

In the mid '90s, he graced the cover of *Black Enterprise* magazine as the most successful Black businessman in the history of the stock brokerage business. His net worth was estimated at better than sixty million dollars. He had offices in New York, Miami, Chicago, and throughout California. He also had international offices in Japan and Toronto.

I was en route to the bathroom to freshen my makeup when he approached me, wearing a Ralph Lauren tuxedo. Ever the businessman, he cut right to the chase, "Wow, you are an attractive woman. Would you have dinner with me tomorrow?"

I accepted his invitation, and that was how we first met. We had dinner at one of L.A.'s finest restaurants, The Slanted Door, known around the world for its authentic Vietnamese food. I suggested the restaurant after learning Vietnamese was also his favorite food. We talked over dinner and drinks.

"So, Haley, I have done some investigating on you."

"Is that right? What you come up with?"

"I've learned that we have a mutual friend."

"Who?"

"Harold McKinley."

"You know Harold?"

"Sure do."

"How?"

"Well he's rich, and I'm rich. We hang in a lot of the same circles."

"I use to work for Harold. He gave me my start in the music business. During the time I worked for him, he was the hottest R&B manager in the music business. He had offices in the Bay Area and here in Los Angeles. He married the singer, Chastity Love, a.k.a., Entice who went on to sell millions of records. He put a million dollars of his money into her, and she blew up. She had the nerve to leave him after she made it. Can you believe that? She acts like what he did for her was nothing. I mean, how can you just dog somebody out who's been good to you, who believed in you the way he did, and not be thankful? Before she met him, she was literally a street hoe, and he took her away from that and married a producer. Then she divorced him and married a football player, and now she's an evangelist."

"Yeah, he did spend a lot of his money on her."

"I'd say he'd paid a lot of money for some pussy."

Tellis laughed. "I haven't seen Harold in years. Do you ever see him?"

"No. Last I heard, he got away from the music business. Been away now for some years."

"Harold is good people, though."

We always got along really well, and over the years had developed a genuine friendship.

Tellis arrived at my house at 6:15. He was driving his Black Bentley with the black convertible top. I got in and greeted him with a kiss on the cheek. This is how we always greeted one another upon first sight.

"Damn, Tellis! I want one of these," I said, looking around at the fine automobile.

"Keep working hard, and you'll get one."

"So, Tellis, are you still seeing Maria?"

"Yeah, its an off-and-on thing, though. I need to find me a good woman and marry her. You know a smart, rich woman who might be interested?"

"You are too funny."

"So how about you, Haley? You still tripping off of dude with the dreads?"

"You talking about DeMarco," I confirmed.

He nodded, remembering. "Yeah, that's his name."

"That's a long story. I'll tell you about him over dinner."

"Like that?" I nodded my head.

As Tellis drove to the restaurant, we talked.

"So, Haley, tell me… what motivates you?"

"People telling me that I can't do something or because I am a woman I have limits. How about you Tellis? What motivates you?"

"Money, figuring out the best way to make it. I don't want to talk about me right now. I want to talk about you, though."

"Okay."

"Back to this guy, DeMarco. Do you love him?"

"What kind of question is that?"

"Just answer the question."

"Tellis, DeMarco's married."

"Yeah, I remember you telling me that."

"His wife was in rehab when we met. She did three years in a drug program at Delancey Street for her abuse of cocaine and recently got out. He claims he's divorcing her. However, I see no proof of that.

"Yeah, if he's married, he's already committed?"

"Exactly. Our falling in love with one another is just one of those things that happened, while we were pursuing our entrepreneurial endeavors together. It really shouldn't have happened, but now I do love him and he loves me… I think. In fact, I think he's in love with me *and* his wife. He contends he doesn't love her, only me."

Tellis nodded. Although he is a very rich man and was as educated as DeMarco, he was a nigguh. A brother from the block, he had his skeletons in the closet, too. Like DeMarco, he had been a block hog. He had used his money to pay for college. But despite his MBA and his JD and his Bentley, and friends and influences in the upper white-boy crust, he didn't forget where he came from.

"Haley, my vibe is that this guy really likes you and I already know how you feel about him. I mean, time will tell. Maybe, weigh it out a little longer. I think he's going to do right by you. Actually, I think he's in love with you, and vice-versa. Give the brother a little more time. Set another deadline, and if he doesn't deliver by then, break it off with him. Haley, I know what its like to be in a relationship with someone and you don't want to be there. Before my divorce, I was in a catch-22 situation like DeMarco…"

Cutting Tellis off, "Do you think DeMarco is in love with his wife, Tellis?"

"No. I think he got love for her, but I don't think he's in love with her. I feel he's in love with you, Haley. That's what I see. Look at his actions. You can tell by his conduct. Haley, you have to remember this is bigger than DeMarco and his wife. His choice affects his children as well, probably even his money to some degree. His choice will alter his life."

Tellis always seemed to know what to say at the right time. The thing about it is, he was always right. So, I guess he was again correct; time would tell…

Thirty-seven

"**What we as** a people need, are more strong sisters like Haley," DeMarco said as he drank Remy from the half-pint bottle. "She ain't like the other females. There's something about her that's different. The way she thinks, her confidence, just the way she is. She can do pretty much anything. She speaks well, writes well. Man, she can write anything. She write business plans, she be interviewing people and writing articles about them and shit. For the magazine she starting, she already interviewed Suge Knight, Master P, Nelly, and it don't even come out until next spring. She is so ambitious, smart, and she down to earth. Usually sisters that got it going on like her be some stuck-up bitches. I believe in her. If she keeps working hard and believes in herself, she is going to do it. Everything she wants will happen for her because she is a smart girl and a hard worker, and I am here to help her in whichever way she needs help. Actually things is already happening for her." DeMarco was double-parked in the projects expressing his thoughts about me to his boys. Kameron was sitting in the passenger seat next to DeMarco. Lil Rob, Quincy, and Scherzo sat in the back seat listening to him… and probably scratching their heads, trying to remember a time DeMarco had last sang the praises of a woman for anything she did outside of the bedroom.

"Man, sounds like you falling in love with Haley, man," Kameron said.

"Man, I was back here just thinking the same thing, but I didn't want to go there, know what I mean," Scherzo expressed.

"DeMarco, you in love with that bitch?" Lil Rob asked.

Quincy spoke up. "Man, leave my nigguh alone. If he in love, he in love, ain't nothing wrong with it. Just cause y'all nigguhs ain't found a bitch to love, don't hate. Appreciate."

DeMarco rumbled, "Man, I am not in love with Haley, she is my business partner." The whole car laughed, including Quincy.

"Man, my nig DeMarco, don't trip, it's cool to be in love. You acting like being in love is a bad thing, my bro," Quincy said.

"Man, I know being in love is a good thing or could be a good thing if you with the right bitch. I don't deny that. But I am not, repeat *not*, in love with Haley."

"My nigguh ain't in love… he mesmerized," Scherzo said around a burst of laughter.

"This nigguh sounding pussy-whipped, if you ask me. Kameron turned to DeMarco. "Nigguh, you pussy-whipped?"

"Yeah right," DeMarco rolled his eyes.

"I don't even think they fucked yet," Lil Rob said.

"What my nigguh, y'all ain't' fucked," Quincy asked. DeMarco didn't respond to Quincy's question. Garrulous laughter filled the car.

"Y'all nigguhs is really dumb. Man, Haley is my business partner and I respect that. Whether I slept with her or not, it really ain't y'all business." More whoops and hollers emanated; a withering look from DeMarco cut them off short.

Scherzo spoke again. "Nigguh, that's another thing I been noticing about you: you never refer to Haley as a bitch. You always call her a woman when you be talking about her. I ain't never heard you not call a bitch a 'bitch.' Yeah, you in love," Scherzo said.

"Man, Haley is my business partner and I ain't gone call her a bitch. She a real woman, she got class and she smart. I don't think about her how I think about other women. Man, them other women can't even compete with her…"

"Damn, she must got some bomb-ass pussy," Kameron interrupted.

"Man, whatever… fuck y'all. Haley is my business partner.

"Who you trying to convince that Haley is your business partner, us or you," Lil Rob asked.

"Hey, I think we better leave this alone. DeMarco up here getting mad and shit and we don't want to make this nigguh mad, cause he get like the Incredible Hulk when he mad," Kameron said.

"Man, I really don't care about the bitch. DeMarco, hand me some bomb back here so I can roll it," Scherzo said. DeMarco passed him a large Ziploc bag filled with dark green chronic.

"Damn, nigguh, where in the fuck this weed from?"

"Humboldt, nigguh," DeMarco, said looking back at him.

"Man, Humboldt got the best motherfucking weed on this planet," Kameron said.

DeMarco shook his head. "Vancouver."

"Man, I heard Chicago do," Lil Rob said.

DeMarco shook his head again and repeated, "Vancouver. Hawaii got some good weed too, but Vancouver got the best weed."

"This nigguh know, if he say Vancouver I wouldn't argue with him, 'cause I don't know nobody who smoke weed like this motherfucker," Kameron said.

"I know, my nigguh do be smoking," Scherzo said.

"You done rolling it, nigguh?" DeMarco asked.

"Almost," Scherzo replied.

DeMarco glanced in the rear-view mirror to see Scherzo's progress, and saw the black-and-white APD car turn the corner behind him. Police officers were riding three deep: one Black man, one Samoan man, and one white female. They spotted DeMarco's double-parked black Range Rover. "Ah shit," DeMarco said, "we got company." He removed the key from the ignition. "Hey, Scherzo, put that bomb away and Kameron, make sure the top is on that bottle of Remy," DeMarco said, pointing to it.

The car pulled up alongside the Range Rover. DeMarco realized the car smelled of chronic. Turning the A/C on to try and blow it out occurred to him, but he realized there was no time. The officers got out of the car. The Black and White officers approached the driver's side, and the Samoan officer approached the passenger side where D sat. DeMarco's window was rolled up. He ignored the officers that were standing on his side. The black officer tapped on the window.

"Roll down the window," the officer demanded.

"Man, this motherfucker really need to quit," DeMarco said.

DeMarco stared at him. He inserted the key in the ignition, started it and rolled down the electric window. He rested his head on the headrest on the back of his seat. The smell of chronic rushed the officers in the nose; despite this, DeMarco had too much game to wince.

"Turn off the engine," the female officer yelled at DeMarco. He looked back at her and hesitated. He turned it off.

"Ain't y'all suppose to be out fighting crime or something," DeMarco asked. He pointed down the street and said, "I just saw an old lady get her pursed snatched. Why don't y'all go and see if she need some help? Ain't y'all suppose to serve and protect? Ain't nothing to protect over here. Man, that old lady, she probably really need y'all." The officers ignored him.

"All right, everybody… out of the vehicle," the female officer demanded. The two back doors of the truck swung open; Lil Rob, Quincy and Scherzo stepped out. DeMarco and Kameron were still in the truck, quite high from the chronic, and taking their time slowly getting out. Pointing to the bottle of Hennessey that sat between DeMarco and Tony, the female officer barked, "Pour out the alcohol."

"Man, these motherfuckers is really taking mines," DeMarco said as he picked up the half-full bottle of Remy. He stepped out of the truck and asked the Samoan officer what he wanted him to do with it.

"Pour it out," the female cop said. DeMarco took the top off and poured the Remy on the ground. "And this is for those who ain't here like my nigguh in Cooley High said," Demarco joked. His boys laughed.

The female officer gave DeMarco a contemptuous look. "So you're the funny one, eh? I need to see your vehicle license and registration." DeMarco sat back inside the truck with the door open. He reached across and opened the glove box and fumbled through it. He took out the small velvet bag that held the pair of soundless stone meditation balls, which he liked because he was able to practice his exercise in public without disturbing people who were around. DeMarco said that the stone balls in some ways were more comfortable than the metal balls, which sometimes produced static. Finally, he found the registration and proof of insurance and pulled them out. Stepping out of the truck, he handed it to the female officer.

She took the registration DeMarco presented. "How much does one of these cost?" She pointed to the car.

"More than you make all year," DeMarco answered. His boys laughed.

"All right… sit on the curb with your friends," the officer said. DeMarco sat. They called in the registration and searched through the truck.

"What you do with the weed in the Zip Loc bag," DeMarco whispered to Scherzo who was sitting next to him on the curb.

"It's stuffed in the back of my pants."

"Goddamn, man, I hope them assholes don't search me, I got like five zips in my pocket," DeMarco muttered. Just as he said that the officer announced that he found some marijuana under the backseat. Wondering whose it was, DeMarco looked around at his boys to search for a guilty expression; peering back, Quincy winced.

DeMarco narrowed his own eyes. "Nigguh, before you got in my car I asked you if you had anything on you and you said you didn't."

Next, the officer walked over to DeMarco and proceeded to search him. He instructed DeMarco to get up from the curb and lean against the police car so he could frisk him.

"Let the bitch search me," DeMarco said, looking at the female officer. She frowned. He winked at her. "I want the bitch to touch my balls." The cop pushed DeMarco onto the car roughly.

"Man, you ain't gone let the bitch search me? I want the bitch to grab my nuts."

"I am going to arrest you," the cop said.

"For what?"

"For being a smart ass."

"Ah, man, come on." DeMarco laughed loudly. People began to come out of their nearby residences. A woman rushed to the scene with a camcorder, videotaping the event.

With DeMarco leaning on the car, the officer patted him down. He reached inside his front coat pocket and pulled out the five zips.

"Well, well, well, what do we have here? Your cannabis club card won't help you this time, buddy," the cop said.

The other officer who stood by read DeMarco his rights while cuffing him.

"Cut up the seats. See if you find any more drugs," the female officer instructed the Samoan after he finished with DeMarco.

"Man, this is really unnecessary," DeMarco said.

"Shut up," the female officer said.

"Bitch."

The cop pulled out a pocketknife and cut a hole in the leather seat on the driver's side. He proceeded around the car to the passenger seat and sliced it open. Then, he went for the back seats. He didn't find anything else.

DeMarco calmly stood with his hands cuffed behind his back as he watched the officers demolish the beautiful look of the seventy thousand dollar Black Range Rover, which wasn't even a year old.

"That's fucked up," Scherzo said.

"It ain't nothing. Fuck it, I'll have it re-upholstered, or I'll just get me another one. I been thinking about getting a Black Cadillac Escalade anyway," he said.

The police officer stood DeMarco up from the curb and read him his rights. Placing him into the back seat of the police car, the black cop snickered. DeMarco took a double look at him saying, "What's the point in taking me in? I'll be out in less than two hours." He turned to Kameron. "Call Haley. Tell her to post bail."

It was around nine when I got the call. I recognized Kameron's voice. I could tell there was trouble. "Haley, you gotta bail DeMarco out. The police rode up on us in the 'jects." My heart started to pound. "We was sitting in DeMarco's truck smoking, they found some weed and they arrested

DeMarco."

I breathed a little easier. "That's all they got him for? Some chronic?"

"Yeah."

"They didn't think he was dealing, did they?"

"No," Kameron said. "He didn't have nothin' on him but a few zips."

That sucked, but simple possession of marijuana was hardly the worst rap DeMarco could have gone down for, as I knew all too well. "Where he at, the county?"

"Yeah."

"Alright, I'm on my way."

An hour and a half-later DeMarco was out. However, he needed to attend court for the marijuana charges. Although it was a misdemeanor, the government always had a thing about pot. DeMarco ended up drawing a ninety-day sentence in the county.

Thirty-eight

It was 7:00 a.m. on Saturday morning. Utopia and I stood in the long line at the county jail to sign up on DeMarco's visitor's list. Not knowing if Nakeesha would show up for a visit with her husband, in an attempt to avoid seeing her, I woke up extra early to make the first round of visits. I figured that if Nakeesha visited DeMarco, it would be for a later visit, seeing as how she had small kids at home. Nevertheless, I uneasily stood in line. I didn't want to go alone, so I brought Utopia along. She gave me some degree of comfort and support. Neither Utopia nor I had ever seen Nakeesha, so we didn't know what she looked like. For all we knew, she could have been standing next to us in line. I leaned over to her and said quietly, "Utopia, when we get up there, I am going to look at one list and you look at the other, and let me know if you see Nakeesha's name on it. See if she signed up already before us. Maybe she's in front of us in this line."

"Alright, I'll check the list the officer on the right has, and you check the list the officer on the left has," Utopia said.

We saw a lot of the females from the 'jects who were visiting their boyfriends or husbands. Finally, we reached the front of the line.

"What is the inmate's name you are here to visit," the officer asked.

"DeMarco Speed."

Starting at the top of the list, the officer ran his pointer finger slowly over the names. He located DeMarco's name. "I need to see your ID or drivers license, ma'am." I handed it to him. He wrote my name next to DeMarco's name on the list.

Utopia quickly glanced at the other note pad while I signed up to see DeMarco. She didn't see Nakeesha's name on it.

"Alright, you can stand off to the side and I will let you know when it is time for your visit." Utopia and I made small talk while we waited for the announcement.

"You know what Utopia? I've been thinking, and I am going to have to stop seeing DeMarco. I can't deal with him anymore, I mean his wife is home now, you know, and I don't see him making plans to leave her."

"That's real talk, girl. You know if you keep on seeing him, it's gone be trouble."

"Yeah, I am going to let him know its over."

"Girl, you gotta be strong, though, and don't let him talk you out of it. You know he's gonna try and talk you out of it, right?"

"Yeah, I know, but I can't live as his mistress. I deserve better than being his mistress."

"Yep, you sure do."

A bored-sounding female voice appeared through a speaker that hung from a wall in the corner of the room. "7:30 visitors line up at the red line." I went in with the first group. When I walked through the doorway that separated the waiting area from the visiting room, I immediately saw DeMarco sitting in front of the big glass window wearing an orange prison jumpsuit. Before sitting down on the brown stool, I stared at him for a moment. DeMarco lifted the receiver off of the white phone that hung next to him on the wall. He pointed at the one on my side. I delayed, because I dreaded the conversation I was about to have. I sat down on the unfinished wooden stool and picked up the phone.

"Hey, baby," DeMarco said excitedly.

"Hey, how you doing?"

"I'm cool. Can't wait to get the fuck outta here, though," he said, looking around.

"Hmmm."

"What? What's the matter?"

"DeMarco, what if your wife comes while I'm here?"

DeMarco humped his shoulders. "I'm divorcing her, Haley, I filed for a divorce last month."

I was speechless.

Breaking my silence, "DeMarco…"

DeMarco held one finger over his pushed out lips, "Shhh,'" he said. I stopped speaking.

"Haley, please don't worry about that. Look, I don't want to talk about Nakeesha. Let's talk about us, forget about her."

"DeMarco, I'm still waiting to see those papers. Really, this is it. It's over between us."

"Haley, how in the fuck you gone say some shit to me like that, and I'm behind bars, and I then put my trust in you? What the fuck that look like? What's your point, Haley? You knew that from the gate before you threw the pussy my way. I'm a man! What the fuck you expect?"

"I threw my pussy your way? What in the fuck do you got, amnesia? You were the one chasing me, remember?! You pursued me, motherfucker."

"Haley, listen, all I'm saying is now we got something. I got something and you got something and you wanna walk away cause of your righteousness. Save the bullshit, Haley. You know what you was fucking with from the gate. I sit up here and I tell you I'm divorcing Nakeesha. I wasn't never happy with that bitch. I married her 'cause it was the right thing for me to do at the time, I done told you that."

"And what, DeMarco? You with me 'cause it's the best thing for you to do at this time?"

"I didn't say that."

"Well, what are you saying?"

"Haley, listen, you got everybody in here looking at us and I ain't about to beg you like a bitch. Now would you let that shit rest until I get out? I'll be outta here in a minute."

"No DeMarco, you listen. It's over between us. Go back to your wife and kids."

"Haley, stop it… now, let's talk about us."

"You don't tell me what the fuck to do! There is no us. DeMarco, I am so sorry, I have to go. I'm not going to continue being your mistress and have you going back and forth between me and your wife! Bye." I stood, hung up the phone, and ran out of the visiting room. Utopia was in the waiting area, reading a newspaper someone had left behind.

"Come on, Utopia, let's go. I got to get out of here. I feel like I'm going to pass out." Utopia put the newspaper on the chair next to hers and followed. I bypassed the elevator, proceeded straight to the staircase, hurried down the seven flights of stairs, out through the white side door, and into the alley. Utopia was a little out of breath as she tried to keep up. We reached her car. I silently got in.

After we had left the county parking lot, Utopia spoke. "How was your visit with DeMarco?"

"I told him it was over." Utopia nodded.

"Because loving him is wrong. You guys were right. My family was right. Maybe in another place and at another time, DeMarco would have been the right guy for me. Utopia, I told him that I deserved more than to be some man's mistress and that it was over. Girl, I love DeMarco, but being with him is wrong.

"I really am through with him this time. I have to stop seeing him."

Utopia was skeptical. "Girl, how do you know this?"

"Because I just do. I know you, Krystal, Camille, and my parents don't believe me, but just watch, you'll see. DeMarco is making me lose focus on my projects, the magazine, the record label, and I can't have that. I have never let a man make me lose focus, and I can't let DeMarco make me lose focus either."

"But girl, y'all comp is about to be out… what are you going to do about that?"

How had I known Utopia was going to point that out? "I am going to finish what I started with him. I just have to separate my personal feelings from business. I can do it. I know I can."

"Haley, I know it doesn't seem like it right now, but you are going to find a guy, a husband one day that you will love and appreciate as much as you love and appreciate DeMarco. And he won't be married."

"You think so?"

"Yeah, it just may not seem like it right now 'cause you going through it."

We reached her place and walked down the street hand in hand. I used my free hand to wipe the tears from my eyes as I walked. "Utopia, I am so glad that God put you in my life."

"Girl, so am I. You are like a sister to me, you know."

"I love you."

"I love you."

Thirty-nine

April 12th

Dear DeMarco,

Since the last time *I saw you, two days ago, I haven't been able to sleep because of the constant thoughts I have of you. I apologize to you if I upset or hurt you—that wasn't my intention when I came to visit you in jail the other day and ran out on you.*

I want to share more with you about the way I feel about us, and why I have decided it would be best for us to both go our separate ways. We can still finish the compilation that we started. However, we don't need to talk until it is time for me to give you your check.

DeMarco, I want to conclude the conversation I started with you the other day when I visited you, but got too emotional to finish. It is easier for me to say what I have to say to you in a letter rather than face-to-face, so here we go.

Somehow, mistakenly, I have fallen madly in love with you. This wasn't supposed to happen. When we first met, I didn't have eyes for you. Nor did you for me. The two of us coming together was about a joint business venture. We were uniting to reach our goals—to make money. We were only supposed to be business partners, but then we became friends, best friends, next thing I know I started liking you romantically and developed deep-seated feelings for you, and then we became lovers. I know it took months, but it seems like it happened about as quick as it reads here.

I ask myself where, how and when did my feelings for you develop. Aside from the fact that you are a good-looking man, I think my feelings evolved over time and as a result of me being so close to you, finding you so fascinating and intriguing—looking at your ambitions and motivations is like looking at a replica of mine. The truth is, I don't know of too many people like us. All I know is I woke up one day and my feelings for you were there. Therefore, I use the word mistakenly to explain how I have arrived at my feelings for you.

Although I didn't see it at the time—you and I have spent way too much time together. Interestingly, those closest to me—my family and friends—saw the love between us forthcoming, even when I didn't. You know, the late nights hanging out together, the long telephone conversations and so on—that was a mistake on our part.

Everybody has a common path on the journey of Life—birth, marriage, children and death. Give or take—these things are pretty much the guarantees that life offers to each one of us if we don't die too young. The one that I am going to focus on in this letter is the meeting of one's soulmate and marriage.

From the time we realize what love truly is, we desire to one day connect with our soulmate. The one person in life we were meant to become one with. The person that destiny brings into our lives. On one hand, I believe that you are my soulmate. But somewhere, nature made a blunder and diverted you from me.

What makes me stop my pursuit of eternal love with you, DeMarco, is your wife and your beautiful children—mostly your wife. DeMarco, I love you and because I love you so much naturally, I love your children and I care about what they think about me. I cannot fathom the thought of them growing up in a home without you, and the idea that they may believe that I took you away from them and their mother, and thus develop a strong dislike of me. I can't accept that. The truth is, I have been selfish with you, and I have regrets about being with you when I think about your family. As it stands, I am the one hurt if I leave now. But if I don't leave now I am afraid that innocent people like your wife and your children will be hurt.

And then there's that other thing that interferes with me loving you, and that is that you're married. I know you don't think it's a big deal, but I disagree. I grew up in the Baptist church. The church—and my parents—taught me that it's wrong to date a married man. According to the Christian Scriptures that I believe in, I am wrong to have these feelings for you, let alone to act on them the way I have. My heart tells me it is all right to love you, to fuck it and just do the damn thang. On the other hand, I can't ignore my conscience and the guilt that's eating me alive. Your marriage, your children and my belief are the things that give me a guilty conscience about loving you and being with you. The burden of guilt is killing me softly. With this said, I can't continue seeing you.

Although I will go on to date other men and I will end up marrying one of them one day, there is only one soulmate for us in life. For me, that was you, but you were intercepted from me. No matter what, no matter how beautiful we might have been, that's the fact.

DeMarco, this has been a difficult letter for me to write. I am weak for you. So don't tempt me. Do not contact me. Accepting the fact that we cannot be is one of the hardest experiences of my life. I am afraid that if you respond to this letter that it is just going to make the hole we need to climb out of—a hole that is already deep enough as it is—that much more deeper to get out of. There is no sense prolonging the hurt and the pain. It is already a difficult task for me to let you go from my life. More importantly, I do not want to get caught up in a game with you, for you are more than entertainment to me. If you love me, you will grant me this wish. No, not my wish—what I know has to be.

There will always be a place in my heart for you, but we cannot be. Sorry.

Love eternal,

Haley

Forty

May 16th

Dear Haley,

I asked my sister to mail you the Los Angeles County stamped copy of my petition for divorce—you'll receive it in the mail it in a day or so.

Haley, I love you. You bring out the best in me. I have never met a woman like you and with you, for the first time in my life I find myself in love with a woman. You are my other half—the half that completes me.

I will end this letter for now, but never the friendship or my love for you.

DeMarco

P.S.

You said I was intercepted from you? In football, when an interception happens, sometimes the other team gets the ball back, so Haley, you shouldn't give up so easily. You said we were only supposed to be business partners. I say, oh well, shit happens. Also, I want you to know that I am seeking joint custody of my children and you will also be a mother to them. With this said, you can erase your doubts of them not liking you. We can all give them the love they rightfully deserve and we can get the love we rightfully deserve. Also, we are going to purchase a big house for us all to live in.

Sincerely,

DeMarco

Forty-one

On a rainy day, when my spirits were rather low, the envelope came in the mail. The return address was to DeMarco's sister, at his grandmother's house. Intrigued, I quickly tore it open. I took the paper out. I'd seen enough legal documents in my life to recognize one when I saw it. The stamp across the top read "Petition for Divorce."

My soul leaped. DeMarco really had filed for the divorce! Here was the document itself; the crisp, original copy, no less, duly endorsed and stamped by the County of Los Angeles. The court's stamp was dated two months after Nakeesha got out of rehab.

Wow, he really did love me. I thought about all the things he'd said. My future brightened as my eyes read over the papers. My future with DeMarco… I really loved DeMarco in the true sense of the word.

Forty-two

May 25th

Dear DeMarco,

I hope this letter finds you well. I miss you so much. I got the copy of the divorce petition you filed in Los Angeles Superior Court that you had your sister mail me. For the record, I never wanted to stop loving you. I want to grow old with you and have lots of babies with you (smile). Just hurry home cause my friend in the closet is not going to do the trick.

Love the hell out of ya.

Haley

Forty-three

DeMarco and I purchased our new home in Anaheim Hills, Orange County, California, an exclusive Los Angeles suburb. Anaheim's demographic was 2 percent African American, 34 percent white, 16 percent Asian and 47 percent Latin. The demographic that made up Anaheim Hills was 92 percent white, 6 percent Asian and probably less than 0.2 percent African American and Asian.

Our realtor showed us a number of homes in L.A.'s exclusive neighborhoods, including Highland Park, Baldwin Hills, Ladera Heights, and Calabasas, before we decided on the two-story, European-style, 3500-square-foot house with the double front entrance doors and shiny round gold doorknobs. The home in the upscale neighborhood boasted a triple garage, a lap pool that extended the entire length of the back of the house, two fireplaces with one each in the family room and the master bedroom. It also had a gourmet kitchen, breakfast area, den, office, formal dining room, living room, and a game room. We purchased our new home with all of the offered upgrades: central air conditioning, a security system, cat-5 wiring, and low-emission windows. Okay, so I didn't really know what low-emission windows were, but hey, they sounded cool.

DeMarco had extra monitors installed in nearly every room in the house, including the bathroom in the master bedroom. Monitors also hung on the walls of our bedroom, the office, and the kitchen. The two-story house, built in 2000, featured an unobstructed panoramic view of Downtown Los Angeles. It was perfect for entertaining, something DeMarco and I both enjoyed doing.

To purchase our new home, I sold one of the homes that my grand-mother left me, and put down $300,000 on the $600,000 house. I deposited the remaining $150,000 into my savings account. After the down payment, our mortgage was a reasonable $2600 per month. DeMarco and I agreed to split the mortgage, utility, cable, garbage, and grocery bills fifty-fifty.

DeMarco and I both liked modern contemporary furniture. The furniture in our new home was therefore modern contemporary. We purchased our bedroom set and most of our furniture from Pottery Barn, Ethan Allen, and the Spiegel Catalog. In fact, our new gray iron king size canopy bed came from the Catalog.

I was sitting up in bed with my back propped against the pillows reading Renee Swindle's novel *Please, Please, Please* when DeMarco came home late one night. Renee was a sister from Oakland who had written a novel about this woman named Babysister, who had an affair with this married guy named Darren. The book reminded me, in a way, of what DeMarco and I were going through, so I was really feeling it.

DeMarco came into the bedroom and gave me his standard "baby, I'm home" greeting: a kiss on the lip. He flung his Fubu jean jacket across the back of the white leather chaise in our bedroom. He then sat down on the chaise, undid the shoestrings on his black and red leather Jordans, slid them off. His white Nike socks followed. He stood up, slid off his black Sean John blue jeans, and headed for the shower.

I laid in bed next to DeMarco, reflecting on the beginning of a new life with him and the blessings that God has granted me: the house, my cars, and him. DeMarco was asleep, snoring loudly in our bed with the new white sixteen-hundred-dollar down mattress and the five-hundred-dollar white down comforter with gold designs. Snoring and leaving the toilet seat up were my pet peeves—both habits of DeMarco- but I accepted DeMarco's irksome ways. I learned to overlook them. I was in love. They say what you won't do, you do for love. I looked at DeMarco, sleeping like a baby next to me, and I thought about how happy he made me and about something my mother used to say. She would always tell my sisters and I that when we chose a man, ensure that he treated us as good as she did; then we would know we had the right man. DeMarco definitely fit her standards. He went through whatever it was he needed to in order to keep me happy.

DeMarco's snoring stopped; he got from the bed in his white Sean Jean boxers. Walking into the bathroom, he sleepily proclaimed, "I gotta go pee."

A few minutes later, he crawled back into the bed, and asked for the time.

"Midnight."

"Man, I'm tired." DeMarco laid on his back with his head propped up on three white and gold pillow shams which matched the comforter, with one arm clasped behind his head, staring up at the ceiling.

"DeMarco, I am so glad that God put you in my life." He smiled.

"How about that," he said sounding excited.

"I guess I should turn of the light so we can get some sleep."

"What… you don't wanna make love, Haley?"

"Uh-uh, not tonight, you wore me out. We been doing it every night this week." We both giggled. "I need a break." I got up and turned off the lights. The drapes in the bedroom were drawn. It was a full moon, and the moonlight shined through the window; you could see our silhouettes. Getting back into bed, I whispered, "Good night, DeMarco."

"Haley?"

"Huh?"

"Good night, don't let the bed bugs bite. That's what my mother use to say to me back in East Oakland when I was a child after she'd tuck me in bed."

"Good night, DeMarco."

Forty-four

DeMarco and I spent most of the day lounging around the house watching television, talking about our families, dreams, and our goals and playing games. We'd played Backgammon, Ace Deuce, Blackjack, and Dominoes. I'd just finish whooping him three games straight in dominoes when the phone rang. "You just got lucky," he said, before retreating upstairs to the bedroom.

I answered the phone.

"Hey cousin, what you doing?" It was Skerz.

"Skerz, what's up, cousin?"

"Just got through whooping DeMarco's ass in dominoes."

Skerz sounded troubled. "Hey, I need to talk to him. The Feds came through the projects tonight, shaking nigguhs down and shit, asking us if we knew where DeMarco lived."

"For real?"

"Everybody was like, naw, we don't know where he live. I asked the cop what they wanted with him."

"What they say?"

"He said that they just needed to talk to him about something. He didn't say what, though. They said that they would be back and to tell DeMarco to come down to the station if we saw him, 'cause they had some questions that they wanted to ask him. Can you put him on the phone?"

"Hold on. He just went upstairs. Let me get him." With the white cordless phone in my hand, I walked to the foyer. "DeMarco? Hey DeMarco! Skerz is on the phone, pick it up. He wants to talk to you," I yelled up the white spiral staircase.

"Alright," DeMarco shouted back. He picked up the phone, "Yeah," DeMarco answered." I hung up the phone.

"DeMarco, the Feds came through looking for you today in the projects."

"Is that right? Which projects?"

"The Downs."

"What they want?"

"They said they need you to come down to the station… something about answering some questions."

"Man, they can kiss my ass. I ain't going nowhere. They'll see me when they see me."

"Huh, I heard that!"

"Who else they talk to?"

"It was me, Skate, Mone, Rico, and Fat Mike posted."

"Alright, right on, Skerz. Thanks for the heads-up."

"Alright. I'll talk to you later." I heard DeMarco hang up the phone.

I walked into the bedroom. DeMarco had a troubled expression on his face. "DeMarco, what's going on?" He was laying on the bed, with the remote control in his hand, flicking through the channels.

"Haley, I really don't know," he said slowly, "but if I were a guessing man, and I am, I'd say that the Feds are looking for me because of what I do. In case you've forgotten, I'm a drug dealer, but we are not the only drug dealers on the block," DeMarco joked. "You know the Millers, over on the next street?"

"Yes?"

"Well, he in the business too."

"What?! Get out of here! You're talking about the middle-aged white couple? The husband drives the white Lexus and his wife has a maroon one just like it?"

"Yep."

"I thought he owned a computer company in Pasadena."

"He does, but he still in the business."

"Well, you learn something new every day. So, DeMarco, what do you think is going to happen?"

"Man, they ain't got shit on me. It's just gone be some technical shit, that's why I expressed to you the importance of keeping the paper trail in our businesses squeaky-clean. That's what we needed. That's what this is all going to boil down to, paper. I'm already knowing."

"So, what are you going to do?"

"What do you mean, what am I going to do?"

"What are you going to do? Are you going to go down to the station and see what they want to talk to you about?"

"Hell, naw! Let them catch my black ass. Like I said, they see me when they see me. Look, Haley, don't worry about it, they ain't got shit on me. We've done our jobs. Whatever they're putting together isn't gone stick. They haven't got shit on me. They just want my black ass. You just make sure that if they come at you that you don't reveal shit to them. You just walk away. Don't answer any questions. If things get real intense you threaten them with your attorney, and don't answer them without an attorney. Haley, you smart, you know how to do it."

"Alright, DeMarco. I am going to take a shower and go to bed. I'm tired." Actually, I hadn't felt tired until after that phone call.

"I'm kind of tired, too. I guess I should be going to bed also."

I took my shower. When I came out, DeMarco was sitting on the white leather chaise, tying the white shoestring on his blue Air Force One shoes. He had his black leather jacket on and a Black Fubu baseball cap.

"Going somewhere?"

"I gotta make a run. I'll be back in a few."

"DeMarco, why don't you just stay in tonight?"

"Haley, please… I do not want to go through this with you tonight. What's the matter with you? When you got with me you knew what I did, you knew how I do, so what's the problem now? I gotta make a run. Damn, we move in together and you acting like… Man, Haley, just chill, please, would you?"

"We move in together and I'm acting like what, DeMarco?"

DeMarco's pager went off. He picked it up and looked at it, reading the number. His cell phone rung.

"Yeah, yeah, yeah, I'm on my way," he said, answering the phone and then hung it up.

"I act like what? You were about to say something and you stopped. You didn't complete your sentence. Nigguh, what do I act like?"

"What?" DeMarco, said looking at the number again on his pager. He focused his eyes back on me. "What did you say? Haley, I don't know what you acting like. Would you please stop?" I started to say something, but DeMarco cut me off. "Not tonight, Haley, I got some other shit on my mind. I'll be back," DeMarco said as he stood up from the white leather chaise. "Let me see the keys to your Range. I ain't got no gas in mines and I don't feel like getting out and pumping none either. Plus, I gotta go to the city and it's gone take me a minute to get there, and that'll make me get there even later."

"They're on the nightstand over there," I said.

"I'll call you from the car. Give me a few minutes." DeMarco kissed me on the forehead and left.

"Be careful."

"You know it."

It hadn't been two minutes since DeMarco left the house when the phone rung. *Damn that was fast.*

"Hey baby," I answered.

"Uh, no… sorry to disappoint you, but its not your baby."

"Krystal?"

"Yeah, girl."

"DeMarco just left and he said that he was going to call me from the car. I thought you were him."

"Oh, girl, I'm calling you because I am near your house. I had dinner with a co-worker at this restaurant in Anaheim, near Disneyland. I was wondering if I could stop by and get that $80 Nordstrom's gift certificate that you said you would let me have."

"Come on."

"Girl, thank you, I want to buy this purse from there. It's on sale for $275. I'm gone use the eighty dollars towards the purchase. Thank ya, girly-girl. I'll be right there. I'm not going to stay, though, 'cause I got to wake up early for work. Plus, I know you got to go to work too… but, then again, you work for yourself, so you can sleep in if you want to. You know what, Haley? All bullshitting aside, I admire the hell out of you. You are attractive, smart, and just a good all-around person. I thank God for our friendship all the time, girl."

"Wow! Thank you Krystal, you good people, too. I also thank God when I pray for our friendship, and I also include you in my prayers."

"Ah, that's so sweet. Hey, Haley? When you and DeMarco's businesses takes off, I wouldn't mind coming to work for y'all."

"Doing what?"

"Duh, I'd be you guys' attorney. I have always wanted to practice entertainment law, I just never really pursued. After law school, I took the first job I was offered and it was in criminal law as a public defender. Then after two years of doing that, I started doing my own thing. I like practicing law, but not criminal. I'm tired of the criminal thing. I feel that entertainment law is the right fit for me and my personality."

"You serious, huh, Krystal?"

"Yep."

"How much would you want to make?"

"Girl, just double my salary. I am making eighty five now."

"Krystal, if everything works out according to plan, DeMarco and I will hire you at double your current salary. Not a problem."

"Haley, I already know you are going to do it. Make it. Girl, I see it, everybody sees it. DeMarco saw it, that's why he sought you out and pursued you as a business partner. Right on, Haley! I love you."

"I love you, too, Krystal."

"I am pulling up in front of your house."

"Alright, I will be right down."

"Haley, just meet me at the door with the gift certificate so I don't have to come in. You know when I come in your house it takes me a long time to leave 'cause we be enjoying each other so much."

"Alright."

I handed Krystal the Nordstrom gift certificate. Despite her being in a hurry, we chopped it up for a minute on the steps before she left. From the front porch, I watched her get back into her car and drive off. I went back inside the house, set the alarm, and got in bed.

Krystal hadn't been gone five minutes when the doorbell rang. At first, I thought it was her doubling back because she had forgotten something; sometimes she'd do that. I started to go for the door when I realized that Krystal hadn't even come into the house. What could she have forgotten? I looked up at the security monitors on the wall in my bedroom.

DeMarco, ever the paranoid one, had surveillance cameras installed throughout the house. Our bedroom, the bathroom, the kitchen, the family room, the game room, and the living room all had monitors. One monitor was in the bedroom; I flipped a switch to view the image from the camera near the front door. Part of me still expected to see Krystal. But instead, I saw men in blue windbreaker jackets, with APD (Anaheim Police Department) written across the back. The blue jackets were everywhere. They even had two dogs with them.

Cursing, I grabbed my cell. It was lying next to me in the bed. I stabbed Krystal's number into the keypad. It rang. It rang again. *Damn it, Krystal, answer your—*

"Hey, Haley."

"Krystal, the police are here, they're outside. There's a lot of them out there."

"What?!"

"Girl, they rung the doorbell. I am looking at a fucking swarm of 'em right now on the monitors. They're all over the place. Krystal, I don't believe this shit… our home is being raided."

"Haley, I am turning around." Even before she said it, I heard the sound of tires squealing in the background. "I will be there as soon as I can. Do not let them in unless they show you a search warrant, okay, girl? And, girl, calm down and don't panic and do not answer any questions." Krystal was gunning the engine. "If *and only if* you see a search warrant do you let them in. Make sure you read it and it is a search warrant

before you let them in, alright?"

"Alright."

The walk from the master bedroom down to the front door seemed to take forever. My feet felt as if they were made of lead; the air itself seemed to grow thick enough so as to slow me down. I had known all along what the consequences were from being with a guy like DeMarco. This was the day I had dreaded and prayed would never come. Because DeMarco was so deep in the game and he did the shit 24/7, the raid was eventually bound to happen. He, too, knew what the possibilities were for a raid of our home to occur. Like a civil-defense warden in a wartime city prone to air raids, he had prepared me for this day. He had calmly told me what to do and say, if and when "Five-O" ever came to raid our home.

DeMarco made it clear to me that there was nothing they could do to me. However, he had warned me that they might try and scare me with their words; he had told me not to buy into it. Now someone was pounding on the door; the intrusion alarm began sounding a klaxon-like tone. I would do exactly as DeMarco instructed me. Exactly as Krystal instructed me. It would be okay. I steeled myself; the long walk to the front door finally came to an end. I pushed in the white button on the intercom.

"Yes?" I forced my voice to be firm, not quivering.

"APD, we have a search warrant to search your home, ma'am," a male voice on the other side of the door said. I turned off the alarm.

"Let me see the search warrant," I said, opening the door a crack. The short, fat cop in the blue uniform handed it to me. It was genuine. A judge had approved the warrant less than two hours ago, giving the cops the right to search our home. I turned and walked away from the door, padded slowly into the living room, and sat down on the ivory leather couch.

For the first time since I had seen those men on the monitor, a smile appeared on my face. DeMarco was no fool. I knew how careful he was to keep anything incriminating outside of our home. I watched the strangers invade my home, knowing they would find no bags of white powder, no notebooks of contacts, or computer disks chronologically detailing DeMarco's dealings. Other than the usual chronic or nade that he regularly smoked, DeMarco didn't keep drugs in the house. If they found that, it really didn't matter all that much because he had a Cannabis Club Card.

I heard a car pull up and screech to a halt. A voice spoke up from outside. "Miss, this is a police scene, please step back."

"And I am an attorney at law, this is my Bar card, and this is my client's home you've just invaded," I heard Krystal's confident voice reply. I heard her high-heels clack on the sidewalk as she approached the front door. Her voice grew louder. "Who's the supervising officer?"

"I am," said the short, fat, white cop by the front door. He made his way toward Krystal. "Who are you?"

"Krystal Robinson, attorney at law," she responded, handing the supervising officer her business card.

The cop inspected it, and placed it into the side pocket of his windbreaker jacket. "What's this all about," Krystal asked.

"We have reason to believe that DeMarco Speed, drug lord, is responsible for a large quantity of the drugs coming into the West Coast, and because of our reasonable suspicion, we are here."

"Drug lord? Mr. Speed is no drug lord," Krystal said. She walked over to the couch I was sitting on and sat down next to me.

"Boss, look at this," one of the police officers said, holding up two small plastic bags of chronic.

"Let's take that into custody. There's probably more in here. Our sources say we should find about twenty pounds in here. Let's find it all," the short stubby cop said. "Oh, I hate drug dealers, they all need to burn in hell. Look at him. The nigger's living like a goddamn king. I'm working my ass off protecting citizens, doing the right thing, trying to stop people like him who are menaces to our society," he mouthed.

Shaking his head, he then opened his pocketknife, walked over to the couch on which Krystal and I sat.

"Excuse me, ma'am, but I am going to have to ask you to move," the cop said to us.

I looked at the knife that was in his hand. "Is that really necessary?"

"Ma'am, if you don't move, I am going to have to arrest you for interfering with an investigation."

Krystal stood up from the couch. Reluctantly, I followed her, walking over to the adjacent matching white leather loveseat, and sat down again. We watched the officer jab the knife hard into the white leather sofa, puncturing the leather. He then dragged the knife from one end of the sofa to the other. Upon reaching other end, he took it out and jabbed into another spot on the edge of the sofa, and walked from that end to the other once more. He repeated his gestures four times, thereby slicing to shreds the entire $5500 Kreiss leather sofa.

Next, he walked over to he matching $2800 chaise, and began the process again. Next was the $4500 loveseat.

I looked at Krystal with a "I can't believe you are letting them do this, don't I have rights" look on my face.

Krystal must have read my mind. "Haley, I know as fucked up as it seems, the law allows this. As angry as I know you are, don't say anything. It will just make matters worse. We will deal with this later. I don't want you to make another case."

The knife-happy officer raised the lid on the White Baby Grand. He scrutinized the inside of it. Another knocked all of the books off of the mahogany bookshelf that ran across the wall; a mountain of books now covered the floor.

The police moved into the kitchen, emptying drawers, peeking inside of the pantry, and throwing boxes of food to the floor. They went into the media room and threw the DVD's onto the white carpet.

After they finished their search on the lower level of the house, the team headed upstairs. This time the knife-happy officer cut all of the mattresses in all five bedrooms. They then went through the closets. I guess they were getting frustrated with not having found a truckload of cocaine or whatever it was they thought was up here.

In the master bedroom closet they found four guns: two .38 Revolvers, a .357 Magnum and a Tek-9. They confiscated every gun.

"Your nigguh is going to be gone for a long time," a Black police officer said to me with a smirk on his face. "He is the kind of nigguh that gives our race a bad name."

I retorted, "No, you are the kind of nigguh that gives our race a bad name, you bastard."

"Where is he," the Black officer inquired. "You might as well tell us. We are going to find him sooner or later. Tell you what, why don't you be a good bitch and call him on his cell. Tell him we waiting on him."

"Go to hell! Fuck you. Kiss my ass."

Krystal narrowed her eyes at him. "Do not provoke my client further. Do you want the press to get pictures of the vandalism you committed here today? Your organization isn't exactly held in the highest of esteem. I'm sure my friend over at KRON would love to get wind of this. You have nothing to show for what you did, and you know it. Cease your slurs against my client, or I will slap a suit on you that would put you all over the press and possibly jeopardize your job… and I know you don't want that." The cop walked away. "Alright, let's roll out." the white stubby supervising officer said. "We got what we need."

"You don't have anything," Krystal said. "We'll see you tomorrow at the station to pick up the *registered* guns and the marijuana you've confiscated that my client's doctor prescribed to him for medicinal purposes."

I called DeMarco and informed him that APD had just left and that our home was raided.

"Did they have a search warrant?"

"Yeah, they came with a search warrant. Krystal's here with me."

"What they find? What they take?"

"Two zips of weed, and your guns."

"My guns are registered and I ain't got no felony. I'm gone go and pick up my shit tomorrow."

"Krystal said she'll go with you if you want.

"You say them motherfuckers took my weed? Did you tell them that I had a Cannabis Club Card?"

"DeMarco, they wasn't hearing that."

"Damn, them motherfuckers got my weed. And they got my guns. Yeah, I'm gone have to go and see them first thing in the morning. I'll be home in a minute. I'm actually about to be getting off the freeway."

The next morning, Krystal came over early. I chatted with her over a cup of coffee while DeMarco was in the shower. DeMarco finished and dressed upstairs, and shortly thereafter walked into the kitchen. "Hey Krystal, what's up?"

"Good morning, DeMarco." He kissed me on the forehead and announced he'd be back in a minute.

"Where are you going?" I wanted to know.

"To get my shit. I'm gone show these motherfuckers my Cannabis Card and that my guns are registered, so they can give me back my shit." DeMarco headed to the door.

"You should take Krystal with you, she's an attorney." DeMarco looked at Krystal.

"It's cool, I got it," he responded.

Krystal stood up. "DeMarco, I really should go with you down to the police station. They came here with a search warrant. That says something. I'm pretty sure they were after more than some chronic and a couple of guns."

DeMarco nodded. "Come on, let's go. Shit, I might end up having to hire you as my attorney."

"Thank you, Krystal," I said as they walked out of the door.

302

Forty-five

The police station smelled of disinfectant and cleaning solutions. With Krystal standing at his side, DeMarco placed his Cannabis Club ID on the counter in front of the tall, lean, white APD police officer behind the counter. The cop peered over his reading glasses, staring at DeMarco.

"Y'all came into my home last night and confiscated my cannabis that I use for medicinal purposes, and I want it back. Also, y'all confiscated my guns. My guns are registered. I am here to pick them up as well."

"Alright. I need to know on what date this occurred on and where," the officer said." When did you say this happened?"

"Last night."

"Where?" DeMarco gave him his address. The officer jotted down the answers to his questions on the yellow notepad.

Still peering over the tiny black square metal frame that rested on the edge of his nose, and smacking on gum, the officer continued. "Hold on, let me get a supervising officer over here. He is the one that is going to have to handle this. Please have a seat." The officer pointed at the empty chairs behind Krystal and DeMarco. Krystal took a seat.

"I don't feel like sitting, I'll stand," DeMarco said.

"He'll be here shortly. He has to finish booking somebody," the gum-chewing officer explained.

A couple of minutes later, an officer appeared, holding DeMarco's Cannabis Card. "Are you DeMarco Speed?"

"Yes, I am."

Krystal interceded, introducing herself. "I'm Mr. Speed's attorney, Krystal Robinson." She extended her handshake. Wavering, the officer shook Krystal's hand. "You have some property that belongs to my client that we are here to pick up."

"Your client was in possession of drugs and guns."

"Yes, but those things were in his possession legally. My client has not broken any laws. The Cannabis Club membership card that you are holding in your hand, officer…" Krystal paused as she read name badge pinned on the officers shirt. She proceeded speaking, "Officer Merit. His medical doctor gave the Cannabis Club membership card that you are holding in your hand to Mr. Speed, and the guns you confiscated from his home are registered firearms in his name. I'm sure you're aware of that by now. Furthermore, my client does not have a felony conviction would prohibit him from carrying a firearm. In fact his record is impeccable.

"As I said, officer, my client, Mr. Speed, and I are here to pick up his property that if you keep any longer you will be wrongfully detaining. Officer Merit, would you please take us to the property room so we may get going? I have to be in criminal court in the building behind this one in an hour," Krystal said, looking at her watch, "and my client likewise has business elsewhere to conduct."

"Let me call over to the property room to let them know that the two of you are on your way over. There is no need for me to go with you." Officer Merit walked away. DeMarco and Krystal headed to the property room. When they got there, Krystal did the talking. She introduced herself and stated their business there. The officer nodded. "Yes, I need DeMarco Speed to sign right here, indicating that he is receiving his property." The officer handed DeMarco the bag that contained his belongings. DeMarco checked through the bag. He took two zips of weed out, placing them in his pocket, and then signed the paper.

"Thank you," Krystal said. She and DeMarco turned and walked away.

"DeMarco Speed… DeMarco Speed," a voice called out from the other end of the hall.

"Shit," DeMarco uttered under his breath.

A plain-clothed cop hurried through the hall toward DeMarco. "DeMarco Speed, I am Officer Jordan. We have some questions for you to answer." He then turned and looked at Krystal. "Hello ma'am, are you his attorney?"

"Yes, I am. What kind of questions do you have for my client?"

"DeMarco, I got a man on lockdown who says that you are his number one supplier and that you are laundering money into a *Rage* Magazine and a *Life Inc. Records*," Officer Jordan said. He was reading off of a piece of paper. Krystal and DeMarco looked at one another. Officer Jordan continued, "I need you to come with me to my office to answer some questions."

Krystal stepped in. "Is my client under arrest, sir?"

The officer's gaze hardened. "Not yet, but I can make that happen. We can do it the hard way or the easy way."

"Mr. Jordan, if my client is not under arrest then we are leaving. Good day, sir." Krystal turned to walk away. DeMarco followed.

"Wait a minute Ms… I didn't get your name?"

"Krystal Robinson, attorney at law." Swinging her dark brown leather Gucci briefcase, she continued to stroll away.

"How do I get in contact with you, Ms. Robinson?"

Krystal stopped. The officer walked up to her. "Here's my business card," she said, reaching inside the front pocket on her beige Jones New York pant-suit and pulling out a card for him.

"Thank you. Let me ask you this, DeMarco. Do you know a Christopher Allen?"

"Yes."

"How do you know Mr. Allen? Did you supply him with drugs?"

"What are you talking about?"

"Was he a client that you supplied with drugs?"

"No, never that. I don't sell drugs. Never have, never will. I *use* one drug, marijuana, that's all. And, my 'drug dealers' are the legal cannabis clubs throughout Southern California. Unless I'm in the Bay Area, then they are the cannabis clubs throughout the Bay Area, Oakland or San Francisco."

"Then how do you know Mr. Allen?"

"Pardon me?"

"How do you know Mr. Allen?"

DeMarco laughed. "I use to fuck his baby's mama and then his sister after that."

"That's not what he says."

"Look, that man is angry with me. He gonna tell you anything."

The officer laughed. "Thank you, that's all for now."

Forty-six

DeMarco and Krystal walked away.
"Hello."
"Haley!"
"Krystal, what's going on?"
"Girl, DeMarco was arrested today."
Oh shit. I wondered why he'd been late coming home. "For what?"
"The charges are for money laundering."
"What?"
"Yeah, I am confident we can beat it. I am sure we can beat it. The evidence against him is weak. I already know they going with the RICO on this one. They're trying to rattle him."
"Can he bail out?"
"There is a bail hearing in two days. Let's see what the judge says. They should grant him bail. He's never been to the penitentiary. It's going before a grand jury. I can't go with him into those proceedings."
"Why?"
"It's the law. Attorneys are forbidden from grand jury hearings."
"What happens after the grand jury's investigation?'
"It may go to trial or it may be dismissed."
"So what the fuck is the whole grand jury for anyway?"

"Haley, the grand jury basically investigates to see if there is probable cause for a trial. About DeMarco's bail, more than likely a judge will grant him the opportunity to bail out."

News about DeMarco's' arrest was everywhere. It even made the front page of the *L.A. Times* and some of southern California's other big dailies. It also made the news in his native Oakland via *The Oakland Tribune*, a daily newspaper, which ran a story about his arrest. His arrest had people talking, even in the projects. The news was also all over the Jordan Down Housing Projects, and was a hot topic of discussion among the residents. When DeMarco first moved out of Compton, he lived in Jordan Downs. Fat Mike, who also had been born and raised in the Jordan Downs, held the *L.A. Times* newspaper with DeMarco's mugshot in his hand. He stood in the projects' parking lot and read the caption aloud to the curious residents that surrounded him,.

Alleged West Coast Drug Kingpin DeMarco Speed Arrested, the caption across the *Times* read. It went on,

The Los Angeles Police Department arrested a resident of Los Angeles County, DeMarco Speed, as he ate dinner at a local restaurant with friends. The charges were money laundering.

"They said he was making ten million dollars a year, and that he had started a record label and a magazine," Fat Mike said with excitement to everyone who was standing around listening to him read the article about DeMarco. He continued reading:

Speed generated a staggering amount of cash from his involvement in the drug trade. His drug network did an estimated $833,000 in business monthly. Unlike most other inner city kingpins, Speed isn't flashy. He wears expensive suits, but he's modest. Daily, he dresses like a businessman gracing the cover of Forbes or Business Times magazines. He drives a $70,000 Range Rover. Speed has never done time in prison, and other than a petty marijuana case that recently landed him three months in the Los Angeles county jail, he's never been imprisoned. Shortly after his release from L.A. County, his record was expunged. Three years ago, after an allegation by an informant who stated that Speed was heavily involved in the West Coast drug trade and was the head of a drug empire, Speed and three of his childhood friends from his home town of Oakland, California were arrested: Latrell Washington a.k.a. Homicide, Kevin Williams a.k.a. Streets, John Santos a.k.a Santos, and Michael Johnson a.k.a. Creature Man, also from Oakland's 6-9 Ville housing projects. The informant implicated Washington, Williams, Johnson, Santos, and Speed in the case. However, he later retracted his signed confession *that had implicated Speed, and refused to testify against him. Because of a lack of evidence, the case against Speed was dropped. However, Washington, Williams, and Santos' case went to trial. Washington and Williams were found guilty of bringing drugs onto the West Coast and money laundering. Each received a thirty-year prison sentence. Santos was exonerated for lack of evidence. Creature Man received a five-year prison sentence. He was released six months earlier for good behavior.*

In another separate case a few years back, a childhood friend and alleged business associate of Speed's, Robert Johnson a.k.a. Mumbles because of the way he mumbled when he spoke, received a life sentence after being caught with twenty pounds of cocaine. The drugs and numerous telephone conversations taped by the FBI locked away for life. He had been serving out that sentence at Pelican Bay State Penitentiary for four years before he was killed by an inmate with a fatal stab wound. The motivation for the attack is yet unknown. Mumbles' funeral included a final tour of his old neighborhood in a gold-and-black, horse-drawn carriage, followed by a procession of five Rolls Royce's, five Mercedes Benz', and five Hummers' limousines with a procession of ushers in black tuxedos. More than two thousand people attended Mumbles' funeral service, and over 800 people attended the sit-down dinner at the Marriott Hotel in Oakland at a cost of $70 a plate. The affair cost an estimated $65 thousand dollars. The funeral was paid for by Speed.

Forty-seven

That Tuesday, the Grand Jury investigations began. DeMarco and I were both brought in at separate times to testify. Although she could not go into the proceedings with us, Krystal prepped both of us for the round of questioning.

I had expected the grand jury to be a bunch of aging white men in black robes with gavels and wigs. But out of the eight members, only five were white: three men and two women. Except for one of the latter, they were all middle-aged; one of the women looked to be around thirty. By their side, there was a petite Asian woman, one balding man who looked Hispanic or maybe Middle Eastern. A black man was the eighth member. He resembled a retired professional athlete. Hell, for all I know, he could have been.

I had also expected the proceedings to take place in a courtroom, but the room in the County building where the hearing took place was more like a large corporate conference room. One of the fluorescent lights flickered annoyingly. Other than that, the room wasn't bad.

The balding Hispanic—I assume he was Hispanic, for he introduced himself as Hernando Cortez- appeared to be the foreman. After everyone took their respective seats, he swore in DeMarco and I prior to each of our questioning periods.

DeMarco was called in first.

Hernando led the questions. "Mr. Speed, what is your involvement in the drug trade?"

"Now ain't that a loaded question," he said with a chuckle. "None."

"Are you telling this jury that you are not presently and have never been involved in selling or dealing drugs?"

"That's what I said, ain't it?"

The Asian woman, Hyun Chang, posed the next question. "Do you use drugs, Mr. Speed?"

"Only marijuana."

"For medical purposes?"

"Yes."

"And what exactly are those medical purposes?"

"Back pain and insomnia."

"Back pain and insomnia?"

"Yes. I went to my doctor told him my problems, and he recommended medicinal marijuana."

"Has it helped?"

"Yes."

The young white woman introduced herself as Marianne Hess. "Mr. Speed, are you the owner of a *Rage* Magazine or *Life, Inc. Records*?"

"No, I am not," DeMarco said, looking into the eyes of each jury member.

"Do you have any involvement with the magazine or the record label?"

"My girlfriend owns both of those companies. I have no responsibility or commitment to a *Rage* Magazine or *Life Inc. Records,* if that's what you mean."

"So let me get this right? You did not and have not funded or worked with the magazine or record label at all?"

"Like I said, I have no responsibility or commitment to a *Rage* Magazine or *Life Inc. Records*."

"You mentioned your girlfriend. Would that be Haley Jones?"

"Yes."

"Does Ms. Jones own *Rage* Magazine and/or *Life, Inc. Records*?"

"From my understanding, she does."

The black man, Rod Storm, jumped in. "What do you mean 'from your understanding?' Mr. Speed, either she does or she doesn't."

"From what I understand she does. I mean, I haven't seen her ownership on paper or anything. She's never shown me that. She keeps her business, her business in that sense." DeMarco spread his hands. "I can't give you information I myself do not possess."

"Has Ms. Jones asked for any money from you?"

"No, she's a real independent woman. Besides she makes way more money than I do. I'm not employed at the present time."

Hyun spoke up, pushing her glasses up onto her nose, peering at some previously written notes. "So how do you survive if you're not working?"

"Actually, Haley's been real good to me, financially supporting me and all. She's a good woman with a good heart."

"Where do you reside, Mr. Speed?"

"Sometimes with Ms. Jones and my brother. I stay between the two places at the present time." Hyun rolled her eyes.

"Your brother—would that be Michael Speed the owner of the Speed Mortgage Company in Beverly Hills?"

"Yes mam."

"You have a rich brother?" DeMarco smiled.

"Yeah he has one of the most successful real-estate mortgage broker companies in Los Angeles. I read in the LA Times Business section that last year his company grossed more than six million dollars."

Hyun continued her firm questioning, "Have you given Ms. Jones any money? Any loans, and say, she paid you right back?"

"No, how could I? I have no income."

"What about dinner? Ever go to dinner with Ms. Jones?"

"Yes."

"Did you pay for those dinners."

"No. She did or we'd pay separately. She's like that."

"So, you are saying that you never even gave Ms. Jones one cent?"

"That's correct."

Rod leaned forward. "State your relationship with Ms. Jones again for us."

"She's my girlfriend."

"Are you married?"

"Yes, but my divorce from my wife is pending."

"So, Haley Jones is really your mistress."

"I guess you could say that."

"How long have you known Ms. Jones?"

"Three years."

"So, I take it you have been dating her since then."

"No, actually for the first two years we were friends in a platonic relationship. We started dating about eleven months ago."

"So, I guess it is fair to say that the both of you have been intimate."

"Yes."

"But you have never given her any money? Not even to go out and buy a dress or some sexy lingerie?"

"That's right. She already has all that stuff and she be shopping all the time, with her money."

Marianne shuffled some papers on her legal pad. "Mr. Speed, please tell us what kind of car you drive?"

"A Range Rover."

"Did you buy it new?"

"No."

"What year is this Range Rover?"

"A 2003."

"A 2003? That's brand spanking new," Rod pointed out. "How much does a fine automobile like that cost?"

"I really don't know. You see, I didn't purchase the truck."

"You didn't? Then who did?"

"My former girlfriend. It was a gift from her."

"Your former girlfriend. She took care of you, too?"

"Actually she did."

Rod chuckled. "Wow, Mr. Speed… you really have a way with women. I need to get some tips from you." The grand jury laughed.

"What kind of job did this former girlfriend have, that her wealth allowed her to purchase this vehicle for you?"

"She's a stock broker, and she's from a rich family. A rich white family, might I add." DeMarco smiled a shark's grin.

"I'm familiar with the background of Ms. Christine Miller, whose family owns the Miller Tea Company, " the younger white man, Scott Hansen, said.

Scott cleared his throat, then continued. "Back to this Haley Jones. What does she get her money from, being that *Rage* and *Life Inc.* are businesses that are still in their development stage and really aren't making any real revenue right now?"

"Haley has a PR company. I assume this is where her money comes from. She could actually better answer your question than I could."

"Oh, I checked with the IRS," Scott said. "It looks like her PR agency had an income of $300,000 last year and the year before that."

"Is that right? You're telling me something I didn't know. Haley is one of those kind of women that you don't ask them their business. She never told me she was clocking like that though! Damn!"

"Thank you, Mr. Speed. It's been good talking to you. You may step down from the stand now."

Malik and Walter also appeared to testify. The grand jury asked them if Tranquility had ever received cash directly from DeMarco. They testified that they had not, personally nor via Tranquility.

I was also brought in to testify. I could tell by this point in time that the jury was just a little bit irritated with not having made any headway. I stood my ground. I must say, I was excellent on the stand. Thanks to the diligence of DeMarco and myself, plus Krystal's tactical advice, I had all the paperwork proving I was the sole owner of the house in Anaheim Hills, *Rage*, *Life Inc.*, and my PR company. I even had Utopia waiting in the wings as my "assistant," simply to help me carry the large quantity of documents we had oh-so-carefully lined up, thereby proving my financial independence down to the last penny. When I was asked to produce proof, I summoned Utopia, who entered with a dolly and five file boxes full of ledgers, tax returns, check copies, forms, and other documents.

Shortly after that, we were dismissed. I heard through various channels that the grand jury investigators contacted the banks, confirming the loan I took out on my house, and they investigated my lines of credit. I'm sure they put my finances and DeMarco's under a microscope; if they had invested less than one thousand man-hours of time, I'd be surprised. But in the end, they conceded defeat. Krystal called to inform us that the investigation was going to be dropped for lack of evidence.

DeMarco and I hugged, went out to Crustacean's, and enjoyed a passionate night together. The ordeal was over. That rather dramatic chapter in life was closed now...

Forty-eight

It was Friday afternoon. I stayed in bed all morning, not really feeling like going anywhere. Yet, dragging myself out of bed, I managed to put on the red Moschino robe that DeMarco had given me for Valentine's Day. It matched the red satin Moschino bra and panties, also gifts from him from a month ago, that I had on underneath the open robe. All items were obtained from the Moschino Boutique on Rodeo Drive in Beverly Hills.

With bare feet, I walked down the white-carpeted spiral staircase with the black spiral cast-iron railing onto the light-colored hardwood floor in the gourmet kitchen. I retrieved the red can of Folger's from the cupboard, measured the coffee, put it in the filter, and slid it into place on the white automatic coffee maker. I turned it on. I absolutely loved the smell of coffee brewing. Usually, DeMarco and I had a cup of coffee in the morning to begin our day. DeMarco always took a sip of my coffee before pouring his; that was routine. I would have given anything right now if only DeMarco could just come and take a sip of my coffee now, as he invariably did.

I walked into the family room and turned on our huge, wide, high-definition TV. Oprah was on. Ironically, today's show was about women who date married men. There was a sister on there, talking about how she preferred dating married men because she didn't want to commit.

Another stated that she enjoyed dating them because the surreptitious

314

relationship excited her. Sex with her husband, night after night, became boring, and that being with somebody different took the monotony out of the relationship. The next two guests were a married couple, sitting side by side. The wife talked about how her husband's cheating had caused her a tremendous amount of grief. Crying, she told Oprah that her husband had commented to a friend that the only reason why he had not divorced her was because it was cheaper to keep her.

"Why do you put up with your husband's cheating," Oprah asked.

"I love him," the woman responded.

The camera cut to a middle-aged black woman in the audience. Shaking her head, she exclaimed, "What's love got to do with it, fool?" Others applauded her. The crowd was slowly stirring itself up.

Oprah regarded the husband with a fixed stare. "When you took your marriage vows, were you serious?"

"Yes, I was serious, and I still am serious. I love my wife. I ain't going nowhere."

Oprah shook her head ever so slightly. "Look at your wife. She is devastated because of your cheating. Look at what you are doing to her. How does this make you feel?" Oprah pointed towards his upset wife while keeping her eyes on him.

The man looked over at his wife, sitting by his side. "Man, she gone be alright, my wife knows me, she knows what I do. She knows I love her." The husband leaned over and whispered in his wife's ear. A slight hum could be heard as a technician behind the scenes ramped up the gain on the guests' clip-on mikes in order to pick up the conversation. "Baby, you know I love you," the man whispered, "but I'm a man and this is what we do." His wife nodded her head in agreement.

Oprah sighed, feeling the woman's pain. The intensity of the moment apparently caused Oprah's eyes to start to water. She fought back the tears. Breaking her silence, Oprah looked back into the camera in front of her and continued her little speech. "Statistics indicate that more than a startling *eighty percent* of married couples cheat on their spouses, and that less than five percent of those affairs end in divorce." Regarding her TV audience with her deep brown eyes, Oprah said, "God, please never let me fall in love with a married man, it's the wrong thing to do. We may not have control over someone we like, but we do have the choice to not date them." The audience broke into applause, and the camera zoomed out, panning over the crowd as it did so. The show ended.

Sitting on the arm of my couch in my family room, I rebutted Oprah. "But, Oprah, it's not so simple. What if you, as the mistress, make the guy happier than his wife does? What if him marrying his wife was a mistake?

What if he had loved his wife, but was not in love with her anymore and he *was* in love with his mistress? What if his mistress could help him advance and he could help her advance professionally? What if each was really the soulmate of the other?"

I respected and admired Oprah; she's a strong woman, but what she had just said had gotten underneath my skin. *She a talk show host. She suppose to be neutral, she isn't suppose to be passing judgment on nobody*, I thought. I know that I took what she said quite personally for a few minutes. Looking back, I know it was silly, but the whole ordeal with DeMarco's hospitalization had really tanked my mood. As I reflected, I realized that Oprah didn't know me and she certainly didn't know DeMarco; our situation was different. Therefore, she wasn't critiquing our relationship. I rationalized with the following logic: if Stedman had been married when the two of them met, I would bet that he and Oprah would have been like DeMarco and I, fulfilling their desires. Feeling better, I got up, poured myself more coffee, and headed back into the living room.

I picked up the Baby Gap catalog that was on the coffee table. My cousin Yvonne, who was expecting, had left it behind after her visit a few days ago. I thumbed through the catalog. All of the clothes were so cute; expensive, but cute.

I thought about the conversation that I had with DeMarco about children. Early in our relationship and well before we were dating, DeMarco commented that a woman couldn't be have his children because he was married. That left me with some feelings of trepidation. However, my thoughts wandered back to a more recent conversation, where I told him that I thought I might be pregnant. He promptly went out to purchase a home pregnancy test from Walgreen's. When the results came out positive, he was happy. He told me he wanted two children with me.

Forty-nine

When it went down, there was no warning. None. I was washing dishes from last night and the phone rang.

"Hello?"

"Haley, DeMarco got shot!"

"What?! You're trippin'… that is not funny." But I knew Skerz wouldn't bullshit me on something like that. The dish I was washing slipped from my hand, plunged into the sink, splashing my shirt with sudsy water. I didn't even notice. Suddenly, time just drew out.

"No, Haley. The ambulance just took him to the hospital!"

"Is he alright?"

"I don't know. They say it's pretty bad. They say he might not make it."

I felt like a deer, with those words coming out of the earpiece like a tractor-trailer barreling down upon me, headlights pinning me to a dark highway. I forced my brain to work, to form words, to react. "Which hospital did they take him to?"

"L.A. General."

"Skerz, what the hell happened?!" I feverishly dried my hands on the shorts I was wearing, one at a time.

"Man, I don't really know. He was just with us, right? Everybody had went to the club in Inglewood, right, 'cause them nigguh's Tay and 40 and 'em had a show, right?" I reached for my car key, which was attached by a ring to my other keys, but bumped them all off of the counter and onto the floor. "I saw DeMarco after the show. He was out front walking to his car, right? We all tried to get him to come with us, 'cause we was all gone hang out in Long Beach at our nigguh Buddha's cousin's house, right?" I reached down, grasped the keys. "DeMarco didn't wanna go with us. He said he was tired and he was going home and go to sleep.

"After the show, everybody go to 7-Eleven. We all in front of there in our cars and DeMarco rolls up. He gets out, goes in the store and buys a bottled water. We all ask him again if he wanted to roll with us again to Buddha's house."

I found the keys, began to move toward the front door, keys in one hand, cordless phone in the other.

"He turns us down again and says that he is going home to go to sleep."

All thumbs, I keyed in the sequence to arm the security system.

"He was like, 'naw, I'm going home,' then he was like, 'you coming by tomorrow evening to watch the Tyson fight with me, right?' I told him I was gone be there. He got in his car and drove off. You know the freeway right there by 7 Eleven?"

"Yeah." I was out the door now.

"We saw him get on it. So, anyway, like an hour later, everybody's pagers start going off, cell phones ringing and shit, and people was yelling that DeMarco got shot. They say that he was on Normandy near the Crenshaw Mall. We all jump in their cars and head to Crenshaw."

I fumbled the cordless phone, caught it, got it back in front of my ear, even as I stuck the key in the ignition.

"By the time we get there, the ambulance had already came and took DeMarco to the hospital. The Range was still there. DeMarco crashed it after he got shot. It was all fucked up, blood was everywhere inside of it, all over the seat, the dash, the floor, the door, even on the inside of the roof."

Savagely, I turned the key, gunned the engine, shoved the transmission into gear. "Oh, my God, no… no!" I cried. "Who was with DeMarco when you saw him last?"

"Nobody, he was by himself."

Now I was at the end of the driveway. Someone had to dodge to get out of my way, giving me an angry beep of the horn. I barely noticed.

"Well, who did he go to the party with?"

"Everybody said he came by himself. Man, the police impounded the Range. I went over and I was talking to the cop, right, that's when I saw all of the blood. I was like, damn! The cop was telling me that something like seven shots was heard."

I was halfway down the block. I could still hear Skerz on the cordless phone. I remembered the clerk who sold me the phone telling me how cool the gigahertz cordless was, with an approximate half-mile range. But I was going fast, and the first bursts of static were already heard while on the line...

"Wait a minute. Let me call the hospital on my cell, I'll get you right back." I tossed the cordless into the back. For a panicked moment I thought that I had left my cell back home, but there it was, plugged into the charger. I had instead, and thankfully, left it in the car. I grabbed it, dialed Information, and received the number to L.A. General. Then I conferenced Skerz back in.

"Hello? Los Angeles General Hospital Emergency Room."

"Hello? A little while ago DeMarco Speed was brought in by ambulance to be treated for gunshot wounds. He got shot on Normandy. I wanna know how is he's doing."

"Hold on, let me find out," the nurse said. Lilting music replaced her voice as she put us on hold.

While we were waiting for her to return, Skerz and I continued to discuss DeMarco's situation. "Man, fuck that, he should have come with us." Skerz said.

"I wish he would've. Man, I hope DeMarco makes it."

"I know."

The music abruptly died as the nurse returned to the phone. "Mr. Speed is in surgery. He's got some pretty serious injuries."

"What exactly are his injuries?"

"Are you his wife," the nurse asked.

"Yes," I said, figuring that to be the best response; the nurse may not have provided more information had I said otherwise.

"He was shot three times."

"Where?" Skerz asked cutting her off mid-sentence.

"Once in the abdomen, the arm, and his leg. The bullet that hit his arm went through; the wound bled a lot but it's just a flesh wound. The bullet in his leg lodged in his femur. That one is going to require an operation to remove. However, it doesn't pose an imminent danger. It's the bullet that's lodged in his abdomen that we are most concerned about."

"Thank you. I'm on my way there right now," I said.

"Ma'am, you may just want to wait... I mean, there isn't much that you can do right now. The doctors are in there doing the best that they can. There is really no need for you to come right now. I can call you if you like after he gets out of surgery. What is your number?"

I gave her the number to my cell. "Thank you."

"What did you say your name was?"

"Haley."

"Alright Mrs. Speed, my name is Nancy. I will call you when there is more news to report." I dropped the nurse off the line, leaving Skerz and I.

"Skerz, I'm driving to the hospital."

"I'll meet you there."

"Alright, I am going to get off the phone now."

"I'll call Krystal, Utopia and Camille and let them know what happened. I'll see you at the hospital," Skerz said.

"Skerz! Wait a minute. One more thing."

"What?"

"I just found out today that I'm pregnant."

"What?! For real?"

"Yep, seven weeks. My doctor called me today confirming the results of the home pregnancy test DeMarco and I did last week that came out positive." I forced back tears, if for no other reason than they would have blurred my vision. I needed to reach the hospital as soon as possible.

"Haley, man, DeMarco gone make it through this. He gone be alright, and then y'all can be a family."

"Oh, I hope so."

When I arrived at the hospital, I was greeted in the waiting room by what seemed like an endless number of DeMarco's friends. Krystal, Camille, and Utopia were also waiting there, too.

The clique closed ranks around me, God bless them. "Are you alright, Haley," Utopia asked. I forced myself to nod. Their eyes were red. All of them had been crying. I went to the nurse station and asked for Nancy, the nurse I'd spoken to over the phone about thirty minutes earlier. One of the ER nurses pointed her out.

Nancy was a short, thin, pale white woman. She epitomized what I imagined a nurse would look like, with her neat white uniform and all. She even wore a white nurse's hat with her short blond hair stuck out beneath it. Maintaining my composure, I introduced myself to Nancy.

Before I could finish my sentence, Nancy said, "Oh, Mrs. Speed, your husband is still in surgery. You can go to the surgery waiting room in the back if you like; it's quieter back there. Plus, it's right next to the operating room where your husband is. When the doctor comes out you'll see him, and you may address your questions to him."

"Thank you."

"Hold on… let me buzz the door for you." I thanked her. Krystal, Utopia, and Camille stood with me by the electric door, waiting for it to open. Buddha walked over and stood next to the women. I glanced over at him. Utopia announced, "there's Skerz." He came over to me and embraced me.

"Hey, Haley… what they say?"

"Not much. I don't think they know much yet. The nurse said that DeMarco is still in surgery. I am going to go and wait in the surgery waiting room in back. It's closer to the operating room," I said.

"Alright," Skerz replied.

"I'm going with you," Buddha said. With him, all of DeMarco's boys left the black vinyl and silver chairs in the emergency waiting room. They followed behind Buddha, myself, and Skerz. The clique was in tow, right behind us.

I really didn't care for Buddha following me around like a lost puppy. I didn't care for him all that much, period, because he treated women like dogs. To Buddha, a woman had no rights, no say in a relationship. Once, I had a disagreement with DeMarco over something, and Buddha was there. He had the nerve to comment to DeMarco—in my presence that I needed to be "broke down."

"I can't believe you're letting her backtalk to you," he candidly said to DeMarco, as though I were a piece of furniture. DeMarco paid him no mind.

However, he later commented to me alone not to ever front him off again. "You know where you stand with me, Haley; that's all that's important. If Buddha want to run his mouth, let him. He ain't hurting nothing."

Buddha treated his girlfriend, Joy, like she was a piece of shit. He was always putting his hands on her, smacking her around like she was his personal punching bag. He even hit her when she was pregnant with their second child.

When DeMarco and I first met, we went to their house. It was around the time that our relationship was blossoming beyond the "it's just my business partner" thing. We pulled up in their driveway. Joy and Buddha were outside, fighting on the lawn. Buddha had a handful of Joy's beautiful, black, silken-wrapped hair in his grip. He was pulling it and dragging her across the lawn despite her kicking, screaming, and cursing.

"Damn, him and his bitch at it again," DeMarco said as they rolled into the driveway.

Pointing at the house, I had turned to DeMarco and asked, "I know we are not going in there." DeMarco didn't think much of it. He turned off the ignition, reached towards the backseat to pick up a six-pack of Heineken, got out, and closed the door. I was apprehensive; I didn't get out right away.

DeMarco walked around and opened my car door. "What's the matter Haley, you coming in?" Buddha was still standing in the yard.

"What's the matter?" I hissed at DeMarco, and made a subtle gesture toward Joy.

"He ain't gonna do nothing to you," DeMarco assured me. He gave Buddha a "what's up." His wife looked at me and mumbled a feeble "hello." Then she went inside. Buddha and DeMarco followed; DeMarco reached for my hand and we went into the house together. Once there, Buddha led us into the living room; Joy was nowhere in sight.

After we sat in the living room for about twenty minutes, Joy came in. She had fixed her hair and changed clothes. "Hey, DeMarco."

"What's up with you, Joy?"

She shook her head as if to say "nothing." She walked over to me and said, "Hello. I'm Joy. It's nice to meet you, Haley. I feel like I already know you because DeMarco always be talking about you." We shook hands. Joy was an exceptionally pretty, dark-skinned petite woman. She was short, at five feet two inches, with a bomb-ass shape. *Everybody said I looked like Halle Berry when my hair was short, but she looked more like Halle then I did. Her features were even like Halle's. They only said that about me cause my hair was cut short.* Joy also seemed to have a cool personality. She gave off a positive vibe. *Why is she with Buddha? She could definitely do better.*

Sitting on a couch across from DeMarco and myself, Buddha tried hitting DeMarco up for some blunts.

"Naw, man," DeMarco said, "I ain't got any. We can go and get some, though."

"Nigguh, the next time you bring your ass over here, bring some blunts," Buddha joked. They both laughed hysterically.

"Nigguh, I got the weed and I brought the drink. You should have the blunts," DeMarco joked back.

"Buddha, nigguh, you got a whole box of blunts upstairs on the dresser," Joy said.

Buddha narrowed his eyes. "Well, then go get them, bitch."

"Yeah, now you need this bitch, huh, nigguh," Joy said, rolling her eyes as she walked out of the room.

Buddha leaned back on the couch. "Man, I'm gone have to find me another bitch and get rid of the one I got. Maybe I can get the real Halle Berry and not this imitation bitch. Yeah, it's time for some new pussy. Fuck that old pussy." DeMarco laughed and repeated the part about getting some new pussy.

I didn't appreciate Buddha's remark. Nor had I appreciated DeMarco laughing along with it. That was a side of him I still didn't like. "Oh, so you think that's funny," I asked DeMarco. He didn't respond right away.

"What?" He acted like he didn't hear me. I shook my head. DeMarco leaned over and whispered in my ear, "Baby, don't trip, its just all in fun." He kissed me on the lip, and I kissed him back.

"Look at the two love birds," Buddha said. "I got a bed upstairs if y'all wanna go up there and fuck. Shit, y'all haven't got to go to all those expensive places y'all be going to fuck… the White Dove, Hotel Bel Air, the hotel on Malibu beach and shit. Hell, pay me $300 a night and y'all can fuck upstairs in one of my bedrooms anytime y'all want. Hell, and if y'all need room service, I get in my kitchen and cook something," Buddha joked. He was fucking obnoxious. *What nerve did he have to say some shit like that*, I thought to myself. DeMarco must have known what I was thinking cause he whispered in my ear, "Haley, don't trip… he just having fun. It's no big deal."

I whispered, "For you, DeMarco I'll ignore him… for now. But he is really getting on my nerves." I tried to keep my voice sweet. "Next time he talks about 'getting a new bitch,' I'm gonna fucking say that Joy oughta get herself a new nigguh, one that ain't such a punk-ass that he beat her. So can we leave soon?"

DeMarco chuckled. "Yeah."

"What y'all two love birds over their whispering about?"

"Don't worry about it," I shouted at Buddha. DeMarco giggled.

Buddha looked pissed. I guess he'd figured I'd said something about him. "Damn, DeMarco, that's yo woman. You let her talk like that to a nigguh?"

"Buddha, ain't like you not been shooting your mouth off. You making her mad. You better cool it." DeMarco's voice was level, but had a steely edge.

Joy returned to the living room. She threw the box of blunts at Buddha, scattering them across the floor as the Swisher box glanced off his head. "Bitch," Buddha yelled at her.

"Yeah, whateva, nigguh," she said.

Now, in the waiting room, Buddha sat next to me. I gave him a look that said, 'if you start any shit with me on a night like this, I'm gonna hand you your ass.' He never did. To his credit, he actually acted like a decent human being. I guess a crisis can bring out the good in people. Truth be told, I didn't think Buddha had had any good to bring out.

"Man, this nigguh gotta make it. He strong. He gone make it," Buddha said aloud. He turned to me. "Your nigguh strong. He's gonna pull through this thing." .

All I could do is nod.

We had our eyes on each other, on the mis-colored TV that was showing "Jeopardy" in weird shades of sepia, and, most of all, upon those big swinging double-doors with the austere sign reading *TO OPERATING ROOM — Absolutely NO Admittance To Unauthorized Personnel*. After about ten minutes, the doors opened. About twelve sets of eyes swiveled to see the doctor walking out of the operating room into the wait area. DeMarco's friends rushed him. "Stay back, give the doc some air," Buddha hissed at them. "How my nigguh doing," Buddha asked the doctor. Then nurse Nancy appeared, shooing the group back into their seats as she walked over to me, along with the doctor. She introduced me to the surgeon.

"Dr. Gretler, this is Mrs. Speed, DeMarco's wife." The doctor turned to me, smiling faintly. "The surgery had went well… well, better than I expected. We'll just have to wait and see. There may be some temporary paralysis. We don't know. But overall, I think we're past the worst now. The good news is that your husband's got no more metal in him. We removed the bullet that was lodged in his femur. More importantly, we removed the one in his abdomen. It wasn't as close to his liver as the ultrasound led me to believe. He's stabilized right now, but it will take him a while to recover given the severity of the injuries he's sustained.

"What's 'awhile,'" I asked. "I don't know," the surgeon said. "It's hard to say. It could take several months or maybe even longer with his type of injuries. He came in here with some severe wounds. He was shot three times with a semiautomatic revolver. It has been my experience that most patients who experience his kind of injuries take more than a year for a full recovery. Judging by those ultrasounds, I wasn't sure he was going to recover. Now I'm virtually certain he will."

"Virtually?" My voice broke.

"Nothing is certain in this profession," Dr. Gretler said. "You want certainty, see an accountant. My profession deals in probabilities. The probability that your husband will fully recover in time is rather high. So, you do have that to be hopeful of. When he does comes home, it's all but certain he's going to need care pretty much around the clock. I have a nurse who can come out and help you, but let's just wait and see how he progresses over the next several weeks."

"May I see him," I asked.

"Not right now. Between the injuries and the anesthesia, he wouldn't even know you were there. Besides, he's been through a lot already and he needs his energy. Why don't you come tomorrow? I will come back and see him around four in the evening."

"Alright. I'll come tomorrow evening. Thank you so much, Dr. Gretler, for every thing."

"Not a problem. I will keep on doing the best that I can, Mrs. Speed, for your husband," he said. He touched me on the shoulder and walked away.

"What did he call her? Mrs. Speed?" one of DeMarco's boys whispered. I heard him. My lip curled.

With everyone in tow, I walked out of the hospital onto the parking lot. The night air helped clear my head. My heart slowed down.

"That's Nakeesha," a voice said. I saw a woman scurrying along, looking like she had just gotten out of her car. She was with Sparkle. She was one of DeMarco's boys girlfriends. DeMarco and I had actually ate lunch with them a while back. I tried to duck behind a row of cars, but most of the group, including the clique, was still with me. Fading into the woodwork with this number of people would have been impossible, even if Sparkle hadn't pointed me out to Nakeesha as soon as she saw me. Needless to say, she did. Nakeesha steamed over towards us. She shouted, "Bitch, what in the fuck is your ass doing here? DeMarco is my husband, not yours."

"Whateva," I responded.

Utopia stepped up, "Bitch, you better get yo ass out of my girl's face. She ain't for yo shit tonight."

Sparkle stepped up, "bitch! I'll mop yo ass all over this hospital, hoe." She turned to Nakeesha. "Girl, fuck that," Sparkle was yelling, "You should just kick her ass now, and get it over with. I never liked that bitch from the gate. She thinks she all that coming between you and DeMarco. I don't see what DeMarco see in the bitch, personally. The bitch think she all that 'cause she been to college."

"This is really not necessary," Krystal said.

"Fuck you, you fat bitch," Nakeesha was yelling.

"No, she didn't," Krystal responded. She drew her fist back and as it rapidly came forward, Skerz caught it, stopping it in mid-air.

Skerz stepped up. "Look Nakeesha, ladies… DeMarco is in there damn near on his death bed. He doesn't need us out here fighting."

"That's real," Buddha interjected, walking up standing at my side. He stared Nakeesha down. If I were a betting woman, I'd bet Buddha didn't like Nakeesha; by the way he mugged her, it was obvious.

A familiar male voice interjected, "But Nakeesha right, though, Haley ain't none of DeMarco's wife." That voice sounded so familiar. Who did it belong to? It was Tyquawn. He was DeMarco's flunky. He was also a producer; at least that's what he called himself with his cheap-sounding garage beats. *Man, them beats ain't taking him nowhere.* He was his own biggest fan. For whatever the reason, Tyquawn never liked me. Seems like the closer DeMarco and I became, the more he hated our relationship. In fact, when DeMarco and I first started working together, he even went so far as to comment to someone that "they" were just using me for my services. I guess he was including himself in "they." He was the weakest link on DeMarco's team, and the weakest link revealed something to me; this is what I thought when I first heard the rumor. I'd confronted DeMarco about it, and he denied it. Even before the rumor, I once suggested to DeMarco that Tyquawn is a latent homosexual. My analyzation of Tyquawn's feelings regarding me led me to think that he had a crush on *DeMarco*. DeMarco hated it when I'd tell him this, and was quick to deny it. DeMarco assured me that Tyquawn was not gay. However, he did say that he could see how someone might conclude that, because Tyquawn was a complainer. He was always sniveling like a bitch, DeMarco had remarked. Finally, I had figured out the snitch in DeMarco's clique. He even went and stood next to Nakeesha during our confrontation.

Some of DeMarco friends were also close to Nakeesha. She was a people's person, and got along well with all of DeMarco's male friends. From time to time, she would invite them over to watch boxing, football, or basketball, plus she'd cook for them. She even played matchmaker between some of them, hooking them up with her sister, cousins, and friends. Yeah, some of them were even loyal to her ass. I used to tease DeMarco and ask him which one of his boys from his camp was the snitch.

"Ain't no snitches in my camp," he'd respond. There was a lot of stuff that Nakeesha knew about us that she was not privy to… that she *should not* have been privy to. *Somebody close to us had to be telling her something*, I surmised. Now I knew who it was.

The incident with Nakeesha made me all the more determined to help DeMarco get healthy and recover. I couldn't wait for him to get better, so I could inform him about his boy. He wouldn't believe it, but there were way too many of his friends who were witnesses to the event. DeMarco would be disappointed, and he is going to check Tyquawn's punk ass about that "bitch" shit he pulled.

Fifty

"*Hello?*"

"Hey, Haley, its us… Utopia, Krystal and Camille. We just calling to say hello and to see how you're doing," Utopia said.

"Did we wake you," Krystal asked.

"No, I'm up. I am just hanging up with the hospital. DeMarco slipped into a coma after surgery last night."

"What?!" the clique all shouted at the same time.

"Girl, why didn't you call us," Krystal asked.

"I just found out. Didn't you hear what I just said? I am just hanging up the phone with the hospital. I was just about to call you guys and then y'all called me."

"Girl, you know we are here for you," Camille said

"I know. Thanks. The good news is the doctor said that an X-ray of DeMarco's brain shows that there is brain activity. Although he's in a coma, it's good sign. Plus, it's not like he's on life support or anything. It's like a really deep sleep."

"Well, that's good," Utopia said.

I yawned. The past twelve hours or so had wiped me out. "Let me get out of bed and take a shower. I am going to the hospital to see DeMarco. I'll call you guys later. Thanks for calling."

327

"Do you want us to go with you, Haley," Camille asked.

"No, I'm alright."

"I love you, Haley."

"I love you, Utopia."

"Love you, Haley."

"Love you, too, Krystal."

"Love you, Haley."

"I love you, Camille."

"Haley, we going with you. Nakeesha might be there," Utopia said.

"No, you guys don't have to come… really."

"We coming. I'm leaving out the door now," Krystal said, "Haley, let me pick up Camille and Utopia and we on our way to get you," Krystal said.

I remembered how Krystal had been ready to take Nakeesha apart. "Uh, Krystal, I really don't think you outta be going. You was about to fuck Nakeesha up last night!" They all laughed.

"Girl, I know, huh? That bitch Nakeesha and her friend, Twinkle, had me acting all ghetto and shit like her ass, making me lose my professionalism. And I'm an attorney about to catch an assault and battery case, maybe even an attempted murder case depending on how things would have went down. I should have known better. Anyway, Haley, I'm cool. If I see that bitch I'm going to ignore her."

"Alright, then, come on. By the time y'all get here I'll be ready. Bye."

Fifty-one

"Hello?"

"Hey, Tellis? It's Haley. I was just thinking about you. I wanted to call you and say hello and to thank you for supporting me with all that I have been going through."

"You are quite welcome. I consider you a real friend, Haley. I'm here for you. I wish you the best. I hope that DeMarco hurries up and get well, so that the two of you and his little bambino you are carrying can move forward with your lives. How is DeMarco?"

"He's out of the coma."

"I heard. I ran into Krystal at City Hall yesterday and she mentioned it."

"Yeah, I hear he's hanging in there. Did I tell you that his wife Nakeesha had my name removed from his visitor's list and she banned me from the hospital?" That had happened four days ago; still my eyes began to puff when I talked about it. "I am not allowed to see him."

"What? Well, it doesn't surprise me. Legally, she's got power of attorney for the moment. Haley, you just hang in there. She can only do what she is doing temporarily, as long as DeMarco is incapacitated. It won't last. When DeMarco is back on his feet he's going to be with you. Just watch and see. I'm a man. I know when a man truly cares about a woman, and DeMarco, he really does care about you and wants to be with you."

"Ooh, I hope so. Sometimes, Tellis I don't know. I wish I could wave the magic wand and just make it all better, you know. Sometimes, I think that DeMarco is not coming back. Maybe our relationship was just one of those things in passing."

"Are you kidding? That man is in love with you. Haley, there is a reason to the madness, and all that has happened. You two met, fell in love, he has a near death experience, goes into a coma and comes out of it, you're carrying his child. Furthermore, you guys have a business that is about to be thriving… all of this is for a reason. DeMarco was put in your life for a reason and you were put into his for a reason. Haley, I wish I could wave the magic wand and make it all better, too, but just hang in there."

"Thanks, Tellis."

"For what? Being a friend?"

"Yeah, thanks for being a friend. Thanks for saying all that you just said. I needed to hear it. And thanks for dinner the other day and for breakfast yesterday."

"Right on. Haley, how's your pregnancy coming?"

"Good."

"How many months are you now?"

"Five."

"What, already? Boy, time sure flies."

"Not to me. I can't wait to have the baby. I have an appointment on Friday. My doctor is going to let me know the sex. At first I didn't want to know, but now I do."

"Who's driving you to your appointment?"

"Me. I'm driving me to my appointment."

"You shouldn't be driving. Let me take you."

"I don't want to impose on you."

"You won't be. What time is your appointment?"

"9:30."

"Alright, I'll see you at 8:30."

"Wow! Thanks, Tellis."

"It's nothing. I'll see you on Friday."

"Alright, bye."

"Later."

Fifty-two

Friday came fast. Tellis called and woke me up at seven in the morning. I picked up the phone and the first thing I heard was his voice. "Wake up, sleepyhead."

Damn, that's what DeMarco use to always say to me, I reminisced.

"Damn, Tellis, you sound like DeMarco! That's what he says to me all the time if he calls me and I'm sleeping. 'Wake up, sleepyhead.'"

"Is that right?"

"Yep."

"Well, get up and I'll be there to get you and take you to your appointment shortly."

"Alright."

"Later."

Tellis arrived at 8:20. He called me from his cell. I wasn't quite ready, so I invited him in. Tellis greeted me with his usual short simple kiss on the cheek.

Today, Tellis was dressed down. He had on a pair of Levi jeans and a dark blue sweater —a white T-shirt hung below his sweater— probably a Versace, Tellis's favorite designer. He definitely had the bucks to afford his clothes. In his closet, Versace designs were everywhere.

"Tellis, nice shoes," I said glancing at his feet on my way into the kitchen.

"I saw them at Macy's men." They had a $500 price tag. I wanted to get a pair for my father on Father's Day; I ended up giving him $200 in a card instead. "Is that Eternity you're wearing?"

"Yeah, how did you know?"

"I know my fragrances."

"DeMarco must wear Eternity also."

"No, actually, DeMarco doesn't wear cologne. Says he can't stand it. I really don't even buy perfume that much anymore now that I'm with him because the scent irritates him. Now, I wear oils mostly. He's cool with the oils. My favorite is actually Patchouli. Hey, Tellis, there's a fresh pot of coffee in here. You gotta have a cup before we leave. I brewed it especially for you." I made my way up the stairs to gather my belongings from the bedroom.

"You made a perfect cup of coffee," Tellis said as I walked back into the kitchen.

"Good! I'm glad you like it."

"Haley, is Krystal seeing anyone?"

"No. She isn't. Why you ask?"

"Oh… I was just wondering?"

"What you like Krystal, Tellis?"

"No. I was just asking. I was just wondering… that's all."

"Yeah, you like her. You can tell me! It's cool."

"I mean, yeah… she's an attractive woman, you know. A strong and smart woman. I'm single, she's single."

I nodded. "Well, you know what, Tellis? I think she also has eyes for you."

"Is that right?"

"Yep," I said nodding again.

"What makes you think that?"

"I'm a woman and I know. I can tell."

"Maybe I'll give her a call and see if she wants to have dinner with me."

"That sounds like a plan. You ready to go?"

"Whenever you are." We left my house and headed to my doctor's appointment.

Fifty-three

Krystal woke up to Utopia banging loudly on her front door. The banging and Utopia's screaming voice excited her, and sent her running down the stairs. She was yelling, "Who is it, who is it?"

"It's Utopia!"

Opening the door Krystal asked, "What's the matter?" Utopia made her way past her into the kitchen. Excitedly waving the premiere issue of Rage in the air, breathlessly, she said, "Have you seen Haley's magazine? It's out, girl, it's out! I was in Albertson's. I needed to get some breakfast food and I went in there to get some eggs and stuff and something just told me to go and look at the magazines and I did. I guess it was meant for me to see, 'cause it was the first magazine that I saw when I looked at the magazine rack. Haley's magazine is out," she yelled. She was ecstatic.

"Let me see," Krystal said, removing the magazine from Utopia's hand. "Oh, my God, this is it." She excitedly flipped through the magazine.

"Here's the Too Short interview! Remember she told us about this interview?!" Utopia pulled the chair from under the round metal glass kitchen table, and took a seat. Standing up and looking over her shoulder together, they read the entire Too Short Interview. The byline read: *The Story of Too Short, Written by Haley Jones.*

"Look… there's Haley's name," Utopia said pointing to it.

Krystal eagerly peered at it. "Wow! Our girl, Haley, she's did the damn thing. Writing has always been Haley's passion. I am glad she followed her dream. This is her dream on paper. Who would have ever thought she would write a magazine, though?"

"I know, huh? Now, girl, we can go with Haley to all those celebrity parties and mess around with some celebrities. I wonder if she can get us in a party with Denzel. Now, that's a man I'd like to get my groove on with, even if it's as Luther said 'only for one night.'"

"Utopia, I am with you on that one. Now that's one guy, married or not married, I get in bed with."

"Huh! I wouldn't mind sleeping with Dre either," Utopia said.

"Dre?"

"Hell, yeah, I'd give him some. Girl, I am about to help her set that interview up. I will do the goddamn interview if she let me."

"You so crazy."

"Let me see that, Krystal," Utopia said, pointing to the *Rage* magazine in her hand. Utopia admired the cover. "So, Haley decided to go with this logo. It's the one we picked, remember?"

"I thought that was the one we picked."

"Yeah, this is it, Krystal." Utopia smiled, "My girl, Haley, she smart. She about to be a millionaire. Hope she give me some money!"

The phone rang. "Get the phone, Utopia?"

"Hello."

"Utopia?"

"Hey, Haley, girl… guess what I'm holding in my hand right now?"

"What?"

"Your magazine, *Rage*."

"Is that right? Where did you find a copy?"

"I went to Albertson's to buy some breakfast food this morning and something told me to stop by the magazine rack and when I did the first magazine I saw was *Rage*. It was sitting right there, staring at me."

"What?! get out of here! So, my distributor Ingram got *Rage* in Albertson's supermarkets?"

"Yeah, girl, it's in there."

"Cool."

From outside, a voice asked, "Who you talking to?"

"Krystal, its Haley. She's on the phone," said Utopia.

"Let me talk to that woman." Krystal grabbed the phone, grinning ear-to-ear.

"Haley, I am so proud of you and I am so happy for you. With all that investing DeMarco be doing in people's projects, I bet he'll be glad to see this one paying off."

"Huh."

"Let's go out and celebrate. We are taking you to Crustacean's in Beverly Hills tonight."

"Girl, y'all ain't gotta do that."

"Girl, we taking you."

"Y'all ain't got to do that! Besides, Crustacean's is too expensive."

"Girl, we all know that it is your favorite restaurant as well as ours, and we going to Crustacean's. Now what you having, the crab and garlic noodles, or the tiger prawns over a bed of garlic noodles, or your favorite, the drunken crab and the garlic noodles?"

"Krystal, with DeMarco still sick and all and me ready to give birth any day now, I really don't feel like celebrating."

" Girl, I love DeMarco, we love DeMarco… but right now I'm concerned about you. Haley, girl, your magazine is out! That is a major accomplishment and this is time for a celebration. Plus, you know DeMarco would want you to go on with your life and have fun. I'm sure that once he's back feeling better, he'll be knocking at your door. Furthermore, about that baby in your stomach, it needs to eat, too. Now, like I said, what you having, the crab and garlic noodles or the tiger prawns over a bed of garlic noodles?"

"The tiger prawns over a bed of garlic noodles," I reluctantly agreed.

"Now that's my girl."

"So, what time are we leaving?"

"Krystal, Haley wants to know what time we going to Crustacean's."

"Tell her let's go around six."

"Haley?"

"I heard, six it is. What you guys doing now?"

"Nothing. I just got all excited and came over here to show Krystal your magazine."

"Alright. I'm about to come over there. Maybe we could hang out and go shopping or something before dinner. I need to go to Macy's. They got some black leather boots on sale that I want to get and I need to find a brown suit."

"Sounds good."

"Aiight. See you in a minute."

Fifty-four

We were running late for church. I put Little DeMarco in his car seat. It was already 11:15 a.m., and church started at 11. Finally, we made it. It was my first time going to church since Little DeMarco was born. He was four months old.

At first, I felt a little uncomfortable going, because some of DeMarco's relatives were members at West Los Angeles Church of God In Christ.

I still hadn't seen DeMarco, and he yet to see his son. I heard through the grapevine that he was doing much better, but still he hadn't called me. Thoughts about DeMarco brought tears to my eyes. They started watering. I felt the tears coming. I excused myself to the bathroom, handing off little DeMarco to Utopia, who was sitting next to us.

When I returned to the pew and sat down, Utopia asked, "Girl, are you all right?"

"I'm cool." *I'd really love to break down and cry*, I thought, *but I have a child now, I have to be stronger than that. Life can bow me, but I will not let it break me.* I removed little DeMarco from her arms and placed him between my own.

I sat in church. I tried to focus on the sermon, but that was a hopeless battle. I kept daydreaming about DeMarco, his son, and I for the rest of the service. After church, Utopia excused herself to the bathroom. "See you outside, Haley," she said. People started coming up to me. "Oh, is that your baby you had for DeMarco?"

"Yes, it is."

"Let me see your little baby… how old is he," they were asking.

"I hear his daddy is doing a lot better now and getting around good. Does he ever come and see the little boy," Sister Carroll asked. She had always been nosy as hell, yet, I couldn't believe she had the audacity to ask me that.

"Yes, he does," I responded sharply.

"Oh, he does? I had heard that he has never seen the baby."

Utopia walked back just in time to hear Sister William's last remark.

"Who ain't never seen what baby," Utopia asked.

Sister Carroll looked at Utopia out of the corner of her eye and continued, "I saw DeMarco's mother in the grocery store the other night and that's what she had told me. She said that DeMarco and Nakeesha had reconciled and were coming over her house on Saturday, which was yesterday, for a family barbecue. She said that all of DeMarco's children were going to be there. Oh, wait a minute… there goes Sister Bridges, she and DeMarco's mom are best friends. I bet she went to the barbecue. Let me get her over here and ask her. Sistah, Bridges? Sistah Bridges!" She waved her over. All the while, I unfortunately thought, *I don't believe this bitch*.

"Hey, Haley, is that the baby," Sister Bridges asked approaching us. "Oh, my God, that little boy looks just like his daddy!" I smiled. Sister Bridges kept talking, "DeMarco spit that baby out. Wait till I tell Ida about this." Ida was DeMarco's mother. She didn't like me. She had a problem with me because I was with DeMarco, and she was close to Nakeesha.

"Oh, my goodness, the family ain't gone be able to deny that that is DeMarco's son when they see him. Well, I do declare," Sister Bridges said.

"Sister Bridges, let me ask you this: did you go to the barbecue at Ida's house yesterday?"

"Yeah, I was there."

"Was DeMarco and his family there?"

Looking up out of the corner of her eye, reflecting on the event, Sister Bridges spoke. "Yeah, they was there, too."

"Was his wife Nakeesha there?"

"Yeah, Nakeesha was there." I looked at Sister Carroll. She was overjoyed.

Sister Bridges quizzically looked at Sister Carroll. "But you know they not married no more."

"Who, who not married no more," Sister Carroll, questioned.

"They say that DeMarco hired a lawyer and had the divorce process underway right before he got shot. They divorced now. The divorce done gone through. Went through while he was laying up recuperating. That's what Ida told me."

I had recently wondered about this; maybe Nakeesha had stopped the divorce proceedings after DeMarco got sick. Now I was overjoyed. And looking at Sister Carroll, who had been oh-so-smug. I've seen plants wilt before, but I didn't think it could happen to a person until I saw Sister Carroll right after she heard about the divorce.

Sister Carroll gamely tried to recover. "Yeah, come to think of it, I did hear something about that. Ida said that with DeMarco almost dying and all of the craziness and all, Nakeesha must have either forgot about the fact that he had put in for the divorce or something and forgot to withdraw the papers. However, I don't think that she could have really legally done anything to stop the divorce, being that it was already under way and all. Whatever the reason, being that she forgot or that DeMarco was adamant, the divorce gone through. Ida was upset. I told her, 'You can't worry about these chillen.'"

"Yeah, but DeMarco was there at the barbecue with Nakeesha and the kids, right," Sister Carroll asked.

"Oh, yeah, he was there, but from what I saw his heart is not into that woman no more. I never saw them talk to one another. DeMarco kept mostly to himself. He stayed in his parents' bedroom most of the time. He was lying down. He wasn't feeling that well, I hear. My daughter told me that when she went to the bathroom, the bathroom is next to the bedroom where DeMarco was, that she heard DeMarco and Nakeesha arguing. She said that DeMarco told her to go home and to not worry about him." Sister Bridges looked out through the nearby door to the parking lot as something caught her eye. "Oh! There go my daughter… she went to get the car. She ready to go now. I'll see y'all later. Bye, Haley, it was good seeing you and that baby!" Sister Bridges got in the car. Sister Carroll looked disappointed and angry.

"I'll see you later, Sister Bridges. It was really nice seeing you," I said, and walked off with the biggest smile on my face.

Utopia met me at the doorway; she had watched and listened to the entire exchange. "Girl, you sure handled that woman well. I would have cussed her out. She came at you file, but you handled her right. Damn, Haley, I am vibing that DeMarco is thinking about you. I bet he calls you soon."

"You think so, Utopia?"

"Yep. I do. Oh, girl, this is what I wanted to tell you. Remember when I talked to you this morning and I said that I had something to tell you when I saw you?"

"Yeah."

"My boyfriend Chris told me that he was with DeMarco this past Thursday. Chris took him to his doctor's appointment. He said that DeMarco talked about you the whole time. Said he wanted to know what was up with you and that he had a lot of questions for him about you and little DeMarco and about Tellis.

"Chris said, it seemed like DeMarco wasn't sure how you would react to him, being that y'all hadn't seen each other in so long and that he was living with his wife and all. He also said that it seemed like DeMarco was preparing himself to see you. Oh yeah, and girl, he said that DeMarco asked him about Tellis. He said that DeMarco had said he heard that you were with him and that you had moved him in to the house that y'all had brought together. Chris said that he told DeMarco it wasn't true and that DeMarco asked him how he know. He said he reminded him that I was his girl, and if that were true he would know because I would have told him. Chris also told him that sometimes he picks me up from your house, and that the times he has gone in he has never seen another man there. He said that when he told DeMarco all of this that DeMarco was like, "Oh. I am going to have to go over there and see Haley and my son. I need to see if Haley's feelings about me are still the same."

I felt about fifty pounds lighter than I had been when I walked into church an hour and a half ago. "Is that right?"

"Yep, so I say all of this to say that DeMarco will be coming to see y'all soon, real soon, so get ready."

Fifty-five

DeMarco felt emotions of both excitement and trepidation as he pulled his new black Range Rover with the white leather seatst that was trimmed in black leather across the driveway of the Anaheim Hills home that he and I had purchased nearly two years ago.

My white 400 Lexus truck with the gold trim and my black Mercedes were in the driveway. He admired the two beautiful automobiles as he made his way up the cement walkway that led to the big white house. DeMarco looked at his key ring with the black and silver Range Rover logo he held in his hand. He had the keys to both of my automobiles on it. They were sitting next to the house key on the key ring. I'd purchased the Lexus truck first, and then, about eight months later, the Mercedes. I'd given him the keys to each vehicle immediately after I purchased them, so in the event that I lost them he'd have a copy.

DeMarco had been out of the hospital for seven months now. He had been at home recuperating for another six months after that. It was his first time seeing the house in more than a year. It took his body a long time to recover from the damage of the bullets, and then from the second operation. He still had some rehabilitating to do, and remained relatively weak. DeMarco could get around okay: he could walk around for a while, but he sure as hell wasn't about to run a five-minute mile or bench three hundred.

Hesitant, he stood outside for what seemed like forever, thinking. He was apprehensive about entering the house, not knowing what to expect once he walked through those doors. Rumor was going around that I had a new man in my life—a stockbroker. They were referring to Tellis, who was a very sincere and strictly platonic friend. Was he playing father to our son? Had he moved into the home that I had purchased with Haley? *Would I enter to find every trace of me removed*, DeMarco couldn't help but think.

He hadn't seen me in over a year. Unintentionally, he'd abandoned me. I had not heard from him in over a year cause of that shit Nakeesha pulled, exercising her spousal rights according to the law, and taking him home with her when he was discharged from the hospital. She knew their relationship was over, and was aware that DeMarco and I had been living together. She should have realized that you couldn't make someone who does not want to be with you, be with you.

DeMarco's mind was occupied by only one question: did I still feel the same way about him that he did about me? He bitterly realized that if I did have a new man in my life, he would have to accept it. He felt cold as he continued to ponder, although the air was warm and today was sunny out on the front lawn which he and I had often looked out over.

At first, DeMarco started to ring the doorbell, but decided against it. Taking a deep breath, he inserted the key into the lock on the door and turned. The key worked; the locks had not been changed. He took another deep breath and pushed the door open. He stepped inside onto the cream-colored carpet, which I loved so much that I had it installed throughout the house. The only part of the house that wasn't carpeted was the kitchen, with its light brown hardwood floors. DeMarco softly closed the door behind him.

Still standing next to the door, he untied the white shoestrings on his red and white Jordan's, and slid them off. My rule: no shoes on the white carpet. He noticed the rapidly blinking red light on the silent burglar alarm on the wall, behind the front door. I had set the silent alarm, and DeMarco inadvertently set it off upon entering the house. He had one minute to turn it off before Brinks would call; if we didn't respond, they would send the police. About twenty seconds had already elapsed; quickly, DeMarco entered the code: 279130. It was my birth date backwards: March 19, 1972. The red light, mollified, stopped flashing. He smiled; *Haley had not changed the code in more than a year*, he thought. For the first time, DeMarco realized I was waiting for his return. The uneasy feeling went away.

The house was still quiet. He walked around the bottom level of the house, noticing that it was immaculate as always. I was a fanatic for cleanliness. I kept our home so spotless that when our friends would visit, they thought that we had a hired housekeeper regularly cleaning it. DeMarco always asked me to hire a maid service to clean the house, even offering to pay for it, but I didn't want anyone cleaning my house but me. I suppose I was a firm believer in the old saying: if you want something done right, you'd better do it your damn self.

After entrance to the house, there were three directions in which one could wander. If DeMarco had gone to the right, he would have walked past the TV room, by the family room, and head en route to our master bedroom. If he'd gone to the left, he'd enter the living room, then the dining room, and finally the kitchen. Should DeMarco chose the straight path ahead, he walk up the black cast-iron spiral staircase that led to the remaining bedrooms. DeMarco took a right, and walked down the hallway to our bedroom. As he drew closer, he could hear my voice; I was on the telephone, speaking with Utopia.

"Little DeMarco, man, he is going to be a heart breaker like his dad. Naw, actually, you know what? I am going to have to stay on his ass. He can't be a womanizer. I ain't having that. Damn, I miss his ass so much, Utopia," I spoke into the telephone. "Girl, Little DeMarco is so cute. He looks just like his daddy. Everyday, he does something that makes me laugh. Did I tell you he's talking now? Yeah, girl. He's a lot like Big DeMarco... stubborn as hell," I laughed again.

DeMarco's head felt somewhere near the ceiling. *Haley really misses me,* he thought to himself. *Damn, if ever there was a cue for me to enter that had to be it...* He showed his face. As soon as he walked in the bedroom, I noticed him. And there was DeMarco.

I did a double-take, as though I saw someone come back from the dead. "Oh, my God, DeMarco?!" I felt giddy. The edges of my vision washed out for a second or two. "I'll call you back, Utopia," I said, abruptly hanging up the phone.

I rushed out of bed and hurriedly walked over to him. For a few seconds, I could do nothing more than check him out, as if he were a mirage that would disappear any second. I touched his shoulder. He was still there. "DeMarco, oh my God!" I didn't know what to do or what else to say, so I tightly embraced him and kissed him. We must have continued kissing for what seemed like a lifetime; he backed up to the king-size bed, pushed me onto the teal green down comforter with the matching bed skirt. I turned the tables on him by rolling us over and climbing on top. Suddenly, I stopped. He remained on his back as I sat up on top of him.

He looked me in the eye. "What's wrong?"

"DeMarco, I missed you so much." I was crying.

He wiped the first tear away.

"Haley, I love you."

My tears fell like rain. The more he wiped, the more the tears were replaced. He embraced my face in his hands, which I also started kissing. With his two thumbs, he wiped my face.

"DeMarco, I didn't think that you'd ever come back. I mean I did… but I didn't."

"Baby, I am so sorry. I know that you really went through it. I am so sorry. I wish that things had not happened the way that they did. I had no control of it. I was out of my body. I am still not yet fully recovered. I would if I could, I'd go back and change everything, baby. If I could, first of all, I never would have got shot, and secondly, I would have came home with you when the hospital released me. But, I am here now, baby, I'm back home with you for good… forever, until death do us part."

"Shhhh," I said. I just wanted to freeze everything exactly as it was. I held my pointer finger over my mouth and then DeMarco's. "I wish this moment could last forever." I laid my head on DeMarco's chest. I had stopped crying somewhere in the last minute. We both laid there, silent, holding on close to each other.

But that blessed moment of reunion could not last forever. Beautiful as it was, I still had issues and unresolved questions for which I needed answers, starting with why I had been made to wait so long.

"What took you so fucking long? I was going fucking crazy over here without you, DeMarco," I said, as I got up off of DeMarco in a flash of sudden anger.

"Haley, I been going through it with my health."

And did he think I hadn't been going through my own hell?

"I know, DeMarco, but you were suppose to be with me recovering, not with that bitch you divorced. You were not even married to her anymore and you stayed with her. Did you fuck her, DeMarco? Did you?" I was screaming as all the bitter heartache, all the waiting, and all the rumors echoing in my head seeped back to the surface.

"Oh, my God, I don't believe you."

"Did you sleep with her, DeMarco?"

He brooded in silence. Then he spoke, his anger rising to match mine. "I'm a man," he shouted back. I was furious. "What do you want? Me to sit here and lie, and tell you I didn't," DeMarco said.

"You did, I knew it. You been fucking her."

"What about you, Haley? Did you fuck Tellis," DeMarco yelled. I glared at DeMarco in disbelief.

"Motherfucker, I dare you to come up in here after more than a year and ask me who in the fuck I've slept with while you was fucking Nakeesha."

"Look, Haley, it really doesn't matter. I don't wanna know if you slept with him or not. It's about us. Haley, baby where am I right now? Where are you at right now? Where is our son at right now? Home. That's all that matters." I quieted down. I felt overcome from the stress of so many accumulated months, months that had seemed like years. I dropped my face into my hands. "Oh, DeMarco," I said, extending my arms out to him, and embracing him again. He kissed my forehead.

"DeMarco… it's just that I missed you so much. The truth is, I was scared. I'm glad you're home. You haven't seen your son." Taking DeMarco by the hand, I pulled him towards another room in the house. "Come, I have something to show you." I led the way to Little DeMarco's bedroom. The door was ajar; I pushed it aside and entered with DeMarco in tow.

The bedroom was decorated in blue and white. Sponge Bob was the theme on the blankets, the walls, and the curtains, even the border just beneath the ceiling.

A little, angelic boy with mahogany brown eyes and chocolate skin laid on the twin bed. "DeMarco, meet your son."

DeMarco quietly pulled the little white wooden chair from the desk that sat in the corner of the room, dragged it next to Little DeMarco's bed, and sat down. Speechless, he stared at Little DeMarco for the longest time. His eyes started to swell. He was crying. Looking up at me standing over him, he said, "Oh, my god, Haley… that's our son. That's little DeMarco. That's *ours*." Wiping his eyes, he said, "He looks like me." I walked over and sat on DeMarco's lap, and we embraced.

"How many pounds was he?"

"Seven pounds, four ounces."

"I was seven pounds too."

"What? Get out of here!"

"I was. Did you have a caesarian?"

"No. Why you ask?"

"My mother had to have one with me. I was just wondering. So, how was your pregnancy?"

"It was cool."

"Yeah?"

"Yeah."

"Damn, Haley, I was suppose to be there." I smiled, nodding my head.

"Just promise that you will never leave us again, and that the next time you will be there."

"I promise."

"DeMarco, remember that conversation we had before your accident? When you told me that all two people had to do was just say that they were married and that's all that mattered?"

"Yeah."

"Well, I believed you. It was such a beautiful idea. But going through all that I have this past year, not being able to see you and all 'cause the law makes it clear I had no rights when it came to you, I have learned that that is not necessarily true." I tried to keep the bitterness out of my voice, but I am certain that some leaked around the edges. "By law, Nakeesha had all of the power when you were in the hospital, and I was left out in the cold. She had me removed from your visitor's list and I couldn't even come and see you. After you were released from the hospital and you went back home to her, I knew that there was no use in me even trying to see you at that point. Whenever I would see one of your boys, I would ask about you, and they kept me posted on how you were progressing."

DeMarco sighed. "You're right, Haley. I can't deny that being married by law, with that neat little piece of paper duly stamped and notarized and all that, does give the spouse a lot of control."

"So, what do we do?"

DeMarco took both my hands in his. "We make it legal."

"DeMarco… are you asking me to…"

"Yes, Haley. I am asking you to marry me."

"Oh, my God!!!" I wept.

"Haley, I want more of these, right here," DeMarco said pointing at Little DeMarco.

I laughed between the tears of joy. "Let's go and make one right now, then."

"Well, let's do the damn thang," he said. I got up from DeMarco's lap. As I stood, feeling warm inside, DeMarco bent down and planted a kiss on Little DeMarco's cheek. Then he bent down further and got on his knees. Looking back at me, he said, "Come here, Haley, say a prayer with me." He reached for my hand. I reached out, took his hand, and knelt down beside him.

DeMarco began. "God, thank you so much for this moment. Thank you so much for putting Haley and Little DeMarco in my life. When I first met Haley, I had no idea that we'd be together as family. I had no idea that she would be the woman that I would find true happiness with, would truly commit to, and would want to spend the rest of my life with. Unlike my last marriage, this time I am marrying for the right reasons. I also pray to you, Lord, that you protect my family, all of my children… and Nakeesha. I wish Nakeesha the best, and I sincerely hope that she can go on and find true love and happiness with a man who can give her what I was not able to give her. Nakeesha is a good mother. She did a lot for me and I will never forget it. I will always appreciate all that she has done. Lord, I also pray and ask you to smooth out the relationship between Haley, Nakeesha, and me. I ask you to humble us, and when necessary, to remind us all that we are human beings. God, foremost, I thank you for fulfilling my request for a bride and I ask that you bless me and Haley's marriage, our union together. Lord, thank you, Lord, so much for putting a woman of understanding and support in my life. Lord, thank you for putting Haley in my life. Amen." I had opened my eyes and stared at DeMarco once he got to the end of his prayer, truly touched by his words.

"Amen," DeMarco said again, and started to get up. I was still holding onto his hand.

"Hey," I said, "I've got a few words, too." DeMarco knelt again, squeezing my hand. "Lord, I thank you so much for giving me a new family. DeMarco was what I needed. I was what he needed. Thank you so much, Lord, for putting us in each other's life. The Bible says, Lord, that we have to order our husband and we have to be patient. God, when I put in that order more than four years ago, the promise I made to you that I would remain celibate until the right one came along, I did not realize that I would get just what I had asked for. Someone who was tall, dark and handsome. And smart. And a good listener. Someone who had all of the qualities of that order that I put in to you, God. Someone who would make me that much happier and my life that much more complete. Lord, I also ask that you help me to be a good mother to DeMarco's children and a good wife to him. Thank you, Lord, for my family. Amen."

"Amen."

As we made our way back to our bedroom, still soaking in the emotions of the moment, I spoke. "DeMarco… Universal, Interscope and WEA offered us a major distribution deal. I went for the one from Universal. They gave us a $20 million advance. They offered us the best deal. The check came about six months ago."

"Wow!" DeMarco appeared as though he wanted to say something more, but couldn't. The "$20 million advance" part was still bouncing around inside his head, not really having yet settled into his brain.

"I deposited it into *Life, Inc.*'s account at Wells Fargo. I put half of it into a brokerage account at Salmon, Smith & Barney, and I opened a Charles Schwab account. The final sales of the Rage comp was $300,000 independently sold, and we generated about $2.4 million from that, thank you very much."

"Haley, we got a twenty-million dollar advance and we got a distribution deal through Universal?"

"Yep, we sold three hundred thousand units independently. That's what got us our $20 million advance. As per our agreement, Universal has redistributed and promoted the comp, and now we are at 600,000 sales three months later. Here look at the ad," I said, handing DeMarco the latest issue of *Rage* magazine.

"Oh my God! This is your magazine? *Rage*! You got Dre, Snoop, and Eminem on the cover." DeMarco looked at me and the cover of Rage, then back at me, then the cover again. "Haley, you did it!"

"Yep, and look at who was on last month's cover."

He snagged up the copy that I tossed at him in mid-air. "No you didn't... baby, you got Master P on the cover!"

"Yep, and the one before that I dedicated to the Bay Area underground music scene. I got C-Bo, E-40, Too Short, and 4-Tay on the cover," I said, handing him another issue of Rage. "And, look, the month before that, Suge Knight graced the cover."

"What? Get the fuck out of here! Haley, damn, you really did it... but I am not surprised. I always believed in you so much. I knew that you would do it."

"DeMarco, I also purchased a four thousand square foot warehouse about two months ago. I spent five hundred thousand for the warehouse. In addition, I put another $180,000 into renovating the place. The construction is still underway; it will be complete in about another two weeks. Wait until you see our new plush offices. I hired an interior designer to decorate the building. We went to Kreiss to purchase the office furniture and the furniture for the recording studio. I hired Utopia to work for us. She's the VP of Marketing. Oh, yeah, and DeMarco, we both need to hire personal assistants. Oh, by the way, we both the CEO's of *Life Inc.* And another thing, Snoop is performing a song produced by Dre on our next comp."

DeMarco laid down on the bed first, motioning for me to lay inside his arms. "Haley, I love you."

"I love you too, baby."

"Thanks to you, Haley, I'm finally out the game. You saved me. Thank you."

"You're quite welcome," I said. I was in seventh heaven.

"I knew the first time I had a real conversation with you at Eastside West that you were different. A strong black woman."

Wow, I thought to myself, *yeah, it's finally happening, thanks to me, and DeMarco was acknowledging it.*

"Baby, I ain't never told nobody this before, but you know for a decade, I've struggled with the opposition of different families and fought them for control of the drug traffic for the entire West Coast and a couple of cities in the Midwest. I escaped poverty. I've obtained the dream everybody in the hood wants... money and power. I've obtained the dream that everybody in

America wants. My boys and me are ghetto stars. I give the title kingpin to the dogs. They can have it. D, Kameron, Creature man and who ever can figure it out, which among them gets to be the next kingpin. I told D and Kam if they wanted to go legit that we'd create a spot for them at *Life Inc.* However, they can't be bullshittin', you know. They either break clean, or not at all. You know what them nigguhs told me?"

"What?"

"They told me that they didn't want to get out of the game. They said they wanted to work with us and Life, but they gone start their own record label especially being that I no longer want any part of the game. I wished them luck. Damn, I wish I had my nigguh Mumbles with me, though. We started all this shit together. Things ain't been the same since he went down. If Mumbles was here, Haley, I'm telling you I know he'd go legit. I've attained all we've ever wanted."

"Who's Mumbles?"

"We grew up in the Ville together… me, him, Creature Man, Sleep, Prophet… man it was a lot of us. Most of them dead or in prison now. That was my nigguh. He died, got killed in prison. They stabbed him to death. I gave my nigguh the biggest funeral. He deserved that. Man, and everybody was there! Former members of the Black Panthers, basketball players from the Warriors and football players from the Raiders… even the mayor of Oakland was there. Mumbles gave a lot of money to the local community in East Oakland. Our neighborhood and they loved him for that, especially the kids. "On holidays, he'd give away turkeys. When the little black boys in East Oakland didn't have clothes to wear or shoes he'd buy it for them. All they had to do is ask. One year, he even sent the entire Boys and Girl's Club to Africa. Paid their airfare, hotel and everything. He even gave them a spending allowance. He said that all black people should go to Africa, said it was an experience of a lifetime. Mumbles had been to Africa several times. He told me that he was going to move there one day, that was his dream. Yeah, Haley, I don't want that shit in my life no more. Damn, that was my clique back in the Ville. Me, Mumbles, Niko, D, Kameron, Antonio, he was half Black and half Italian, Streets, Homicide, and this nigguhh we use to call Sleep. Haley, I came up in the game with them under me. A man couldn't ask for better soldiers than them. They were true to the game. Them nigguhs never ratted on me. I mean, they did time and never ratted. They some real nigguhs. I put in work to build my empire and the shit wasn't easy. You know, Haley, like everybody who really in the game, I really didn't care if I lived or died. It was like I was on a suicide mission. I mean that's really what it is when you out there on the block, suicide, but you get so caught up in the day to day you really don't see it that way. You see things through a different eye. You see it as survival, and that's really what it is living in the inner city and living a thug life, it's all about survival of the fittest. You know, a thug really doesn't have many options, so we make the best out of a bad situation and we come up and were admired.

"Sleep use to study with the Muslims and go to the mosque. Sleep ended up changing his name to Knowledge, said that the white man no longer kept him asleep. Most of us still kept on calling him Sleep. In the beginning, he use to correct us, but I guess he got tired or something cause he stopped. Sleep never got out the game. He died about three years ago… that was when I first met you. Sleep was crazy, we should have called him Homicide rather than calling Homicide, Homicide. That nigguh Sleep was really homicidal. He was a real killer. His reputation is what got him killed. It preceded him for bad. I'm lucky. Yeah, Haley… I've thrown in my belt. I'm going to give it back to the dogs. Haley, I'm done with that life, the thug life. I wish I could make the little black boys in the hood and on the block realize that just because it looks like gold doesn't mean it's gold. But, then again, you can't get on a man for what he has to do to survive and that's what it's about in the ghetto, surviving. It's really a catch-22 situation, you know. Man, I have been so fucking lucky not to have been taken out by the streets. I am so lucky to not have gone to prison. Shit, not everybody in the game gets a chance like I got. I was lucky."

DeMarco stopped speaking. When the silence persisted I looked up at him. It was good listening to him and hearing the way he was talking. He really had learned something and he was serious. He returned to the conversation. "Haley, I'm starting a not-for-profit organization called the Inner City Foundation. Through the Foundation, I'm going to buy abandoned homes in the hood, starting right here in Compton and my hometown east Oakland, and renovate them into neighborhood community centers. When the youth and young adults go there instead of feeling like they're in a community center, they will feel as if they are in a home. Through the foundation, we can provide them with after-school tutorial services and sports activities to fill the young peoples' free time. From time to time, we'll bring a celebrity or famous athlete through for a pep talk, and so that they can meet them, and hopefully be inspired. We can sponsor sleepovers, block parties, and buy clothes and shoes for the local inner-city teenagers who participate in area youth sports."

I smiled. "Let's call Krystal first thing in the morning and have her set up the non- profit organization for us. She can handle all of the paperwork that is necessary to make the foundation happen.

And she did.

Krystal found a 3400-square-foot home in Compton in need of renovation. It had been on the market for over two years and had been partially burned out; currently, it was inhabited by a succession of drug dealers and homeless people. The home was on the market for two hundred fifty thousand dollars. She found another in East Oakland, two blocks from where DeMarco grew up in sixty-nine Ville. It was on the market for two hundred thirty thousand dollars. It had a history similar to that of the house in Compton.

Krystal had no problem getting the respective city governments to expedite the paperwork to allow the Foundation to purchase the homes; both places were designated public nuisances. The city of Compton even managed to get us $10,000 in grant money from an urban renewal program. Along with Krystal, DeMarco and I flew out to Oakland to purchase the home. We met with the Black-owned Smiths Construction Company, and immediately hired them to do the repairs. Their sister company in Los Angeles took care of the Compton home.

Three months later, "A Place Like Home" opened, serving disadvantaged youth and young adults in the East Oakland and Compton neighborhoods where DeMarco had once lived. The ribbon-cutting ceremony for the home in East Oakland took place first, on a Saturday. The following weekend, we had the same ceremony for the home in Compton. The mayor and the president of the NAACP were at both ceremonies. In Oakland, Antawn Jamison of the Golden State Warriors was present; for L.A., Shaq was there. Even music mogul Suge Knight was present for the second ribbon-cutting ceremony. He was also from Compton. An ABC News crew was there, too. Jamison donated a $25,000 check to A Place Like Home; Shaq handed over another $25,000 to complement Suge's $25,000 check.

We had our eyes on another abandoned home in each neighborhood.

Fifty-six

A Place Like Home was well-received by residents of East Oakland; even the local politicians praised it. The Channel 2 News, with anchor Dennis Richmond, ran a special segment about the program and how it was taking youths and young adults off of the streets, thereby filling their free time. There were more positive reports applauding a drop in violence in the neighborhoods where the centers opened.

In addition to serving as a recreation place for youth and young adults to hang out while playing pool, ping-pong, air hockey, and basketball, the Centers had more structured programs designed to expose urban youth to culture and academic improvement opportunities such as tutoring sessions, sporting events, and cultural enrichments found in museums and plays. The Centers helped young people find jobs after school, provided counseling for drug addicts as well as teenage fathers and mothers, and legal advocacy and intervention for young offenders. There was even a cultural summer enrichment program where attendees were exposed to other cultures abroad. The youth traveled outside of the U.S. for three weeks, visiting faraway places like Senegal, South Africa, London, and Amsterdam.

When the Oakland chapter of Zeta Phi Beta Sorority heard about A Place Like Home, they volunteered and worked with us to build a female social discussion group aimed at mentoring girls and building self-esteem.

The group, called Sistah to Sistah, discussed current affairs and relationships. Occasionally, they'd even invite the males to attend a session when they dealt with issues on why they cheat or wanted a male point of view on a particular topic. The males' social discussion group was called The 100 Black Males Club, operated by the Oakland Chapter of Phi Beta Sigma Fraternity, who, like their sorority sisters in Zeta Phi Beta, volunteered their time for the enhancement of the community and its people. Both focused on gang prevention and diversion programs, and each program offered scholarships to black colleges. All participants had to do was indicate their desire to go to college, follow the normal entrance process, and A Place Like Home paid their tuition for all four years.

This particular day was special because DeMarco was in town, and had stopped by the Center to see how things were going with "his baby." I was with him. The after-school tutorial program was in session, with the middle school and high school students in attendance when DeMarco and I arrived. DeMarco stuck his head inside the room of the large house that served as a classroom, to say hello to the director, Ali Williams. Ali, too, was a former drug dealer and friend of DeMarco's who grew up in East Oakland's 6-9 Ville. I stood at the door observing and admiring the happenings of the place. With DeMarco greeting Ali and informing him that we were there, the whispers started. DeMarco ignored them.

"That's DeMarco," a voice whispered.

"Where?"

"Right there," a boy pointed in his direction. All eyes in the room were focused on DeMarco.

"With the dark blue slacks on and blue sweater," someone asked.

"How do you know?"

"'Cause I saw him before. He friends with my uncle."

"Yeah, that's him," another voice said. DeMarco had left his suit coat in the car. It was a hot day in Oakland.

"He fine," Tiffany, who was fifteen, said.

"Sure is," another girl agreed.

"Um hum," the murmurs of agreement among the girls spread across the room.

"So, that's DeMarco Speed, from where we from."

"Yeah, girl, that's DeMarco from 6-9 Ville."

"He looks rich, and he fine. I'd be his baby's mama. Plus I heard that if you his girl he spends money on you," another voice spoke softly. We left the room and the questions for Ali started.

"Wasn't that DeMarco Speed," Anthony asked.

"Yes," Ali responded.

"Can we all meet him and talk to him?"

"I have always wanted to meet him," Omar said, echoed by a roomful of "me too's."

"We wanna thank him for starting this place," Chanelle said.

"Ooh, please, Ali… can you tell him we want to meet him and chop it up with him," Jason asked.

"He's my mentor, I want to be a baller like he is," another boy voiced. The look on Ali's face was one of disbelief. Here, DeMarco has cleaned up his act and he's still being accused of being a dealer.

"He don't do that no more! That's why he started this program for us, dummy," Jason expressed.

"I'll see what I can do. I'll be right back." Ali left the room momentarily. When he returned, he announced that DeMarco would come and meet them during the last thirty minutes of the program. "He'll be here at seven."

Everyone was excited.

Like clockwork, at 7:00 p.m., DeMarco entered the room, carrying the day's edition of the Oakland *Tribune* newspaper. I was with him. I took a seat at one of the desks while DeMarco kept towards the front of the room with Ali. Ali Introduced him. DeMarco sat down on the large table, placing the newspaper down beside him.

John was the first student to speak. "DeMarco, we know about you, Mumbles, and Creature Man. We heard the stories and we love them."

"What stories are those?"

"That you built an empire, you got heart and you are a sav."

The expression on DeMarco's face indicated that what these youth were saying took him by surprise.

"We know that you was a block hog," Clarence said.

"Is that what people are saying about me?"

The room broke out in nods and "yes" and "uh-huh."

"I tried to tell these fools you ain't about that no more, that you changed and that's why you started this program for us," Jason said.

John shook his head. "Man, whatever. We know that you had love for your boys and that when you made it you took them with you. They all moved with you down to L.A. and they all balling. That's what I want to do, DeMarco. I want to follow your footsteps. You're my mentor… you all of our mentors from the Ville. You are the perfect example of success. I want to be just like you."

Another young man started talking. "DeMarco, I have always wanted to work for you. A lot of people saying that you opening this center is a front—"

DeMarco cut him off. "Who's a lot of people?"

"Just people, they be saying—"

DeMarco cut him off again, a look of disgust on his face. "Man, me opening this center ain't no front. I've changed my life. I've gotten older and I see life differently than I did when I was a youngster. This is real," DeMarco said, standing up from the table and pointing his two fingers down at the floor. "You tell 'them,' you tell those 'people,' whoever the hell they are, I said that. Also tell them I stopped bamboozling my people."

Many in the room looked perplexed.

DeMarco continued, his voice gentler but no less genuine. "About the stories you've heard about me and others, let me tell you something. I'll start by saying this. Selling drugs and putting guns in our community is a setup. If I knew back when I was a youngster, if I knew what I'm trying to teach you all now, that you have options, I would not have sold drugs. All I want to do with A Place Like Home and all of the programs we offer here is present those options to you. It's your choice. Whatever bed you make is the one that you are going to have to lie in. Be it life in prison, in a casket or doing right. I don't want you guys to ever forget this.

"About these glorious stories you say you've heard about me. They may be true and they may not be, but I can honestly say that I'm not proud of them. Do y'all know that most of those guys you've heard these so called 'glory stories' about, are dead or in prison for the rest of their lives? Like I said, I was one of the lucky ones."

"DeMarco, you say there's options for us, what options? We thugs! Don't nobody care about us. We gotta make it the best way we can. You know that, you know it's about surviving in those streets," John asserted.

"I care." DeMarco paced the front of the room. "That's why I started this program. Look, our environment, the space we live in, plays an important part in our development. It makes us who we are. We respond to situations based on what we learn in our environment. People who grow up in an inner-city community, we are products of our environment. This is the environment that creates us, it is the environment that creates our thug mentality and the way we think and the way we see things. It is an environment where you become immune to losing those close to you, your friends and family members. Attending funerals becomes a regular part of your routine. Death no longer fazes you because it is common occurrence in your community. We become immune to it.

"When you in the game, you figure 'death happens to us all,' and at some point it will be your inescapable destiny. And you can believe nine times out of ten, people in the inner cities throughout America are dying for two reasons: money and drugs.   "Basically that's it. All this killing has to do with economics, narcotics, and turf wars. Most of these drive-bys are done when the shooter is high. Trust me, I know… there's no way somebody who isn't out of their body is going to commit a premeditated crime like murder. Without drugs or alcohol in you, you'll think twice about pulling the trigger, unless its in the heat of the moment. The sad thing about it is the drug dealers, addicts, the pimps, the boosters, and those committed to a life of crime and violence who become our heroes. They are what we want to be because they have what we want: money, nice places to live, nice cars, Mercedes, BMWs, Escalades, and Hummers. And why do they become our heroes? Because our mothers and fathers and some of our grandparents who should be our real heroes are strung out. It doesn't make sense for us to have to look outside our families for role models, but if you from the inner city, often times you do."

"Man, what you say sounds good, but we thugs, like he said, and don't nobody other than probably you care about us. I mean I'll give you that, you trying. But the truth is, DeMarco you got this organization and shit cause of your money you made in the game," John said.

In defense of DeMarco, Jason chimed in, "Man, my nigguh own *Life Inc.*, he got major fucking rap artists on MTV, BET. That's how he got his money to start this."

John nodded. "Man, whateva, I ain't hatin' on the nigguh. Hell, I admire him. I wanna be just like him. When I'm a balling drug dealer one day, I'm gone give back to the community too."

"Young man, you better hope that you are around to give back to the community," DeMarco said. "Can't give much of anything to anybody if you wearing a toe-tag or a number."

"Then answer me this," John said to DeMarco. "I hear you saying we should give up the thug life, but the thug life is the life where those who are your friends you display loyalty and support to. It's like, if somebody is messing with you or disrespect you, and you are my friend, then they disrespecting me, too. Then we gone deal with it together. It's like when two people are married, they become one."

DeMarco shook his head. "How many brothers you got?"

"Me, "John said pointing to himself looking around.

"Yeah, you."

"Two."

"Let me ask you this. If your two brothers are arguing or fighting and you're around, how do you respond to them?"

"I either ignore it or I step between them and stop it."

"That is exactly my point. But you don't ride on them. Now I got a question for everyone in here. If you had two brothers who were fighting and pulled out a gun, what would you do?"

"I'd take it," Calvin said.

"It wouldn't go down like that," another voice shouted.

"I'd intervene," someone else declared.

DeMarco smiled. "Now you guys get the picture. We need to all learn how to be our brother's keeper even when our brothers don't have the same mother or father that we do."

DeMarco fixed his eyes on John. "Yeah, I see what your saying, you're right. But—"

DeMarco cut John off before he could complete his sentence. "I just want you guys to think about the advantages and disadvantages of living a thug life, and weigh it against the options you have. The options that A Place Like Home presents to you, that's all. You need to understand that, even though you come from a confined and fucked-up environment, you have options. You need to realize that, and if you walk away with nothing else from this conversation, please remember that. You need to realize you can have a nice car and a nice house by building things, by doing positive things that add value to the world around you. It might not be as 'easy' as the thug life, but you don't spend your life looking over your shoulder.

"You also need to realize that pretty much all drug dealers and people in the game either end up in jail… or dead. But, hey, don't take my word for it." He picked up the newspaper and slapped it down on the table, in front of everyone. "If you don't believe, go and do your homework. Find out who all the kingpins were and the balling drug dealers were, and see what they are now doing. I want y'all to come back and tell me what you learn. Whoever comes back with the info will get $100 bills from me."

DeMarco picked up the day's issue of the Oakland Tribune newspaper. He spread out the pages, and held up a two-page spread. The pictures of 107 Black faces were laid out on the pages.

DeMarco's voice rose, became almost staccato in its restrained fury. "Do you know who these people are, who they were? Yeah, I see some of you nodding your heads. You, in the back there… tell me who these people were."

A young man shifted uncomfortably in his chair. "They… they are the 107 murdered this year in Oakland."

"Anybody want to dispute that," DeMarco proclaimed, with the voice of a drill sergeant. "No? Good, 'cause that's exactly what this waste of life on these pages is.

"Know anybody on here?" Again, nearly every hand in the room went up in the air.

"How many of you in this room attended the funeral of one of the people behind the faces on this newspaper?" Every hand in the classroom was raised.

"How many of you are looking forward to the next one," DeMarco demanded. The hands wilted away.

"I got three little cousins on the pages of these newspapers. I attended all of their funerals. I paid their burial expenses, 'cause they parents didn't have the money to bury them. Do you know how much a funeral costs?"

The youth before him shook their. "Eight Gs, that's how much. Does your family have $8,000 to bury you if you die today or tomorrow?" Heads before him were again shaking "no." "I know from firsthand experience that living life in the ghetto is so fucking hard. All the negative shit we go through, especially as black males. I mean, we know all too well the feeling of being hit by a police baton against our heads, our bodies. The ghetto and all the shit that plagues it can re-fashion a harmless person into a slayer, if agitated, disrespected, forced or roused in any way.

"How many people in here like Tupac?" The hands sprang back to life.

"Yeah, he was our ghetto prophet, wasn't he? When we listen to Tupac's music, this is what he talked about. In his songs Hail Mary, So Many Tears, Trapped is representative of this and of the life and thoughts of the inner city Black male who got caught up. Understanding the psychology of individuals, we realize that Tupac's ideals on this subject were created. He wasn't born that way. Violence is a learned behavior. Observing the background of an inner-city male especially allows us to see how his thoughts could develop in such a way.

"Like 'Pac, I grew tired of it. Like him, I, too, said I was through with the thug life. If someone else wants it they can have it. Me and 'Pac and people like us, we are no longer disillusioned. We see the life for what it really is." DeMarco voice faded, although all eyes remained intent on him. He looked into the eyes of all before him, including Ali's and my own, and continued. "We need to bring our communities back to the way they were during the late 1960's, and early 1970's. Before drugs and guns were abundant in the black community, we saw a community of people uprising, hitting their stride despite all the obstacles. Self-esteem and confidence were rising, and more Black-owned businesses were forming. We were organized, going to school, and as a community of people, understood the importance of education, unity and black power.

"Unfortunately, somebody out there didn't like all that. The confinement and attacks our community has experienced from outside forces have taken their toll. Once drugs were introduced into the black community and we partook of them, using and dealing to each other, we saw an overwhelming increase in violence and the beginning of the decline of a race." DeMarco looked back into each set of eyes before him. "Yeah, and when I was younger, I was a part of all that shit. I used youngsters, males and females alike, such as yourself, to sell for me. I'd set you up, put you in the game, even front you the money to be in the game, but you could believe I was getting something out of it.

"Today, I do kind things for you guys, and don't expect anything back. But back then, if one of y'all crossed me, or stole from me, don't think I'd just let it ride; I was all about my money. But when I started having daughters and shit, I woke up and realized it wasn't cool to treat females the way I was treating them. When I started having sons, I realized what it meant to be a father, and I didn't want my sons to be 'ballers,' to have to go visit them in prison, or see their faces here." He gestured to the newspaper.

DeMarco looked around the room. "Yeah, I see it in your eyes. There are some of you who want to square up like me and 'Pac did, and there are some of you whose funerals I'll probably be attending. And for those of you who die and whose families are unable to afford your funeral costs cause you succumb to the game, I'll probably be even paying your burial service. I believe that everyone deserves a decent burial.

"But maybe some of you will listen to what I'm trying to tell you, learn a lesson without having to go through hell to get there. Maybe some of you will wise up, and square up, and I'll be paying for you to become doctors, lawyers, or engineers instead. If that happens, then what I'm doing here won't have been wasted. It's your choice."

With that, DeMarco rose up, grabbing the paper on the way. He stopped at the front of the room, and tacked it up to the wall. Looking back, he quietly stated, "It's your choice. Do you want your face up there next year?" Then, after giving a long, silent gaze at the young faces in the room, he walked out.

I sat there in my chair, flabbergasted. I was amazed with this side of DeMarco, which I witnessed for the first time. After what DeMarco had just so articulately expressed, I admired him and loved him just that much more. I knew he'd apply the same kind of persuasion, motivation, and brainpower toward this new venture as he had applied to the old… and succeed at it. I knew he was going to be a tremendous force for good. Yeah, he was the kind of man I could marry. The kind of man I could have children and grow old with. The kind of man with whom I could spend the rest of my life.

Epilogue

I am so tired. DeMarco and I made love three times last night. We did it once before we went to bed, twice during the middle of the night, and again early this morning, just as the sun began to rise.

Our lovemaking on top of the bed was like a ship cruising at sea after a storm had calmed: riding the waves up and down, so pleasantly.

Before DeMarco brought me out of exile, I'd been celibate for three years. Since his one-year absence from me, it was my first time having sex. I was committed to our relationship. Why is doing it again with a guy that you haven't done it with in a long time the best sex in the world, so good it can even make you cry?

This morning, I went to get out of bed. DeMarco tugged me back down and planted a kiss on my lip. I turned my neck to the side. He kissed it again. Then to the other side, and he kissed there.

"Where you going," he whispered in my ear.

"To put on Al."

"Yeah, put Al on," he said. Lying on his back, he rested the back of his hand on his forehead. His other arm was laying on his chest, the teal comforter with the white sheets underneath rested below his waist. His bare chest showed. I put Al Green's song, Simply Beautiful, in the bedroom's CD player. DeMarco and I sung along with Al.

Keeping with family tradition, as my sister and three brothers did before me, DeMarco and I danced to the song at our wedding. And we didn't dance to a record; no, it was Al himself. He sounded even better live than he did on a recording.

Our wedding was a black-and-white wedding. The bridesmaids were my clique, of course; my sister and my three cousins walked down the aisle in short-sleeve, body-hugging, long, white silk dresses with free-flowing ruffled hems at the bottom. With their bomb shapes and protruding behinds (thanks to the design of the dress), they looked like a million dollars. The flower girls—DeMarco's five and seven-year-old daughters- walked down the aisle with pink and white roses in their hands, wearing white sheer-above-the-knee dresses. Krystal was my Maid of Honor. She promenaded down the aisle wearing a long, free-flowing, white dress also made of silk. Alexander McQueen designed all of the ladies dresses.

I walked down the aisle with Tellis in tow; he gave me away. I wore an elegant, backless Bob Mackie wedding gown. The top was white sheer, trimmed in pearls, and the bottom was a combination of both satin and sheer. I admit that I looked quite extravagant in the $8000 wedding gown. For the cocktail and dinner parties, I changed into a $5000 long, simple, pure white silk spaghetti-strap dress. The popular designer Bob Mackie designed the party dress as well. The tight-fitting garment hugged my shapely body. Like in the dominatrix suit, I towered in the white silk dress.

DeMarco wore a traditional Bob Mackie black tuxedo. With his dreads held back in a ponytail, and wearing the tux, he stood there looking fine as hell. D was his best man. His brother Michael and all of his henchmen, including Creature Man and Kameron, were groomsmen. The best man, groomsmen and ring bearer—Little DeMarco, a.k.a. Lil D, who was now two- donned black tuxedos. While everyone else's tux varied a bit, his was identical to the one that his daddy wore. "If there is any man or woman who feel that these two should not be joined together, please speak now," the reverend said. I looked back and caught Utopia nudging Camille. I looked over at Krystal who was standing at an angle behind me, and then towards Utopia and Camille; all three of them laughed under their breaths. He proceeded, "DeMarco Speed, do you take Haley Jones as your wife, to love and to cherish till death do you part?"

"I do."

I was crying uncontrollable tears of joy. I looked back at my mom, who sat next to my uncle. He had escorted her to the wedding because my father was in the hospital. She was also joyfully crying. "Haley Jones, do you take DeMarco Speed as your husband, to love and to cherish, until death do you part?"

I was nervous. I thought I was going to collapse right there at the altar. "Uh huh." The church laughed.

"Baby, you're suppose to say 'I do,'" DeMarco leaned into my ear and whispered.

"I mean, I do. I do! That's what I meant to say," I nervously explained. The church belted out another laugh. I felt like I was on some strange trip.

"Now, Demarco, turn to the bride, look into her eyes and repeat these words. 'With this ring, I thee wed.'" DeMarco spoke the reverend's words and slipped the rare pink four-carat rock, made in Italy, on my finger. It was so big and beautiful, that I believe even Elizabeth Taylor would have died for it.

Now the preacher was smiling, looking at me. "Now, Haley, turn to the groom and repeat these words after me. 'With this ring, I thee wed.'" I repeated them, looking directly into DeMarco's eyes as he had done for me, while holding on to each word as if it were my last. I slipped the precious two-carat Tiffany wedding ring onto his finger. His wedding ring was elegant and simple, just the way he liked his jewelry.

The preacher turned to DeMarco, "Now, you may kiss the bride." DeMarco lifted the white veil and planted a long kiss on my lip. We wouldn't stop kissing; we basked in this moment that so much stress, energy, time, and love had been building up to.

I don't know how long we were kissing, up there, in front of God and everyone. At some point, D tapped DeMarco on the shoulder and said, "Can y'all finish that later? I got a cocktail party and dinner party to go to!" The whole church heard him and laughed. I was blushing as DeMarco smiled.

After the wedding service ended, we led the wedding party out onto the steps of the church to the parked white Hummer limousines. As we walked through the doors, one hundred white doves were released into the air, and people were throwing rice on us as photographers from some of the music publications, the *L.A. Times*, and *Sister to Sister* magazine took snapshots as we exited the church. They also captured pictures of DeMarco's famous supermodel cousin Chyna who had flown in from New York to attend our wedding. Krystal, Utopia, and Camille were happily crying, overcome by emotion. Later, one of those pictures of DeMarco and I was entered into both *Macavelli* and *Ebony* magazines, showing us among the hottest Hollywood celebrity couples. I guess this is what being CEO of an entertainment conglomerate got us.

Oh, yeah… guess what? I noticed Krystal and Tellis holding hands when they got into the Hummer, between the time that we left the church and they entered the cocktail party. They became further acquainted with one other throughout the entire night. I looked over in her direction a few times during the celebration, and when she would look in my direction, I gave her a huge smile. Her smile, in turn, was so huge that she could have been in one of those Colgate commercials. Need I say who caught the bouquet?

The wedding had been small and intimate, but the cocktail and dinner parties were huge. More than one thousand people attended the Pacific Palisades cocktail party, which overlooked Malibu beach. But eventually it tapered off and wound down. As the full moon soared high in the sky over the beach, people drifted away. At last, the celebration was down to two…

If you enjoyed reading *The Problem Is, I Fell In Love*,
Macavelli will soon publish Pamela M. Johnson's fourth novel, *Protégé*.

MACAVELLI PRESENTS A NATIONAL INDEPENDENT BESTSELLER

Protégé

A NOVEL BY

PAMELA M. JOHNSON

BESTSELLING AUTHOR OF I'LL CRY TOMORROW

The following is the synopsis and the first two chapters.

Protégé
a summation

In Protégé, Kennedy Kelly is an assured and savvy vice president of Land Acquisitions for a real estate development company on the brink of bankruptcy who, at the encouragement of Robert F. Bennington—a handsome, affluent, shrewd, and ruthless real estate tycoon, becomes a real estate developer. Robert is at the top of his game: with persistence and dedication, he's made all the right connections and has built an empire of wealth. He soon becomes Kennedy's mentor. Under his leadership and guidance, Kennedy launches her own real estate development company and learns to gracefully navigate in the property business. She follows in the footsteps of Robert, climbing the ladder of success and escalating to the top where she finds success. The road that leads to her success, however, is a bumpy one. Problems arise when Kennedy, who is the epitome of a woman who needs both sex and commitment in a relationship, falls for Robert, a married man who, unlike Kennedy, can easily separate the act of sex from love. Inexorably, Kennedy finds herself plagued by desires that cannot be reciprocated. In protégé, we see confirmation of the explanation of enlightenment that John Gray shed light on in *Men Are From Mars* and Women *Are From Venus*. *Protégé* also explores the secrete lives of black men who, unable to reveal their sexual orientation, are on the DL: the down low.

One

The first time I saw the handsome real estate mogul Robert F. Bennington was on the cover of *Macavelli*. He was an older, good-looking, well-groomed black man whose handsome face and impeccable attire caught my eye, as did the half-smile mixed with ease, pride, and confidence. Impressed, I studied the cover intently. I admired everything about him, especially his suit. He had on a nice and expensive looking dark blue suit. Beneath it, he wore a crisp white shirt with gold cufflinks, and a blue and yellow striped tie hung around his neck.

Subsequently, I took notice of his close-cropped haircut that had traces of gray hairs seeping through the top and along the sides. I found that the gray affectionately made him distinguished looking and that much more handsome. With the exception of his neatly trimmed, full mustache that, too, had bits of gray, he was clean-shaven.

Pulling the magazine closer into view, I gazed at the gold chain on his wrist and over at the posh gold Presidential Rolex lying next to it. Knowing the twenty-thousand dollar price tag the watch carried, I voiced beneath my breath, "Damn, I bet that watch cost more than the clothes he's wearing on his back." In my mind I debated about which one cost the most, his clothing or his watch. I did a quick guestimate and concluded with the watch. I'd been to the Gucci Boutique in San Francisco about two weeks ago and saw a suit that looked identical to the one Robert was wearing in the picture. It carried a six thousand dollar price tag.

Next, I gawked at his nails. They looked manicured. My eyes gravitated back up to his beautiful face. The poise of self-assurance that rested on it and the strength of his personality captured in the photograph was unmistakable. I admired him. Unabashedly, I brushed the back of my fingers along the square and beautifully structured jaw line of his dark brown chiseled face. Next, I touched the dimple in his chin. I stared at the bits of gray in his hair coupled with his chic look that made him strikingly attractive. I continued studying the picture of the man I marveled in the moment, who looked to be in his fifties, that the editors of *Macavelli* had decided deserved this month's cover. "Wonder what his story is," I thought to myself. Obviously, to earn such a spot on a trendy and popular magazine cover, he must have been a man of respect and admiration. I shifted my eyes to the headline on the left side of his picture, *Construction Mogul Robert Bennington, Who Built His Empire from the Ground Up, Speaks on How to Keep Your Millions.* I glanced back at him. "He's a millionaire? He built an empire?" I questioned if he was happy. It was just a thought that crossed my mind. I vibe that, beneath the money and fame, he wasn't. Truth is, I think rich people have more worries than everyday common people. There was something about his eyes that seemed sad. They say the eyes are the truth of our soul. They don't lie. But, I dismissed those thoughts and once again beamed. I felt a rush of adrenaline, "Daaaaang, he fine," I yelled out. I sighed. A sense of nervousness overcame me as I shuffled the magazine from one hand to the next. This is the affect that he had on me. I was in awe. I wondered if he was as good-looking in person as he was in the picture.

I'll never forget that day as long as I live. I'd just entered the building of my condo and retrieved today's mail from the silver mailbox that hung on the wall in the lobby. It was a Tuesday night, it had been a long day, and I was exhausted. I'd been dealing with the stress of the recent death of my paternal grandmother whom I loved dearly. My father, who died when I was in high school, was her only child and I was her only grandchild. I had been putting in 7-day weeks, fourteen hours a day for more than two months at Castellazzo Development Corporation, an Italian owned real estate development company. The company had been a family owned and operated business for more than eighty years. Its current owner, Mario, was the founder's grandson. I'd work for the company for five years now, starting as a land acquisition manager and becoming VP of Development and Land Acquisition two years ago. I got the job after passing my brokers exam. Before joining Castellazzo, I'd worked as a real estate sales agent and, for three consecutive years, I was the top sales agent in the office. That day, I'd worked all day at Castellazzo.

The company was in financial trouble and if we didn't find an investor soon, we would have to file bankruptcy. Understanding our negative cash flow, that the business wasn't self-sustaining and that we were clearly operating in the black, I told the owner that he really needed to think about whether or not he had a viable business, and, if not, it was time to close shop. Once a burgeoning and thriving business, Castellazzo Development Corp. had an impeccable reputation. However, the owner before Mario was his uncle Polly, who really mismanaged the company that his father founded and was largely responsible for its down fall. It was eventually learned that Mario had a gambling and drug problem and his notorious habits caused the company to plummet even further, almost to the point of no return. For the past five years, the company had been operating in the red, hanging on by a thread. Fortunately, those days were pretty much over with, but, as always, Mario didn't take my advice. Instead of going to work for another developer after Castellazzo I'd considered starting my own real estate development company where I'd focus on land acquisition, funding it with a four-hundred thousand dollar inheritance I had recently received from my grandmother's life insurance policy that she willed to me. There was also the two six-unit apartment buildings she left me that she owned free and clear in San Francisco that she'd purchased in the early sixties.

When I finally arrived home that night, I stood in the foyer and thumbed through the mail: letters, bills, and magazines, one by one. I grew excited when I saw my new Essence followed by my favorite, *Macavelli* Magazine. I was always excited to see those magazines every time they arrived. I placed *Macavelli* on top of the mail stack. I wanted to read that one first after I took my shower. Inside the elevator I pushed the number 3 button that led to my floor. As soon as I checked my messages and settled into my place, I headed to the shower. Afterwards, I sauntered to the kitchen, poured me a glass of red wine and retreated to my bedroom. I propped four pillows against the head-board, got in bed and rested my back on them. I read the *Macavelli* article about Robert F. Bennington lying in bed that night. I thumbed through the magazines pages, glancing momentarily at the article about Beyonce' and Jay Z "Is marriage in the air," and the one about the self-published author Pamela M. Johnson, "African-American author launches publishing company, *Macavelli* Press to fill void in lack of black published authors," until I came to the feature article about the mysterious man on the cover. I read it from beginning to end. I learned so much about him. For one, he was from humble beginnings in Louisiana. He'd grown up poor. Although he came from poverty and was dealt a bad hand in life, like a great deal of successful black people before him, he beat the odds in a racist society and excelled. I, too, had come from poverty. Yeah, I wanted to be like him, extremely successful. Robert was the youngest of five. He was the only one in his family to graduate from college. He simultaneously earned an MBA and law degree from Stanford, made millions in real estate as a developer and, in addition to owning Bennington Development Corporation, Inc., he owned a few other businesses. The article mentioned that he had a net worth of four-hundred and fifty million dollars. Robert was so rich that his wealth put him in the top ten percent of black people in this country. In the article, he expressed his disappointment with black millionaires who go broke. He talked about how it made no sense for people such as Mike Tyson and others to make hundreds of millions of dollars and end up going bankrupt. To avoid this, he suggested that celebrities set up trust funds for themselves that would allow them to get monies at different intervals during their lifetime. That way, for those who don't know how to manage their money, they wouldn't die broke, but would leave their families financially secure. He said that if rich black people like the young rappers or athletes making quick money took his suggestions on how to hold on to their money, invest it and make it grow, then his formula would work for them too.

Reading further into the article, I learned that Robert was caught up on a scandal eight years ago. He'd invested in a dot.com company at the beginning of the dot.com phenomenon in the Bay Area. He'd taken the company public. Eventually, he would sell off more than eleven million in stocks and it was alleged that he informed his friends who had invested in his company that the stocks would split three to one. He would become the probe of a two year FBI investigation when other stock holders began complaining about his sell of his stocks and his insider trading. It was said that he got a tip from a stock broker who was on his payroll. His ex-girlfriend, who'd been his mistress for three years, testified against him in court, revealing that he'd forked out an eighty thousand dollar down payment on a home for her in Miami before he broke off their relationship. She said that he had confided in her about the tip he'd received from the stock broker, saying that it was the reason he sold his stock and warned his friends about what was going to happen with the stock. It was also alleged during the trial that he'd been verbally and physically abusive to his mistress. When the prosecutor pointed out the rumor, she confirmed it. Needless to say, Robert denied the rumor, saying that he was a complete gentlemen at all times with women. The judge could have sentenced him to serve up to seventy years in the penitentiary, but ended up sentencing him to eight months in a Colorado prison where he was reduced to mediocre chores like washing the dishes and cooking in the kitchen for the other inmates. He actually became a trustee while incarcerated, but was prohibited from running his businesses. However, it was later learned that while he was incarcerated, his businesses still pulled in about a million a month. The article also talked about a former girlfriend who was a model that had sued him for sexual harassment. It said that she used to work for him and had become one of his mistresses. She alleged that because of his position as her boss, she knew if she didn't do what he wanted her to that he would fire her and that because she had a young daughter she couldn't risk that chance, so she complied with his sexual advances. A lot of thoughts ran through my mind and I wondered many disappointing things. In the end, though, I concluded that the real crime of Robert F. Bennington committed was being a rich and probably arrogant black man to white people here in America.

Reading even further into the article, I discovered that the impressive man I had just learned so much about resided in my very city, San Francisco. He lived in an exclusive neighborhood called Sea Cliff, a community where the home prices start in the low four millions and went up as high as eighteen million. The neighborhood is located on the northern edge of the city. Other well-known residents of Sea Cliff included the CEO of Oracle, actor Sean Penn and actress Sharon Stone, as well as famed attorney Melvin Belli, a.k.a. The King of Torts, before his unfortunate death. I couldn't believe that this successful man on the cover of *Macavelli* lived in the same town that I did and yet I didn't know him. I concluded that this remarkable and inspiring man defied the odds. People told him that he wasn't going to be anything in life and he proved them wrong. White people told him that he couldn't live in Sea Cliff, but again he proved them wrong. Everything he was told he couldn't do, he did it; and anytime you beat the odds and achieve what they told you you couldn't, that's success in America.

As the next couple of years passed, I ran across the name Robert Bennington a lot in both local and national newspapers and magazines. A recent article in the San Francisco Chronicle mentioned his donation for one hundred thousand dollars to his Alma Mater. Robert was inspiring, impressive, and so motivating to me. Finally, in April, nearly three years after reading the first *Macavelli* article, I decided to write him a letter, introduce myself, and ask if he'd be interested in investing in my record label and the music group that I was working on at the time. Interestingly, I sensed, even then, Robert's difficult personality that I'd come to know all too well. Nevertheless, I knew that he was real like me, and would appreciate my intelligence and assertive nature. I just knew we'd get along. I had a knack for getting along with people who had difficult personalities that other people couldn't get along with, especially men.

There was an annual Real Estate Development Conference coming up in Los Angeles that I decided to attend. I'd seen the itinerary and knew that Robert Bennington would be there, he was presenting on a panel at 2 p.m..

I had it all planned—I'd approach him after the panel and introduce myself, tell him how much I admired him.

It was a hot summer day, the weather in Los Angeles was beautiful. It was about 85 degrees when my flight landed at LAX and I was standing at Passenger Pickup awaiting a taxi. I spotted one sitting down a ways and flagged it on. As I got inside the car and sat on the back seat, I glanced down at my watch. It was 12 noon. The flight from San Francisco to L.A. was a short one, fifty minutes. "Where to?" the taxi driver inquired. "The Biltmore, and then the L.A. Convention Center. I need you to wait for me. I just need to check in to the hotel and drop off my luggage in my room, and then I'll need for you to drop me off at the Convention Center," I replied from the back seat. The Biltmore was the official hotel accommodating lodging for the event. They had advertisements in the Development Conference brochure. Today was Friday, and I decided to stay in L.A. and visit friends through Sunday. "So where are you from? I hear your accent," I voiced to the taxi driver.

"I'll give you a hint," he kindly joked, "it's a country in Africa. Guess."

"Keep on talking," I said. "I'll figure it out.

"The U.S. is a land of opportunity. The Big Apple, New York City, they call it, the land of opportunity," he spoke.

"Nigeria, you're from Nigeria."

"That's correct, ma'am." He smiled. I smiled back at him. We drove for a few more minutes in silence. "The Biltmore," the driver called out as he made way to the entrance door. The door man approached the taxi and opened the door. "Would you like me to take your luggage for you ma'am?"

"Yes, please." I handed him the bag and reached inside my Coach bag and pulled out my wallet, followed by two twenties. I turned to the driver, extended him the money, "I need you to wait, for me," I repeated. "I'll be right out." A huge smile covered his face. "No worries, ma'am, I'll be right here when you return," he spoke in a thick Nigerian accent. I exited the taxi, returning to it shortly.

The L.A. Convention Center Parking lot was packed. As we traveled across it I took notice of the large crowds. People from everywhere had come to attend the annual event. "Okay, ma'am, this is it, the L.A. Convention Center," the driver asserted. I looked at the meter, $85.00. I fumbled through my wallet and pulled out the monies due to him. I included in it a nice tip. A smile, bigger than the one he displayed earlier when I pulled out the monies at the Biltmore, erupted across his face. He licked his lips. I handed it to him. "Thank you ma'am. Will you need a taxi anymore while you're in town? I don't usually do this, but I could give you my cell number and if you need to go somewhere you can call me," he said.

"No, I'm cool. I leave in two days and I'll be hanging out with friends here in L.A. They have cars. But thanks for asking." I glanced down at my watch again, it was twenty minutes before Robert's panel was set to begin. I exited the car, headed inside the building and located the room where the panel would take place. The moderator and the panelist appeared on the stage. I spotted Robert, he was wearing a dark blue suit similar to the one he sported on the cover of *Macavelli*, but the suit had a different design. They took their seats and over the course of the next hour discussed how they'd entered the industry, their success and their advice to other developers. Afterwards, the panelists had all gathered in front of the stage, talking to those in attendance. I walked in Robert's direction. He noticed me approaching and flashed me a nod. My question was answered—he was as good-looking, if not better, as his picture on the cover of *Macavelli*. As I got within arms reach, two men came out of nowhere and pushed their way in front of me. "Excuse the lady," Robert expressed. He reached for me and pulled me around one of them. I was standing at Robert's side while one of the guys, an Asian guy asked him, "Mr. Bennington, I was wondering if you possibly had some time to sit down and talk. My brother and I started our own development business and I'd like to get some advice from you."

"No, sorry, I don't. I have a plane to catch in less than an hour."

"Oh, I see." The eager look on the guy's face changed to a solemn one. "Well, how about five minutes, could I have just five minutes of your time?" Robert shook his head no.

"I don't have time, sorry." The guy walked away. The other guy, who had observed the interaction between Robert and the Asian guy, now stepped forward and extended his handshake. Robert took hold of his hand. "Mr. Bennington, I'm Tim Roth with Newsweek. We are interested in interviewing you for an article that will appear in our magazine, not this coming issue but the next. Here's my card, I can do the interview over the phone if you like, or if you have time we could do it now."

"Let's do it," Robert replied. He turned and looked in my direction.

"You don't mind if I do this interview first, do you?" he asked. I shook my head no. "I'm Robert Bennington, and your name?" he asked extending his handshake. I took hold of it, "Kennedy, Kennedy Kelly."

"What do you do, Ms. Kelley?"

"I work for a developer, or maybe I should say I worked for a developer, as vice president of Land Acquisitions."

"What developer might that be?"

"Castellazzo." Robert's eyebrows rose.

"Oh yeah, your boss has been having some troubles lately," he spoke softly. I nodded. Robert looked in the direction of the reporter. "Let's go and do the interview in a restaurant, I could use a cup of coffee. He motioned with his hands for me to walk in front of him and lead way to the restaurant inside the building. I'd passed it en route to the room. When we got there we all got a cup of coffee, Robert didn't argue with the reporter who offered to buy them all. "Hey, I thought you had a plane to catch in less than an hour?" I commented after the interview ended and the reporter had gone. Robert pulled the sleeve of his blazer back slightly, it was covering his watch. He shrugged his shoulders and then uttered, "It's my plane and my pilot, so I can leave pretty much whenever I want, that is after I get clearance by air traffic control to fly."

"You headed home?" I asked. Robert shook his head. "I'm off to Tennessee to purchase four hundred acres of land for a new development I'm building that I'm the lead developer in."

"Wow," I voiced.

"Yeah, it's a pretty big deal," Robert expressed. Robert kept commenting that he had to leave, but we sat in that restaurant and talked for two hours. What struck me about him is that he sounded much different than I had imagined. His speech was proper. He sounded like a white man. I was shocked. "So how do I contact you?" Robert asked.

"Here, lock my cell number in your cell," I instructed him. He removed a Motorola from his suit pocket and locked my number into it. Next thing I knew, his business card was staring me in the face. As I reached for it, Robert asserted, "Wait a minute, let me see that card again." I gave it back to him. "Here's the direct number to my office—it bypasses my assistant—and here's my cell number'" he said as he wrote on the back of the card. He handed me the card and was staring at me hard as hell. "Why are you staring at me like that?" I asked. "I was just looking at how beautiful you are. Your beauty is amazing." I blushed. I'll be in San Francisco Monday after next, I'd like to take you to dinner. Would you go with me, to dinner?"

"Sure."

"Okay, I'll call you." When I got to work that Monday I decided to write Robert a letter, you know one of those standard business letters that business people always write to people they appreciated meeting at a conference. I dropped the letter in the mail.

Robert called me that Monday when he returned, as he said he would. I was at work and had just returned to the office from lunch, when I saw the red light on my cell phone blinking, indicating that I had a message waiting for retrieval. I'd forgot my cell on my desk when I'd left for lunch. I proceeded to the silver coat hook that was behind my door, removed the brown wooden hanger and hung up my cashmere coat. I headed over to my desk where I sat down and pushed the speaker button on the cell phone before dialing the number to get my messages. "You have one new message sent today at 1:05 p.m.," the computerized, female voice on the message machine greeted me. It was now 1:30 p.m.

"Hello, Kennedy, this is Robert Bennington. I received your letter and wondered if you'd like to have lunch. Call me on my direct line—here's the number..." he repeated it. My eyes widened and my mouth dropped open at the sound of his name. I sighed. Now, I was smiling. "*The* Robert Bennington called me," I was flabbergasted. I reached for a pen from my Zeta Phi Beta coffee mug that I had purchased at my sorority's last national meeting in Las Vegas. I hit the replay button on the phone so that I could hear the message once more and write down Robert's number. Pushing the speaker button off, I hung up the phone and, with a smile fixed on my face, stared into the distance. I was happy that he'd responded to my letter and sounded just as interested in meeting me as I was in meeting him. I glanced back at the black AT & T phone that sat atop my mahogany colored desk. It matched the three tall bookshelves that stood next to one another across the room. After gathering my thoughts, I hit the on button again and dialed his number. The phone rang five times before he answered.

"Hello?"

"Hello… Robert…?"

"Yes."

"Hey, this is Kennedy, Kennedy Kelley."

"Oh, hi Kennedy, I received your letter. There are a lot of restaurants around here. I was wondering if you wanted to grab lunch."

"Yeah, I got your message about lunch. I'm actually just returning from lunch. Had I known you were going to call and invite me to lunch today I would've taken a later one."

"Well, how about later this evening…say after 5:30. Are you available then? We could meet somewhere."

"That sounds great."

"Good," Robert expressed. He kept on talking "Yeah, I got your letter and read it." He grew silent as if he were waiting on a response from me. I was nervous. I didn't know what to say. I said a lot in that letter and although I sensed he liked it, I didn't really know the details of what he thought about it. Yet, he was calling me and that was a good sign. Still, not knowing how to respond, I sat silent on the other end, playing nervously with the black telephone cord, twisting it around my finger. Robert was silent, too. After what seemed like a lifetime, he broke the silence, "Okay, I'll be leaving my office at 5:30. I'll call you when I get in my car."

"Okay, I'm off at 5, but I'll stick around and leave then, too."

"Okay, bye, I'll talk to you then."

"Okay, bye Robert, I'll see you later." Like clock work my phone rang at 5:30. I'd just exited the parking garage downtown on 5th Street and was now crossing Mission Street when I heard the ring. "Hello?" I answered.

"Hey, Kennedy?"

"Hey, Robert."

"Okay, I just left my office. I'm in my car now. Where would you like to meet?"

"What's your location?"

"I'm at Union and Fillmore."

"I'm at Mission at 9th Street."

"We're not that far from each other. So, where do you want to meet?" he repeated.

"Where do you want to meet, Robert?" I asked, answering his question with a question.

"You pick the place," he said.

"Okay, let's see… do you like Sushi?"

"Yes, Sushi's cool."

"Let's meet at Ozumo's Japanese restaurant on Stewart Street. "It's between Mission and Howard. Do you know the place?" Ozumo's reputation preceded it. Their food is authentic and represents excellence. It was the best Japanese restaurant in the city with thousands of fine dining choices. It was one of my favorite places to eat. I had recently read in the food section of the San Francisco Chronicle Newspaper that San Francisco had more restaurants than New York City. My friend Monica, a student at San Francisco's Culinary Academy who was an excellent cook and aspiring Restaurateur, corroborated this statement.

"Yes, I know where it is."

"Okay, I'll see you in, say… ten minutes?"

"Alright."

"Bye, Kennedy, I look forward to seeing you."

"Bye, Robert. I look forward to seeing you, also."

Two

I arrived at Ozumo's before Robert. There was an available parking stall in front of the restaurant that I pulled my blue Audi sedan into. I exited my car and entered the restaurant. Once inside, I looked around the beautifully designed and dimly lit restaurant. It was crowded, as usual. In addition to the good food, what I also really liked about the restaurant was its great atmosphere and inviting ambiance. Subdued light filtered through rice paper screens embedded with leaves and twigs, and matching lampshades sat on the tables, setting a wonderfully romantic and dramatic mood. It was amazing. I glanced at my watch. It was twenty-seven after the hour. You have a few minutes, I thought. Better head to the restroom to check my appearance, my hair, touch up my make-up and freshen up a bit. I'd just gotten a new short, feathered and layered haircut. I wanted to make sure I was looking good when Robert saw me for the first time. You know the saying, first impressions are lasting impressions. I had to make a good impression on him. Fortunately, that morning I decided to wear my black Inc. suit with the wide legged pant. I had on a black knit top beneath my blazer and I was sporting some black Kenneth Cole boots. Accentuating all the black was a pair of gold loop earrings, a gold mesh three tier ruby bracelet that my mother had given me last year for Christmas, and a gold Eclissi watch that I got from Macy's the last time they had their White Sale. It may have not compared to the gold presidential watch that Robert owned that I saw on the cover of *Macavelli*, but it was within my budget. I must admit I was looking pretty damn good, if I do say so myself. Eagerly, I stepped out of the restroom and looked around for Robert's face. There was a time when he wouldn't have known me from Tom, Dick or Jerry. However, thanks to our meeting in L.A. he knew what I looked like. My eyes traveled across the restaurant, scanning the room. He hadn't arrived yet. "Excuse me, miss, do you have a reservation? " the hostess inquired, interrupting my thoughts.

I shook my head, followed by the words, "No, I don't."

She was quite pleasant and friendly, "No problem, I can seat you. How many people in your party?" she said in a thick Japanese accent. I held up two fingers, and voiced, "Two, but he hasn't arrived yet." She pointed in the direction of the bar that sat in the middle of the floor. "Would you like to have a drink at the bar? We have excellent Sake and cocktails, and when your friend arrives I can seat the both of you."

"Sure," I replied. She reached for a cocktail menu in the wooden rack on the wall and walked in the direction of the bar. I followed her. She sat the menu on top of the bar, and before walking away turned to me and said, "All of our cocktails are excellent, you couldn't make a bad choice if you wanted to." She smiled. I took seat on the bar stool. I read the cocktail menu and the ingredients in the drinks; everything sounded good. The two Sake Sampler's that offered three different Sake's in miniature sizes for the customer to try sounded enticing. I wondered if I should try the Nama Ichiban Sampler that included three sample size Sake's. The menu described the sampler Ohyama Nama, a fruity tasting drink that had peach and apple in it and medium dry Sake. The other sampler, Ichinokura Nama, the menu described as having an aroma of Koji rice and fruity scents with a savory taste. Then there was the Umenishiki Nama, another fruity aroma drink, and the Tokyo Glow made with Absolute Citron, fresh lemon juice, sugar, and Mandarin liquor, served up with sugar rum. There was also the Sake Cosmo with Triple Sec, lime, and cranberry juice. Next on the cocktail menu was the Lemon Ginger Sake Martini with Sake. Its ingredients included, ginger, lemon juice and a splash of triple sec served up with a sugar rum. The hostess was right: there wasn't a bad choice on the menu. I glanced over the menu again and decided on the Sake Cosmo. I sat the menu down, signaled the bar tender over and ordered my drink. Now, I was staring through the huge slate glass in front of me looking at the passersby heading to their destinations. I spotted a tall, medium built, good looking black man. He was wearing a charcoal gray suit with a white dress shirt. He didn't have on a tie. I took a second look as he entered the restaurant. He looked cool, calm and collected. His hands were inside his pant pocket. He looked around the place. My heart fluttered looking at that handsome man. I lifted the small glass that contained the Sake casually in the air. It caught his attention. I waved him on. He took notice of me. He nodded and headed in my direction. When he was a few feet from the table, I stood up and extended my handshake, "Hello Robert, it's nice to see you again." He extended his hand to meet mine. I took notice of the Marina two-toned silver and gold Rolex. It was nice.

"It's nice to see you, too, Kennedy. Seems like you are even more beautiful than the last time I saw you." I smiled at what he'd said and pointed at the empty barstool next to mine. We both took a seat. "What are you about 5 feet 8?"

"I'm 5 feet 9, you're close."

"So what are you drinking?" Just as I asked that, the bar tender appeared, "Would you like to see our cocktail menu, sir?"

"Yes, please," Robert replied. He sat the menu on top of the bar in front of him. "We have a great Sake menu," he continued and Robert nodded. He scanned the menu with the tip of his finger, going down, up, over and across, pointing to each item as he read it. Still looking down at the menu, he voiced, "I'll have the Sake Sampler." The bartender shook his head and asked which one. Robert lifted his head from the menu and looked at the bartender, "The Nama Ichiban Sampler."

"I almost ordered that one, too," I said.

"But then changed your mind?" I nodded. Now Robert focused his attention solely on me. He pointed his index finger in my direction. "You know Kennedy, you are a hell of a writer. After I read your letter I knew that I'd meet you, but I didn't know it would be today!" I nodded at what he'd said. I'd been told for years how well I expressed myself on paper and about how excellent of a writer I was. Just then, the hostess approached us and asked if we wished to be seated at a table. She led us to a cozy table at the far end of the restaurant. Promptly, a waitress appeared to take our orders.

Placing his open palms on his chest, "May I take the liberty and order for us?" Robert politely asked.

I nodded, "Surprise me."

He looked at the waitress. "For our appetizers, we'll begin with the Futago, the Kani Kani Kani." The Futago was this thinly sliced beef tenderloin, with garlic sautéed spinach and Japanese Eggplant, drizzled with a miso-sesame sauce; and the Kani Kani Kani was this appetizing Dungeness crab cake with spinach aioli. "We'll also have the Tempura Crab Salad." Robert peered around his menu and looked directly at me, "Kennedy do you like Duck?" I nodded. He went on, "We'll also have the Sonoma Muscovy Duck Breast with Scallions and Jasmine Rice." As we waited on the arrival of our food, Robert and I made small talk. The conversation soon turned towards my work at the real estate development company.

"So, what is it again that you do for Mario?"

"Basically, I'm running the company as VP. You know, we are looking for investors."

"I see. So you are looking for an investor for him…Mario?"

"The company has employees and I'm one of them. I'm looking for an investor so we can keep our jobs."

"What's your security?"

"What do you mean?"

"If I give you the money, what's your security? I mean you could save this guy's company and he could dump you?"

"He wouldn't do that."

"How do you know?"

"Because he's loyal to me.""Sweetheart, loyalty in business is money, don't you ever forget that," he said sternly.

I nodded. "Trust me, he wouldn't get rid of me…he wouldn't do that to me," I said defensively. A disbelieving look appeared on Robert's face.

"How much money are you looking for an investor such as myself to invest in your development company?"

"Five million."

"How would you spend the money, if I gave it to you?" he wanted to know.

"First we need to purchase a lot of land and subdivide it, put some houses on it, build a small community, you know."

"Huh."

"Huh, what?"

"I'm just wondering…"

"Wondering what?"

"Well if you are as good as I think you are as a businesswoman and if you're as smart as I think you are, why would you want to do all the work, build someone else's company, and only make a salary while they are making millions."

"Having your own business, it's too risky," I retorted. "I don't want the headache."

"But you already got it." Robert said. "Your boss, and him not understanding how to manage money along with his other problems, are responsible for his downfall and you know this. I understand that you are trying to save him, but honey, you can't save him if he doesn't want to save himself." Robert repositioned himself on the bar stool. "From what I see, he doesn't want to save himself, if he did he'd be in somebody's rehab program," Robert said without blinking an eye.

I threw my hands up in the air and looked Robert in his eye, "You're right, you're absolutely right. Why am I trying to save him?" I asked myself out loud.

"Because I think you're scared, scared of being out there on your own, maybe even scared of success," Robert said. I thought about what he'd said, maybe he had a point.

Kennedy take your education, your background and your experience and start your own development company. You will excel at it, trust me. When I say something—and you can ask anyone that I know to vouch for this—you can take it to the bank. I know talent when I see it and I see something in you Kennedy. Look, I am here sitting across from you, and I'm not an easy person to get, but you got me. Go and make it official and incorporate your business with the secretary of state, Kennedy Kelly Development Corporation. I can show you how to set up your business if you want." I nodded. A few thoughts ran through my mind. Maybe Robert was right that if I helped Mario out of his bind by finding an investor that he'd get rid of me after I saved his company. He was married and his wife didn't like me. In fact, she'd been on him lately about getting rid of me. In her mind she thought that I was sleeping with her husband. In her mind she thought that every woman wanted him, but this wasn't the case. It was just her insecurities that led her to believe this.

"So what do you like to do Kennedy?" Robert said, cutting short my thoughts and changing the subject.

"What do you mean?"

"You know, what do you like to do?"

"I like to write and watch TV and … "

"No, you know, what you like to do in your free time to have fun," he cut me off.

"I like doing a lot of things, like going to the movies, to restaurants, I like to go walking on the beach, socializing with my friends. What do you like to do, Robert?"

"Make money." He lifted the glass to his lips and sipped his drink.

"No, Robert, as you said to me, what do you like to do in your free time to have fun?"

"Make money." I gave him that don't play with me look. "No really, that's what I like to do. It's all I think about," he chuckled.

"Really?"

"Really."

"Well, besides that, what do you like to do?"

"Really nothing else." He locked me in his stare. He went on. "Hell, I don't know, I like to play golf, travel. Have you ever been to Africa, Kennedy?"

"No, I haven't, but I'd like to visit."

"You have to. Every black person should visit Africa at least once in their lifetime."

"I agree, that's why I'm going to go one day."

"The women in Africa, they have these really big butts. I mean, like wow, the biggest butts I've ever seen."

Robert picked the small glass back up, took a sip of the Sake, and set it back down. The Sake was beginning to have an effect. "I mean really, Kennedy. I ain't ever seen a woman with a butt as big as the ones on African women. You ain't ever seen a woman with a butt as big as the ones on African women. With enthusiasm, he carried on. He reached his hand behind him and demonstrated how big African women's butts are. It almost felt as if I was in a college lecture with a professor giving a lecture on African women and their big butts. All the while he's talking, I'm not quite sure how to respond, so I don't. Speechless, I just smile at him and look around the restaurant. Finally, he changed the subject, bringing the focus back on me. "Yeah, Kennedy like I was saying, I think you should be your own boss you've got the intelligence to do it with." I nodded.

"Okay, here are your appetizers," the waitress appeared, setting the two sets of ivory chopsticks and plates of Futago and Kani Kani Kani on the table. "I hope you enjoy. I'll be right back with your Tempura Crab Salad."

"Excuse me, would you also be so kind to bring us some Tempura and California Rolls?" Robert asserted.

"Yes, sir," the waitress responded.

We both picked up our chopsticks and dug in. "Hmmm," I said as I tasted first the Futago followed by the Kani Kani Kani. They were both so appetizing. Robert followed my lead as I looked up to see the waitress approaching our table with the Sonoma Muscovy Duck Breast with Scallions and Jasmine Rice. That was delicious, too. As always, the food at Ozumo's was superb.

"Why are you staring at me like that, Robert."

"I'm just admiring how beautiful you are, that's all. Don't pay me any attention. You work out?"

Now I was talking with food in my mouth, "No, but I should."

"So, your body is natural?"

"Yes," I said followed by a head shake.

"Wow, a lot of women would have to work out to get a body like yours. I mean look at you, you are a perfect size, flat stomach and everything."

"Would you stop," I said. However, I couldn't stop smiling. I loved the flattery.

"When I spoke to you earlier on the phone I really had no idea how beautiful you were. Wow, amazing. You have beautiful smooth brown skin, not a blemish on your face." I stared at him. "And your eyes, they're beautiful. I like big eyes. You know, you kind of remind me of Kelly Rowland from Destiny's child. That's exactly who you look like, but I'd say that you are about a shade lighter." I smiled and commented, "I actually hear that a lot. I wish I had her money."

"So how did I do, did you like my food choices?" Robert wanted to know, gesturing his open palms at the food on the table.

"Not bad," I joked. "Next time I get to do the honors and order," I said, pointing one of the chopsticks in his direction.

"Okay, I'm going to hold you to that." I smiled. "So when's next time, when do I get to see you again, Kennedy?"

"Not this Friday, but next Friday night."

"Okay, and where are we going, might I ask?"

"Post Trio, it's on Post Street near Union Square."

"Yeah, I know the restaurant."

"You like it?"

"It's cool." Robert and I sat there making more small talk and drinking Sake. We talked the night away until the restaurant closed.

"How was everything? Did you enjoy your meal?" our waitress showed up and wanted to know.

"The food was excellent," I responded.

"Can I get you any desert or anything else?"

"No, I'm fine. What about you, Robert?"

"Can you have the bar tender make me a Martini?"

"I sure can," the waitress responded.

"Kennedy, are you sure that you don't want anything else?" The waitress stopped in her tracks and looked at me. "No, I'm fine."

"I'll be right back," she said. A few minutes later she retuned with the Martini, placing the glass before Robert along with the black wallet that contained the bill. "Dannngggg, she didn't waste anytime in bringing the bill," Robert joked. I smiled. He finished the drink, opened his wallet and pulled out his American Express card, glanced at the bill and placed the card on top of it. He told me that he never carries cash. "I'd be lucky to find five dollars in here," he whispered as he folded the wallet closed.

"Come on, let's go," Robert said, standing up from his chair. "Where did you park?"

"I got lucky and found a space right outside."

"I'll walk you to your car."

And that's the story of how I met Robert Bennington and became his protégé. That was three years ago. We've been friends ever since.

ORDER A MACAVELLI BOOK

Macavelli Press accepts credit cards (including debit cards with the Visa or MasterCard logo), money orders and checks. To order a book by phone using your credit card call 1-888-281-5170. If you prefer to submit your order by fax and pay with a credit card, copy the order form below and fax your order to us at 1-620-229-8978. If you prefer to pay by check or money order you may copy and send the order form on the following page, along with your check or money order, via U.S. Postal Mail to us at the address below:

QP Distribution
22167 C Street
Winfield, Kansas 67156

The ever-growing Macavelli Press Catalog currently consists of three novels:

1. *From a Hard Rock to a Gem: a Memoir of a Lost Soul*
2. *I'll Cry Tomorrow*
3. *The Problem Is I Fell In love*

We are currently taking advance orders for Pamela M. Johnson's forthcoming novel *Protégé* due *to* hit book stores in January 2006. You may also pay by credit card, money order or check for pre-orders. At the time that your order is placed your credit card will be billed and/or payment will be required. If you pre-order the novel now, *Macavelli* ensures it will arrive by November 1, 2005. *Macavelli* also insures that for all orders placed after November 1, 2005 for *Protégé* will arrive within 3 weeks of the order being placed. To pre-order Protégé follow the guidelines above that explains how to order a *Macavelli* Book; you may also use the toll-free number above or send a copy of the order form below indicating your order to QP Distribution at the address shown above for them. If you have any questions regarding pre-orders you may email preorders@macavelli.com.

Info for *Protégé* is as follows:
Price: $14.95
ISBN 0974657220

Library of Congresss Preassigned Control Number: 2005925739

Novel price	$14.95
Tax (8.5%) San Francisco, California	$ 1.27
Shipping & handling	$ 4.00
Total amount per book	$20.22

For novels shipped directly to prisons deduct 15% ($3.03) = $17.19

Special discounts up to 25% are given to schools and non-profit community-based organizations. For more information email sales@macavelli.com.

Purchaser Information

Name: _____

Inmate ID #: (if you are incarcerated)_____

_____

Address: _____

_____

_____

_____

City:_____

State: _____

Zip Code: _____

Please fill in the name and quantity of book(s) you are ordering below

Name of Book   Qty.

_____

_____

_____

_____

_____

CREDIT CARD TYPE

Visa   MC   Other: _____

Expiration Date: _____

Approval No.: _____
(see back of card)

Signature: _____

For questions about your order, you may email sales@macavelli.com

About the Author

Pamela M. Johnson received her Associate of Arts degree in Liberal Studies, completed a triple undergraduate degree major, simultaneously earning Bachelor of Arts Degrees in Public Relations, Organizational Management and Speech and Communications. She went on to earn a Master of Arts degree in Humanities and Leadership with an emphasis in Organizational Leadership. She published her debut urban fiction novel *From a Hard Rock to a Gem: a Memoir of a Lost Soul* written in urban vernacular in January 2004. For her second novel, *I'll Cry Tomorrow,* a spin-off novel of *From a Hard Rock to a Gem,* she switched to a different genre, a spiritual based love story that deals with the theme of HIV and AIDS in the Black community. Her third novel is titled *The Problem Is I Fell In Love,* is a romantic love story and her fourth novel *Protégé'*—a love story and mystery is schedule for a spring 2006 release. She has completed her fifth novel, *The Autobiography of Antaawn Sing, Drug Lord* (a release date has not yet been set for this novel) and she is currently at work on two more novels, *Birthwhistle and Without Father.* She is presently soliciting writings for two forthcoming anthologies *Ghetto Prophet: The Ideas, Philosophies, & Opinions of Tupac Shakur* and *Azar Zanta* that she will edit and publish. *For more information about the anthologies and submission guide lines visit www.macavellipress.com*

Johnson is also the founder and publisher of Macavelli Press and CEO of The Johnson Agency, a pr agency with a niche in literary pr, and book marketing (www.thejohnsonagency.net). Forthcoming—is a global urban culture magazine, *Macavelli* that Johnson will publish.